Crime, Fear and the Law in True Crime Stories

Crime Files Series

General Editor: **Clive Bloom**

Since its invention in the nineteenth century, detective fiction has never been more popular. In novels, short stories, films, radio, television and now in computer games, private detectives and psychopaths, prim poisoners and overworked cops, tommy gun gangsters and cocaine criminals are the very stuff of modern imagination, and their creators one mainstay of popular consciousness. Crime Files is a ground-breaking series offering scholars, students and discerning readers a comprehensive set of guides to the world of crime and detective fiction. Every aspect of crime writing, detective fiction, gangster movie, true-crime exposé, police procedural and post-colonial investigation is explored through clear and informative texts offering comprehensive coverage and theoretical sophistication.

Published titles include:

Anita Biressi
CRIME, FEAR AND THE LAW IN TRUE CRIME STORIES

Ed Christian (*editor*)
THE POST-COLONIAL DETECTIVE

Paul Cobley
THE AMERICAN THRILLER
Generic Innovation and Social Change in the 1970s

Lee Horsley
THE NOIR THRILLER

Susan Rowland
FROM AGATHA CHRISTIE TO RUTH RENDELL
British Women Writers in Detective and Crime Fiction

Crime Files
Series Standing Order ISBN 0–333–71471–7
(*outside North America only*)

You can receive future titles in this series as they are published by placing a standing order. Please contact your bookseller or, in case of difficulty, write to us at the address below with your name and address, the title of the series and the ISBN quoted above.

Customer Services Department, Macmillan Distribution Ltd, Houndmills, Basingstoke, Hampshire RG21 6XS, England

Crime, Fear and the Law in True Crime Stories

Anita Biressi
Senior Lecturer in Media Studies
Buckinghamshire Chilterns University College
High Wycombe
Buckinghamshire

palgrave

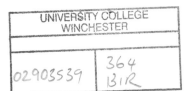

First published 2001 by
PALGRAVE
Houndmills, Basingstoke, Hampshire RG21 6XS and
175 Fifth Avenue, New York, N.Y. 10010
Companies and representatives throughout the world

PALGRAVE is the new global academic imprint of
St. Martin's Press LLC Scholarly and Reference Division and
Palgrave Publishers Ltd (formerly Macmillan Press Ltd).

ISBN 0–333–74547–7

This book is printed on paper suitable for recycling and
made from fully managed and sustained forest sources.

A catalogue record for this book is available
from the British Library.

Library of Congress Cataloging-in-Publication Data
Biressi, Anita, 1965–
    Crime, fear, and the law in true crime stories / Anita Biressi.
        p. cm.
    Includes bibliographical references and index.
    ISBN 0–333–74547–7
    1. Crime in popular culture—Great Britain. 2. Crime in mass
media—Great Britain. 3. Crime in literature. 4. Crime writing—
–Social aspects. 5. Fear of crime—Great Britain. I. Title.

    HV6947 .B57 2001
    364—dc21
                                                    2001021869

10   9   8   7   6   5   4   3   2   1
10   09 08 07 06 05 04 03 02 01

Printed and bound in Great Britain by
Antony Rowe Ltd, Chippenham, Wiltshire

For my parents,
Alfredo Carlo Biressi and Ruth Lina Biressi

Contents

Preface

This book examines contemporary true crime narratives produced in Britain since the late 1970s. It unpacks the relationship between true crime, its popular fascination and appeal and the moment of its recent commercial success. It argues that an analysis of the ways in which true crime picks up and works with discourses of law and order, crime and punishment, violence and vulnerability provides valuable insights into the production of the modern social subject. It maintains that the real experience of violence upon which non-fiction draws must be taken into account by cultural criticism if critique is to move beyond a purely relative textual reading of true crime.

This work begins by signalling the generic antecedents of true crime literature, arguing that new literatures of crime arise partly through new knowledges and new practices and partly through the collision of a range of mainly non-fiction popular genres. It charts the emergence of modern notions of 'lawlessness', the divisions between the criminal subject and the law-abiding citizen and the creation of the 'dangerous individual' demonstrating how these become the main objects of scrutiny in contemporary true crime literature.

The rhetorical division between the criminal and the good citizen is interrogated through an examination of the discursive relationship between British true crime and the social construction of crime and criminality since the late 1970s. Topical discourses about home security and rising crime are unpacked in order to demonstrate how these intersect with dominant notions of individualism, citizenship and social responsibility. This analysis emphasises how subject positions such as the 'moral subject' are constituted through a range of discourses about crime, and also considers the likely pleasures offered by true crime. Illustration, humour and a popular vernacular all contribute to an understanding of true crime as a popular reservoir of experience and knowledge about crime and its social context and that the pleasure of recognition is a significant one.

An examination of the newer collect and keep true crime partwork magazines demonstrates that anxieties about agency, progress and mortality, which are central to an understanding of true crime in general, are particularly pointed in the new true crime. For while true crime presents the development of modern technologies as inherently progressive, the images and stories of the destroyed body which lie at its core, suggest a profound ambivalence about the role of 'man' in the order of things. The book concludes by examining through close textual analysis the discursive clash between a literary aesthetic that elevates and privileges the murderer as a powerful agent and a moral imperative that aims to condemn him (rarely her) for turning victims into objects of atrocity and abuse. The overall argument is that the discursive conflicts played out across the range of true crime forms constitute a locus of fascination and repulsion with crime and criminality that says much about the production of the modern social subject.

Acknowledgements

My gratitude goes to the British Academy, the University of East London and Buckinghamshire Chilterns University College for funding various stages of the book. Particular thanks also go to the Faculty of Arts, Social Sciences and Humanities at BCUC for funding the sabbatical that gave me the opportunity to complete this work. Thank you also to friends and colleagues at the Department of Cultural Studies at UEL and at BCUC for their help and friendly support throughout the period of this work.

I wish to thank staff at the following institutions for their help in locating materials. The British Library, Bloomsbury and St. Pancras; the Rare Manuscripts Reading Room, The British Library, St. Pancras; The British Newspaper Library, Colindale, North London; The Guildhall Library, London; Learning Resource Centre, University of East London; Senate House Library, University of London; The St. Brides Library, London EC1; Barking Central Reference Library and the Bodleian Library, Oxford. Thanks goes also to Research Editor Lucy Wildman and Librarian Victoria Kearns, both at the *Reader's Digest* Archive, to Elizabeth Munroe, P.A. to the Director, Crimestoppers Trust and to Sergeant Bob Gray at the Press Office at Thames Valley Police.

Many friends and colleagues contributed to the development of this book, by reading manuscripts, offering criticism and new insights, collecting press cuttings, listening to my complaints and passions, cooking me meals and ensuring that I enjoyed a good night out once in while. Particular thanks go to Dr. Caroline Bainbridge, Professor Andrew Blake, Professor Clive Bloom, Pat Burn, Miri Forster, Dr. Laura Marcus, Bert Nunn, Sylvia Nunn, Berni O'Dea, Professor Alan O'Shea, Dr. John Parham, Professor Kenneth Parker, Bill Schwarz and Kathryn White. I owe a special debt to Dr. Susannah Radstone whose patience, commitment and untiring enthusiasm pushed me forward and to Heather Nunn without whom this book would not have been written.

Introduction

> We all seem to be interested in murderers these days. They are our truth and our fiction; they are our truth *as* fiction, and vice versa.
>
> Wendy Lesser (1993: 2)

As Wendy Lesser notes, extreme crime, especially murder, exerts a particular popular fascination. From conventional press reportage to the controversial death row images featured in the billboard advertisements for the Italian knitwear company Benetton, it is more than apparent that real-life crime sells. True crime entertainment, then, is just one contributor among many to the media debate about crime in society. Today, British true crime books and magazines address a heterogeneous range of criminal activity including multiple and domestic murder, gang warfare, grand robbery and serial rape. The genre may be broken down into sub-genres authored by detectives, relatives of murder victims and relatives of criminals, in addition to books written by journalists and other professional writers. Alternatively, these narratives may be organised by theme, according to type of killer, mode of killing, region or period – for example, 'Women Who Kill', 'Doctors of Death', 'Classic Murder', 'Crimes of East Anglia' and 'Victorian Poisoners'. These stories are non-fiction narratives based on actual events, packaged and promoted for entertainment as 'leisure reading'. They may be of any length from a feature article to a full-length book study but, unlike reportage, the event does not have to be contemporaneous or currently newsworthy. Again, unlike news or documentary, true crime is promoted primarily and explicitly as a leisure pursuit. For example, the 'Summer Special' editions of the monthly true crime magazines are promoted as 'holiday reading', a way to 'put up your feet and relax'.

1

As will become apparent, the basic paradigm of the true crime narrative is built upon and modified in different ways by individual true crime writers, publishers and even readers. True crime is not, therefore, a single, monolithic genre. On the contrary, it is made meaningful to its audience precisely because it yokes together stories of the bizarre and the horrible with changing discourses of contemporary and immediate interest. The different forms of true crime entertainment are significant precisely because they produced and still produce knowledges of crime and criminality that intersect with the 'social experience of crime'. John Cawelti (1977) has argued that looking at the formulas of popular literature illuminates a range of fundamental questions, shedding light on how crime is defined in different periods and cultures, how crime literature is related to other elements of culture and the story patterns deployed to embody popular fascination with crime (Cawelti 1977: 52). This book examines formulas, codes and conventions, but then moves on to explore how these intersect with, and inform, a more complex problem – how the discourses of true crime help to produce the modern social subject who is both fearful and vigilant, but also intrigued by crime.

The main focus of this book is contemporary true crime literature in Britain since the 1980s. True crime publishing began to expand significantly at this time and only showed signs of entering a mild decline towards the late 1990s (Thorpe 1997). This decline demonstrates, perhaps, that the boom in true crime was congruent with the particular social, economic or political co-ordinates of the 1980s and early 1990s. In a commercial climate where all leisure interest magazines need to compete vigorously for shelf space, new true crime titles continue to enter the market successfully. Clearly, there is a significant readership for a variety of true crime magazines and indeed there is some evidence that the number of readers may have increased during the past two decades. *Master Detective* and *Master Detective Summer Special* (both established 1950) and *True Detective* and *True Detective Summer Special* (established 1952) are the longest running magazines. 1981 saw the launch of *True Crime* and its Summer Special and ten years later, in 1991, the quarterly magazine *Murder Most Foul* came on the market.[1] These magazines hold in common their distinctiveness in the marketplace as purveyors of non-fiction. The magazines' promotional material and front covers stress the authenticity of the material addressed in each edition. The cover of *Murder Most Foul*, for example, boasts the slogan 'NO FICTION' and 'EVERY CASE TRUE'.

Magazines are mainly sold in newsagents and by annual subscription.[2] Also, they frequently carry advertisements for other true crime periodicals and books, especially sister publications, suggesting that readers probably buy two or three titles per month. Circulation figures are approximate or in some cases completely unavailable.[3] However, the publisher's statements for a typical year claim that their three main titles – *Master Detective, True Crime* and *True Detective* – have a circulation of 24,000 each.[4] Their stated target groups are men and women between 25 and 85 in all socio-economic groups, a rather vague assertion whose commercial optimism is presumably intended to entice advertisers.[5] Other research estimates that the combined readership for the three publications is 195,000 plus, with many readers probably buying all the titles each month (Cameron 1990: 131).[6]

These long-established monthlies frequently recycle stories across publications and from US to British magazines, retelling period or 'classic' cases and using rehashed press reports (ibid.: 133).[7] This eclecticism is indicative of the non-specific geographical constituency of readers. Like national papers they both define what is of national concern (the 'big stories') and stress that these stories are meaningful to readers everywhere (Soothill and Walby 1991: 35). These sources, together with the often crude reproduction of monochrome photographs and drawings, recall the conventions of tabloid reportage (conflated, however, with the codes and conventions of generic fiction). The structural and formal resemblance of these magazines to newspapers suggests therefore that they may be viewed as 'ephemeral best-sellers' or one-day books, quickly read and soon to be discarded (Anderson, B. 1983: 39).

In February 1993 Eaglemoss Publications brought out a weekly, numbered series entitled *Real-Life Crimes ... and how they were solved*. This magazine is innovative because unlike many earlier publications it is designed to collect and keep in clip binders. *Real-Life Crimes* is published with colour photography, graphics and charts that contrast strongly with its competitors' monthly publications, which are entirely in monochrome and crudely produced on low-grade paper. This magazine resembles more closely other 'quality' leisure interest and self-instruction magazines such as those for cooking and DIY. It employs colour-coded sections, clear layouts and the higher production values of reference periodicals. The stated target readership of *Real-Life Crimes* is 68 per cent female, aged between 16 and 34 and occupies the C1, C2 bracket (a higher socio-economic bracket than that estimated for the more traditional magazines and a confirmation of the high numbers of female readers). The series was scheduled to run for approximately 120 issues and achieve a circulation of 300,000 (Campbell 1993: 13). These figures suggest that a far larger market than that reached by more traditional magazines is potentially receptive to true crime.

March 1993 also saw the arrival of two more crime-related magazines: *Murder Trail* and *Crimesearch*. *Crimesearch* (anticipating an initial print-run of 80,000 copies) least resembles the traditional true crime magazine because it invites the reader to help resolve recent police inquiries by offering rewards for details of unsolved crimes, including recent murders. Its contents suggest that it is tapping into the 'law and order' market created in the main by television programmes such *Crimewatch UK* and *Crimestoppers*. *Murder Trail*, promoted as 'frighteningly realistic', is a bi-monthly publication for armchair detectives. It contains elements of a puzzle book or murder mystery, providing forensic details, clues, maps and so on, to enable the reader to investigate crimes (Campbell 1993: 13).

This market was mined further when, in April 1994, *Killers – The Murder Magazine*, subtitled '*Shocking True Stories of the Ultimate True Crime*', was launched. It was immediately successful enough to be issued as a monthly publication. It began with an initial print-run of 50,000 copies, double the circulation figures of its more established rivals, and is expected to make a profit for the foreseeable future (Nadelson 1994: 18). It is possible, however, that the novelty of the arrival of these new-style publications in a previously long-established market may account, in part, for these commercially promising figures. *Killers* soon changed its name to *Ultimate Crimes*, ostensibly in response to reader concern that *Killers* was too 'hard' a title for them to be seen reading on public transport or to leave lying about the house (No. 10 editorial). However, the title had also received some negative coverage in an *Observer* article accusing the magazine of pandering to a growing 'cult' interest in vicious crimes in Britain (Roe 1994: 18). In an interview the editor defended the magazine rather inarticulately by arguing: 'People are interested in murder today. It's the last frontier of violence. Women are interested in reading about sex killings' (ibid.). *Ultimate Crimes* was followed three years later in January 1997 by the Marshall Cavendish Reference Collection series *Murder in Mind*. This fortnightly glossy publication, launched with the faces of Fred and Rose West, is designed to collect and keep. Its high production values and reference to 'consultants' already well known to true crime fans and even to the public in general, constructs an image of responsible non-prurient interest in crime. Its promotional material reinforces this image:

> This unique series has been written to set out the facts clearly. *MURDER IN MIND* allows the reader to examine the evidence of each case and draw his or her own conclusions and ultimately to comprehend the incomprehensible – the act of taking another life.[8]

In addition to these, dedicated articles about true crime are now part-and-parcel of other mainstream periodicals such as newspaper supplements, *Reader's Digest* and women's leisure and lifestyle magazines. New magazines launched in the 1980s such as *Chat* and *Bella* adapted the traditional woman's weekly into a new-style cheap tabloid package that delivered both women's issues and human interest news features, including true crime (Winship 1987: 148–62). The women's weekly magazine, in keeping with its generic relationship to tabloids and newspaper supplements, commonly deploys the language of the confessional and of sensation to let readers into a story of personal suffering or despair. Stories such as 'Let Me Bury My Son', an interview with the mother of a Moors Murder victim in *Chat* (Johnson J. 1992), provide an opportunity to revisit notorious crimes from the perspective of the victim's family. Other stories are presented in a murder-mystery format such as the story of one woman's discovery that her missing daughter had, in fact, been murdered, described in 'The Secret of the Sands; the dunes concealed John Cooper's crime – until the sands shifted', featured in *Bella* (Taylor E. 1994). *Chat* also ran a series of period true crime stories featuring Victorian female killers entitled 'Deadlier than the Male' (e.g. Mortensson 1992a and 1992b). These features are luridly illustrated in red and black, with scareheads and a sensational vocabulary in keeping with the flashy traditions of tabloid reportage. Their presence signals, above all, the ubiquity of the true crime feature article and its attraction to a broad range of readers. As a crime story loses currency it often moves away from the news pages and enters the arena of leisure reading, revealing in this transition a constituency of female and/or younger readers interested in reading about crime and its consequences for the people involved.

The launch of new book imprints also signals an expansion in true crime publishing. The early 1990s saw the peak of true crime's success in Britain, with the launch of true crime series by Virgin, Headline, Nemesis and Creation Books, the re-issue of Penguin's *Famous Trials* series and Music Collection International's true crime audio books. More recently, notorious murder cases such as that of Fred and Rose West and Dr Harold Shipman have inspired a number of both well-researched and 'instant' books. The commercial success of British true crime also parallels the tremendous public interest in true accounts of crime in the United States (Provost 1991: 7; Stasio 1991; Nadelson 1994). Since the late 1980s, true crime in the US has achieved sufficient popularity to justify a spate of reprints and the retrieval of older or more obscure cases (Jenkins 1994: 92). These reprints, also appearing in Britain, are clearly indicative of consistent popular interest, which stands in stark opposition to critics who have generally regarded true crime as ephemeral, of limited interest and even somewhat distasteful.

A survey of *The Bookseller* catalogue from 1979 onwards indicates a notable increase in the numbers of true crime books published during the 1980s. However, the categorisation of books as 'true crime' is problematic for librarians and booksellers alike, which in turn confounds any attempt by the researcher to make a clear-cut assessment of its presence in the marketplace. *The Bookseller*, for example, collates its books under the heading 'Law and Crime' without differentiating between true crime, legal textbooks and investigative journalism by writers such as Paul Foot.[9] One indication of the shifting borders of the genre may be the recent reissue of the Penguin *Famous Trials* series (originally Hodge and Hodge 1941–64). Covers bear a red and black margin-strip of an elongated fingerprint that renders them easily identifiable. An entry in *The Bookseller* of 12 August 1994 promotes the series as 'the classic series of true crime books', a claim that retrospectively locates them in a more lucrative category than that of 'legal history'.[10] Penguin have also re-issued 'classic' individual accounts such as Sybille Bedford's *The Best We Can Do* (1958) as part of their *True Crime* imprint.[11] Other books in the series tend to focus on 'classic' or period murders such as those perpetrated by Crippen,[12] Mrs Maybrick,[13] and so on. Otherwise they may feature more contemporary but little-known British murders such as the deaths of the elderly Luxton family on their isolated farm in 1975, analysed by John Cornwell in his book called *Earth to Earth* (1984).

Relying on publishers' own book promotions leads to inconsistency in identifying true crime books. For instance, in 1994 Penguin published Alexandra Artley's *Murder in the Heart*, the story of sisters June and Hilda Thompson who killed their father in 1988 after years of severe abuse. The story of 'one small, ordinary family gone completely mad' (cover notes) won the Crime Writers' Association (CWA) Gold Dagger Award for Non-Fiction. Yet Artley's book is packaged somewhat differently. Its subtitle, *A True-Life Psychological Thriller*, elevates the book into 'Current Affairs, Psychology/Psychiatry' (cover notes) rather than the more stigmatised genre of true crime. But the book carries all the signifiers of 'quality' true crime: the CWA award, eleven pages of monochrome photographs, including a police Blue Book[14] shot of Mr Thompson lying dead on his bed, and a foreword by the acclaimed true crime writer Brian Masters. Its packaging and promotion also signal a hierarchy of taste and distinction within the industry itself, where high production values, an acclaimed author or a quality newspaper or publisher can be drawn upon to signal a true crime product as uniquely 'serious', 'thoughtful', 'objective', 'judicious' and so forth.

Since the early 1990s true crime books have also appeared under imprints which more clearly signal their target market, – such as Time Life's *True Crime* series or the new imprint by Virgin, also called *True Crime*. The mid-1990s also saw the successful introduction of the true crime audio book from publishers such as Music Collection International which issued a series in December 1994 narrated by the true crime specialist and radio celebrity Martin Fido.[15] Cases here included profiles of Peter Sutcliffe,[16] John Reginald Christie,[17] and so on. During the years 1992–96 17 imprints consistently carried true crime books, a number which is in itself indicative of the perceived capacity of the market for these publications.[18]

A flurry of books often follows close behind the trial and conviction of notable British criminals such the nurse Beverley Allitt,[19] Rose and Fred West[20] and the Newell brothers.[21] In 'Making a Killing in the Bookshops' (1994), a review of the books published after the sentencing of Roderick and Mark Newell for the murder of their parents, the journalist Alexandra Duval Smith investigated the notion that 'murder pays' in the publishing industry. She noted that three paperbacks telling the story of the Newell family would be available after sentencing, riding on the back of the very useful publicity generated by the case.[22] Each book would have a 10,000 print-run and as 'instants' they would have a large, if short-lived market capitalising on public recognition of the case. She also observed that serialisation in the national press might well be as remunerative as an entire print-run of books. Cases such as the Newell brothers are small fry compared with that of Fred and Rose West where at least six books were commissioned, including two books co-authored by the Wests' own children (Oxford 1995: 4–5).[23]

The mid-1990s continued to see some expansion of the true crime industry, creating a publishing 'boom' noted even in the 'quality' press. The crime journalist Duncan Campbell's feature article 'How Murder is Putting New Life into Publishing' (1993) was written in response to the 'newly invigorated true crime industry'. According to Campbell the industry consists not only of books, which constitute the bulk of popular mainstream true crime, but also the new part-work *Real Life Crimes*, and more obscure items such as a circulating tape of a murderer's confession, collector's cards and a Jack the Ripper fanzine. A year later Giles Gordon (1994) of *The Times* again noted the increase in true crime books, even going as far as to suggest that the British tradition of reading crime fiction was being undermined by true crime books where 'reality has learnt to mirror fiction'. The suggestion that detective fiction fans are moving over to true crime is questionable, although it is indicative of the perceived attraction of true crime narratives. Maxim Jakubowski, the owner of the specialist bookshop 'Murder One', said in an interview for *ES Magazine*: 'Britain produces more crime fiction per head than anywhere else and more and more writers make a living from it' (Martin, A. 1995: 20). But Jakubowski also notes the significant numbers of true crime readers. Ten per cent of 'Murder One's sales are true crime, with some 'excellent' authors such as Brian Masters as well as a lot of 'exploitative, scissors-and-paste stuff' (ibid.).

In recognition of this patently popular but critically neglected genre, this work undertakes a textual analysis that unpacks the relationship between true crime, its popular fascination and appeal, and the moment of its recent commercial success. Examining the often conflicting knowledges that inform the various forms of true crime and how they are articulated opens up to scrutiny the accounts that they offer of crime and criminality, progress and mortality. An analysis of the ways in which true crime picks up, articulates and interrogates discourses of law and order, and crime and punishment, can provide real insights into the production and inflection of the social and, more especially, the legal subject in a particular historical moment.[24] For the commercial success of British true crime publishing since the early 1980s is congruent with other politicised debates about crime, disorder, disciplinarity and the legal and social responsibilities of the individual citizen. Historically, the rhetorical tenor and the discursive boundaries of these debates stem from the late 1950s and 1960s. Then 'public opinion' aired in parliament and in the media addressed anxieties about a perceived decline in moral standards and family values. This decline was discursively linked to increasing 'permissiveness', liberalism, a growing affluence and the Americanisation of the mass media (Hoggart 1957; Weeks 1981: 232–63; Hebdige 1982; Sutherland 1982; Davies and Saunders 1983: 13–50). These debates about permissiveness, affluence and media influence quickly crystallised around highly visible, public crimes of social disorder and also around the more private, hidden crimes of individual murder and atrocity.[25] They continue to form the discursive bedrock of current, particularly conservative criticism and concern over rising crime, the importation of American-style criminal activity such as serial killing, gun crime and drug cultures, together with the portrayal of sex and violence in popular entertainment. Integral to these debates is the spectre of the dissolution of the 'family' as the lynchpin of civilised society. These debates, evident in the national press and in popular journals such as *Reader's Digest*, frequently return to fundamental questions of law and order, punishment and retribution and the calibration of justice for the victims of crime, issues which are of genuine public concern. It is important to explore the ways in which true crime functions as a potential arena for the articulation of these common fears and anxieties. How much can true crime and its related forms tell us about how these fears are figured, contained and directed?

It will become clear that the social construction of crime and violence that informs true crime entertainment is, by definition, important to readers. The fact that the cases narrated involve *real* people who actually experienced violence and abuse should not lead automatically to the condemnation of true crime readers and fans as voyeurs or as readers of poor taste. Readers too have a 'lived' relation to the true accounts of crime which they encounter everywhere; public fears of street crime, burglary and even random violence also demand critical recognition.[26] In view of this there is a need to explore the landscape of fear against which true crime is set, to understand contemporary fears of crime and random violence that form the social backdrop of the current popularity of true crime books, magazines and television programmes.

Popular concern about crime is amplified in political discourses and in the discourses of the popular press and television (Cohen, S. 1973; Hall, S. *et al.* 1978; Chibnall 1977; Hough 1988; Schlesinger *et al.* 1992). These anxieties are rendered explicit in the successful implementation of a number of pro-law and order initiatives aimed overtly at the active citizen. Neighbourhood Watch schemes, the Crimestoppers initiative and the boom in home security goods and services during the 1980s all demonstrate a willingness by some sectors of the public to participate in security and surveillance practices (Traini 1984; Hough 1988; Taylor, I. 1997). The fuelling of social anxiety about crime and public safety is the result of a complex interaction of personal experiences of crime and the variety of discourses through which crime in general is apprehended. Readers, therefore, bring to true crime their own fears and experiences of crime, of random violence and more generally of injury, abuse and death. The underscoring of 'truth', authenticity and actuality in the promotion of true crime stories about violence and atrocity arguably signals to the reader that these are not foolish fears but patently grounded in verifiable and often notorious fact.

This analysis of true crime narratives will address all these issues of definition, interpretation and evaluation, mainly through models of discourse and discursive practice. Here 'discourse' is taken to be an identifiable group of statements which together, produce a particular type of knowledge. True crime, like any genre which has established codes and conventions, typically deploys a number of related themes, registers and knowledges to produce its own particularised understanding of the social experience of crime, violence and criminal justice. In this sense, true crime conforms to the notion of the 'discursive formation as a network or corpus of statements' where 'the statements all support a common "theme" ... a "strategy", a common institutional, administrative or political drift or pattern' (Cousins and Hussain 1984: 85). However, a discursive formation is not isolated or impermeable to other discourses; rather it contains traces of past discourses and accrues elements of others which are adjacent to it. True crime, in its attempt to interpret or explain the notorious criminal and the violent event within society (for this is its 'common theme'), draws upon the discourses of medicine, psychiatry and jurisprudence, all of which have themselves helped to establish the limits of how a criminal subject is to be perceived and understood. This book looks at the pattern of discursive practices that constitute different forms of true crime entertainment, looking at how and why some forms of true crime emphasise themes that others subdue. It also examines how these discourses, far from being contained, are actually made hybrid through their marriage to other, quite different literary, theological and political models of the criminal subject and criminality. For example, an analysis of contemporary true crime narratives offers insights into the kinds of power relations produced by the discourses of law and order, citizenship and individual responsibility and how these are articulated in popular literature. The recent forms of these relations of power, embodied in

Thatcherite discourses of individual responsibility and law and order rose to prominence at the same time as true crime found significant commercial success. This conjunction invites the question of how true crime (and forms adjacent to it) articulates the nature of Thatcherism and its ideological legacy. I explore the ways in which true crime's recent commercial success may be related to its ability to harness, explore or even challenge the dominant discourses of the period.

The book falls into two parts. Part I Issues, Histories, Contexts, establishes the questions that are encountered and addressed throughout; questions of definition, of development and change and of the inter-relationship of true crime and broader professional and popular knowledges and practices. Chapter 1 presents a preliminary indication of the complex relationship between the four coordinates central to this book: generic true crime, its appeal and fascination, its intersection with the political moment of its production and consumption and its production of particular understandings of the modern social subject. This last issue, of the modern social subject, arises in different ways throughout the book and is partly dependent upon the form and address of true crime and also upon the social and political discourses that inform it. The network of discourses of crime and punishment, law and order, social breakdown and moral responsibility that knit together political comment and true crime entertainment, jurisprudence and popular journalism, all help to produce and promote recognisable modern social, more specifically, legal subjects. These include such figures as the moral subject, the responsible citizen, the agent of the law, the dangerous individual, the habitual criminal and the innocent/vulnerable member of the public. Chapter 2 traces the emergence of some of these figures through discursive shifts and historical transformations that pre-date contemporary true crime. It unravels some of the historical discursive formations that produced earlier forms of true crime entertainment and the new kinds of social subjects that they articulated. Chapter 3 examines the inflection of these subjects in the political climate of the 1980s and early 1990s, looking especially at how the rhetorical division between the criminal and the good citizen is articulated and sustained in the language of law and order, true crime programming and popular journalism.

Part II Stories, Bodies, Criminals, adopts a much closer textual reading of popular true crime forms. Chapters 4, 5 and 6 are case studies of different kinds of true crime magazine. The first two chapters consider the development, enduring appeal and relevance of the traditional monthly magazine, analysing its deployment of a popular verbal and visual vernacular, its revelry in the bizarre, the comic and the grotesque and its dependence on period stories. Chapter 6 moves on to inspect the quite different pleasures of the new-style collect and keep partwork magazine, focusing on the centrality of forensic science and the emphasis upon the dead and decaying body of the murder victim as both spectacle and clue. Chapter 7 concludes with an examination of the centrality of the murderer to true crime biography. It looks at the collision between a literary aesthetic that elevates and privileges the male murderer as a powerful agent of action and destruction and the moral imperative that impels the biographer to condemn him utterly for turning his victims into objects of atrocity and abuse.

Part I
Issues, Histories, Contexts

1
'True Stories Only!'

> Doctors who use their medical knowledge to kill make chilling criminals. And there have been quite a few of them in our century dating back to Dr. Crippen. We all like to think that stretched out on the couch in the privacy of the doctor's surgery we're going to be in soothing, healing hands. With the benefit of hindsight, though, we wouldn't have been too happy in the surgery of Dr. Robert Clements. Here was a veritable upright citizen by day, a real Dr. Jekyll; and a cunning killer by night, Mr. Hyde himself. Clements used his extensive knowledge of poisons gained during a long sojourn in the East to kill no fewer than four of his wives for money. We open this *Master Detective Summer Special* with the compelling story of this ruthless GP and his tragic victims. *Master Detective Summer Special* presents lots of other true stories which we hope will give you hours of fascinating holiday reading – come rain or shine!
>
> (*Master Detective* Editorial for Summer 1996: 1)

Reading true crime, like reading fiction, may be a leisure activity, a holiday diversion or a keen pastime. It is frequently sold alongside detective fiction and police procedurals and is often consumed by the same readers, dissolving the always straining divisions between fact and fiction. Yet above all, true crime promotes itself as 'actuality', as 'realism', 'as existing in fact'. Magazines address the potential buyer with the promise of 'true stories only', 'no fiction'. Publishers themselves generally define the genre of true crime as consisting mainly of true stories of sensational and dramatic murder, with gangsterism, armed robbery, kidnapping and so on as mini-genres or virtual sub-genres in their own right (Provost 1991: 5ff). More broadly, true crime may be understood as a form which proffers the reader stories of *lived experiences* of crime, violence and murder. It mediates disturbing social realities and experiences of violence, abuse, atrocity and death. But usually this is already a secondary mediation of crimes that have been recycled from reportage, anthologies and encyclopaedias of crime. It is these mediations (both primary and secondary) that articulate the very stuff of fantasy, fear and anxiety around crime. Moreover, the experience of murder and violence within society has become naturalised, especially within the popular press, as timeless and universal, with notably heinous acts of violence and atrocity further abstracted from their historical context through concepts of the 'evil' and the 'monstrous' (see Oppenheimer 1996). Despite, or perhaps because of, this tendency to mythologise extreme criminality in the media, true crime generates its appeal specifically through its attempt to capture the distinctive experience of particular crimes and the uniqueness of their perpetrators. It makes sense, therefore, that a critical examination of the genre should at least begin by turning to the actuality of the originary, historically grounded event of violence or murder that forms the basis of the true crime story.

An acknowledgement of the brute actuality of the events which source this literature of crime allows one to consider how these are reshaped and fashioned into the images and narratives of true crime entertainment and the implications of this fashioning for critical work. Two issues are at stake here: an acknowledgement of the transformation of actuality into pleasurable forms and leading on from this, the question of how cultural critics engage with and politically interpret that troubling pleasure. This pleasure may be considered 'troubling' in the sense that 'experience' and 'reality' disrupt or trouble the processes of representation which attempt to articulate and confine them. Here the potential violence of representation comes into question. Most simply, non-fiction and barely fictionalised representations of violence, atrocity and murder have been challenged in the media for exploiting the lives and experiences of those who have already been exploited too much.[1] Also, true crime may be analysed and contested for reiterating rather than challenging the conventional power relations played out between victims and criminals, between criminals and the law and between the state and its citizens. Finally, the horror of murder, rape and atrocity is both represented and unrepresentable, spoken and unspeakable even within the arena of a genre whose business it is to give them visual representation and narrative form. A study of true crime reveals how popular literature can make the difficult and disturbing accessible to the reader, through its narrative representations of the criminal justice system and of the society which it serves, of the criminal and of the victim and of atrocity and abuse.

The acknowledgement of the brute actuality of the events that form the basis of the true crime genre presents some difficulties for the cultural critic. For even as we, critics or general readers, acknowledge the extra-textual experience of particular crimes we still know of them only through the textual evidence of trial transcripts, interviews, newspaper features, and so on. Any 'event' is accessible only via the form of its retrospective construction. Even visual recordings (most famously perhaps the Zapruder video of Kennedy's assassination, the Rodney King affair and, in Britain, the CCTV recording of James Bulger being led to his death by two older boys) offer filmic constructions of shocking events whose interpretation is open to dispute. The issue here is that both the 'criminal event' and crime narratives are apprehended through a variety of differently weighted discourses. In the end, it is only the reader who remains to evaluate their veracity as a representational form. The reader, like the critic, has no choice 'but to work with the reality we have: the reality of the paper print, the material item' (Tagg 1988: 4). It is true crime's anchorage to real events, people and experiences that defines its very form and substance. There is an overt relationship between representation and the represented here; a bond which affords true crime and other true stories of adventure, travel, mystery or romance, a very direct appeal. True crime is both testament and also an aestheticisation of brute violence. The point and appeal of true crime is its role as a purveyor of uncomfortable reality and nasty historical fact through the accessible devices of popular story-telling.

Looking at the Thompson family

> The act of representation no longer seems as clear cut as it once did. The issues of specificity and corporeality bring to a focus tensions within the domain of representation. They sharpen questions of magnitude posed by the felt tension between representation and represented.
>
> Bill Nichols (1994: 2)

The idea of a present but elusive cognitive relation between the crime event (the happening or sequence of happenings which informs true crime) and its textual representation demands closer scrutiny. For the actuality of the crime event is both the essence of the true crime story and the fulcrum upon which issues of both academic principle and media ethics have been mobilised. An examination of the case of the Thompson family begins the task of unpacking the critical implications of true crime's claim to represent the real (through actuality) and its ethical implications for critics and readers of true crime stories.

In 1994 the Barbican Art Gallery in London held a photographic exhibition called 'Who's Looking at the Family' which focused on diverse photographic representations of the family, displaying images dating mainly from the mid-1980s. One set of photographs, some taken and some selected by John Heatley, commanded particular attention from visitors who scrutinised his row of images, halting at the concluding explanation, and then returning to the beginning of the sequence to study them anew. These seemingly innocuous photographs were of the Thompson family, Hilda and Tommy and their two daughters, June and Hilda. The sequence included family snaps of the children standing with their parents in the back garden, their smiling faces screwed up in the sun, pictures almost indistinguishable from my own and many others' childhood photos. Others showed the happy faces of June and Hilda as they entered their teens, as young women sitting in the pub wearing identical coats and finally several interior photographs of the Thompsons' extremely neat and ordered home. The final picture was of Tommy Thompson lying on a bed in the scrupulously tidy front room. Only then, in the written addendum, were visitors told that Mr Thompson violently abused his family all their lives, until in 1988 his two daughters (both then in their thirties) each shot him while he lay helpless, suffering an epileptic fit. The photographs of the house interior and of Thompson's dead body turned out to be documentary evidence of the scene of the crime taken by John Heatley in his professional role as police photographer.

Over a period of 40 years, in Chorley and Preston, Lancashire, Mr Thompson cruelly abused the Thompson women. The house where Thompson died in Preston was evidence of the family's strange and constricted lives. It was organised like an institution, with barrack-like living conditions. To some it was 'an eerie amateur museum of one small, ordinary family gone completely mad' (Artley 1994: 11). Tiny notices covered the house, recording the minutiae of everyday life – when the budgie was due to moult, when the new soap dish was opened. Throughout their lives June and Hilda Thompson, together with their mother, suffered relentless aggressive physical, mental and sexual abuse by Tommy in this domestic environment. During their trial at Liverpool Crown Court in November 1988 June and Hilda received a token two years' suspended sentence for the crime of murdering their father. Mr Justice Boreham said: 'I accept that in many ways your life has been a form of torment and in a sense you have taken your punishment before the event' (ibid.: ix).

In the light of this knowledge the gallery photographs, which seemed to reveal the quaintness of the domestic interior of a small Lancashire family home and the narrative of a growing family, now appear to mean something else entirely. Val Williams (1994: 62) writes in the exhibition catalogue: 'Like a cartographer mapping some alien and terrifying land, he [Heatley] identified the surface of dysfunction and exposed a terrible history.' Here is representation as revelation and exposure; the photographic process allowing an access of light both technically and metaphorically upon the subjects of representation. Newly informed, we understand differently Mr Thompson's military and obsessive neatness and what turns out to be the scene of his violent demise in the front room. Now these domestic interiors seem to be quite clearly 'criminal evidence', like that displayed in the police Blue Book which trial juries are invited to view.[2] The photographs become records of the 'scene of the crime', where the subjects of photographic practice are important or notable because they have been the subjects or objects of horrific violence and finally murder.

As 'records' of the Thompson family both the police and family photographs gain specificity of time, place and function which seems to narrow the gap between the subjects and their representation. For although the photograph can be propaganda, misinformation or fakery, there is usually some definite iconic and indexical relationship between the photographic image and its referent. In the same way, the true crime story can never be wholly severed from the events that it purports to relate, since the genre defines itself most simply as a true story of a crime. To borrow a phrase from Roland Barthes, in both cases 'the referent adheres'; in both cases representation and its referent are glued together 'like the condemned man and the corpse in certain tortures' (Barthes 1984: 6). While the practice of reinterpreting the Thompson images in the light of new information is a reminder of the dubiousness of any claims that the photograph represents a fixed reality, none the less for the viewer this knowledge of a horrific family drama seems to set a seal upon interpretation. This sequence offers up a narrative of domestic life that becomes re-inscribed as a narrative of murder.[3]

In 1993 Alexandra Artley used some of these same images to illustrate her true crime book *Murder in the Heart*. Both front and back cover of the paperback edition bear images of the smiling girls, juxtaposed with their family portraits. But unlike the Barbican photographs which catch viewers unaware, here readers are probably more familiar with the conventions of the true crime genre. With the help of the jacket notes it is already clear that readers should expect a tale of a 'terrible domestic tyranny and of the unreason that can rule people's lives', a tale that ends in murder.

In Artley's book the photographic images are already anchored by captions. Under a monochrome image of the grinning Thompson girls, Artley writes:

> June and Hilda Thompson entering teenagerhood, around the time when Tommy Thompson first began to sexually abuse June. Photography was an element of his sadism. Whatever unpleasant event had just preceded the taking of the photograph, he always insisted that the subjects smile very enthusiastically. (1994: fig. 14)

Here attention is drawn to a layered reading of the Thompson photographs; even as they illustrate and enhance the true crime text they are also 'evidence' of the disturbing crimes that occurred within that family. Tommy Thompson's photographs are in this context artefacts of the 'real', evidence not only of the truth of the true crime story but also of the true nature of Thompson's criminal behaviour. Here the interpretation of images is no more or less fixed than those in the gallery but a different relation is established through the generic codes and conventions of true crime. If the photographs help to reinforce a sense of place and time, they also provide the reader with faces to link with the central figures in the narrative, building identificatory bridges between text and reader. This construction of empathy and identification with either the murderer or the victims of crime also helps to circumvent the accusation that reading true crime is morally dubious or voyeuristic. Up-market true crime books in particular claim to 'close the gap' between subject and reader through point of view and empathy. In the foreword to *Murder in the Heart* Brian Masters writes:

> The writer may expand beyond bald chronicle to engage the reader in an exercise of imaginative empathy, to do that which is forbidden in the courtroom – namely, to make the audience *feel* what it

was like to live under the same roof as Tommy Thompson. (Artley 1994: x)

This imaginative empathy helps to defuse the ethical implications of reading either the distressing diary entries of the Thompson women or the more objective authorial accounts of the violence they endured over a number of years.

Bill Nichols (1994: 44) has noted with reference to the phenomenon of reality television that the 'combination of raw and cooked, evidence and story, produces a spectacular oscillation between the sensational and the banal'. In true crime, details of the ordinary and the banal, of everyday life in 1890s Whitechapel or in 1960s Hell's Kitchen, bind the ordinary and the bizarre together. The story's roots in the quotidian reinforce the empathy already constructed through photography and address to the reader. The banal is everywhere present in Artley's book: facsimile extracts from the scribbled diaries of the Thompson daughters, the retrospectively poignant family snaps, the reassuring presence of tea-drinking rituals and cuddly toys for the women who survived Tommy Thompson. These things temper the sensational 'violence, superstition and mental illness all bound together by a terrible love' which the story aims to reconstruct (1994 cover notes). They help to ground extraordinary violence in the everyday.

These representations of the Thompson family in both the gallery and the true crime book, their oscillation between actuality and reconstruction, between the quotidian and the bizarre, exemplify the chief difficulty and challenge of the critical analysis of non-fiction genres. To engage critically with true crime is *critically* to engage with the fact of its reference to both banal and exceptionally disturbing social realities and their transformation into mass entertainment. True crime narrates crime-events (already mediated by personal accounts, diaries and the stories produced by the law, journalism, and so on) and transmutes them into new kinds of stories, into mass-produced entertainment, into 'leisure interest' products. The narrative frame arguably renders palatable the distasteful and unpleasant aspects of real lives which true crime attempts to reconstruct. None the less the up-market true crime writer usually carefully negotiates questions of taste and decency. For example, Alexandra Artley writes that she has passed over one especially harrowing detail of the Thompson women's experiences in silence. By drawing attention to this omission Artley underscores her tale's credibility as both an accurate (she knows that there is more to tell) and morally scrupulous endeavour (she is not going to tell it).

Surveying the press coverage of the case she notes that by Christmas 1988, 'the three women were left without a rag of private or public dignity between them' (Artley 1994: 7). Artley, despite being a journalist herself, roundly condemns the press's descent, 'straight down to sex, violence and freshly ground screw of the grotesque' (ibid.). This distancing strategy presumably permits author and reader to proceed together in good conscience, albeit more delicately, to weigh up the finer details of the 'truth' of the Thompsons' lives.

The notion that the media constructs and mediates social reality is a legitimate and wholly acceptable commonplace. So too is the notion that these constructions and mediations are never definitive, nor are the ways of reading them fixed. As Heatley proved in the Barbican exhibition, the Thompson photographs may be read and understood in diverse ways, depending upon the information at one's disposal, the devices used to frame the images and the context in which they are placed. Even the preferred reading cannot be the final or only reading. Likewise Artley can construct a literary interpretation of the 'truth' of the Thompson case only by contrasting it with the grotesque distortion of the 'truth' in tabloid press reportage. Another true crime book, programme or magazine article might construct the narrative quite differently, offering us other 'truths'. The question of truth here impacts upon this work because any discussion, for example, of the aesthetics of true crime runs the risk of closing down the brute reality of the original crime event and its social and personal consequences for real people. To acknowledge this 'truth' (even though we as readers and critics cannot directly apprehend it), is to occupy a position, for no matter how reflexive the criticism, the critical gesture is always threaded through with assumptions, with criteria of taste and value rooted in what we perceive the *facts* of the story to be.

Defining the true crime book

Artley acknowledges the delicacy sometimes required in investigating and telling a potentially nasty story of violence and incest; she chronicles her circumspect approaches to the victims of Tommy Thompson, her carefully prepared interviews with neighbours and police officers and refers to atrocities that she will not detail. With careful writing such as this it is easy to forget the broader picture of true crime publishing within which Artley's work finds a place as a saleable story, as a marketable journalistic commercial endeavour. Turning to the publishing industry and its perceived market reveals, more fully, what true crime aims to do and where the ethical boundaries of the genre are to be drawn. For here at least publishers, authors and booksellers must select criteria for economic success and decide what constitutes a good true crime book within the context of the market place. The American true crime author Gary Provost writes in his book *How To Write and Sell True Crime* that entertainment is the primary objective of the successful true crime book and the reason why people read them. He himself understands the process of reading true crime through the conventional metaphors of escape and immersion: 'We are writing for readers who want to escape, who want to be transported into another world, another place. ... They want colour, character, emotion' (Provost 1991: 90). Provost understands true crime reading as a pleasure related, rather than in opposition to, the pleasures of consuming other popular forms such as romantic fiction (which he also writes under a female pseudonym). Clearly, however, there must be features specific to true crime, which generate the particular experience and pleasure of the genre. Actuality is most obviously a prerequisite. Provost (ibid.: 129) observes, for example, that pseudonyms are sometimes employed for reasons of confidentiality and that although these do not alter the substance of the text in any way, readers are 'put off' by them. Real names and real places are badges of authenticity; powerful signifiers that help to differentiate true crime from 'novelised' stories of crime. Photographs, usually in monochrome, also reinforce the 'worldliness' of the true crime text, with most true crime books including about eight photographs (ibid.).

The publishers interviewed by Provost exhibit fairly consistent views about what constitutes true crime. Carolyn Reidy, president of Avon Books, well-known publishers in the American true crime field, identified three common themes in the genre: 'There are murderers among us. ... Money can't hide evil or buy happiness. ... Do I have the potential for this evil in me too?' (ibid.: 10). These themes situate true crime within a broader philosophical context that is also characteristic of other 'true' story genres such as the 'true romance'. First, the true story must be an exemplary parable about the relationship between worldly aspirations (avarice, ambition, sexual desire) and metaphysical aspirations (happiness), and second, stories about other people are also about 'us'. In fact, although greed or jealousy often motivates crime, many true crime books focus on atypical and inexplicable violent crime where motivation is obscure or psychologically complex. What is clear, however, as Reidy herself observes, is that for most publishers and readers the central theme of true crime has been and continues to be murder. The publisher Charles Spicer comments on the genre: 'It's not about art theft, it's not about governmental cover-up. It's really a case involving a murder in which there's an investigation and usually a trial' (ibid.: 9). While true crime is sometimes defended as exemplary parable, it is also thrilling. Reidy notes: 'People these days feel threatened by their perception of increasing violence all around. There is both a desire to understand and a vicarious thrill in reading about violence' (ibid.).

An editor at Dell is more flexible about the crimes which define the genre, citing the book *Perfect Victim* as an example of a good true crime read. Here the story concerns a woman snatched from the road in 1977 and kept as a slave in appalling conditions for seven years before finally being rescued (ibid.). The virtue of the crime for this publisher is its 'abnormality', its novelty carrying more weight than the more 'everyday' murders that fill every newspaper. Spicer goes on to identify insight into the protagonist (usually the murderer) or 'psychological realism' as an important feature of these stories. Psychological realism enables the reader to move some way towards understanding character and motivation, as well as providing a way into a potentially disturbing or alienating story. Indeed emotional, psychological and narrative truths are considered to be fundamental to a well-crafted true crime story. Also, several editors argue that a strong sense of place and evidence of in-depth research is also essential (ibid.: 9–10). Provost himself strongly agrees, contending that the setting is virtually a 'character' in its own right. He observes: 'the reader is left with the feeling that if all the characters in the story were exported to another state or region, the story would not have happened, at least not in the same way' (ibid.: 93).

True crime: professional ethics

It is an indication perhaps of the extent to which the modern true crime market has established and consolidated itself that there are now three books in print aimed at new authors interested in the genre. Both the Provost book and the audio book *How To Write True Crime That Sells* (Kolarik and Kennedy 1993) published in the US are also distributed in Britain.[4] Again, the implicit assumption behind GeraLind Kolarik and Dolores Kennedy's audio discussion is that murder is the subject of choice for true crime that sells and that, somewhat vaguely, true crime sells because it caters to 'public fascination' (Side A). Kolarik notes that violence is not enough in itself to sell copies. The narrative also needs to achieve closure, preferably with the conviction of the criminal protagonist. This offers the reader the reassuring sense of a 'good ending', both aesthetically and morally.

Both of these 'how to' books attend to the ethics of true crime writing only in the most pragmatic fashion. Provost, for instance, indicates that the case of a murderer who committed post-mortem atrocities on the body of his female victim could have made a successful story. However, 'it seemed that the alleged murderer was such a raving psycho-wacko that even total co-operation from him would be almost worthless' (Provost 1991: 25). No further comment is proffered on the ethics of interviewing disturbed alleged murderers, or indeed on the suitability of the proposed topic of investigation. Instead he advises writers to 'go for the emotions' when interviewing people involved with criminals or victims (ibid.: 75). Of the eight potential stories that Provost considers for a true crime case, none is rejected for ethical or moral reasons. Provost, Kolarik and Kennedy all employ a wholly professional discourse, emphasising the need to consolidate the author's legal security through taped interviews and release forms. The latter, however, are more forthright about techniques employed to locate and approach suitable sources. In cases with a high media profile they recommend attending the victim's funeral, although this should be done 'softly' (Kolarik and Kennedy, Side A). Again, police officers and family members of both victims and criminals will want to tell their side of the story if they are 'approached carefully' (ibid.). None of these three authors addresses questions of taste or decency or offers advice on how much or what kind of detail is acceptable for publication.

To understand the complexity of the journalist/subject encounter in true crime writing it is more useful to read Janet Malcolm's *The Journalist and the Murderer* (1990), an investigative account of a true crime writer and his subject. Malcolm's book reproduces a letter written in 1975 by the former policeman and well-known crime writer Joseph Wambaugh. The letter was to Dr Jeff MacDonald, a man accused of the slaughter of his wife and two small children, who was seeking a collaborator to write a book about his defence campaign. Wambaugh was bluntly honest about what this would entail:

> You should understand that I would not think of writing *your* story ... It would be *my* story. Just as *The Onion Field* was *my* story and *In Cold Blood* was Capote's story. We both had the living persons sign legal releases which authorised us to interpret, portray, and characterise them as we saw fit, trusting us implicitly to be honest and

faithful to the truth as *we* saw it, not as *they* saw it. With this release you can readily see that you would have no recourse at law if you didn't like my portrayal of you. Let's face another ugly possibility: what if I ... did not believe you innocent? (Wambaugh, in Malcolm 1990: 29)

As it turned out Wambaugh did not take on the book. Instead the project was taken up by the journalist Joe McGinniss who befriended MacDonald and agreed to follow MacDonald's defence team as they struggled to prove his innocence. However, McGinniss's book, entitled *Fatal Vision* (1983) (published after MacDonald was found guilty), damned him unequivocally as a psychopath. MacDonald, in spite of being found guilty, sued the journalist for breach of contract because he had deliberately feigned a sympathetic friendship while writing a work of character assassination. Malcolm's account of the case was written in response to the ethical issues that arose from the breach of contract court case in the United States – *MacDonald* v. *McGinniss* 1987. MacDonald and his publishers eventually settled for a large sum out of court. The case became a *cause célèbre* illustrating the conflict between the rights of the subject of a book versus the freedom of the journalist to dissimulate in order to tell his/her 'true' crime story.

The problem highlighted in the case, as Malcolm sees it, is one of the interdependence of writer and subject in the production of the non-fiction narrative. As will be seen in my later discussion of Brian Masters' (1985a) book on the murderer Dennis Nilsen, while the writer strives 'to keep the subject talking, the subject is worriedly striving to keep the writer listening. The subject is Scheherezade. He lives in fear of being found uninteresting' (Malcolm 1990: 19–20). Malcolm's incisive account illustrates how the problem of providing 'interesting' characterisation constitutes a literary problem. The true crime writer must make the biographical subject into an appealing criminal protagonist.[5] It is a literary challenge which also becomes ethical jeopardy with real consequences for the people involved in the case. McGinniss decided that MacDonald was guilty (as did the jury); his book therefore naturally substantiated this view of the case. Consequently, argues Malcolm, McGinniss was obliged to portray MacDonald as vicious, evil, violent and manipulative in order to justify not only his condemnation of MacDonald as murderer, but also his 'bad faith' or deception in claiming to support his subject while working to reveal the 'truth' about him.

Malcolm anatomises the complex relationship between a variety of discourses: journalistic, legal, psychiatric and fictional, examining how they were used in order to transform the banality of the biographical subject into the dramatic and mythic figure of true crime – a figure whose authenticity convicted murderer MacDonald decided to challenge in court. The fact that this mythical figure is more meaningful, more comprehensible and more appealing to both writers and the general public than the ordinary man in the dock throws open to question the 'ontological status of a character' within and without the true crime text (ibid.: 80). Malcolm puts forward the example of Dr Michael Stone, who was called in as an expert witness to support McGinniss's depiction of his subject as a narcissistic psychopath. Somewhat bizarrely, Dr Stone made a medical assessment formulated on the basis of the account of MacDonald *as presented in McGinniss's true crime book.* For example, Stone describes in conventionally dramatic terms his first reaction to seeing MacDonald in the courtroom; his perception apparently coloured by the material he had read: 'I was highly nervous about being in the presence of this man. ... I had the feeling his eyes could bore holes through a tank. The steely stare of this hostile man!' (ibid.: 79–80). Malcolm confronts Dr Stone, pointing out 'the dangers of subjecthood': 'You talk about him as if you really knew him, as if he were a real person. ... But actually he's a character in a book. Everything we know about him we know from McGinniss's text.' But Dr Stone seems unable to perceive a problem with his text-based diagnosis (ibid.: 79–81). So Malcolm illustrates the everyday slippage between the 'life-world' and its representation in true crime journalism, the ways in which literary discourses have real effects on the way in which the dangerous individual is perceived. For she signals the ways in which the discourses of true crime are picked up and brought into the broader arena of debate about crime and the perception of the dangerous criminal subject.[6]

Malcolm argues that the journalist, unlike the novelist, draws on a narrow range of ready-made literary figures in order to shape his/her narrative. Certainly, literary figures including Raskolnikov, Count Dracula, Dr Jekyll and Mr Hyde and Dr Frankenstein's creature appear with tedious regularity in true crime reportage. In fact, both the notorious murderer and the writer of true crime narratives draw on these codes in order to comprehend the nature and meaning of atrocity and the nature of the killer himself (see Chapter 6). The non-fiction writer needs to reconcile what Hannah Arendt (1963) called the 'banality of evil' with the publisher's and indeed reader's expectation of a credible and readable account of atrocity and those that carry it out. It is Malcolm's convincingly argued contention that since MacDonald did not appear to have an exciting or overtly disturbing 'personality', the true crime writer had a 'literary problem' to solve. The solution is often to turn to the codes of romantic literature[7] or to the 'vivid characters' of criminal psychiatry as an effective shorthand in the portrayal of the notorious homicide since this allows for a romantic depiction of medical pathology, of something 'bad' hidden beneath the apparently normal exterior (Malcolm 1990: 71–3).

McGinniss sought his solution in lengthy psychiatric textual profiles of what 'pathological narcissists' tend to be like. The intention, alleges Malcolm, was that: 'some of the aura of those characters would come off on MacDonald – that by extension, their interesting horribleness would become his' (ibid.: 73). For McGinniss the appearance of an uncompromising normality had to be presented as indicative of a serious and dangerous disorder, and psychiatric literature was drawn upon to substantiate this. He wrote:

> We are dealing here not with a complete man but with something that suggests a subtly constructed reflex machine which can mimic the human personality perfectly. ... So perfect is this reproduction of a whole and normal man that no one who examines him can point out in scientific or objective terms why he is not real. And yet one knows or feels he knows that reality, in the full sense of full, healthy experiencing of life, is not here. (in ibid.: 75)

In this way, through the deployment of psychiatric literature (which is also 'literary' literature), suggests Malcolm, the romantic myth of the innate goodness of man is perpetuated and the problem of evil is not engaged with but is circumvented. MacDonald may resemble you and me, but this is only because he is able to replicate ordinariness (and innocence), not because he is ordinary (or innocent). As Tom Gunning (1995: 41) demonstrates in a different context, the categorisation of the criminal subject is not about substantiating the truth of criminality, but rather it attempts to pick out the criminal from the general population and allocate blame. Writing of the nineteenth-century development of new technologies of criminal identification such as photography, which attempted to combat criminal disguise, Gunning notes suggestively, 'the criminal who could hide beneath an assumed identity functioned like a forged banknote, exploiting the rapid exchange of modern currency while undermining the confidence on which it depended' (ibid.: 20). In the MacDonald case, the dangerous criminal subject is not even human, but is portrayed merely as a ragbag of human characteristics, a creature replicating the human persona, a phantom, an *assumed identity*. He arguably becomes a foil, both *undermining* and reinforcing the tenuous integrity of the reader's own subjectivity since the reader knows that he or she is 'real' and present even if MacDonald is not. The role of the true crime writer, however, even if he/she presents the reader with this patch-work simulacrum, is in conflict with this representation, since the writer-investigator's declared purpose is to go beyond the mask in order to reveal something authentic and even revelatory beneath. It is the circular impossibility of such a task that is addressed in the final chapter of this book.

True crime: literary merit

Authors such as Provost, Wambaugh and McGinniss say little or nothing about literary merit despite the inevitable 'literariness' of true crime. Usually the subject is said to 'lead' the true crime writer to the book, providing the focus of good true crime writing. For Gary Provost, normal people committing abnormal criminal acts are the inspiration for writing well about crime. In this context crime is not in itself 'abnormal', but particular forms of crime such as murder may be. True crime writing is not about hard news or artistic truths, it simply seeks to entertain the reading public. Novelistic techniques are therefore used to tell a story to the same readers who read novels (Provost 1991: 90). Having said this, Provost still chooses to begin his book, pre-dictably enough, with a genuflection at Truman Capote's *In Cold Blood* (1966), the work with which 'the true crime book was elevated to liter-ature' in the United States (Provost 1991: 7). Capote's book, which focuses on the near-random murder of a Kansas farming family by two apparently unremarkable misfits, was famously presented by its author as a 'non-fiction novel'. These murders were 'abnormal' not only because they were homicides, but also because they happened in an ordinary 'safe' community, occurring, in other words, where they were least expected. The axis of Capote's book is the enigma of the 'mean-ingless' murder and the inevitability of the murderers' encounter with the law. The book is pivotal in American true crime because it seemed to show that real-life crime, even random 'meaningless' murder, could be made meaningful in imaginative non-fiction, approximating even the 'great American novel'.

The point for Provost (ibid.: 117) is that narrative non-fiction should not be regarded simply as journalism but as a unique form that offers a 'pleasurable reading experience' – a non-fiction novel. The true crime writer must provide the 'truth' and a 'good read', a combination that demands the judicious use of 'creative license'. A precarious balancing act ensues as the writer creates a scene 'so explicit that the reader can step into it and get lost in the reading dream' without violating 'the promise of truth' (ibid.: 118). Publishers interviewed by Provost tend to leave the question of licence to the author and his/her lawyer unless there is obviously some detail in the text that the writer could not know and which will therefore be likely to 'disturb' the reader's confidence in the authenticity of the work. Finally, then, creative licence is based upon a professional judgement of the facts and of general knowledge of a case and the people involved. Where individuals cannot be expected to recall precise details of something that may have occurred several years before (e.g. clothes, dialogue), a writer must be at liberty to make an educated 'guess'.

Provost claims that literary non-fiction is much more open to criticism about inaccuracy than film or television because of its generic alliance with print journalism. It is certainly the case that the adherence to the unwritten rules of literary licence is important to the reader. The potential for controversy over fictionalised non-fiction is epitomised neatly in David Lodge's literary investigation of Capote's short story 'Handcarved Coffins: A Non-fiction Account of an American Crime'. In his article 'Getting the Truth' (1981) Lodge checks the veracity of Capote's claim to be presenting non-fiction. He attempts to challenge its 'authentic' presentation by foregrounding the structural similarities between Capote's tale and the stories featuring Sherlock Holmes, discovering similarities that brand 'Handcarved Coffins' as fiction. He also challenges its implausibility and assesses the implications of the 'absence of circumstantial data' surrounding the events of the story. The text is critiqued because it relies upon the 'emotional charge' of its status as a true story in order to sustain its fictional narrative appeal (ibid.: 185). In other words, the story comes with 'extra-textual support'. The implication is that true crime is inferior because it is dependent upon an external referent to orient itself as a readable text; its worldliness taints its literary aspirations. The insinuation is that good literature does not need the sales pitch or the prop of an appeal to the 'real' event to pull in the reader.

Lodge enters the field as the critical detective resolved to undermine Capote's textual claim to authenticity. But for what purpose? The article could have approvingly located Capote within a distinguished story-telling tradition that knowingly constructs tales of mystery, crime and adventure as memoirs or testimonies, including the hugely successful crime stories of Conan Doyle.[8] Instead, Lodge chooses to take Capote to task for what is in fact an established and popular literary trope. His criticism here is symptomatic of the 'problem' with true crime at a moment when readers and critics seem to be seeking guarantees of authenticity from the media. While some critics have noted the increasingly playful and reflexive nature of representations of history and real events in literature and on film and television (e.g. Sobchack 1996), 'deliberate border violations' between 'fact' and 'fiction' continue to incite concern (Nichols 1994: x).[9] It is likely that Lodge's investigation reveals more about the reader's need to be secure in the knowledge that a non-fiction story is what it purports to be than it does about false claims or bad faith on the part of the crime writer. Lodge's critique does, however, signal usefully the essential ambiguity and appeal of the true crime story. It trades upon the extra-textual event which informs the narrative, while at the same time it transmutes facts into a 'story', into 'entertainment', and both of these must be held in concert.

The assumption inherent in Lodge's critique is that the writer who relies on the extra-textual event as a prop to support the emotional charge that underpins effective story-telling is in some way *morally* as well as aesthetically compromised. Jack Miles' (1991) evaluation of true crime goes one step further by attempting to make a comparative assessment of the 'moral ante' of American true crime books and their fictional counterparts such as Bret Easton Ellis's notorious yuppie slasher-novel *American Psycho* (1991). For Miles (1991: 59), true crime literature is analogous to 'true sex' literature (that is to say, pornography): both are venal exposures of 'real people' for profit or entertainment. The argument is that fictional narratives are simply more likely to be able to explore violent cultures and subjectivities successfully (the relationship of profit and entertainment to these more 'successful' texts remains unexamined). For Miles a successful text performs a precarious balancing act, scrutinising the centrality of violence within American culture without pandering to it. Both the generic conventions and contractual obligations of true crime writing, argues Miles, precludes the necessary imaginative leap which novelists sometimes attain in the representation of the 'national imagination' (ibid.: 64). If violence is central to the American 'national imagination', popular interest in this violence is regarded by Miles as part of the problem, rather than as a reaction or engagement with the problem. He suggests that true crime writing and pulp fiction 'should almost certainly be seen as symptoms of some kind of national obsession', an obsession presumably less pandered to by ('quality'?) fiction writers (ibid.: 64). This media obsession, according to Miles, is peculiarly American and to be differentiated from the 'gentler literatures' of safer countries.[10] The commercial success of true crime is symptomatic of a national, peculiarly North American malaise. Having noted the prominent role of true crime writing in the US as a crude conduit of collective fantasy and imagination, he rejects it as unworthy of further critical attention except as the bottom line against which more serious fictions of violence may be measured. He concludes:

> Lingering critically over the lingerers over crime-as-spectacle serves little purpose. Much crime fiction and perhaps most 'true crime' non-fiction is so entirely without an agenda that there is little to discuss: there is only a questionable entertainment to promote. (ibid.)

Two issues need to be foregrounded here. First, the articles by both Lodge and Miles explicitly link the ethical problem of true crime with questions of quality and value.[11] True crime's explicit connection to the 'emotional charge' of reality, to 'spectacle' and to entertainment, together with its apparent refusal of an artistic 'agenda', seems to condemn it utterly. Second, true crime's mass readership is rendered suspect and distasteful, 'lingering' over murder stories as the subjects of a Weegee photograph would over the wreckage of an automobile accident.

A number of British true crime writers have worked to counter the perception of true crime as formulaic, trashy or distasteful. Respected British true crime authors such as Jonathan Goodman have done much to promote a positive image of British true crime as a literary genre with a respectable pedigree that harks back to the essayist Thomas De Quincey (see also Roughead 1943).[12] The aesthetic rewriting of crime engendered a tradition of 'cultured' *aficionados* of 'great British murders' that is quite different from its American counterpart. These writers, with the moral and aesthetic advantage conferred by historical distance and/or European cultural heritage, narrate 'classic' murders in an 'inverted hierarchy of its own, with the villains ranked in order of dishonour' (Cyriax 1996: ix). In his essay 'The Fictions of Murderous

Fact', Goodman (1984) acknowledges the problematic inclusiveness of the word 'crime' as a defining term, unequivocally presenting murder as the central and most important act within crime literature. As a literary epigone of De Quincey, Goodman (1984: 21) acknowledges the need to discover quality or 'picturesque' cases that constitute worthy subjects for the true crime writer. At the same time, he accepts the suggestion that it is not the quality of British murders that make them famous within the literature but the quality of the British writers who take them on. Clearly, then, Goodman believes that one can differentiate between quality true crime literature and hack writing. In stark contrast to Provost, he draws on the romantic notion of the artist producing truth, in this case 'readable truth' (ibid.: 25). Goodman acknowledges the need for the imaginative leap of fictionality, seeing the best true crime as 'a grim novel in action'.

The placing of the boundary between fact and fiction in true crime, is however, less than clear-cut. For example Robert Graves' book *They Hanged My Saintly Billy*, first published in 1957, together with numerous speculative works on the identity of Jack the Ripper, stand condemned by Goodman as examples of fraudulent writing which deserve some name other than 'true crime'. Yet Graves' work shows that he explicitly acknowledges that the book detailing '*The macabre life and execution of Dr Wm. Palmer*' is an imaginative reconstruction. Graves states: 'In reconstructing Palmer's story, I have invented little, and in no case distorted hard fact. But the case is so complex that to argue it out in historical detail would have made a very bulky and quite unreadable book' (Graves 1962: x). He is therefore open about the need to draw on the narrative devices of fiction in order to structure the story in a readable way, creating copious dialogue and picaresque description in keeping with the period. He also makes a point of stating his primary sources for the story. In this respect, as will be demonstrated later, Graves differs little in his approach to his subject from other 'responsible' true crime writers and is in any case rather more scrupulous in this regard than most. It is impossible therefore to identify unmoveable criteria upon which a judgement of 'quality' true crime writing may be based, even in the writings of an author like Goodman, whose profession is true crime. As will be seen throughout the book, these judgements by book reviewers and journalists slip back and forth between valuing the 'imaginative' and the 'dispassionate' as criteria of good writing and often these two qualities are held in concert, albeit differently weighted.

Thinking through true crime

If the question of the 'quality' of true crime as literary entertainment remains to be explored, so too does its role in the dissemination of models of understanding of crime and punishment in everyday life. The growing popularity of true crime has attracted increasing academic attention in the US but very little in Britain, aside from the work of Cameron and Frazer (1987). Work in the US has focused upon the mythic figure of the serial killer and his (rarely her) construction through a variety of texts. These may include those of true crime, but more usually focus upon the press, fiction and film (Jenkins 1994; Oppenheimer 1996; Tithecott 1997) or upon the serial killer as emblematic of the postmodern turn or of traumatic spectacle (Seltzer 1998). The emphasis upon the figure of the serial killer (as opposed to the domestic murderer for example) by academics can be attributed to the high media currency of this figure since the 1980s in the US. This currency stems from the popular perception that serial killers are a peculiarly North American phenomenon. The term accumulated popular currency through true crime books during the 1980s (see especially Ressler 1992), the commercial success of the film *The Silence of the Lambs* (Demme 1992 USA) and the notoriety of Brett Easton Ellis's novel *American Psycho* (1991).

Work by Philip Jenkins (1994), in particular, has illustrated the range of social and political issues that may be illuminated through analyses of the social construction of serial homicide as a putative social problem. Controversially, perhaps, Jenkins argues that the high profile of serial murder cases in the US has mobilised a range of special interest groups and official agencies, which formulate agendas that are ideologically and politically self-interested. According to Jenkins, these can include radical feminists, advocates of black rights, white supremacists, critics and defenders of homosexual rights, law and order campaigners and government agencies seeking increased funds for policing, and so on (Jenkins 1994: 3–4).[13] Most important is the scope of Jenkins' analysis which addresses the inflection of the serial killer 'problem' through popular forms such as slasher films, true crime books and the press. The range of these representations usefully illustrates the shifting, shape-changing construction of the notorious criminal, a figure who is so often portrayed in fact as well as fiction as clear-cut and monolithic: white, highly intelligent, socially competent and male (e.g. Jacobson 1985; Harris 1988).

In *The Lust to Kill* (1987), Cameron and Frazer have signalled the role of true crime in picking up and reproducing particular knowledges of crime and criminality. Their work focuses upon the social implications for women of the media construction of male murderers as heroic figures within modern society. Here the links between murder and misogyny are made explicit through studies of the historical construction of the murderer as 'deviant' or as existential anti-hero, as well as through closer analyses of texts such as national newspapers and true crime monthly magazines.[14] The work of Cameron and Frazer, together with studies by feminist critics and historians such as Judith Walkowitz (1992), Nicole Ward Jouve (1986) and Joan Smith (1989), chronicle the 'political effects' and material consequences of myth-making in the cases of the Whitechapel murderers in 1888 and the Yorkshire Ripper murders from 1975 to 1981.[15] The argument common to these writers is that the mythologisation of the murderer who kills women can mask the real material conditions of gender relations, relations that arguably form the basis of women's experiences of crime and the fear of crime.

Sara Knox's book *Murder: A Tale of Modern American Life* (1998) investigates the gendered appeal and function of stories of murder within the context of the US. Her study includes fiction, medico-legal texts, press coverage and true crime accounts of notorious homicides. Knox devotes considerable thought to the often neglected position of the victim in the narration of contemporary murder, focusing particularly on how racial and gendered power relations are made overt in the actual perpetration of violent crime and then reinforced by its media coverage. Here she signals the political importance of acknowledging the reality of the crime and its aftermath that informs true crime entertainment and crime journalism. Knox argues that there are (albeit very few) contemporary writers who do try to place the victims at the centre of their true crime account and who try to refuse the common tendency to aestheticise discourses of murder (Knox 1998: 10).[16] The exceptional presence of these politically aware writers foregrounds the highly conventional aesthetic processes of mainstream true crime writing. For even thoughtful true crime writing, even writing that chooses to critique some aspect of the society within which a crime takes place, must appeal to the reader within the terms of engagement prescribed by the genre.

Also relevant is Knox's analysis of the coverage of a murder case whose protagonists became known as the 'Honeymoon Killers'. The couple, Martha Beck and Ray Fernandez, were sentenced to death on 7 March 1951 for a series of notorious murders. Also known as the 'Lonely Hearts Killers', Beck and Fernandez, posing as brother and sister, reputedly killed up to 20 women after Fernandez befriended and seduced them in 'lonely hearts' clubs (Wilson and Pitman 1961: 235). The killers were as notorious for their passionate love for each other as for the crimes that they committed together. Knox traces the ways in which the facts of the crime as they were recorded were variously reworked into 'true crime', mainstream film, and so on. What is striking in her work is the delineation of the ways in which the structure of the true crime narrative seems to secure a definitive and authoritative reading of the case. The events of the Beck and Fernandez case lent themselves readily to the framing discourses of both crime and romance. The drive to produce a story that stayed within the perimeters of these two genres necessarily marginalised the mass of conflicting detail and opposing voices that arise from a crime case of any complexity. Knox's interrogation of the case is based upon the interdependence of the two genres (crime and romance) during the period and how their deployment increased the potential audience for such a story. It will become apparent throughout this book that the parameters of the true crime genre, as with any genre that survives historical and social change, are flexible. True crime, like biography, reportage, television programme or specialist magazine feature, can be an adaptive and hybrid form. While its organising discourse will always be that of crime and its consequences, this discourse will often take on the colour of others that seem to fit most closely with the material under discussion, its potential audience and its cultural context. For example, studies undertaken later show how discourses as various as melodrama, psycho-biography, the gothic and the romantic inform and direct true crime magazine articles (Chapters 4 and 6) generating stories that attempt to make sense of gendered and other power relations played out in the perpetration of crime and its aftermath.

True crime and the production of knowledge

Concerns about the problem of representing violence are also more broadly articulated in the arenas where public opinion is formed.[17] Network television and the press in particular frequently provide fora for journalists, critics and lobbyists (and even members of the public) to debate the political bias, effects, ethics, taste, decency and quality of cultural products such as true crime. Media representations of violence and criminality from *The Terminator* (Cameron 1984 USA) *to Natural Born Killers* (Stone 1994 USA), from Marcus Harvey's notorious portrait of Myra Hindley (Royal Academy, London 1997)[18] to true crime books and television programmes have all been challenged on some of the grounds listed above.[19] In order to understand the cultural impact of denigrated forms like true crime, it is necessary to recognise the high media currency of these frequent debates and how they intersect with, and even produce, common concerns about the potential (bad) effects of certain media products.[20] Acknowledging and understanding the concern and occasional disapprobation generated by true crime is more productive than succumbing to the argument that if audiences (or indeed cultural critics) do not like something, they should simply look elsewhere.[21] Integrating critical analysis with recognition of the ethical issues of cultural form and process enables academics to avoid the shift towards mainly descriptive analysis.[22]

Broadly speaking, true crime entertainment is undoubtedly a popular form: it is commercially successful, it has a wide appeal, it is often demotic, sometimes 'offensive' and 'vulgar' and it *appears* to 'follow public tastes' (Fiske 1989). Yet in spite of its plebeian generic origins it is not made by the people for the people. In spite of the space it provides for exploration of oppositional positions in regard to the law and its executives, it is situated firmly within dominant discourses of law and order, punishment and retribution, surveillance and control, social conformity and disciplinarity. The dominant presence of these discourses within much true crime may offer the reader conservative interpretations and solutions to the 'problem' of crime and punishment but to say that these discourses are present and that they constitute part of the appeal of true crime need not contradict the view that meanings are contested, ambivalent or contradictory, or that true crime is open to a variety of reading positions.[23]

The central problem is that the critic needs to engage with the 'disrespectable, easy text' critically, but without foreclosing on its role as a source of contrary meanings and sometimes ambivalent pleasures (Fiske 1989: 121). In his influential book *Understanding Popular Culture*, Fiske advocates the adoption of a 'double focus' that does not shrink from identifying the ideological traces of consumer capitalism in mass-produced culture, but that also allows for the contradictory meanings and pleasures that 'escape control' (ibid.: 105). The categories of the popular that are most offensive to high culture – the sensational, the excessive and the obvious – are integral to certain sub-genres of true crime literature, such as the true crime monthly magazine (see ibid.: 114ff). The propensity of magazines to show rather than tell, to illustrate rather than explain, to engage in hyperbole, melodrama and the discourses of the tabloid press, signals their central function as popular entertainment. One way into an understanding of the value of these texts, then, is to consider the ways in which they might intersect with the experiences of their readers; to inquire into the ways in which they invite recognition as much as amazement.[24] Fiske, looking at the sensationalist *Weekly World News*, whose headlines speak of aliens, ghosts, bizarre deaths and incongruous love matches, sums up the way in which this recognition works: 'Every headline on the page is a sensational example of the inability of the "normal" (and therefore of the ideology that produced it) to explain or cope with specific instances of everyday life. The world it offers the reader is a world of the bizarre, the abnormal' (ibid.: 116).

These hyperbolic texts, texts that closely resemble in form and address the true crime monthly magazine, throw into doubt the rationalist claims of modernity. The lurking suspicion that the world is more complex, less knowable and less controllable than dominant discourse allows is confirmed by the 'revelation' of bizarre and unlikely events. This book interrogates the way that true crime harnesses contemporary knowledges and concerns about a range of crime-related issues to produce its own generically distinctive narratives of crime, investigation and punishment. It examines the ways in which true crime throws open and interrogates broader questions of subjecthood, agency, progress and mortality, arguing that true crime tests the boundaries of the very notions upon which it depends – common sense, the triumph of law and the responsibility of its citizens in the maintenance of the good society.

True crime, then, is a genre that produces particular forms of knowledge and – lest it be forgotten – pleasure. The discourses of true crime, like all popular narratives, produce relations of power, establishing and exploring the place of subject and object, agency and will in modern life. However, power is not merely repressive but productive: 'it doesn't only weigh on us as a force which says no ... it traverses and produces things, it induces pleasure, forms knowledge, produces discourse' (Foucault 1980: 119). We need to ask then what pleasures, as well as knowledges, are produced by the various forms of true crime entertainment and how these might intersect with broader public debates about taste and censorship, criminal behaviour and individual responsibility in everyday life.

The textual analysis of true crime stories as sites of discursive conflict and negotiation is made meaningful and useful if true crime is read within the social context of everyday life. This project does not regard 'texts' as commentary or exegesis on the social, but rather as one way among many in which the social is produced, one way in which the social experience of crime is both rendered meaningful and disseminated. This is possible because Foucault's notion of discourse refuses to distinguish between thought and action, language and practice, it aims to show 'that to speak is to do something – something other than to express what one thinks' (Foucault 1969: 209). The fact that Foucault refuses to distinguish between these elements does not mean that the difference between discourse and actuality is collapsed, rather that one can only apprehend the latter through the former. Foucault's work does not therefore rule out the material basis of human experience, which is given due recognition in this project, instead it is the perception of that experience which is structured through discourse (Mills 1997: 50–1). If there is the potential for a socially committed critique within discourse theory, it lies in demonstrating the relations of power and knowledge that inform and shape perceptions of human experience and help produce subjectivities.

As already noted, Cameron and Frazer (1987) undertake just such a demonstration of the power relations produced through the discourses of true crime and reportage. Their work, written in a highly accessible way, demonstrates the critical strengths of discourse analysis, showing how it can provide a key to understanding the meaning of modern sex murder and its representation. They demonstrate the ways in which discourse both produces real relations of power and is the ground upon which a critique of power can be made. To say that a discourse constitutes the core of any understanding of crime and criminality does not imply that actuality and discourse are one and the same, but simply that the relationship between them is infinitely complex and inextricable. For instance, the authors demonstrate that murder and the discourse of murder are irretrievably linked so that the representations available to the criminal can help to shape 'the form of his killing and the way he understood it' (Cameron and Frazer 1987: xiii). This linkage between murder and the discourse of murder does not mean that representations directly incite people to kill. But rather that criminals (no less than the 'general public') clearly draw on discursive models of criminality in order to describe and comprehend both their own and other criminals' behaviour, offering a concrete example of how discourse produces relations of power (see Chapter 6). The implication here is that it is only by understanding how discourses produce behaviours – as well as models of understanding behaviours – that both perceptions of crime and the actions of criminals and victims may be altered.

Foucauldian initiatives tend to be suspicious of the notions of both accessible experience and social progress. Indeed, they constitute a rather grand narrative of the decline of 'progress', 'idealism' and 'universal values'. Yet acknowledgement of the reality of crime and its aftermath and of the material conditions of individual experience has to be accommodated in a critical analysis of true crime literature. True crime narrates the individual's experiences of crime and punishment. It is also a forum for exploring the more general fear of crime and public concern about the processes of criminal detection and the effectiveness of the criminal justice system. An analysis of the discourses of 'law' and 'justice' aimed at revealing their intimate relation to the subordinating strategies of power, control and disciplinarity must not be undertaken at the expense of ignoring this popular investment in the power of the law. The common experiences of crime and social inequality which lead to calls for equality, rights and justice before the law and safety in the streets, also have a place in the story of crime (see Hunt and Wickham 1994). In the Thompson case, for example, it must be possible to say that the abuse of the Thompson women happened, that June and Hilda Thompson did murder their father and that the law delivered some kind of justice by failing to imprison them for this crime.

2
Histories of True Crime

True crime literature and its antecedents

The popular consumption of true accounts of crime is not a recent phenomenon. A long line of literary and popular antecedents informs various kinds of modern true crime entertainment. The great mass of popular street literatures and their more respectable counterparts such as the Newgate collections, newspapers and the novel have all made some mark on contemporary true crime. Antecedents matter here for a number of reasons. Most simply, they are evidence that modern true crime, like crime fiction, consists of codes and conventions whose appearance is explicable, not only in terms of current knowledges and practices, but also in terms of the traces they bear of earlier knowledges and practices. It is difficult to understand how these conventions and the discourses which they support alter, shift or are even dispensed with altogether, without a knowledge of their earlier literary and non-literary influences.

The purpose here is to signal the discursive shifts and transformations that occurred from form to form and thereby look forward to the emergence of contemporary true crime. This signalling also begins the task of exploring how fact-based entertainment produces discursive models of crime, criminality and the purposes of the law, together with the modern social subjects posited by them. In other words, a mapping of early types of crime-inspired writing can help discover the productive relations between crime, true crime and modern subjects; to learn how 'discourses produce something else' (Mills 1997: 17). For the discourses of true crime may be understood as 'practices that systematically form the objects of which they speak' (Foucault 1969: 49). True crime, together with a range of related forms, contributes to the discursive production of criminal subjects and moral subjects, positing complex relations between them. In this context, a study of true crime involves discovering what kinds of relations are produced between popular criminal literature and the social order.

The concept of the antecedent, while it usefully helps to substantiate the generic relationships between earlier and more recent true crime literatures (and between true crime and other discourses about crime), has attendant theoretical problems. Its definition – a preceding thing or circumstance – posits firm, *a priori* links between earlier and current forms of true crime literature which sit uncomfortably with Foucault's advocacy for historians of the introduction of 'discontinuity' into history (Foucault 1969: 8). For example, the assumption of a linear model of causation may marginalise any evidence of gaps and discontinuities in the production and consumption of these literatures and in their discursive treatment of crime. The recognition of gaps and discontinuities brings new relations of power and knowledge to the fore by revealing, for instance, the influence of the novel form on modern criminal biography. This may arguably be achieved by refusing what Foucault (ibid.: 4) calls the search for 'silent beginnings' and what Lennard Davis (1983: 2–4) calls the 'evolutionary' explanation of the (dis)appearance of literary form, genre and narrative.[1] This may be achieved by a stronger (albeit somewhat schematic) emphasis upon the different, the discordant and the discontinuous in the production of crime narratives. For example, true crime literature may accommodate the somewhat awkward juxtaposition of older discourses of divine providence, with newer discourses of prevention and detection in stories of crime. This emphasis on the awkward and discordant also counteracts the tendency of causative and linear models of literary heredity to assume that the development of literature, whether popular or elite, stems solely from earlier literatures of similar status and not at all by other forms such as the press or oral story-telling (Davis 1983). An additional problem is that while the search for true crime antecedents suggests, fairly accurately, that murder was and continues to be the dominant crime in the popular imagination, it might also imply, quite erroneously, that murder is always the frequent and typical object of fear and concern about crime in everyday life. It is important therefore not to map any imaginary or literary discourses of crime directly and evenly onto actual experiences of crime and criminality. Crime narratives are not, of course, analogues of the social experience of crime.

Having made the above caveats, the search for antecedents, when undertaken with caution, arguably augments an understanding of true crime literatures, not simply as texts, but also as discursive formations which produce and disseminate knowledge about crime, punishment and other material conditions of everyday life at particular historical moments. Also, while one might turn to a recent true crime text to learn how it orders, to a lesser or greater degree, knowledge of its historical moment, it is helpful to recall that it will also bear traces of earlier knowledges, practices and literary conventions, since there is no clear break between older and newer forms of popular literatures. Knowledge of these earlier conventions, and of how they have become sedimented into the genre, will therefore enhance analyses of current forms. Their traces, for example, will inflect present meanings and pleasures in different ways and this needs to be taken into account.

Understanding change in true crime literature

It is arguable that the apparently consistent popularity of true accounts of crime, in all their variety (but especially of murder), lends itself well to speculation that the discourses of true crime change little and its readership is relatively constant. The discourses of true crime seem at first sight to develop and change incrementally along with the discourses that inform and construct our notions of crime, law and punishment and with the broader transformations of Western society. These transformations from religious to secular society, from feudal-agrarian to industrial-capitalist society characterise Western modernity and may be read as largely progressive in nature, as part of a permanent revolution (Berman 1982). This view would allow that true accounts of crime in the 1680s, 1840s and 1980s have more in common than not, especially as they are all produced within the broad sweep of a progressive Western modernity. This progressive view would be substantiated by technological and cultural developments that contributed (albeit unevenly) towards the successful development of mass literature and mass culture, including true accounts of crime in its various forms.[2]

Likewise, the story of crime, jurisprudence, policing and penal reform has also been conveyed as moving progressively towards an ideal balance within modern society.[3] This ideal is a putative middle way between the calls of civil liberty and the requirements of crime prevention, crime control and national security. This positive view is epitomised in the title of T. A. Critchley's police history *The Conquest of*

Violence (1970) whose interpretation of the changing relationship between policing and the state is entirely progressive.[4] This interpretation is overtly reiterated in today's true crime literature and television, which draw upon and celebrate every refinement of the technologies and strategies of detection, as an aid (rarely a threat) to the security and integrity of the individual citizen or community.

However, in opposition to this progressive history of the law is a history of ideas and practices, 'of discontinuities, ruptures, gaps, entirely new forms of positivity, and of sudden redistributions' (Foucault 1969: 169). Foucault's vision of modernity is an alternative, bleaker view, which, as indicated in Chapter 1, vigorously undermines the predominantly optimistic humanist vision of history. At its most despairing it views the trajectory of modernity and the discourses of the Enlightenment which support it, as simply spreading and diffusing surveillance and 'carceral' techniques throughout society (Foucault 1975: 297). Foucault argues that penal and police reform – the development of more 'humane' punishments and methods of social control – is simply more insidious than its spectacular, more overtly cruel predecessors. Instead of Critchley's optimistic vision of the conquest of violence, Foucault perceives an increasing occlusion of violence through a gradation of disciplines that become naturalised and therefore incontestable, moving from the externally imposed through to self-scrutiny and self-discipline (1979: 302–3; 1980). From this perspective the emergence of new forms of knowledge (e.g. psychoanalysis, psychiatry, forensics, sociology) and new disciplinary strategies (e.g. penal reform, policing, photographic documentation) in the nineteenth century produced a subtle redistribution (not an 'improvement') of the purposes of criminal investigation and judicial inquiry. This alternative vision of the shifts and transformations within history allows one to examine the antecedents of true crime in a different light, as discursive formations that both draw upon and help to produce new subjectivities and new modes of objectification before the law.

The purpose of this chapter is to seek out a constellation of 'beginnings', rather than the 'origin' of what is now recognised as true crime literature and the subject positions that it constructs (Cousins and Hussain 1984: 4). It will certainly persist in trying to trace the formal relationships between earlier forms of true crime entertainment and contemporary true crime, taking into account the broader changes of capital and consumption which produced new kinds of readers and new kinds of popular entertainment. However, in addition it will explore the discursive shifts which characterised the various beginnings of true crime, shifts in knowledges and practices which true crime narratives took up and made their own.

This chapter engages with true accounts of crime in two stages. It begins by examining the early formulaic true crime entertainment of the late Elizabethan and Stuart periods, whose construction of the criminal, of justice and of the social order was firmly embedded within the discourses of retribution, redemption and divine providence. It will ask how new and emergent discourses began to encroach upon this vision of social order in response to the growing secularisation of society and the increasing importance of personal property and individual liberty. Finally, it will examine how this growing displacement of the religious by the secular, the feudal-agrarian by capitalist enterprise and so on, crystallised in the nineteenth century as a result of material changes and new knowledges. These changes, including developments in systems of knowledge such as psychiatry, psychology and medicine, informed jurisprudence and produced a new kind of criminal subject – the dangerous individual (Foucault 1988; Wiener 1990; Hunt and Wickham 1994: 42). It is this medicalised, specularised figure who has been allotted a central place within crime literature and who remains familiar to today's readers of true crime.

The triumph of God's revenge: the place of providence in true crime narratives

Real life crime has been a source of narrative entertainment in both literature and popular entertainment since at least the early modern period. The popular formulaic literature of the sixteenth, seventeenth and eighteenth centuries, in the form of broadsheets, pamphlets and, later, in collections of accounts, were simple melodramatic tales, 'stressing the providential order through which the criminal was inevitably punished' (Cawelti 1976: 53). This street literature generally aimed at humble people who supposedly required the moral certainties that enabled the world to retain its ethical meaning (Gatrell 1994: 169).[5] In addition, trial pamphlets, often written by clergymen, presented accounts of the circumstances of the criminal, including the details of his/her crime, capture, trial, confession and/or scaffold speech. Murder, in its more unusual forms, was the most popular subject matter. Peter Lake notes that pamphlets were as sensational as any modern horror movie, leaving little to the imagination. He quotes for example a pamphlet from 1606 in which a female robber turned 'tragical midwife' ripped open the belly of a pregnant woman with a knife and severed her child's tongue (Lake 1993: 259). Pamphlets not only describe acts of murder and atrocity but also dwell in some detail on the state of putrefaction of corpses and other unsavoury details. For example, Lake (ibid.: 260) cites a 1614 story that tells how a murdered baby is discovered thrust down a privy, 'all besmeared with filth of that loathsome place'.

These stories were read alongside tales of the depraved gentry and the obscene acts of the city low-life such as those recalled in Henry Goodcole's *Deeds against Nature* pamphlets (ibid.: 260). According to Lake these tales were basically exploitative, albeit framed with religious and moral polemic. However, as Garthine Walker (1996: 124) makes clear, a strong moral framework was a prerequisite of the genre: 'Whatever the sensationalist intent and appeal of rehearsing shocking doings, the central organising theme of the genre was not disquieting titillation or violence, but the restorative and comforting trilogy of sin, divine providence and redemption.'

The actual function of these stories is to inform readers of the awful consequences of the breakdown of authority and duty within the social structure (ibid.: 266–7). Here a struggle to maintain authority and to ensure that the humblest embrace the duties of their position is played out in the struggle between good and evil, piety and sin which structures narratives of crime and of scandal. Chronicles such as these voice the concerns of a pre-capitalist society where the production of commodities is still local and small scale. In these circumstances everyone is required to conform to the needs of the community at large, for the greater good of the community (Mandel 1984: 4).[6] These stories tell of law-breaking at a time when the location, pursuit and capture of criminals was dependent upon the community itself, if not upon chance (Sharpe 1980; Kent 1986). Here in Ernest Mandel's (1984: 4) terms, there were no 'specialists' either to police society or to detect and pursue wrongdoers, only an invocation for all to attend to the lessons of Christian piety. Implicit in this model of the community is a Christian world-view in which people were categorised according to their potential for social inclusion and their familiarity with local ways, with the good citizen placed in strong contrast to the criminal who abjures honest labour and has turned away from sustaining Christian values (McMullan 1998: 96). At this stage, true crime tales in the form of chapbooks, ballads and broadsheets portray the transgressor of Christian values as one who, faced with an inevitable punishment, can be redeemed only through the embrace of Christian values. Most popular formula stories of this period were not interested in either complex ideas of individual motivation or broader questions of social causation; instead their trajectory was one in which the criminal, discovered through error or guilt, was made to face his or her just punishment (Cawelti 1976: 54).

The above characteristics – Christian rhetoric, the intervention of providence and the inevitability of punishment – were not confined to ephemeral street literature. The notion of the criminal act as essentially a crime against God as much as an offence against the law was naturally present in collections aimed at educated readers. Here also the eye of God presided over the doings of men and women, His centrality encapsulated in the title of the first English collection of murder accounts, *The Triumph of Gods Revenge agaynst the Crying, and Execrable Sins of Murder in Thirty Tragical Histories* by John Reynolds (1621–2). This collection of 30 stories divided into five volumes went through a number of editions. It was so successful that the 1662 edition was avowedly issued to stamp out a plagiarised edition 'lately patched and pilfered' called *Blood For Blood* (Reynolds 1662: Address to Reader). These tales were not about contemporary English criminals; rather, they resembled synopses of dramatic stage tragedies. They were set in the past and located on the continent, lending them perhaps an air of respectability lacking in the cheaper formats and a diversion from more local troubles (such as the civil war, which ended only nine years before the 1662 edition). Despite the common complaint that 'we can scarce turn our ear or eye anywhere' without confronting crime and iniquity (1679 Preface), the 1679 edition is pleased to note that fortunately our own island is not very productive of murder and adultery so that foreign examples must be sought (Dedication).[7]

Here the messy business of revenge, adultery and murder is structured through the discourses of retributive religion so that Providence intervenes to ensure that God's justice prevails. Reynolds notes:

> For these are crying and capitall offences, seene in heaven, and by the sword of his Magistrates brought forth and punished here on earth. A lamentable and mournefull example ... may we all read it to the reformation of our lives. (Reynolds 1679: 105)

Thus before the onset of centralised policing and the science of detection, the discourses of religion and social conformity explain the solution of a crime and the capture of the criminal as 'revelation' through the miraculous discoveries of God. This religious paradigm presupposes that transgressors are always caught, an event whose inevitability is portrayed graphically in the illustrations for the 1679 edition. Here line drawings take the form of strip cartoons depicting various points in the story but always finishing with the punishment scene.[8] The punishments depicted are various; they include common-or-garden hangings, burial alive between two walls and the severing of limbs prior to being impaled on a stake.

The Newgate Calendar

It could be argued that it was the judicial response to crime in the form of public executions that formed the basis and central attraction of the great mass of crime literature.[9] 1773 saw the publication of the first edition of the still famous compendium *The Newgate Calendar or Malefactor's Bloody Register*. This assembled and repackaged the stories told in prison broadsheets into handsome bound volumes, again for the monied classes, who consumed them in greater numbers than they did some well-known periodicals (Knight 1980: 9; Gatrell 1994: 157–8). The *Annals of Newgate* (1775) by Reverend John Villette also fictionalised these same sources (Senelick 1987: xviii). These stories, unlike those in the Reynolds' collection, had the added *frisson* of being both indigenous and part of popular memory. Again, the Newgate stories were promoted as publications intended for moral edification, undertaking the same moral agenda that imbued the individually published pamphlets aimed at the semi-literate (Knight 1980: 9).

Let us turn to the 1773 edition. This ran to five volumes, each of about 400 pages and carried around a dozen illustrations, covering a range of crimes dating from 1700 to the time of publication. As in the Reynolds' collection, the spectacle of murder, adultery and, most dramatically, public punishment is both highly commodified and rendered respectable by its high production values and its rhetoric of duty and piety. At the beginning and end of each tale the editors stress the instructive nature of the text. As will be seen later, the construction of the *Calendar* anticipates many of the characteristics of the true crime monthly magazines produced towards the end of the twentieth century. The stories themselves resemble reportage, recording events and making judgements without any obvious authorial voice, except in its concluding comments. It is this common absence of an identifiable authorial voice which signals the inferior status of true crime as 'genre writing', and its considerable distance from canonical literature (Palmer 1991: 5–7). Stephen Knight comments:

The stories relate to each other by mere juxtaposition and by having the same underlying principles – *The Newgate Calendar* is no more than the sum of its parts: stories can easily be added or removed, their order can be changed and the whole is not in any real way different. (Knight 1980: 17)

Or, in the words of the historian J. A. C. Gatrell: 'read half a dozen and you have read them all' (Gatrell 1994: 175).

The agenda of the *Calendar* is ostensibly one of moral instruction. The frontispiece for Volume I is exemplary in its depiction of the courtroom. Through the windows of the court the reader spies figures hanging from gallows, the image anchored with the words: 'Behold and see the Reward of the Wicked' and 'The whole tending to guard Young Minds from the allurements of VICE, and the paths that lead to DESTRUCTION' (1773: i). The typography itself, larded with upper-case characters, is a rather attractive invitation to shudder at the horrors to come. The avowed intention to form young minds is even more explicit in Norman Birkett's selection from *The Malefactor's Register* (1951). Here the reproduced frontispiece of a late eighteenth-century edition depicts a domestic scene of mother and child, subtitled: *A Mother Presenting The Malefactor's Register and Tenderly Entreating Him to Regard the Instructions Therein Recorded*. Here the mother and her son, ensconced comfortably in a domestic setting, turn (together with the reader) to look through the window at the unlikely sight of a nearby gibbet on a hilltop. These engravings of punitive spectacles were part of a broader programme of visible punishment as edification and deterrent wherein 'punishments must be a school rather than a festival; an ever-open book rather than a ceremony' and places of punishment could be conceived of as a 'Garden of Laws that families would visit on Sundays' (Foucault 1975: 111). In this edition all the engravings offer a tour of this garden, depicting the scene in which the criminal's sentence is carried out. In the 1773 edition the anonymous editors call attention to the 'salutary purposes' of such stories which pay 'careful attention to the events of Providence' (1773: iii–iv). As in the frontispiece described above, the language of deterrence is deployed as a caution to those who are easily influenced: 'Here the giddy thoughtless youth may see as in a mirror ... the absolute necessity they are under to practice the duties of religion' (1773: iii). None the less, like the true crime stories of today, edification is tempered with entertainment. These editors at least are happy to concede the *Calendar*'s role as a source of diversion, useful to pass the time on long sea journeys, as well as to instruct families morally (ibid.: v). Like the newspapers and journals that spring up from the early years of the eighteenth century, these stories transform the parochial into events of universal interest and notoriety. This edition even assures readers that the range of stories is great enough so that everyone will be sure to find crime stories set in their own locality (ibid.: vi).

The accounts in these editions are between 900 and 1,500 words in length and usually deal with cases of murder. The account of the murderer Thomas Hunter is quite typical of the simple structure of these stories, which belies the complexity of fear and fascination they actually articulate (1773 Vol. 1: 43–8). The account is mainly descriptive and to the point, chronicling briefly Hunter's developing role as tutor and mentor to the three children of the Gordon family in Scotland. Hunter, a divinity student, is discovered making love to his mistress by the two boys and their sister while the parents are away (ibid.: 43). The children report Hunter to their father who banishes the woman and severely reprimands the tutor, leaving him vengeful and 'full of malice' (ibid.: 44). Later, Hunter attacks the two boys while out walking and promptly slits their throats with his penknife. To modern readers it might seem strange that Hunter is immediately apprehended by a passer-by to whom he then confesses, but this is in keeping with the commonplace that providence intervenes to ensure justice is done. Contrary perhaps to expectations in a genre that deploys the language of deterrence, the engravings in this edition depict the moment of the crime rather than the scene of execution. Here the spectacle of the scaffold, so ubiquitous in other editions, gives way to depictions of the actual atrocities committed by the protagonist, substantiating Lake's view that thrill and titillation were central to their production. Beneath the Hunter engraving is the simple sentence: 'the Revd THOMAS HUNTER kneeling on one of his pupils, while he is cutting the other's throat, near Edinburgh' (ibid.: between pp. 46–7).

Again, perhaps surprisingly, in this account Hunter is not seen to display contrition, but rather he expresses regret that he did not have an opportunity to despatch the boys' sister as well (ibid.: 47). Albeit unillustrated, the description of Hunter's sentence is graphic enough:

> He was carried to the place, and his right hand first struck off at the wrist with a hatchet, after which, to be drawn up by a rope to the gallows, and when dead to be hung in chains betwixt Edinburgh

and Leith, with the penknife stuck through his hand, and fixed over his head, on top of the gibbet. (ibid.: 47)

Here execution stands as a kind of mimesis, a physical representation or tableau of the nature of Hunter's crime. It illustrates an 'art of punishing' whose 'analogical penalties' lend themselves well to true crime literature (Foucault 1975: 104–5). In Foucault's terms it 'established a set of decipherable relations' (ibid.: 44) between public torture and the crime itself. As such it proved too much for the children's father who asked for Hunter's remains to be removed to another place so that he did not have to pass them daily on the public highway.

For contemporary readers the Hunter story is of horror heaped on horror. Hunter did not simply murder; he violated the social order in which his place was pre-ordained. He seemed suitably qualified in religion to tutor children, to reside with a respectable family and to care for his charges during their leisure time. The implied question asks, 'when someone like Hunter fails to occupy his station honourably, who then can be trusted?' The story is in one sense a story of the complexity of power relations between a well-to-do family and their employee. The children in Hunter's charge, although ostensibly of a lower status than their adult mentor, exhibit considerable power over him which they demonstrate by reporting his sexual liaison and thereby undermining his career and concomitant social standing. His destruction of the children, without apparent compunction, is also therefore an assault on the social order and of his role within it.

The account concludes with some brief reflections upon Hunter's story. The editors emphasise the cleric's dangerous religious radicalism which marked his inevitable decline into criminality and social anomie. Most notably the piece does not end with the reprobate's professions of regret but something far more terrible to contemporary readers. At the point when his hand is severed Hunter is heard to cry, 'There is no God', a scene which surely added a final seal of horror to an already horrible narrative. Hunter's defiance arguably conjures both fascination as well as repulsion, suggesting that the closure offered by the restorative trilogy of sin, divine providence and redemption described by Garthine Walker above may be eluded or even defiantly refuted by the criminal protagonist. Hence what Foucault (1977: 68) calls the 'true stories of everyday history' not only worked to justify the violent spectacle of capital punishment but they could also (albeit inadvertently) glorify the criminal who refuses to capitulate.[10]

As just demonstrated the spectre of social anarchy, as well as the specific taboo of murder, is often central to the narrative construction of these crimes and their social effects. Sometimes, however, the scandal of the social, as well as theological, consequences of murder appear to leave commentators bereft of words. For these reflections, although moral in tone, are often fairly perfunctory. For example, Volume II of the *Calendar* presents quite a detailed account of the infamous Catherine Hayes who was convicted of the murder of her husband John, an act known as 'petty treason' (1773: 185–211). The term 'petty treason' (that the murder of one's husband is an offence against one's sovereign) is indicative of the broader threat which violent married women constituted to the social order.[11] Indeed Walker (1996: 125) notes that these pamphlets reveal less about how women were actually viewed in society and rather more about 'the conceptualizations of assaults upon the model of the social order which underpinned religious and political hierarchy and control' (see also Knelman 1998).

In this case it was both the manner in which Hayes disposed of her husband's body and the manner of her own death which generated such notoriety. Hayes dismembered his corpse with the help of two assistants, who then disposed of his head for her. The head was discovered by the Thames and lodged on a pole in the town so that it might be identified. Here again the engraving depicts the crime scene rather than the execution: 'Hayes, with her helpers, Wood and Billings, decapitating her husband' (ibid.: between pp. 192–3). For this crime she was sentenced to be burnt at the stake. The text notes that it was customary for criminals to be strangled first as a kindness, but the executioner was tardy and Hayes died screaming as she tried to push the burning faggots from her. Like the Hunter case above, the shallow viciousness of the crime as it is presented seems to leave the editors at a loss for words, since Hayes apparently killed her husband simply because he bored her. None the less the 'serious address to married women in general' which follows the account is cursory and half-hearted, merely advising resentful wives to 'put their trust in the power of the Almighty' (ibid.: 211).

The events related in these compendia (aside from treatments such as the earlier John Reynolds' collection addressed above) are usually straightforward crimes committed by ordinary people who turn their backs upon their allotted familial or social roles; a rejection which constituted a still greater symbolic threat to the social order. In these tales the criminal's apprehension and punishment is presented as the inevitable result of the ordered community living according to God's laws. The intense sociability of the early modern citizen was the main safeguard against criminality and disorder (McMullan 1998: 95). In these circumstances it is error or guilt itself which must reveal the murderer to the community. So, for example, the head of John Hayes is fixed on a pole in plain sight of the community and seems itself to accuse the culpable and lead to their capture. The small-scale and reciprocal social surveillance and individual guilt which informed these narratives originated in a profoundly Christian model of the social order, a model which was crumbling just as these stories were being consumed in such vast numbers (Knight 1980: 13). William Godwin (who did much in *Caleb Williams* [1794] to explore 'the entrails of mind and motive' which crime narratives consistently ignored) observed that this emphasis upon surveillance was indeed theologically informed. On reading an edition of the Reynolds' collection with a recommendatory preface by the Reverend Philip Batteson, Godwin comments on the latter's efforts: 'the beam of the eye of Omniscience was represented as perpetually pursuing the guilty, laying open his most hidden retreats to the light of day' (1794: 352 n2). In these stories the social control of crime is presented as direct, unmediated and inescapable (Knight 1980: 13), although it must be added that the flagrant defiance of the conventions of confession and redemption exhibited in some stories is also related in lingering detail.

Policing, property and the dissolution of the old order

As noted above, the discourses of retributive religion that strongly informed the conceptualisation of crime produced a coherent vision of a social order which was actually changing quite profoundly during the seventeenth century when many of these narratives were circulating. Mutual and continuous surveillance could not easily accommodate the social changes engendered by plague, poverty, vagrancy and a rising population. A surplus and under-employed itinerant population acquired a new 'dangerous moral resonance' (McMullan 1998: 96–7). Consequently, the last half of the eighteenth century and the early nineteenth century witnessed increasing pressure to transform its policing from often haphazard and voluntary local forces into a centralised, organised system of social surveillance and control.[12] As these new discourses of policing and social control entered the public domain they too found their way (albeit tentatively) into true accounts such as the *Calendar*. These were often juxtaposed quite awkwardly with the theological discourses that were still reproduced from earlier editions.

The editors of the late eighteenth century *Calendar* sampled by Norman Birkett make a particularly strong bid to present the collection as a serious endeavour and as a worthy contribution to current debates upon crime and criminality (Birkett 1951). The preface sets out an appeal for the 'improvement of the police of this country' as well as the deployment of the strongest penalties as deterrence to others (ibid.: 13). The mere mention of policing exemplifies a discursive shift typified by a new lexicon of law and order; a lexicon which is familiar enough to the modern reader of both true crime and the newspapers where public opinion is still deemed to be formed. In this edition the demands include that 'the law operate its *full force* against every housebreaker', that the 'execution of *ten* women would do more public service than that of a hundred men' and that 'notorious defrauds should be rendered capital felonies' and so on. Only forgers, who are deemed to be a better class of person, usually fallen upon hard times, attract a gentle word. As for murderers and those who commit 'unnatural crimes': 'it is only to be lamented that their deaths cannot be aggravated by every species of torment!' (ibid.: 14). This edition then is marked by the emerging discourses of the new science of policing which were beginning to enter the public domain during the last few years of the eighteenth century. Here there is a discordant juxtaposition of discourses, grafted as they are onto the older discourses of retributive religion addressed above.

The science of policing gained widespread attention in Britain via a well-publicised treatise by Patrick Colquhoun. This work entitled *A Treatise on the Police of the Metropolis* (1797), appearing in the wake of anxieties produced by the French Revolution of 1789, garnered great acclaim, running through seven editions in ten years (Critchley 1970: 38). Drawing on systematic statistical evidence Colquhoun produced lurid accounts of criminal activity. His aim was to construct a police force that would locate and control delinquents who were putatively produced by a convergence of idleness, poverty and crime (McMullan 1998: 105). Colquhoun maintained, contrary to popular opinion, that the prevention of crime could indeed be accommodated with the inviolable right to personal liberty and individual freedom which characterised the English nation (Tagg 1988: 72). As T. A. Critchley observes, his language was revolutionary:[13]

Next to the blessings which our Nation derives from an excellent Constitution and System of general Laws, are those advantages

which result from a well-regulated and energetic plan of Police, conducted and enforced with purity, activity, vigilance, and discretion.
(in Critchley 1970: 38)

According to Colquhoun, these advantages included the encourage-
ment, protection and control of those whose recreation is innocent: 'to
preserve the good humour of the public and to give the minds of the
people a right bias' (in McMullan 1998: 105). In essence, the notion of
the active prevention and detection of crime itself posited a professional, organised and, most significantly, perhaps, centralised police
force. These objectives would, of course, produce a different kind of
relation between the social and the law. For the criminal would no
longer be revealed through the offices of Providence (and the uneven
efforts of the parish constable system) but identified through the
organised practices of the new science of detection. Colquhoun harnessed the pioneering ideas of John and Henry Fielding together with
Enlightenment thinking in order to advocate the twin strategies of surveillance and education. His plan included the creation of an intelligence service, the maintenance of a register of known offenders, with
classified information on certain groups and finally the publication of
a journal to aid detection and promote moral education (Critchley
1970: 39). The journal would 'excite a dread of crimes', commenting
'on the horrors of a gaol; on punishments – whipping, the pillory, the
hulks, transportation and public execution' (in Critchley 1970: 40). In
this respect its discourses of horror and deterrence would resemble the
language of the true crime literature which was already in circulation
and which had not, demonstrably, deterred anyone at all.

These formidable ideas for a modern police system were not immediately taken up, possibly because of opposition from the city to what
was viewed as a usurpation and misuse of state power (Emsley
1987/1996: 222). However, policing in France, to which Colquhoun
looked for inspiration, had already paved the way for the 'administrative machine' which would eventually police England (Foucault 1979:
213). Here throughout the eighteenth century 'unceasing observation'
became the strategy for anticipating social disorder and preventing
crime; observations had to be documented, organised and easily
retrieved, creating an 'immense police text' (ibid.: 214). Foucault notes:
'unlike the methods of judicial or administrative writing, what was registered in this way were forms of behaviour, attitudes, possibilities, sus-
picions – a permanent account of individuals' behaviour' (ibid.: 222).
In the light of these strategies it can be seen how the Enlightenment,

which discovered liberties, also invented the disciplines, thereby producing an egalitarian framework haunted by its shadowy underside (ibid.).

The new discursive formation of policing then contained a set of statements about how the prevention and detection of crime might be professionalised and also a moral condemnation of the idle poor. It emerged in response not only to fears of violent crime and social disorder, but also to meet the needs of the growing property-owning classes whose goods needed to be protected. For contrary to the popular memory of murder as the pre-eminent crime, the increasing reification of property was pivotal to the production of both law-making and law-breaking during this period (Hay 1975: 13; Foucault 1979: 75). As a consequence a new kind of moral subject began to emerge, the property-owning citizen, whose assets distinguished him/her as someone in need of the law's protection. Even as calls for the scaling down of capital punishment proliferated in the second half of the eighteenth century, the number of non-violent offences for which one could be executed continued to burgeon. Property crime inspired most of the capital statutes, which grew in number from about 50 to over 200 between 1688 and 1820 (Hay 1975: 18). Capital punishment was therefore increasingly invoked, not for the so-called 'true crimes' of murder, rape and so on, as defined by modern criminologists, but for new crimes which were previously regarded as innocent or venial acts (ibid.: 13). Indeed Hay (ibid.: 19) contends, it was through the ideology and practice of the law, which transformed licit into illicit acts, that property became 'officially deified' within modern culture and property crime a public scandal.

Modern criminal subjects: the delinquent

As already indicated, the eighteenth century witnessed a gradual shift in attitudes towards criminality; whereas a certain amount of illegality had been tolerated within the population, this gradually gave way to the marginalisation of the criminal as a 'limited' but 'skilled' delinquent (Foucault 1979: 75). This shift towards the modern conception of skilled delinquency and organised criminality is one that is still familiar today.[14] As Foucault comments: 'A general movement shifted criminality from the attack of bodies to the more or less direct seizure of goods; and from a "mass criminality" to a "marginal criminality", partly the preserve of professionals' (ibid.: 75). Here Foucault spies the emergence of discourses which produce an essentially modern criminal subject; a criminal who might be urban, is probably skilled and may well be situated within a broader subculture of criminality – the criminal underworld (Chesney 1970; Salgado 1977; McMullan 1984).

The growing deification of property and its discursive links to this new kind of criminality are epitomised far more explicitly in the developing novel form of the early eighteenth century than in true crime itself. For the true crime industry, as already indicated, relied on reprints and was consequently slow to shed its earlier discursive construction of the contained community bonded by religious piety and mutual surveillance. According to Ian Watt's landmark study of the origins of the novel, a new brand of criminal subject, produced by economic conditions, soon found his/her way into literature, most notably in the novels of crime reporter Daniel Defoe (Watt 1987: 95). Famously, Watt identifies *Robinson Crusoe* (1719) as the emblematic product of the rise of economic individualism. The argument is that Crusoe himself is the product of both the new economic imperatives and a Puritan individualism which together constitute a peculiar internalisation of conscience (Watt 1987: 74–5). Defoe's novels usefully exemplify the literary shift from picaresque subject matter to a prose which articulated the rise of individualism and the establishment of the distinct criminal class already noted above. The growing discursive construction of poverty as a shameful condition, rather than one which merited charity, meant that Defoe's characters 'would rather steal than beg, inveigle rather than remain poor' (ibid.: 95). The increasing centrality of notions of the individual subject is arguably evident in the structure of these novels, which are determined by the shape of an individual life. Defoe's stories of moral reprobates and criminal types, including *Moll Flanders* (1722), *Colonel Jaque* (1722), *Roxana* (1724) and *Authentic Memoirs of John Sheppard* (1724), are all essentially biographical in construction, straining the always unsafe divisions between fact and fiction.[15]

According to Lennard Davis (1983), criminality is central to the establishment of the novel form. Money and felony go hand in hand, both highly charged words in the lexicon of the eighteenth-century novel (ibid.: 128–9). Certainly the early novel bears some relation to earlier ballad forms, especially criminal biographical ballads whose claims to facticity, currency and news were echoed in the early novel (ibid.: 44ff). As Davis demonstrates, our current distinction between fact and fiction held no water in the early modern period. Histories, stories and news were all important for the lessons they taught and the interpretations they offered, not because of their avowed proximity or distance from the 'truth' (ibid.: 69). Like the popular literature already addressed above, the novel's treatment of the whore, the cutpurse and the villain employs a 'double discourse of both deterrence against sin and a nostalgic reaction against power and property' (ibid.: 125–6, 136).

Here, then, the discourses of individualism and the deification of property epitomised in the novel produced a peculiarly English bourgeois sensibility; one that chose to reject any organised policing. By the first part of the nineteenth century the great majority of the middle classes and the intelligentsia was still wholly hostile to the police (Mandel 1984: 12). Where the state was already bourgeois (Britain, Belgium, France, Holland and the young US) the middle classes preferred that the state remain weak, confident that the laws of the market were strong enough to perpetuate its rule. Moreover, state spending was a waste. The police were a necessary evil encroaching upon the rights and freedoms of the individual (ibid.). It is also overlooked in today's true crime writing on period crime that the bulk of the prison population in Britain was made up of bankrupts, rather than murderers or even thieves. Individuals from all class groupings were guilty of business and financial fraud, forgery and pilfering in the workplace (Emsley 1996: 121ff). The middle classes, therefore, were painfully aware of the short step from model citizen to convict and they tended to be hostile to the forces of the law and to the 'system' which orchestrated them.[16]

Modern criminal subjects: the mob and the notorious criminal

Paradoxically, perhaps, the objections to organised policing bled away with the emergence of classical liberalism. Indeed John McMulllan (1998: 109–10) contends that the liberal state had to police more in order to govern less:

> Liberal rule did not abandon the quest for an administered society so much as redefine and innovate new means to achieve it. ... Rather than being displaced, police science seems to have merged directly and decisively into the great social interventions of the nineteenth century.

Hostility towards the proposed 'police machine' did, therefore, finally diminish; it diminished as result of broader threats to the social body than that of the spectacular murders described above.[17] Workers suffering from widespread unemployment and the high price of bread turned to the radical press for diversion and explanation. Broadsheets with titles such as 'Flare-up! and Join the Unions' (Birt *c.* 1840) signal the presence of activist discourses at street level as well as among middle-class reformers.[18] 'Flare-up!' contains a wryly humorous dialogue between an activist and various workers who lament the poor conditions of their labour. It ends with an uplifting ballad, including the incendiary verse: 'Now one and all they have combin'd, and swear to hold communion. They say they'll bring the masters down, so Flare-up! and join the Unions!'

These major disturbances within the nation-state were clearly class-based or tied into various kinds of mass movement. Hence, as Anthony Giddens (1987: 184) notes: 'the "criminal" is specifically no longer a rebel but a "deviant" to be adjusted to the norms of acceptable behaviour as specified by the obligations of citizenship.' Having said all this, it was the individual criminal subject, whether thief or murderer, who remained the central attraction of true crime in the nineteenth century and into our own century. If anything the declining number of executions from the 1830s onwards made individual criminals even more notorious and fuelled the commercial success of broadsides. The increasing rarity value of executions caused publishers to concentrate on fewer cases in far greater detail, and the *Newgate Calendar* continued to recycle older cases in much the same way as do the true crime magazines of today. Indeed by the early 1800s the *Newgate Calendar* was still overwhelmingly popular. New collections were issued in 1809–10 (enlarged 1826–28) and in 1841 (Altick 1972: 4). In addition, the publication of George Borrow's retrospective collection *Celebrated Trials ...* (1825) ran to six volumes, proving the market longevity of older stories of crime (Altick 1972: 4). Alongside these up-market successes, self-sustaining growth was achieved in popular publishing with the introduction of new technologies such as the iron frame press (Gatrell 1996: 158–9). Sellers of broadsides (or 'death-hunters') continued to watch sales of almanacs, broadsheets and ballads rise until the 1860s (Altick 1972: 4). Cheap reprints of the *Newgate Calendar* far outsold books by 'popular' authors such as Ainsworth, Thackeray or Dickens (Hollingsworth 1963; Byrne 1992). The prolific London printer James Catnach produced the most remarkable sales figures during the period. His pamphlet 'Last Dying Speech and Confession' of the murderer of Maria Marten, sold 1,166,000 copies (Williams 1961: 165). Sensational cases could command sales of up to two million sheets, even without the extra material which might follow on its heels, replicating and embellishing the original story (Gatrell 1996: 159).

The historian J. A. C. Gatrell (1996: 175) describes this literature, which altered little in its overt moral posture for over 200 years, as repetitive, intrusively moralising and formulaic. As he observes, the unappealing rhetoric of moral certainty with which these were infused was unlikely to constitute their primary attraction to ordinary readers. Yet vast numbers of people chose to purchase them and to hear them read aloud. It is likely that it was the power of the broadsheets' gallows imagery that commanded the greater attention of readers. Yet a few stark, crudely cut, images of the gallows were frequently recycled by printers and made to do for a range of narratives. Gatrell suggests that the repetitive use of these illustrations, far from becoming hackneyed, actually became increasing iconic and resonant to readers. Gallows imagery fused the 'psychic energy of the spectacle and emblematic power of the gallows' to produce 'totemic artefacts'. As such they performed a complex office of defusing the horror of public executions (ibid.: 175).[19]

Certainly, execution narratives commanded considerable public interest, presumably as much for their memorable verses as for their illustrations. By the 1830s true accounts might include a sorrowful lamentation and particulars extracted from press reports or police intelligence. In addition the execution day might see a full or double broadsheet carrying details of the trial, confession, execution, verses, woodcut portraits or gallows scene. Something for everyone, no matter their level of literacy. In sensational cases a 'book' of 4, 8 or more pages would follow, which summarised all the preceding publications (Gatrell 1996: 158–9).

It could be argued, however, that the moral import of these broadsheets was defused in other ways not explored by Gatrell. For example, the impact of the retributive discourses borne in most true crime broadsides would have been softened or counterpointed by the overall complexity of tone in the variety of news and views disseminated by street literature. Broadsheets arguably resembled popular journalism, purveying details of boxing matches, natural and man-made disasters, comical neighbours, musings on love, death, wealth and oddities, such as the case of the husband who, on his death, was discovered to be a woman.[20] When taken together, the cornucopia of visual and written texts which were even then available to the illiterate and semi-literate, arguably produced a carnivalesque vision of society in which aristocrats can be obscene, women can be men and judges can be fools.

The majority of crimes reported in broadsheets continued to be of a cruel or unusual nature. Headlines such as 'Account of a dreadful

MONSTER, cutting and maiming FEMALES' (Catnach 18–)[21] and 'Eight Persons Murdered!' (Catnach 18–) which tells of two women who poisoned their families bore the news values of crime reporting still familiar to contemporary popular journalism.[22] Likewise the report of the 'Execution and Confession of J. Simpson a boy aged 15 for Robbing a Dwelling-House' (Catnach 18–) concentrated on the length and variety of his short criminal career wherein he committed upwards of 40 crimes from the age of seven years old. Cases such as that of the Simpson boy constituted part of the spectre of juvenile delinquency which had been haunting educated opinion since the beginning of the century and which constituted a full-blown moral panic by the 1840s (Pearson 1983: 157). Educated opinion, however, was quick to blame the parents of such children, whereas street literature such as the above tended to regard parents with considerable sympathy. Moreover delinquents frequently referred to as 'human vermin' and 'moral sewage' by the educators and journalists of the day were regarded as the precursors of political insurrection among the lower orders (Pearson 1983: 158–9).

On the whole street literature continued to condemn the murderous criminal and juvenile career criminals such as the Simpson boy, emphasising their monstrous and unnatural characters. As such their tone seems broadly in keeping with educated opinion. However, a closer look at the variety of true crime broadsides reveals a greater degree of complexity or ambivalence in their treatment of other types of criminals and lawlessness than suggested by the examples above. Some criminals were regarded with considerable sympathy by the broadsheets, especially those whose death sentences were somewhat haphazardly reviewed by the body known as King in Council (see Gatrell 1996: 543ff). A sheet entitled 'Execution of the unhappy men who suffered this day at Newgate' (Catnach 18–) is typical. It informs readers that 13 prisoners (all listed by name in the sheet) had their death sentences reviewed by the King and that all but three were given 'respite'. The text which details the latter's crimes (John Edmonds stole a horse, William Austin stole a letter while working at the Post Office and Richard Jasper forged a Bill of Exchange) looks upon the condemned men sympathetically. It concludes with a short emotional letter purported to have been written to Anne Jasper by her husband the day before his execution. The regretful tone employed in this broadside and others of a similar nature constructs a criminal who, far from being monstrous or 'other', is an ordinary citizen like the reader, suggesting perhaps that 'there but for the grace of God go I'. As Gatrell demonstrates it was certainly not unusual for friends, neighbours, employers and even jurors to petition the court recorder and Home Secretary for clemency, and the men named in broadsheets might well have had strong support from local readers. The implication in these stories is that the executed men (all convicted of property crime alone) were the victims of the capriciousness of the judicial system which reviewed their cases, perfectly illuminating the well-known phrase 'the glorious uncertainty of the law'.[23] Richard Jasper would have commanded special sympathy in any event as the general public regarded forgers with leniency.[24] Fraud and embezzlement were often perpetrated by wretchedly poor white-collar workers, increasingly faced with the temptations of the growing world of business, investment and insurance (Briggs *et al.* 1996: 132; Emsley 1996: 121ff). The social boundary was firmly drawn between the individual and financial temptation: 'It was here that English society chose to fight the battle for the control of the new, traditionless, unpredictable urban communities emerging out of the Industrial Revolution' (Briggs *et al.* 1996: 122).

Other types of criminals could also be treated with some affection by broadsheets, particularly when they made a mockery of the police, whose increasing presence found its way into true crime. For example the 'Extraordinary Life and Death of Mary Anne Pierce, alias LADY BARRYMORE' (Catnach 18—) tells the history of a woman who, formerly the mistress of a lord, turned to gin with dramatic consequences. While drunk she became 'the terror of Police-officers and Publicans. Had been 150 times at Bow-street, and confined in every Goal [*sic*] in London'. The text delights in Pierce's unusual physical strength when intoxicated and the manner in which she wrecked gin shops. Indeed, 'such was the extraordinary strength of the woman that she has been known to beat down three watchmen in succession, without any great effort.'

On a more sombre note, the police begin to appear in broadsheets as a source of authority and power within local communities, albeit usually called in as a last resort. It was extreme cases where criminal incidents could not be resolved privately or within the community, which were referred to the constabulary. 'Cruel Barbarity: To a female Child only Nine Years of Age' (Phair *c.* 1830) is an account of how a woman named Pascoe was brought to the watchhouse at Shadwell and Wapping for mistreating a child whom she had bought from a workhouse. In this case neighbours, hearing the child's screams, apprehended Pascoe and dragged her to the station. In cases such as these the examination of suspects at Bow Street Police Station inevitably became another regular source of intelligence for true crime broadsheets.

Modern criminal subjects: the dangerous individual

Two constructions of criminality then, the radical mobster and the thief, produced an association between popular illegality and the lower classes, the two arguably leading to a class-based concept of delinquency. Foucault argues that the prison in particular succeeded in producing and reinforcing a recognisable delinquency that permanently marked the criminal subject:

> [Prison produces] a specific type, a politically or economically less dangerous – and, on occasion, usable form of illegality; in producing delinquents, in an apparently marginal, but in fact centrally supervised milieu; in producing the delinquent as pathologized subject. (Foucault 1979: 277)

A number of penal and juridical moves underpinned the construction of the working-class delinquent. The release of prisoners on licence (known as ticket-of-leave), the common usage of the term 'criminal class', the criminal record and the formalised notion of the 'habitual criminal' all reinforced class-based notions of criminality.[25]

The most explicitly pathologised criminal subject was not, however, the proponent of social disorder (since this was perceived as a somewhat collective activity) or the perpetrator of property crime, but the criminal who committed spectacular or 'unnatural' acts or murder, rape or atrocity. This criminal, as will be seen throughout the course of this book, continues to be the favourite object of true crime's attention and scrutiny. A conflation of the offices and discourses of law and medicine arguably produced this type of dangerous individual. From the eighteenth and more particularly the nineteenth century onwards this criminal would have been identified variously as suffering from dementia, homicidal mania, moral insanity, diminished responsibility or a psychopathic disorder (Cameron and Frazer 1987: 92–3). Hence the appearance of the 'dangerous individual' as a new kind of criminal subject arose partially from debates about the fixing of personal responsibility within the criminal law, particularly in the last decades of the nineteenth century. Martin Wiener (1990: 265) notes:

> The operation of the criminal law became a locus for conflict between, on the one hand, a new inclination, encouraged by science, success, expanding social ambitions, and the difficulty encountered in practice in precisely locating legal responsibility, to replace the

moral fixation of the law by extending an administrative role and, on the other hand, a continuing anxiety on the part of many about the social dangers of the law's losing its moral boundaries.

Attempts to calibrate personal responsibility were most easily dispensed with in cases of infanticide and suicide. The criminalisation of the self-murderer and child murderer gradually gave way to prevailing medical opinion that mental disturbance played a significant part in these acts (Wiener 1990: 266ff). This medical view of criminal responsibility also impinged upon other types of homicide. Violence was increasingly being linked to mental abnormality and the acting out of a 'moment of madness' (ibid.: 265). *The Times* in 1881 summed up the perception that not greed but uncontrolled impulses were behind most violent crime:

> It is clear that with all our boasted progress in civilisation we have not yet got rid of the brute. In these days the creature who figures most frequently as the murderer does not belong to the criminal classes. ... His neighbour's purse may be in no danger from him, but for life or limb, when passions stir him, he has absolutely no regard. (in ibid.: 272).

It has been argued that the pathologised criminal, conceived as an unpredictable threat to society, is produced via the psychiatrisation of crime that prioritises the criminal's character above his/her crime. In his lecture on 'The Dangerous Individual' Foucault (1988: 126) contends that from the early nineteenth century the procedures of court examination came to demand more than a confession of guilt, but rather 'a revelation of what one is'. In other words, in addition to the offence and the penalty, there was the character of the criminal to be reckoned with:

> At first a pale phantom, used to adjust the penalty determined by the judge for the crime, this character gradually becomes more substantial, more solid and more real, until finally it is the crime which seems nothing but a shadow hovering about the criminal, a shadow which must be drawn aside in order to reveal the only thing which is now of importance, the criminal. (ibid.: 127–8)

For Foucault the nineteenth-century coincidence of psychiatry and notions of 'dangerousness' created the 'great monster' of criminal and popular lore: 'criminal psychiatry first proclaimed itself a pathology of the monstrous' (ibid.: 129–30, 31). Crimes against nature, crimes without reason, paradoxical crimes stemming from a derangement which would have no symptom other than the crime itself and which could disappear once the crime had been committed, 'were the terrain upon which medics and lawyers met and sometimes clashed' (ibid.: 133).[26] These crimes themselves became the totem and preserve of a dangerous criminal subject whose place within modern true crime entertainment has yet to be challenged.

Robert Louis Stevenson's 'shilling shocker' *The Strange Case of Dr Jekyll and Mr Hyde* (1886) is perhaps the best-known fictional exploration of the criminal whose deviance is only made manifest at the moment of the crime. Influenced by multiple personality theory, criminal anthropology and Darwinism, Stevenson's novella features the outwardly respectable figure of Dr Jekyll who comes to realise that man is neither good nor evil but 'radically both'. Jekyll explores this dualism through the chemical creation of an alternative persona called Mr Hyde who commits unmotivated crimes of singular ferocity. Mr Hyde is the literal embodiment of the monomaniacal criminal whose crime is the only symptom and therefore evidence of his madness. He epitomises late Victorian fears of recidivism, of a lapse into criminality and bestiality, fears which arose from the publication of Charles Darwin's 1859 *Origin of Species* (Jackson 1981: 116). In addition, the novel graphically challenged the 'fixity of moral boundaries' by underlining the ways in which nature failed to adhere to the moral distinctions that culture and civilisation had formulated (Wiener 1990: 253). Here the discourse of Darwinism and of the new criminology epitomised by the work of Havelock Ellis pit nature against culture. As Wiener (ibid.: 253) observes:

> Thus, while naturalizing discourse served to conceptually (and emotionally) isolate the criminal offender, in the long run it tended to blur the dividing lines between degrees of criminality and respectability, as more generally between the normal and the abnormal, because both categories were now being derived from a naturalistic continuum rather than the either-or typology of moralism.

Dr Jekyll and his *alter-ego* were to be invoked (among others) as the psychological model for the 'maniac' who ripped up women in the Whitechapel district of East London only a couple of years after the publication of Stevenson's book (Frayling 1986; Walkowitz 1992:

206–7). For the story helped furnish the idea that the Ripper might be 'respectable' and therefore untraceable. The 'Whitechapel Murderer' or 'Jack the Ripper' committed gruesome, anatomically precise and apparently ritualistic murders of at least five women within the district between August and November 1888 (Odell 1965; Rumbelow 1981). As Cyriax (1993) notes, during the killings journalists besieged Whitechapel. Eight daily papers, middlebrow magazines and penny dreadfuls all picked up the story.[27] Indeed, in both popular memory and in true crime accounts the figure of the Whitechapel Murderer is seen to typify the unreasonable dangerous individual, an individual whose cover for madness is assumed to be his everyday normality, even his 'respectability'. He is deemed by some to be 'the benchmark by which all sex killers are judged', a murderer who 'stands at the gateway of the modern age' (Cyriax 1993: 281). If the Ripper is marked as 'modern' it is not only because of his appearance near the *fin de siècle* but because of his construction as a 'sex killer', 'sadist' or 'erotomaniac', labels which accrued to him via the popularisation of psychiatry and more specifically of sexology (Walkowitz 1992: 207). It has been suggested that at this time criminals and other designated groups were invited to speak and confess their sexuality, producing the 'setting apart of the "unnatural" as a specific dimension in the field of sexuality' (Foucault 1976: 38–9). If this is so then the unavailability of the Ripper for scrutiny and interview truly stamped him as an enigma to be solved rather than simply as a criminal to be apprehended.

It was not, however, contemporary press and true crime coverage of the case alone that guaranteed its longevity in the public mind but Marie Belloc Lowndes' 1913 best-seller entitled *The Lodger*.[28] *The Lodger* tells the dramatic tale of a couple called Bunting who, facing poverty, rent out a room to a stranger during a public scare over a series of vicious murders. The book is perhaps most remarkable for its exploration of female fascination with murder and the macabre; both Mrs Bunting and her stepdaughter Daisy are attracted as well as repelled by the so-called 'Avenger' murders. It becomes clear, much to Mrs Bunting's growing horror and fascination, that the stranger must be the 'Avenger'. Lowndes firmly situates the killer within the discourses of the dangerous individual. For it emerges that the killer is an escaped lunatic who, although suffering from religion-inspired erotomania, passes as normal through his apparent respectability. Educated and financially secure, the killer pores constantly over his Bible and Concordance, keeping to himself, silent aside from the misogynistic commentaries which he offers up to his increasingly suspicious landlady.

Lowndes' book helped to popularise questions of individual psychology and the implications of mental disorders on sentencing policy; both issues which were directly relevant to the construction of the 'dangerous individual'. In addition, her portrait of the educated, mobile, deranged sex killer helped to establish the Whitechapel Murderer as 'dangerous individual', as a modern phenomenon and the model against which subsequent random killers have been measured. It is this type of dangerous individual, who became conspicuous at the cusp of the twentieth century most notably in novels such as those by Stevenson and Lowndes, rather than in journalism or true crime, who became the central attraction of late twentieth century true crime magazines and criminal biographies.

The Moors Murders as a landmark case

If the Whitechapel Murderer foregrounded the establishment of the dangerous criminal subject as part and parcel of the modern English cultural landscape, the Moors Murder case of 1957 gave it a contemporary inflection in keeping with the new emphasis upon sex crime. Here the stranger killing indicative of the 'dangerous individual' and sex crime indicative of the 'pervert' came together to produce a new spectacle of murder. Ian Brady and Myra Hindley were tried at Chester Assizes from 19 April to 6 May 1966. In the words of the true crime writer Colin Wilson (1971: 144):

> The bare facts have a quality of nightmare, like the dreams of a sadistic pornographer: a young man who admires Hitler and de Sade seduces a religious and rather ordinary girl, and persuades her to join with him in kidnapping, torturing and killing a number of children.

The couple had been accused of the murders of Lesley Ann Downey, Edward Evans and John Kilbride. Brady was found guilty of all three killings and Hindley of the first two, but found guilty of being an accessory to the Kilbride killing. Both were sentenced to life imprisonment. In January 1985 Brady also confessed to the murders of Pauline Read and Keith Bennett which, although suspected, had remained unproven. All except one of these victims were children. The manner of the children's deaths provoked public outrage. Ten-year-old Lesley Ann Downey was stripped, gagged and photographed before her murder. Her screams were tape-recorded with music superimposed, including the songs 'The Little Drummer Boy' and 'Old Saint Nicholas' (Johnson 1967: 14). The fifth and final victim Edward Evans, aged 17, was battered to death with an axe in the couple's own home. The couple's unsuccessful attempt to recruit Hindley's brother-in-law to murder added to their notoriety.

The 'Moors Murders' case, as it came to be known, was a landmark in a number of ways relevant to this book. Certainly, it continues to command significant media attention as a case that is emblematic of the modern British sex crime (Soothill and Walby 1991: 87–91). These acts of random murder conducted by two highly dangerous individuals seemed to confirm the perception that a new brand of criminality was at large. As a 'sex crime' it seemed both to invite and affirm the explanatory discourses of psychology and psychiatry (ultimately affirmed by the onset of Brady's mental illness while in prison). As a 'modern crime' it was regarded as a barometer of increasing social malaise and the haemorrhaging of 'traditional' values and mores. As a crime committed by a modern young couple it seemed to encapsulate and direct contemporary anxieties about social mobility, consumption and the growing presence of the mass media. Finally, it inspired what has been regarded as a classic of modern British true crime, Emlyn Williams' novelistic account of the case entitled *Beyond Belief* (1967).

For Colin Wilson (1972: 161) the case as 'sex crime' was paradigmatic of the role of the psychological motor in modern murder. He regards murder as a 'field of expression' for untapped intellectual energy and sexual drive. Within these parameters acts of murder and depravity perform a cathartic function, acting as a release valve for misdirected drives. Even where the catharsis hypothesis has been explicitly refuted by cultural commentators one can see how it became wedded to contemporary anxieties about permissiveness, moral decline and criminality. For journalists of the time such as Pamela Hansford Johnson the Moors case crystallised public concern over a constellation of issues that continue to inform current debates about crime and the representation of crime. The case summed up the social consequences of growing permissiveness, of increasing affluence and of the effects of the mass media upon weak minds. As a crime apparently rooted in the triad of sex obsession, the crumbling of the social bond and an increasing social mobility, it finally provided the markers against which more 'moral subjects' could be established and measured. For example Johnson's book on Brady and Hindley entitled *On Iniquity* (1967) overtly challenged psychological and cathartic explanations of criminal behaviour, suggesting that the dominant explanatory model of 'sickness' should make way for the older concept of 'wickedness' in accounting for murder and atrocity (Johnson 1967: 7). Johnson argued that this wickedness is rooted in the new atmosphere of 'permissiveness' that has infected English society. Even the ancient English town of Chester, the location of the trial, is tainted and sordid. Walking around the town, Johnson (ibid.: 19) notes:

> I climbed the narrow, dank stairs to the ramparts. ... A light drizzle was falling now, bats flitting in the russet-coloured dusk. ... I saw a couple closely embraced against the sweating stones. ... Almost at once, they unlocked. ... As they passed by me, I saw that both were men ... [I] had not gone far when I realised that I was being dogged by an elderly man ... whispering dirt in my ears.

Here the modern notion of permissiveness is elided with gothic horror. But it is also wedded to notions of misdirected sexual drives, of sexual desire that has escaped the confines of the family and of domesticity. Desire and eroticism have 'gone public', the link between permissiveness and modernity rendered explicit through the visibility of sex in the streets, of same-sex couples and whispering men. If the Moors murders are regarded as symptomatic of desire misdirected, they are also perceived to be symptomatic of an 'affectless society' in which any emotional investment is refused (ibid.: 35ff). Johnson suggests that the population is conditioned by sick jokes, media pillorying of those in authority, boredom and a sexual permissiveness finally sanctioned by the successful legal defence of *Lady Chatterley's Lover*, into an abnegation of emotion and social responsibility.[29] Johnson, like Q. D. Leavis (1932) before her, felt that the 'semi-literate reading public' could not cope with the 'full liberties' of the mass media. Here was a dangerous new marketplace in which Krafft-Ebing may be bought from railway bookstalls, and violence may be consumed via television in the comfort of one's own home (ibid.: 28–9). In this arena intellectual energies are as misdirected as sexual energy, seeking out literary avenues best left open to the highly educated (ibid.: 28). Hindley and Brady epitomised the fears signalled here, fears of the 'swinging society: under its Big Top, the whole garish circus of the new freedom to revel, through all kinds of mass media, in violence, in pornography' (ibid.: 17). If Brady and Hindley seemed to embrace (along with many other working-class people) the 'shiny barbarism' of the new permissive society, they also became a gaudy emblem of that barbarism.

Public fascination with the Moors case turned upon the questions of how to demarcate the boundaries between the criminal subject and its others (the responsible citizen, the bystander, and the reader of true crime). A contemporaneous two-part feature on the case in *The Observer Supplement* (Ferris 24 April 1996a and 1 May 1966b) justified its coverage of the case with the argument that an insight into the 'mind of the murderer' is also an insight into ourselves. Its author Paul Ferris (1966b: 9) notes:

> Others I know, have these strange dreams of murder they have not committed but fear they might have. What we read on the subject is more than an account of an eccentric Them, safely remote from normality on the far side of the fence. It is about us.

Here Ferris deploys a post-Freudian vocabulary that accounts for individual criminality but which also allows for a collective sense of guilt.[30] The criminal subject and its others are linked in a chain of associations that hark back to the stories of Hogg (1824), Poe (e.g. 1839), Stevenson's *Dr Jekyll and Mr Hyde* (1886) and Lowndes' (1913) story of the psychopathic 'Avenger' (discussed above) and forward to the modern true crime biography.[31] These are stories of *doppelgangers*, *alter-egos* and fractured selves. As narratives of the instability of the danger-ous criminal subject (who is banal and exceptional, ordinary and dangerous), they throw into question the very stability of the subject.

Beyond belief

The Moors Murderers case became the benchmark against which many subsequent cases were to be measured.[32] It also inspired Emlyn Williams' book *Beyond Belief* (1968): a 'classic' of modern British true crime which was itself to become a benchmark and inspiration for its countless successors (Oxford 1995: 4–5). Williams' book, which sought to mix 'history' with 'imaginative understanding', helped establish the reflexive tone of modern British true crime. The book was immediately received by reviewers as the definitive, if flawed, work on the subject (Playfair 1967: 160). It was also favourably compared with that American landmark of true crime, Truman Capote's *In Cold Blood* (Fowler 1967: 17) (see Chapter 1).[33] In Williams' book, and in the many true crime books that followed in its wake, criminal biography became essentially an anatomy of the human psyche through the exemplary analysis of the dangerous individual. The author (Williams

1968: 52) asks: 'What are the spells which are woven after birth, the subtle processes working from day to day in the darkness of the young head, as it grows from childhood to adolescence and maturity?'

This is a self-consciously literary encounter with murder and depravity. It seeks to explore both the depths and the resilience of the human psyche within a post-Darwinian world. In an appendix to the book Williams describes a meeting with Hindley's brother-in-law David Smith and his family.[34] Here the author constructs a model of the natural relationship between life and death. He notes that the family uses the baby's pram that had once been used to transport one of the corpses. Smith laments the death of Hindley's dog Bobby, before mentioning that the cat has given birth to five kittens, saying, 'Ye can't go against nature, can you?' (ibid.: 351). Williams spies a copy of *The Monsters of the Moors* on the coffee table just before he is informed that the Smiths have a second child on the way. The strategic juxtaposition of dialogue and observation underlines the casual and apparently thoughtless proximity of life with death. More importantly, the family scene serves to illustrate the resilience of human nature in the aftermath of an unnatural crime. Humanity can penetrate the external world and go against nature in the most spectacular of ways: 'The world advances, how it strides! Yearly, monthly, weekly, yet another mystery of the universe laid bare. Dare-devils from Omsk or Oshkosh frisk like drunken balloons in outer space, a billion miles from home' (ibid.: 51). But for the true crime writer the individual human subject remains the terra incognita, the epitome of unnatural action:

> We advance. But the one mystery we shall never solve, is the enigma of human identity. What am I? What are You? I spell You with a capital because to you, you are as real as I am to me. (ibid.: 51)

This notion that true crime biography may assume an educative function, exploring questions of identity and subjectivity, is founded upon the idea that, as in philosophy, the human subject is the only significant object of scrutiny. In the foreword Williams defends the book against potential accusations of bad taste and the unnecessary revelation of sordid fact with an allusion to Pope's *Essay On Man*. He notes: 'but some of us do want to know, and it is salutary to inquire: the proper study of mankind is Man. And Man cannot be ignored because he has become vile. Woman neither' (ibid.: vii).[35] Pope's essay also gave the injunction to 'know thyself', an injunction that is integral to the double-vision of true crime project; a project that scrutinises the murderer in order to hold a mirror up to the reader.[36]

Concluding comments

These histories of true crime, of popular accounts and of the knowledges and practices that they articulated, map the emergence of different inflections of modern subject through the discourses of crime and criminality. Here it can be seen how the practices and knowledges that speak of, and regulate, law and order help to produce what could be described as a new lexicon of political subjects. These include the professional agent of the law, the law-abiding citizen, the property owner, the habitual delinquent, the radical member of the mob, the dangerous individual and the sex criminal. These figures, as familiar as they might seem when enumerated in an historical overview such as this, are also inflected differently at specific moments in time. For example the law-abiding citizen of the 1890s has different duties and concerns from his/her 1990s counterpart. None the less as tropes or rhetorical figures these subjects, once produced, continue to inform current debates about crime and punishment, policing, penalty and jurisprudence and the following chapters' discussion of true crime and its articulation of contemporary concerns about crime make most sense when set against this backdrop.

3
Discourses of Law and Order in Britain from 1979 to 1995

'Keeping 'em peeled' – the vigilant citizen as moral subject

> It is curious that in the last two decades increases in recorded crime, falls in detection rates and a squeeze on funding have been met by what seems at first sight rather like a return to eighteenth century values: more emphasis upon the role of the victim and the community in responding to crime, the expansion of the private security industry, and deterring criminals through severe penalties rather than through detection.
>
> Philip Rawlings (1999: 173)

> We wanted a society of autonomous citizens, and we have created a society of frightened human beings.
>
> Ralf Dahrendorf (1985: 4)

This chapter aims to understand the political context of contemporary British true crime and the conditions that fostered its resonance for readers and viewers. The argument is that true crime exhibits in popular form an extension or amplification of the political discourses that have come to dominate the political landscape since the late 1970s. This chapter documents and analyses these discourses in order to set the scene upon which the drama of true crime is played out. I examine the ways in which certain television programmes and mainstream publications (law and order series and *Reader's Digest*) discursively construct a 'moral subject' who stands opposed to the criminal subject of true crime and who is also emblematic of a particular sociopolitical moment in Britain. An examination of the discursive construction of the moral subject and its intersection with dominant public discourses of citizenship and responsibility reveals much about the political moment of its elaboration, a moment that forms the backdrop of the consumption of specialist true crime publications such as those examined in the following chapters.

In general, media debates about rising crime and other law and order issues are supported by the assumption that it is the natural rights of life, liberty and the possession of private property, (all rights bound up with the development of modern British individualism) which are under threat from the criminal.[1] Of these three rights, the threat to life is deemed to be the pre-eminent crime within specialist true crime and within fictional forms such as television crime drama and the detective novel (see Cohen 1988: 236–40; Sparks 1992).[2] As already shown in the discussion of early true crime, the trajectory of true crime stories tends to follow the pursuit of the criminal and how she/he is brought to the gates of justice and indeed sometimes beyond to her/his execution. Here the criminal, having broken the bonds of the social contract through acts of murder, rape, mutilation and so on, rarely manages to evade detection and punishment. When a crime achieves notoriety because it remains unsolved it is usually presented as a rare phenomenon meriting the particular scrutiny of the true crime buff.[3]

The context of these homicide-oriented forms of true crime is a public sphere within which broader issues of law and order, citizenship and responsibility, security and risk are circulated. John Keane (1996: 5) has noted:

> The democratic zone of peace feels more violent because within its boundaries images and stories of violence move ever closer to the citizens who otherwise live in peace, due to risk calculations and safety requirements of insurance companies; the eagerness for publicity of policing authorities; [and] campaigns to publicise violence and to mobilise criminal process (against rapists and child murderers, for instance).

As already noted, in popular literature and reportage the criminal subject is constructed not simply as an aberrant individual, but by extrapolation, as a threat to the values of the liberal society and of the modern state whose duty it is to preserve life, liberty and property. Having said this, the freedom to own and to defend property is largely unaddressed in true crime magazines. Property and white-collar crime occupy a more important role in what might be called 'law and order' programmes[4] such as *Crimestoppers* (ITV), *Crime Monthly* (LWT),

Crimewatch UK (BBCl), and its two sister productions *Crimewatch Unlimited* (BBC1) and *Crimewatch File* (BBCl), and in mainstream journals such as *Reader's Digest*. The programmes are usually anchored by journalists who present a number of unsolved crimes that require 'help' in the form of information from the viewing public.[5] The crimes are presented and discussed via a mixture of interviews with police officers, reports and dramatic reconstructions. *Crimewatch UK* (BBC1 1984–), the best known of these programmes, maintains audiences figures of 11–12 million with a format that includes interviews and dramatic reconstructions of (usually) violent crime and sex crime. Although it ignores white-collar crime, it regularly features an item entitled 'Aladdin's Cave' which displays merchandise recovered by the police from thieves and fences. The programme lays some emphasis on the distress caused to the individual citizen through property crime. It looks not only at burglary and credit card fraud, but also at less stigmatised crimes such as shoplifting, forgery and duplicate designer clothing. Its range of reference performs an office rarely undertaken by specialist true crime publications, producing a broad and diffused vision of a criminalised Britain where criminality operates at every level of society.[6] The programme's spin-off book substantiates its depiction of the criminal quotidian, warning of a 'subculture, almost an industry' which thrives on the circulation of stolen goods and recommends careful precautions against theft (Ross and Cook 1987: 142).

Within law and order programming organised crime (e.g. armed robbery) and random crime (e.g. stranger killing) are counterpointed with the initiatives of the individual citizen. In the opening sequence of *Crimewatch UK* various members of the public (together with the viewer) see, for example, a suspicious-looking man pass by as he runs through suburban streets. The sequence concludes with an interior shot of what might be construed as the 'good citizen' spying the runner from his window and reaching for the telephone, presumably to call the programme (or the police). This sequence, together with the opening music and graphics (which includes blue flashing lights reminiscent of a police car rooftop lamp), juxtaposes official policing with self-policing in a manner that elides the differences between them. Here the citizen-viewer and the police are both established as monitors of the community space and with the same function – the detection of crime and the pursuit of the guilty. As such this scenario suppresses the ways in which detection (especially on the part of the ordinary citizen) is naturally quite random and contingent.[7]

It could be argued that it is this picture of both vigilance and worry about crime that characterises programmes such as *Crimewatch*. The programme seems to reveal the messy consequences of careless lifestyles: the girl who leaves the club with a stranger, a kitchen window left open, a shopkeeper who uses the same route to the bank one time too many (see Weaver 1998). Law and order programmes, by showing us the unpleasant consequences of individual action or inaction, invite an imagined community of viewers to review the measures which they themselves might take in order to shore up their own defences. The programme's depiction of the consequences of inaction or lack of vigilance on the part of the individual returns the problem of crime to the private citizen rather than to the state, 'constructing a new citizenship through fear' (Palmer G. 1998: 12). These programmes exhibit no interest in the causes of crime and criminality; instead they present themselves as an instrument through which the private person (pictured in the opening sequence of *Crimewatch* reaching for the phone in the *domestic space*) can help the police to solve specific crimes. The perceived need to formalise the vigilant neighbourliness which is already evident in more affluent communities, through the adoption of Neighbourhood Watch and the like, is arguably congruent with a broader perception, aired by the media, that we need to 'bolt down Britain' (Rayment 1996: 12). In fact, of course, this cohort of programmes portrays many atypical crimes, which are unlikely to be prevented by community initiatives, consisting mostly of murder, violent robbery and sex crime (Schlesinger *et al.* 1992: 408; Schlesinger and Tumber 1993). *Crimewatch* presenters Nick Ross and Sue Cook describe how the makers of *Crimewatch* have a very shrewd idea of what is wanted in the show: 'with a quarter of a million crimes recorded every month you would think *Crimewatch* would be spoilt for choice. In fact it is remarkably difficult regularly to find three crimes worthy of reconstruction' (Ross and Cook 1987: 29). The programme seeks to solve cases with the aid of the public, but it is also a 'show', a successful entertainment. It is dependent upon the very crimes that it seeks to solve. By the time it is ready to go on air this paradox is painfully apparent: 'frankly, at this stage, with all this investment in time and effort, not to say the BBC's resources, we pray that the crimes are not solved just before we go on air' (ibid.: 34).

The public investigation of crime as both spectacle and information has become a genre in its own right. 'Infotainment' programming is itself a mini-industry, with law and order programmes aiming to situate themselves as essential sources of information for the informed citizen. It could be argued that these programmes adopt a defensive stance, which deliberately situates them as an extension of the arm of the law, buttressing the law-abiding majority against the excesses of both individual rogue criminals and against the criminal classes in general. Indeed *Crimewatch UK* presenters Nick Ross and Sue Cook have stated: 'Moreover, any crime that has hit the headlines is followed up for, though the motive may not be entirely virtuous, we believe it is in the programme's interests to be seen at the centre of the crime detection business' (ibid.: 29).[8] However, elsewhere in the programme's spin-off book the authors stress the programme's deliberate difference and distancing from the police and the crime detection business (ibid.: 156). Yet the programme's opening sequence with flashing blue light, police presenters and the use of evidence such as CCTV film and e-fits, which are strongly coded as the productions of law enforcement agencies, signal *Crimewatch*'s alliance with the institutional forces of law and order.[9] Clearly, this does not mean that the programme's material always conforms to the police perspective in every case but rather that the general tenor of the programmes obscures the significant differences between law enforcement agencies and law and order programming.[10] The programme's emphasis upon teamwork and variety – its joint presenters, visible ranks of telephonists and its coverage of diverse crime-related topics – reinforces its role as a cog in the machine of law enforcement. These features, along with its police force guests, signal the notable structural differences between *Crimewatch UK* and investigative report programmes such as *Beam and Da Silva* (Carlton UK 1994–) or *The Cook Report* (ITV/Carlton UK 1987–).

Privatisation and individual responsibility

> In the modern State, the *citizen*, in so far as he is separate from the *private* man and the *productive* man, becomes externalised in terms of his own self. He plays a part in a political community in which he sees himself as social. Whereas he is also social, and more so, in another context. The citizen – the man who is well-informed about public manners, who has reasoned opinions, who knows the law – has become a political fiction; for there are necessary political fictions just as there are necessary legal ones.
>
> Henri Lefebvre (1958a: 89)

Crimewatch's depiction of the viewer as active, autonomous and socially responsible positions him/her as a citizen whose status entails duties as well as rights. The term 'citizen' is used advisedly here. Citizenship has been the emblem of late modernity: an instrument and symbol of progress, equality and liberty. As Henri Lefebvre argues in the above quotation, the citizen is both a necessary agent of the modern state and also a necessary signifier of its political success. In addition, the effective and consistent adoption of the role of the good citizen by individuals within the state arguably subtends the broader manageability of the social body. The requirements of active citizenship meet the criteria delineated by Michel Foucault (1975: 216) for the ordering and manage-ment of what he refers to as 'infinitesimal distribution of power rela-tions'. For the injunction to be a good citizen arguably fulfils three criteria of power: it obtains 'the exercise of power at the lowest possible cost', it extends the effects of 'social power' and, finally, it increases the usefulness and manageability of the individual within the political system (Foucault 1975: 218). Philip Wexler's (1990: 165) suggestion, however, that the concept of citizenship belongs to a 'bygone era' needs to be considered within this specific socio-economic context. Although Wexler argues that the prerequisites of *ideal* citizenship have failed (autonomy, participation, influence) I persist in using the term since the discourses of law and order persist in invoking these very modern ideals when they enjoin the populace to police their society and them-selves. During the 1980s a particular discursive regime came to the fore in which populist notions of citizenship dovetailed with a broader New Right emphasis upon individual responsibility with regard to health care, education and law and order. Since 1979, New Right political dis-courses have colonised the discourses of law and order, returning the problem of crime to the lap of the individual citizen:

> Crime prevention no longer simply meant government or its agents stepping in to moralise the poor or to detect crime; at its core was individual responsibility. Individuals not only chose to be criminals, they also chose to be victims by not taking measures to protect themselves ... and their property. (Rawlings 1999: 163)

In this sense it is the duty of the citizen not only to be law-abiding (to 'know' the law) but also to be a custodian of the law. Consequently, the government has encouraged the public to 'walk with purpose' and to organise Neighbourhood Watch schemes in order to defend private property and the way of life upon which it is predicated. In addition, cit-izens are invited to participate in crime prevention and detection initia-tives sponsored by non-government money.[11] The Crimestoppers campaign launched in 1988 is exemplary here. Its slogan 'Uniting against Crime' fronts a national network of voluntary boards to create partnerships between the public, business, the media and the police. It is a registered charity with the financial backing of a range of companies including Securicor, Racal-Chubb and Barclay's Bank (companies whose widely recognised names are already signifiers of both financial and physical security). It solicits the public to phone in information anonymously and also publicises a different crime each week via the media. It operates a cash reward system regulated by the multinational organisation 'Crimestoppers Incorporated' (Johnston 1992: 138–40). One leaflet sets up the invitation: 'Fed up with criminals around you? Tell us what they're up to.' Another leaflet challenges, 'Robbery, murder, assault, rape, drug dealing are happening everyday in our community ... do you care enough to do something about rising crime?' The uncontested presence of such schemes is evidence of a growing acceptance of (or lack of resistance to) a new emphasis upon individual responsibility in conjunction with state policing and private enterprise. For Les Johnston (1992: 137ff) the high profile of television programmes such as *Crimewatch UK* and quasi-corporate initiatives such as Crimestoppers also relocates notions of 'responsible citizenship' within a broader re-articulation of the relationship between the public and the private sphere. Johnston (ibid.: 140) comments: 'These examples of commercial and media sponsorship demonstrate that active citizenship is not just about encouraging individuals to give information about crime. It is also about bodies acting as "corporate citizens" to shape agendas in the public sphere.' In this way the discourses of law and order and of citizenship became newly inflected, combining with a broader and more diffused emphasis upon enterprise, corporate responsibility and privatisation.

John Major, Margaret Thatcher's successor from 1991, sought to strengthen the strategic alliance between 'responsible citizenship', state and private policing. The mobilisation of the concept of citizenship as autonomous agency rather than as collective endeavour was part and parcel of this alliance. A desire to suture the rights and responsibilities of individual citizenship into state policing of the civil realm had already been rendered explicit with the deployment of the phrase 'active citizen'. This phrase, deployed by the Home Secretary, Douglas Hurd, in 1989, was used to signify a more vigilant and interventionist moral subject, a subject who could fill the 'gaps' between public services (Hurd 1989; see also Johnston 1992: 223–4). This notion of citizenship as policing was arguably dependent upon a vision of the financially self-sufficient individual: 'Without property, a citizen cannot be independent; without the income of property, an individual will not have the leisure necessary to be a good citizen. Without property the citizen is passive' (Ignatieff 1991: 26). As Stuart Hall and David Held (1989: 174) suggest: 'In this discourse, citizenship is detached from its modern roots in institutional reform, in the welfare state and community struggles, and re-articulated with the more Victorian concepts of charity, philanthropy and self-help.'

The formulation of the Citizen's Charter in the early 1990s explicitly harnessed this resurgent notion of citizenship to the philosophy of privatisation and individual choice. The Charter initiative was intended to be 'one of the central themes of public life', sustaining the momentum of privatisation and managerialism inaugurated under Margaret Thatcher in the 1980s and giving new powers to the citizen (HMSO 1991: 2, 51). With regard to issues of law and order the emphasis was upon producing measurable standards and targets in the police and judiciary's dealings with the public in order to strengthen public confidence in the law and more specifically in the police as agents of the law. The Charter was to facilitate the opening up of the police service to competition through Compulsory Competitive Tendering (CCT) and performance-related pay (HMSO 1994: 111, 118). This built upon the efforts of the Thatcher government to introduce business skills and attitudes to the police (Sullivan 1998: 342). The public themselves were encouraged to extend the deployment of Neighbourhood Watch schemes (HMSO 1991: 24)[12] and in 1994 Hurd's successor, Michael Howard, encouraged the Watch to develop street patrols in order to complement the work of the police (Reiner 1995: 3).[13] Most tellingly, perhaps, one of the earliest publications was a statement of the rights and expectations of victims of crime, a Victims' Charter (HMSO 1991) which attempted to counter the public perception that criminals and their families received more state assistance than their victims. As will be demonstrated later on with reference to the discourses of *Reader's Digest*, this perception is amplified in the press and popular journals, along with the broader perception that the dead hand of bureaucracy and statism often impedes the good citizen's pursuit of justice.

'A very modern sort of watchfulness': security and surveillance

The advocacy of active citizenship is part of a broader discourse of self-policing and privatised security. Since the 1970s 'protective service occupations' including those of private policing have become a fast-growing area of employment, to the extent that 'private police' now outnumber state-employed police (Taylor, I. 1997: 53–4, see also Campbell 1992; Johnston 1992; Gill and Hart 1997).[14] As indicated above, the Charters of the early 1990s sought to render the police services more competitive with the private sector, opening them up to market competition. So too the decades since the late 1970s have witnessed the increasing privatisation of security for the individual citizen and for corporate business. The rise in home security goods and services during the 1980s is at least indicative of a growing market ready to invest in locks, entry-phones, alarms and even cameras rather than rely on community policing and other official measures to stem a perceived deluge of property crime.[15] In *Home Security and Protection*, one of a rising tide of advice manuals on home defence published in the 1980s, the author notes:

> Security is really an attitude of mind and the techniques now available to translate that attitude into physical protection can be effectively employed only if *all* the risks are recognised and each separate measure is carefully assessed and introduced to form part of a total security plan. (Traini 1984: 8)

The idea of security as an 'attitude of mind' conjures up preparedness rooted in personal motivation and psychological resilience. Here the vocabulary of co-ordinated risk assessment and militaristic planning elide dominant notions of DIY, home-making and domestic responsibility with those of military defence and siege management.

Several factors contributed to the boom in the sales of home protection goods and services. The development of burglar alarm systems tailored specifically for the home rather than as adaptations of commercial systems allowed the consumer greater and more appropriate choice (Traini 1984: 7). Government campaigns such as the highly successful 1982–83 drive by the Home Office to promote window locks also spurred householders into making other home security purchases (ibid.: 18). The home security industry itself has exerted pressure, sometimes unethically, to encourage the consumer to invest in their services by sending out unsolicited sensationalist literature which fosters fear of crime (ibid.: 8). There has also been a growing acceptance of privately funded street patrols paid for by local authorities, businesses and residents (see Boothroyd 1989a and 1989b; Johnston 1992).

Surveillance in the form of close circuit television has also entered public fora: the shopping mall, the housing estate and even residential suburbia. The paradoxical nature of modern individualism is revealed by the gradual and occasionally rapid colonisation of public space by the instruments of surveillance. The concern over the safety of persons and property has engendered what Andrew O'Hagan (1996: 163) has called a 'very modern sort of watchfulness'. This newly inflected vigilance informs the construction of the moral subject. The contemporary moral subject is enjoined to consent to this surveillance not only in the interests of the community but also as evidence that he/she has nothing hide. If this citizen is innocent of wrongdoing he/she can have no objection to the TV monitor, the speed camera or the personal identification card. For this watchfulness manifests itself not only in the visual recording of everyday life but also in its administration and documentation.[16] Certainly, Britain is already a highly administered society where the 'visible body' is clothed in paperwork to such an extent that the idea of women or children permanently disappearing into a Cromwell Street nightmare seems incredible (O'Hagan 1995: 183).[17] Gitta Sereny, in the revised (post-James Bulger) edition of her first book on the child-murderer Mary Bell, expresses her dismay that irregularities of behaviour may remain unnoticed in such a highly administered society:

> The fact is that, in a modern state at the end of the twentieth century, it should be impossible for social services to remain unaware of crises in crisis families; it should be impossible for children who behave conspicuously in school not to be noticed and attended to. (Sereny 1995: xiv)

This call for attention to – and intervention in – situations where normative guidelines, boundaries and practices have been transgressed in terms of *behaviour* naturally begs the question of how the state establishes and polices norms without prejudice and without contravening individual liberty. It is a commonplace that individual liberty has to be measured against wider concerns about the security of all citizens. Paradoxically, surveillance, instituted in part so that the populace can live freely and without fear, is incompatible with individual liberty, leading to 'a progressive erosion of the area of liberty and a corresponding retreat into what private world is left' (Abercrombie *et al.* 1986: 151).

This private world, for those who can afford it, is the world of home ownership. During the 1980s the Conservative government's objective was to facilitate home ownership and reduce dependence upon public housing, with the intention, among other things, of fostering greater 'self-reliance' among citizens (Hutton 1995: 203).[18] As public housing faded from the landscape new communities arose through house buying. Indeed, as early as 1974 Jonathan Raban (1988: 90), in a commentary on the movement which was soon to be called 'gentrification', observed that 'community is becoming an increasingly expensive commodity'. These government initiatives created a new class of homeowner, determined to defend their property and happy to join neighbourhood vigilance schemes. Indeed, evidence seems to indicate that in spite of the shift in housebreaking towards poorer areas, where none the less audio and video equipment may be present, it is usually the more affluent consumer who actively secures his or her home. As will also be noted later, in the case of Neighbourhood Watch schemes, it is the people most vulnerable to burglary who take the fewest security precautions (Traini 1984: 11).

The growth of Neighbourhood Watch schemes during the 1980s is a testament to generalised fears of rising crime and a concomitantly strong perception of increased personal vulnerability.[19] It reinforced the division between the responsible moral subject and its others. The role of the schemes is precisely to increase vigilance and therefore diminish both crime and the fear of crime. The emphasis here on self-motivation and personal responsibility accords with the broader tenets of individualism articulated in political and popular discourses since the early 1980s; namely the capacity for 'transformative action, responsibility and self-motivation' (Abercrombie 1986: 81).[20]

In terms of visibility alone these schemes have been hugely successful, with 90 per cent of people having heard of the initiative by 1988 (Mayhew *et al.* 1989: 51). Surveys have found that members tend to come from more affluent groups, often owner-occupiers, who are already well informed about crime prevention measures. Areas where the risk of burglary is far greater (poorer council estates, social housing, ethnically mixed city areas) have the fewest schemes with far fewer people eager to participate in them (ibid.: 60). None the less, for those that take up this scheme, researchers have noticed that the enhanced precautions taken against property crime, together with the increased surveillance undertaken by the Watch, still failed to alleviate worries about being burgled. They conclude:

NW [Neighbourhood Watch] has achieved its aim of making members more alert to the risks of crime. They are, though, more worried about burglary. This was no doubt a factor in their joining the NW, and schemes may inevitably sustain this worry in trying to foster an awareness of the risk. (ibid.: 61)

Neighbourhood Watch offers individual subjects the chance to situate themselves within a broader community of concerned citizens. The concept of vigilant neighbourliness is attractive because it offers citizens the chance to take proactive measures, to form alliances with the police and perhaps even the chance to recuperate a positive community ethic which stands in direct opposition to the demonised street culture of youth gatherings. It appears to offer people a measure of autonomy and direction in controlling their own environment. Having said this, the ethos of Neighbourhood Watch is often at odds with what it manages to achieve. As Johnston (1992: 148) argues:

The mechanisms whereby such lofty ideals might be realised are often unclear. In practice, therefore, schemes have tended to focus on the more limited goal of opportunity reduction, by having participants act as 'the eyes and ears of the police'.

This concerted effort to police public space and defend private property is overtly flagged by street signs, posters and door stickers, which signal the formalised vigilance of local people. Here organised preventative measures are established in an attempt to repel or warn off the perpetrators of street crime and burglary. As Stuart Hall (1976: 230–1) has argued, reactions to both these threats are usually founded upon unexamined judgements about present and past experiences as the victims of crime, wherein the wish is to return to an idealised past when people felt secure in their neighbourhoods. Hall also contends:

What is violated is in fact a social and historical construction, not a physical entity: it is ourselves as persons, to which the whole historical development of safety, of the spread of the rule of law and order, have contributed: or our public-communal spaces. (ibid.: 230)

Clearly there exists genuine and sometimes well-founded fear of the potential physical and emotional damage caused by street crime or burglary. Hall seems to be suggesting that beyond this there exists a less tangible popular perception that the social order, and our own security as subjects, which should both vouchsafe public safety, have also been violated. It is this social order, and its maintenance, to which the moral subject is rhetorically attached.

The citizen versus the criminal subculture

From the 1980s onwards the construction of the citizen as an active, autonomous participant in the fight against crime (via *Crimewatch UK*, Neighbourhood Watch, Crimestoppers and the Charters) was opposed to that of the passive citizen, the 'sponger', 'fraudster', benefit 'scrounger' and also to the recidivist criminal (see Hall 1983: 29). The notion that state dependency promoted moral laxity was advanced through New Right discourses which quickly became diffused into the 'common sense' of the public opinion. The long-established concept of a subculture of crime was given a new political inflection, continuing the work of patrolling the divide between the good citizen and his/her others. This notion of crime as performed by an 'autonomous criminal class' serves, as Foucault (1980: 41) has argued, to inhibit commerce between ordinary people (citizens) and the criminal element and to construct the populace as a 'moral subject'.[21] The moral subject, like the 'healthy' subject or the sexually 'normal' subject, is produced through practices that classify people and divide them each from the other (Foucault 1982: 77).

Prior to the discursive construction of criminalised subjects as a 'class' or semi-autonomous group, the practices of those who committed crimes within the community would have been understood differently or rather within different terms of reference. Foucault notes, for example, that within the French feudal system, spaces of tolerance were inevitable where centralised administrative systems did not yet exist to permeate and regulate village life within a consistent judicial economy (1975: 82–3). In practice, each 'social stratum' had its margin of non-observance, of tolerance, exceptions to the rule of law, and so on. This mode of living cheek-by-jowl in relatively restricted areas where everyone might notice a stranger or a suspicious happening gave way with the rise of capitalism, the modern state and rapid urbanisation to a more precarious sense of lawlessness.[22]

It has been argued that the carceral organisations, including the penitentiary, assumed their modern form at this very point when traditional states changed into nation-states (Giddens 1987: 183).[23] These changes initiated a new configuration of 'coercive relations' which may be discerned most clearly in the move to 'sequestrate' certain elements within society (the mad, the sick and the criminal). These regulatory acts produced new subject positions, wherein subjects were more clearly demarcated as within or without the social order of the law. As Giddens notes: 'The creation of a perceived need for "law and order" is the reverse side of the emergence of conceptions of "deviance" recognised and categorised by the central authorities and by professional specialists' (1987: 184). It is the construction of deviance and its corollary, the perceived need for law and order, which is the basis of the administrative state and its prerogative to deploy the instruments of violence (ibid.). Thus it is only in the seventeenth century, with the onset of urbanisation and the establishment of the nation-state, that the idea of a general 'lawlessness' becomes common currency (ibid.: 189–90). As noted in the previous chapter, these conditions allowed the development of new types of policing, which in conjunction with the criminal law, began to differentiate criminal activities from other types of 'social strife'. With the disruption of this equilibrium of tolerance those that participated in illicit activities become criminalised, symbolically and sometimes literally, ostracised from the community. In this sense, as argued by Tony Parker in his 1963 case study of a recidivist law-breaker, the petty criminal becomes an 'Unknown Citizen', only meeting the threshold of visibility at the points where re-offending occurs (1963: 148–9).[24]

Current debates in the media about crime and punishment persist in demanding the maintenance of prisons that, it has been argued, produce and reproduce the cultures of criminal apprenticeship, delinquency and recidivism. As Philip Rawlings (1999: 173) noted in the quotation that opened this chapter, this renewed emphasis upon individual responsibility, private policing and deterrence recalls the values of a much earlier age. During the 1980s and early 1990s the conviction that 'prison works'[25] through deterrence fuelled a programme of prison building and increased prison security (Norrie and Adelman 1989: 114; Rawlings 1999: 148ff; see also Tumin 1997: 23). These penal cultures in turn underpin the discursive split between citizens and the 'criminal element' within society, arguably fostering recidivism and social division (Foucault 1975: 272). Increasingly then, the 'rehabilitative ideal' was jettisoned, replaced by a growing pessimism founded in the belief that prison did indeed 'work', but only in the limited sense that it removed, for a period, criminals from the mainstream of society (Rawlings 1999: 154). This failure of the rehabilitative ideal meant that the crime is not deleted once the sentence has been served. The prison and the prison record set the criminalised subject apart from the community, instituting divisions within communities where earlier there had functioned 'a whole equilibrium of tolerance' (Foucault 1975: 272–3).

The perceived schism between ordinary people and the criminal element has also been reinforced through the discursive practices of law and order professionals who, for example, aided the media construction of urban 'No-Go' areas, particularly after the public disorder incidents in Brixton, Toxteth and Southall in 1981 (Keith 1991; Campbell, B. 1993: 97–122). Sir Kenneth Newman, who was the Metropolitan Police Commissioner for most of the 1980s, coined the phrase 'symbolic location' precisely to encapsulate the physical location of relentless criminality within urban centres. His 1983 annual report identified four such areas (Rose, D. 1992: 31). For him it was territorial black youths themselves who mapped these areas as symbolically free from the law (ibid.: 32). However, these areas were and continue to be 'symbolic' in ways not noted by Newman, as reservoirs of popular fears and anxieties about ethnicity, poverty and civil unrest. They are politically sensitive, ethnically mixed areas where a predominance of 'non-whites' apparently signalled for Newman a reversion to an earlier era of lawlessness. For example, in the rhetoric reminiscent of the nineteenth-century social explorer, he positions these areas as breeding grounds of criminality; equating them with 'the criminal rookeries of Dickensian London' where the 'neighbourhood bobby' would routinely be attacked (ibid.).

It has already been shown in some detail how the rise of the New Right formed the backdrop to these often racially-driven scenarios (Hall *et al.* 1978; Keith 1991; Keith 1993). The opposition between the good citizen and black/immigrant youth subculture has been amplified through the national press and television coverage of street robberies and related law and order issues since the 1970s. The discourses of some forms of true crime entertainment work from and reinforce this notion of an ethnic (white or black) criminal class, underclass or subculture. Racialised 'gangs' such as the Triads, Yardies or 'steamers' were, and continue to be, thoroughly condemned in true crime and reportage. Here Yardie and Triad gangs are often counterpointed nostalgically to the notorious and much mythologised London gangsters the Richardsons and Krays who operated during the 1950s and 1960s. Dovkants and Davenport (1997: 13) note of the 'old style gangsters':

> Their power inspired respect, not just among their peers but also among lesser crooks who might otherwise prey on people on their patch. In south London the Richardson brothers ruled with an iron

hand. 'No one would dare mug an old lady on Charlie Richardson's manor,' a veteran detective observed.

Here white working-class gangsterism and criminal subcultures are largely portrayed as the inevitable counterpart of growing affluence and the 'good' society.[26] Portrayals of the gangland violence of post-war criminals like the Krays are imbued with nostalgia, as a period when working-class communities were white, criminals kept order and only other criminals got hurt. In this myth serious criminals really were 'organised', they looked after their own, were no less corrupt than their colleagues in the force and even policed their own streets (see Taylor 1984).[27] The rhetoric of individual responsibility which underpins the myth of the white East End gangs and which underwent a resurgence in popular representation during the 1980s, was part and parcel of this broader discourse of self-policing and private policing evident within Britain since the late 1970s.

Public centurions: investigative and true crime programming

As already noted, programmes such as *Crimewatch UK* discursively reinforce the contemporary construction of criminals as a *class* who respect neither life nor property. The audience is schooled in the differences between the criminal 'subculture' and the lives of ordinary people. Yet paradoxically viewers are invited to call in if they recognise a voice, know this person or can identify an e-fit portrait. In this way criminals are portrayed as both inside and outside of the community. The audience is enjoined to remain vigilant, to 'keep 'em peeled' in the interests of themselves as potential victims of crime within their own region or neighbourhood. But they are also provided through networked programmes with portraits of alleged criminals living on the other side of the country; criminals whom they could never spy except on their television screens. This fosters a broader vision of a generalised national lawlessness, continuing a process of the dissemination of true crime accounts that was inaugurated with the establishment and consolidation of the national press (Williams 1961: 173ff; Altick 1972; Lee 1976; Chibnall 1977).

Sometimes this generalised lawlessness may be transmuted into a paranoid view of the everyday which conveniently shores up the authority of those individuals in the public eye who construct themselves as the guardians of the honest citizen. One of these public centurions is the investigative reporter Roger Cook who fronts the public interest/consumer affairs programme *The Cook Report* (Central Television/ITV 1987–). This programme was at the forefront of popular current affairs programming, pioneering a style of television journalism that could be relied on by viewers to present scenes of confrontation, secret cameras, 'sting operations' and doorstep interviews. Cook is discursively located as the people's (more particularly the consumer's) representative. For example, a trailer for a new series of *The Cook Report* (ITV 10 October 1997) presents him standing with his hand on a globe; a voice-over informing us that 'the guilty are everywhere'. Here Cook is described as 'the eyes and ears of a nation', a man engaged in the relentless pursuit of an intimidating list of criminals ranging from forgers and fraudsters to racketeers and robbers. Cook, a proxy of the autonomous, self-directed citizen, is the epitome of the proactive moral subject. His visible outrage and determination to pursue every avenue of inquiry on behalf of the viewer reinforces his alignment with this subject position. However, his belligerent, confrontational persona suggests a man acting not wholly within the parameters of the law. Like the fictional private detective, Cook *appears* to work alone, he can be relied upon to doorstep suspects, set up 'stings' and seek out whistleblowers and stool pigeons. In this way he acts, on behalf of the viewer, as a progenitor of action. He seems to go beyond the reaches of conventional policing while at the same time always returning the target criminal to the arms of the law. When Cook invokes the law, which he tends to do with a righteous flourish, he invokes it on behalf of the citizen as 'moral subject', not on behalf of the state at large. In this way he stands in concrete opposition to media representations of the vulnerable citizen who can only secure his/her home or 'walk with purpose' as a defence against the statistical likelihood of becoming the victim of crime. The trailer which stresses the ubiquity of criminality is needful for it underlines the necessity of Cook's repetitive active pursuit of criminals and fraudsters. The image too of a single man as the eyes and ears of the nation returns the problem of crime to the lap of the individual subject.

The Cook Report is exemplary of the move in British factual television during the 1990s from issue-driven to 'people-based' and 'story-based' programming designed to appeal to a broader audience (Holland, P. 1997: 152). As Raymond Williams (1991: 12–3) has noted, the dramatisation of experience in general has become 'a new form and pressure' in modern society, where the 'slice of life' that had formerly been the business of naturalistic drama has become a 'basic need'. This last decade has seen the advent of new genres and innovative styles of non-fiction programming that seem to meet this 'need' including 'hybrid' programmes that mix reconstructions of actual events with straight-to-camera address (Holland, P. 1997: 158–9).[28] These include many law and order programmes such as *Crimewatch UK* and *Stop! Police! Action!* (Carlton) and reality programming such as *999* (BBC Bristol 1992–), together with more conventional true crime series.[29] As Richard Sparks (1992: 156) has noted, it is no trivial matter that they, 'in a very real and particular sense employ the same syntax of depiction, narration and editing as crime fiction do' (see also Reeves 1993; Petley 1996). For it is the medium of television that has perhaps most fully undertaken the function of oral story-telling in order to dramatise real life crime and reinforce the division between the moral subject and its others.

True crime series such as *Michael Winner's True Crimes* (ITV), *In Suspicious Circumstances* (Carlton), featuring Edward Woodward, and *Expert Witness* (LWT), featuring Michael Gambon, all begin with an introduction made directly to the audience. These series comprise self-contained 30-minute dramatisations of serious crimes (usually murder) with *In Suspicious Circumstances* being the only one of the three to focus on 'classic' crimes of the past.[30] In these programmes the presenter sets the scene and then invites the audience to join him in viewing the ensuing tale:

> Tonight's story takes us on the emotional roller coaster that the police and the relations of a kidnap victim are put through when a loved one is snatched from his family. ... It is an extraordinary account of technique and perseverance pitched against a determined evil man who had all the aces. (*Michael Winner's True Crimes* 27 March 1994)

The presenter is therefore established as the source of knowledge about the crime and as an omniscient story-teller who reassures viewers that the criminal will be caught at the end.[31] Like the Ancient Mariner, each presenter seems to look the viewer unwaveringly in the eye as he begins the story; his rhetoric addressing viewers directly. Underlying the introduction to these stories is a sense of immediacy ('tonight's story takes *us* on the *emotional roller coaster*') which is reinforced by the way in which the cases are dramatised. Here the drama cannot lie with the intellectual mystery of 'whodunit' because the presence of the story-teller is there precisely to reassure viewers that the case has already been solved and the perpetrators of crime brought to justice. Instead the drama lies in the unravelling of the investigation and pursuit of the criminal to the gates of justice (and no further). The psychological and social questions that form the basis of up-market criminal biographies (e.g. Masters 1985a), popular academic studies (e.g. Canter 1994) and 'quality' documentaries[32] are generally absent. For example, in *Expert Witness*, trailed as representing 'the long arm of forensic science', Gambon stands as guarantor of the efficacy of policing technology in tracing the criminal. The cases related in this series are presented without question as evidence of this efficacy. In one programme (broadcast 3 May 1996) Gambon warns: 'What you are about to see really happened ... her killer was driven by simple emotions of hate and jealousy. He would have done well to note that a mind clouded by emotion is no match for the cool logic of science.' At the close of the programme he notes reassuringly, 'A classic chain of evidence brought him [the murderer] down. ...With Michael Kite's conviction Wiltshire Constabulary maintained their hundred percent success rate in bringing murderers to justice.'

Like Roger Cook, these presenters are established as exemplary moral subjects. Usually in later middle age, they embody a masculine authority that is reinforced by an extra-textual knowledge of their public personas. These speakers appear to 'have counsel' for the audience (Benjamin 1992a: 86). Their wisdom stems from age, gender and media status. The presenter is naturally located on the side of law and order, but more particularly it is his alliance with natural justice that reinforces his position as an authority figure.[33] Finally, the presenter is afforded a certain gravitas through his proximity to death. At the end of the account of the kidnap case (cited above), a case that also involved murder, Michael Winner turns to the camera. He appears to be holding a large leather volume, perhaps an old storybook. The book, however, turns out to be an advice manual on how to commit the perfect crime. This manual, we are told, was found at the home of the murderer. In this and many other ways the presenter's status is weighted by the authority that he borrows from death and its emblems (e.g. the crime manual) which subtend the veracity of his account. As Walter Benjamin has remarked: 'death is the sanction of everything that the storyteller can tell. He has borrowed his authority from death' (1955a: 93–4)

The personas of these presenters bear contradictory messages about the role of law within society, arguably revealing the contradiction at the heart of dominant constructions of the moral subject. Winner, in particular, draws on Old Testament discourses of good, evil, providence and retribution in the programme, presenting the law as a bulwark against chaos in order to frame the narrative to come. Winner is best known as the director of the controversial *Deathwish* (USA 1974–) films and more recently of the revenge film *Dirty Weekend* (UK 1992); all these films celebrate a righteous vigilantism that is clearly outside of the rule of law but that is also presented as its necessary supplement. In contrast, Winner's well-publicised work for a police memorial fund firmly situates him within the confines of officially sanctioned modes of justice.[34] Winner's public persona reveals the ways in which the moral subject of law and order is itself fissured and contradictory. This subject is both aligned with the institutional discourses of law and order (required to collaborate and to conform) but is also required to supplement or complement the procedures of law and order (to be an 'active citizen'). This dual role of the moral subject is epitomised in the opening sequence of *Expert Witness* which visually represents the audience's collaboration with the surveying eye of both institutional and individual justice. The programme opens with a grid of small boxes filling the screen; each box houses a single pale blue eye. It soon emerges that the eye belongs to presenter Michael Gambon and also in a sense to us as viewers, since we oversee a case that we already know has been solved through forensic science.[35]

These programmes provide a moral world-view, which sanctions a law and order economy of a punishment to fit every crime and the notion of just deserts and natural law rather than the 'economy of suspended rights' (Foucault 1977: 11) which characterises modern sentencing and its aftermath. Thus the programme must present itself confidently as being 'beyond reasonable doubt'. For these narratives dramatise the execution of violence by the criminal in order that there is no question of doubt as to the rightness of the subsequent arrest, the (unseen but clearly implied) punishment and the ultimate re-creation of the event as a media spectacle. In this sense then these stories are 'modern morality plays' (Hall *et al.* 1978: 66), rehearsing and underpinning the 'populist moralism' that is inherent in discourses of law and order (Hall 1983: 37–8). Stuart Hall has noted the ways in which the discourses of law and order speak so powerfully to the citizen. The play on 'values' and on moral issues in this area strengthens the law and order crusade's grasp on popular morality and common sense conscience:

But it also touches concretely the experience of crime and theft, of loss of scarce property and fears of unexpected attack in working class areas and neighbourhoods; and, since it promulgates no other remedies for their underlying causes, it welds people to that 'need for authority' which has been so significant for the right in the construction of consent to its authoritarian programme. (ibid.: 38)

In contrast to Benjamin's (1955a: 101) reader of the novel, viewers may not 'warm their shivering lives' with the deaths which are dramatised for them, but instead they are invited to focus on the *process* by which law and order is reinstated and the status quo resumed. The presenters, as temporary personifications of 'authority', invite the viewers' consent to a narrative of crime and punishment that offers no solutions except vigilance and discipline. In these narratives the act of murder (together with the law's response) is the prime mover and the central pivot of the story rather than the somewhat two-dimensional characters ('jealous husband', 'solid detective', and so on). In a sense, the viewer is external to this televised true crime story because he/she knows it has already been resolved.

The moral subject of *Reader's Digest*

> 'It must be true. It says so in *Reader's Digest*.'
> (in Harman *et al.* 1992: 5)

Public discourses of law and order, the role of the citizen and the role of the state, and the ways in which these inform the construction of the moral subject and its others, may be effectively explored in Britain's best-selling non-fiction magazine *Reader's Digest*.[36] Although perhaps not an obvious source of generic true crime stories, its relentless pursuit of real life stories and 'practical values for everyday life' (June 1994: 1) means that personal experience of crime and issues of law and order are topics generously represented within its pages. Moreover, *Reader's Digest* is exemplary of the ways in which the popular press embraced and amplified New Right discourses of self-reliance and individual responsibility, producing a 'moral subject' who stood as a bulwark against that 'new folk-devil', the scrounger (Hall 1983: 29), and also the recidivist criminal. Popular journalism was responsible for the diffusion of these ideas. Hall (ibid.) notes: 'the colonisation of the popular press was a critical victory in the struggle to define the common sense of the times.' Here was undertaken the critical ideological work of constructing around 'Thatcherism' a populist 'common sense'. This chapter concludes by charting the complexity of these debates within *Reader's Digest*, a magazine whose broad spread of features frequently explores issues of law and order and the relationship between the state and its citizens. Here the frequent portrayal of criminality and the treatment of law and order issues need to be understood within the organising framework of the *Reader's Digest* philosophical and political formula. For as will be seen in some detail, the ideals and values instituted with the establishment of the magazine continue to structure the stories that it tells.

The discourse of *Reader's Digest*: individualism and responsibility

Popular magazines have occupied a significant place in British literary culture since the founding of journals such as *Blackwood's*, the *London Magazine* and the *Westminster Review* two centuries ago. Even today a book serialised in a national newspaper will usually reach a greater audience than book sales alone (Erickson 1996: 12). Despite this, magazines and especially newspapers continue to remain at the bottom of the intellectual hierarchy of written formats (ibid.: 13). Indeed, adult leisure reading, especially illustrated reading, comics and readers' digests have been dismissed as 'evoking nothing so much as pre-digested food' (Lefebvre 1958: 33). It is for this reason, perhaps, that a dramatically successful magazine such as *Reader's Digest* can remain largely unaddressed in literary cultural studies.

Reader's Digest was set up in 1922 by an American couple, DeWitt and Lila Wallace, who aspired to produce a monthly compilation of articles in pocket-book form that would be available through subscription. The first international edition arrived in Britain in 1938. By 1988 its world-wide readership per issue had reached 100 million ('50th Anniversary Album', 1972: 109–11). According to its own handbook the British *Digest* currently has a circulation of 1.5 million and a readership of 6 million. 96 per cent of buyers purchase the magazine through subscriptions and half a million readers subscribe for three years of more. Perhaps even more impressive are the 250,000 readers who have subscribed for more than seven years, a figure which clearly indicates a strong degree of loyalty and familiarity with the *Digest* formula (indeed if not also the commercial advantages of a subscription system for periodical sales) (Harman *et al.* 1992: 2).

The philosophical vision of individual initiative and self-instruction and its concomitant bolstering of a specific political individualism, was determined at the magazine's outset. The *Digest* emerged at a moment in American cultural history when leisure reading was becoming imbricated with a broadening base of consumer-led culture. It anticipated by four years the equally successful Book-of-the-Month Club founded in 1926 by Harry Scherman. This mail-order book business also sought to provide the 'middlebrow' consumer with pre-selected enlightening reading, although this time in the form of unabridged novels (Radway 1992: 512). The Club tapped into the increasingly predominant notion at that time that reading could be enjoyed as a form of relaxation rather than as a mode of instruction alone. However, as Radway notes, this pleasure was uneasy. She contends that readers still found it necessary to regard the consumption of fiction as a useful activity: a 'pleasure that also fostered edification and uplift' (ibid.: 519).

The vision of leisure consumption as a preferably constructive and active pursuit remains integral to the *Digest's* philosophy, leading to a number of subsidiary enterprises such as the Reader's Union, a group of 16 special interest book clubs, mail order music, videos and language courses (Harman *et al.* 1992: 22). In a feature celebrating 50 years of *Reader's Digest* the authors state: 'The editors themselves derive genuine satisfaction from their participation in what they regard as an exciting and continuing experiment in popular education' ('50th Anniversary Album', 1988: 115). The ethos of popular instruction by example requires that the frivolousness of fictional representation be discarded in favour of stories that are clearly identified as actuality. This ethos of self-help, popular education and autodidacticism in the US is part of a broader, more explicitly political trajectory: '*Reader's Digest's* cold-war anti-communism – [was] homely, old-fashioned, communal, friendly, *family orientated*: mass production with private, domestic consumption values built in' (Bloom 1990: 15). This tilts at a broader political ideology that is embedded in the post-Second World War opposition between the free capitalist society of the West and the restricted state communism of the East. This is political ideology, which although it clearly informs *Reader's Digest*, remains diffuse since it is retranslated into notions of the everyday: consumption, advice for living and 'commonly held' aspirations. The promotion of the free economy within its pages is articulated through the discourses of individualism, self-reliance and consumer choice, which are, in turn, set firmly within the context of the family as a model of exemplary citizenship.

The magazine's emphasis upon domestic consumption as intrinsic to modern family life is reflected in its advertisements and in its consumer investigations, as well as in the general political philosophy upon which the magazine is built. The first foreign language edition (in Spanish) was explicitly designed to counter pro-Axis propaganda in South America. Indeed, by the 1960s DeWitt Wallace (1972: 108) could proudly claim that: 'The *Reader's Digest*, more than any other mass circulation magazine, has consistently exposed the evils of communism, and has as consistently portrayed the blessings of the free-economy system.' By the 1960s the idea that individual liberty was linked indissolubly with the free economy had become common currency. It began to gain an even stronger populist ideological foothold from the late 1970s onwards when Reaganite and Thatcherite discourses opposed the free, energetic consuming individual entrenched in the domestic space against a range of deviants, subversives, criminals and outsiders (including the communist bloc). As Charlie Leadbeater notes, the philosophy of consumption inherent in Conservative individualism meant much more than simply buying and selling:

> It incorporates those everyday acts within a much wider social philosophy. It has asserted the possibility of individuals becoming agents to change their worlds through private initiatives. Aspirations for autonomy, choice, decentralisation, greater responsibility, which were met with mumbling paternalism by the post-war social democratic state, have been met by Thatcherite encouragement in the 1980s. (Leadbeater 1989: 142)

This model of self-determination and personal responsibility through choice 'implies that individuals have a measure of power over an external world' (ibid.), an idea that is central to the philosophy of *Reader's Digest*.

Reader's Digest and the language of common sense

The magazine has a well-tested ethos of bringing informative entertaining articles to the reader's attention. Their tips to potential article writers include the conviction that: '*Digest* articles are definitive. They include, somewhere in the text, every fact that readers need to know' (Harman *et al.* 1992: 2). This self-proclaimed harnessing of the definitive is needful if the magazine is to provide a condensed and therefore 'essential' range of material for the informed general reader. It is arguable that by defining the limits of knowledge and presenting its essence alone, *Reader's Digest* offers a consoling distillation of the general knowledge that might be relevant to the reader. Here there is an avowed attempt to render an

unruly and aleatory world safe and knowable through the presentation and privileging of fact above all else.

These facts are presented through articles structured to *demonstrate*
the points being made. This is achieved through the use of dialogue,
illustration and personal stories. The editors state: 'Readers are not
simply *told* the facts, they are *shown* them, through anecdotes and
examples. We are storytellers, and our printed pages are as visual as a
television screen. The writer's experience must become the reader's
experience' (Harman *et al.* 1992: 3). This accent upon personal experience and what Richard Hoggart (1957: 94) calls 'the close detail of the
human condition' is the foundation of *Reader's Digest's* immense
appeal. Here the editors present the idealised close identification
between the reader and the writer as virtually unmediated. Their
voicing of the common-sense assumption that television operates as a
window on the world points to the supposedly mimetic possibilities of
representation, including that of the written word. This impetus
towards mimesis impedes, at least in theory, any move by the reader to
adopt a critically distant position. Like the popular papers of the 1950s
described by Hoggart, the *Digest* attempts to demonstrate its world-
view rather than explaining or interpreting it. Hoggart (ibid.: 94–5)
argues that this strategy is typical of popular art that is:

> a presentation of what is known already. It starts from the assump-
> tion that human life is fascinating in itself … the staple fare is not
> something which suggests an escape from ordinary life, but rather it
> assumes that ordinary life is intrinsically interesting.

The idea of popular magazines presenting what is already known is
crucial to an understanding of the ideological aspirations of *Reader's
Digest* and its amplification of prevailing media notions of the problem
of crime and the role of the individual. In part the already known is
clearly a tribute to the quotidian and ostensibly transparent values of
everyman and everywoman. These values are already known, since
they are the putative products of common sense that is looked to as
the arbiter of all dispute and the measure of all knowledge of the everyday. It also posits a unitary vision of what is important and meaningful
to the *Digest* reader. The brandishing of common sense, in conjunction
with representational realism, invites the reader to participate in the
apparent consensus of public opinion. As Catherine Belsey (1980) has
argued, common sense is humanistic and therefore based upon an
empirical and idealist interpretation of the world. Belsey notes:

'common sense urges that 'man' is the origin and source of meaning, of action, and of history' (1980: 7). For this reason it becomes important that magazine articles which deal with complex and sometimes rather abstract issues should above all be made meaningful through the deployment of personal experience, illustration and anecdote. In *Reader's Digest* individual action tends to be constructed as both the motor of crime and also of the solution to crime. Even those articles which launch their examinations of crime with statistical information on crime rates present crime rises as rooted in the baser instincts of human nature; they rarely seek structural social, cultural or economic explanations.[37]

Active citizenship and defensive individualism

Reader's Digest, although international in circulation, tailors its special features to the market in each target country, arguably constructing a vivid 'imagined community' of like-minded readers (Anderson 1983). For example, the British magazine's essentially and sometimes explicitly conservative rhetoric articulates an individualist philosophy of personal striving for success bound to a highly defensive stance on Englishness, heritage and citizenship. This perspective is propagated most clearly from emblems of Englishness such as 'our ancient meadows' (June 1994), saving traditional hymns and the establishment of D-day museums (both May 1994). It is usual therefore for exemplary material to focus on the 'British' and therefore 'universal' experience of crime rather than say crime in the East End of London, Doncaster or Govan. For instance, the story 'Anatomy of a Burglary' (Watkins and Fletcher 1985) (see below) underlines the likelihood of British readers becoming the victims of house-breakers, noting that burglary is 'striking a home in England or Wales every 35 seconds' and that a report from *Which?* magazine 'puts the chance of your home being burgled this year at one in 25' (Watkins and Fletcher 1985: 58). The article finishes with the routine *Reader's Digest* exhortation, urging readers to become proactive in order to anticipate and combat the potential threat that it has just delineated. Suggested precautions include fitting quality locks, using time switches, marking property and joining or starting a Neighbourhood Watch scheme (Watkins and Fletcher 1985: 61).

This standardised positive conclusion reflects the magazine's overall US-inspired philosophy that well-produced popular reading can motivate readers towards self-improvement (and indeed even self-defence). When stories deal with more disturbing themes such as child abuse or rape, the formula of a positive ending may seem somewhat incongruous. For example, the features 'If Your Child is Molested' (Jacoby 1982) and 'Let's Stop Punishing the Victims of Rape' (Watson 1982) both end with positive advice on coping with sexual assaults or with the aftermath of an assault. Typical too is the deployment of statistics as objective evidence of the problem of the form of crime under discussion. For the *Digest* statistics are the hallmark of sound research and a guarantee of objectivity. Julia Watson's article on rape cited above is a model of this kind of reporting. The feature opens with the story of 'Angela' raped after she accepted a lift from a regular customer at the fast food outlet where she worked. Watson (1982: 146) then steps back to provide the reader with the statistical probabilities of rape incidents: 'Scenes like this occur with frightening frequency throughout Britain. ... Last year, 1,238 rapes were recorded – more than three a day. Estimates suggest that anywhere from two to twenty times as many rapes actually take place as are recorded.' After quoting Thatcher's call for the law to protect women, she briefly recalls the history of myths and prejudices about rape. The article then returns to 'Angela' and the aftermath of her experience. A short piece at the end entitled 'How to avoid, or combat, sexual attack' offers a range of measures from checking ID when answering the door to techniques of self-defence (ibid.: 151).

This article and many others conform closely to a model of magazine journalism that is itself structured through the discourses of individualism and self-help. It is exemplary of a formula which seeks to avoid confrontation with the overtly political while none the less operating within purview of a New Right ideology which espouses both individual free choice in the market and a form of social conservatism. For the *Digest* tips, whether for personal success, self-defence or consumer rights, are based upon the privileging of individual initiatives over collective action. In the case of rape the typical scenario is one of an individual woman taking measures to protect herself against a rapist whose motivations are rooted in personal pathology. For instance, in an abridged version of the estate agent Stephanie Slater's book (she was kidnapped, but lived to tell the tale) published in the *Digest* there is only one assessment of the kidnapper, Michael Sams, a quotation from the judge who called Sams dangerous and evil (1995: 155–79). In the spirit of *Reader's Digest* the emphasis here is upon the determination of the individual victim of crime to survive against all odds. Here popular feminist and other academic discourses of the collective reclamation of public spaces or of the reinterpretation of pathology as misogyny are generally absent.[38]

Within *Reader's Digest* the individual subject who combats such powerful foes as crime, big business or government bureaucracy is a
modern-day hero. As indicated above, the magazine tends to privilege
personal experiences, particularly those that fit well into scenarios of
struggle between 'us and them'. These are especially evident in the frequent feature-stories of 'Fighting Spirit' in which the little man or
woman makes a stand for common sense against an institutional
Goliath, for example, the 'extraordinary battle' of a murder victim's
parents to instigate The Bail (Amendment) Act of July 1983 so that
habitual criminals are not easily given bail (April 1994: 137–8).
Subtitled 'Heart-warming stories of ordinary people who win extraordinary battles' the article is typical in its advocacy of petitioners and
campaigners and in its suspicion that the law, in its weakness, favours
wrongdoers. The Bail story is juxtaposed with two others: the story of
three formidable women campaigning to defend their valley from a
water company and Welsh villagers' determination to save their local
store (April 1994: 138–40). The juxtaposition of these diverse stories
privileges the theme of self-help over and above the incidents that they
relate, pointing to the importance of individual action as the bedrock
of *Reader's Digest*. The structuring of crime-related stories into scenes of
individual or limited community action in the face of an 'industry' of
criminality or the blinkered procedures of the law chimes with this
vision of ordinary people beating the odds.

'Neighbourhood Watch foils the burglars' is exemplary of the kind of
crime-related issue where individuals can be seen to be taking
affirmative action in the face of threats to the community (Hodgkinson
1995: 152–6). Again, as with the Neighbourhood Watch schemes discussed earlier in this chapter, the emphasis here is not upon collective
political action but single-issue initiatives that temporarily unite and
mobilise private individuals for action on a single front. Hence these
stories of neighbourhood initiatives follow a similar structure to stories
of individual heroism. This special report begins with the familiar
mantra of statistical vulnerability, noting that there is a burglary every
35 seconds. This disturbing information is countered by an illustration
of a glass-panelled door bearing a triangular Watch sticker with an eye
at its centre. The feature is then launched with the story of a particularly ferocious break-in at a middle-class home in Macclesfield,
Cheshire (ibid.: 152). The two female occupants were assaulted and
held at knifepoint. But, notes the author, before Neighbourhood
Watch the gang would 'probably' have got away with it (ibid.: 153).
Here Cheshire is lauded as the first county in Britain to pilot a commu-

nity watch scheme and as such it is an ideal vehicle for the *Digest*'s ethic of self-help. There is little doubt expressed here about either the efficacy of the Watch or any interest in the broader socio-economic issues surrounding property crime. Indeed, the article provides a seal of approval with a quotation from a recidivist housebreaker who vows that he will never go near a Neighbourhood Watch house (ibid.: 156).

Often these scenarios of David and Goliath (of ordinary people versus relentless criminality) are used to depict the determined individual over-turning the spectre of overweening state control or bureaucracy. Again these stories retain and perpetuate Thatcherite discourses which resolutely positioned the Conservative government against the overweening state and therefore on the side of the people. This discourse is in fact paradoxical since it can constitute a reassertion of the forces of law in opposition to liberty. Articles on personal finance and consumption are strongly situated within a discourse of individual consumer rights, often in the face of intractable and sometimes criminal bureaucracy. For example, 'Private Clampers: Public Menace?' by Tim Bouquet (April 1997: 76–81) is couched within the language of threat and personal vulnerability, suggesting that private parking wardens are in fact 'legalised muggers'. The story opens with the frightening tale of a diabetic woman whose car is clamped while she seeks urgent medical help. Further on a small photograph of a clamped wheel is anchored with the quotation: 'You've got to intimidate the owner. It doesn't matter if the driver's disabled or pregnant' (ibid.: 79). The 'heart-warming' tale of personal triumph in the face of serious odds sits uneasily with this more pessimistic portrayal of leviathan bureaucracy. Although it is the 'embattled dissenting individual in a bureaucratic world' who is lionised, the monthly publication of the magazine needs the abstract forces of bureaucracy to resurface in new forms for the next edition (Abercrombie *et al.* 1986: 145).

The inadequate functioning of public-run legal institutions in the face of 'common-sense' arguments is frequently addressed in the magazine. For example the *Digest* offered two detailed treatments of the perceived failings of the Crown Prosecution Service (CPS) in June 1990 and December 1995. 'The soft arm of the law' (Bouquet 1995) begins with two separate examples of valiant women who, faced by the obstruction of the CPS, none the less persisted in the struggle to bring their rapists to justice (ibid.: 61). Here the number of plea-bargained or abandoned cases is imputed to an unreasonable drive for cost-effectiveness within a service where bureaucracy is 'unchained' (ibid.: 64). The scareheads that pepper the article reinforce the proposal that the service is riven with dangerous inefficiency: 'Abandoned cases', 'Justice on the cheap', 'Fall in convictions', 'Victims ignored', 'Wasting money', 'Bureaucracy unchained' and so on.

The demonisation of bureaucracy and of state-run institutions fits easily within the liberal free market ethos of the magazine. This characterisation of red-tape public institutions as over-regulated and unbending is occasionally couched in more explicit language when calls for personal security and individual privacy produce troublesome oppositions. Features on the call for identity cards foreground the ambivalent position of the magazine in relation to surveillance and privacy. These features are, I suggest, indicative of a general unease about the extent to which the state penetrates the everyday in its documentation of its citizens. They represent the contradiction that is at the heart of the relationship between the modern state and the private citizen. On the whole, however, surveillance; capitalism and industrialism are presented as ultimately necessary since they are clearly fundamental to the rise of the modern nation-state which requires an administrative system in order to function smoothly (Giddens 1987: 57–8). Clearly, then, *Reader's Digest* constructs an ambivalent relationship between the citizen and the state, a relationship that is brought into sharp relief by the 'problem' of crime. The magazine's consistent support of the active, responsible citizen in opposition to crime and bureaucracy (which hinders justice) reinforces the division between the moral subject and its (criminal) others. It constructs a defensive individualism that is entrenched in the domestic and shored up against the threat of crime. This notion of the defensive individual underpins the Thatcherite philosophy wherein: 'the private space, provided for by hard-earned income, is sacred, to be protected against the unwelcome encroachments of the state, with its spurious claims upon individuals' resources' (Leadbeater 1989: 143).

Criminality and entrepreneurialism

What is remarkable about *Reader's Digest* is the way in which it draws on the discourses of Thatcherism and enterprise culture not only in order to understand the good citizen and his/her duty as a moral subject, but also to understand the criminal subject.[39] Its celebration of individualism is ambiguous. It is always bound up with anxieties about potentially negative by-products of the individualist ethos – the breakdown of the ordered society and the unlimited and unpoliced freedom of the rogue individual. In *Reader's Digest* the limits of individualism

are defined, explored and made accessible to the reader through empirical examples in which boundaries are exceeded or transgressed by
both enterprising criminals and privatised policing. An article entitled
'Anatomy of a Burglary' by Watkins and Fletcher (1985) illustrates this
point. The first page is vertically divided between an illustration of a
shifty-looking man thrusting his arm through the smashed window of
a domestic entrance and a column of text:

> Martin Hutton, 32, has an average annual income of £75,000. He
> lives with his wife in a £250-a-week flat in London's West End,
> drives a new Mercedes and takes holidays in The Bahamas. His
> neighbours believe he is a successful entrepreneur in a growth
> industry. ... Certainly he is successful and in a growth industry ...
> Martin is a burglar. (ibid.: 57)

In this article the figure of Hutton is the personification of a distorted
or rogue version of the free enterprise culture that was to revitalise
British capitalism during the 1980s (see Heelas and Morris 1992).[40]
Through stories such as these the *Digest* renders accessible the philosophical difficulties inherent in 'individualism' and the conceptualisation of culture which is posited by it. But it does so by displacing these
difficulties onto the criminal subject – a subject who has in fact learned
the lesson of the individualist ethos far too well. If venture capitalism
entails opportunism, a readiness to be proactive and above all the
ability to take risks, the figuring of criminality as venture capitalism
out of control, or wrongly directed, signals the limits of acceptable risk-
taking and sets it against a backdrop of broader social fragmentation.
The motif of criminality as enterprise culture gone awry occurs on a
number of occasions in the magazine. For example, in 'Watch out!
There's a burglar about' burglary is presented as a business with tax-free
profits (Watkins 1982: 48–52) and in 'How to beat the car theft pros'
the multi-million pound 'industry' of car crime is investigated
(Cunningham 1990: 39–42). It seems that while the magazine in other
contexts expresses admiration for the entrepreneurial spirit of the
period and the political discourses of Thatcherism, the story above
evokes a rather different, certainly more suspicious, vision of entrepreneurialism as an action that pushes at the boundaries of individual
liberty at the expense of other citizens. It suggests also that appearances may be deceptive and that even the most outwardly respectable
of communities may be sheltering professional criminals: in the 1980s
and 1990s criminal difference can hide itself among the newly monied

classes. The burglar, through his conspicuous consumption of the goods and services associated with upward mobility (West End flat, holidays, cars and so on), appears to offend the good taste and inherent decency of ordinary citizens. Consequently, the article deploys a prevalent discourse of the 1980s – the free individual aligned with capitalism – but distorts it so that the entrepreneur (often championed politically as the logical choice to improve and support public and suburban spaces, including through crime prevention – see above) is presented as a hazard to the community.

The choice of Martin Hutton as the human face of housebreaking also precludes a very different model of criminality and how it may be understood. The presentation of this particular burglar as an avaricious, socially mobile and highly organised *individual* sets the key-note for a feature which is thereby unable, or refuses, to frame its discussion within the broader socio-economic context of burglary in the mid-1980s. Instead it presents a model of criminality which chimes with the moral and punitive discourses of the Thatcher and post-Thatcher years (Kettle 1983). In this way it closes off other ways, from right across the political spectrum, of understanding crime as symptomatic of broader social divisions. For example, in December 1985 the *Faith in the City* report, produced under the aegis of the Archbishop of Canterbury, sparked controversy by arguing that urban poverty and its attendant problems such as crime, was partly the result of a Conservative philosophy that over-emphasised the role of the individual (Young 1989: 416–17). Again only a year later, in 1986, the confidential annual internal appraisal report of the Metropolitan Police was agonising over the need to police 'two Londons' divided by the political and economic stress of social polarisation between the rich and the poor (Rose, D. 1996: 96). This document stated:

'Whilst fear of crime in the outer ring of more affluent boroughs is a pervasive problem ... the same fear is increasingly proximate to reality in the inner London "twilight boroughs".' There, if people were in fear of crime, it was because they were in genuine danger.

In this last instance the police, as a state agency endorsed by Thatcher, became itself a site of contestation. It both underlined its role as a manager of social order but was also cognisant of social inequities engendered, but rendered invisible, by the emphasis upon the free market and the individual as the basic unit of society. It seems then that the *Digest*'s treatment of crime-related issues tends not to address poor people's experience of crime (and crimes often committed by the poor), but instead speaks most strongly to – and about – their *perceived* readers' fear of the rogue criminal subject. In most cases the statistics offered are not ordered through geographic, economic or social grids but generalised until the likelihood of any individual reader becoming the victim of crime is simply a question of the odds. In this way *Reader's Digest* replicates broader political discourses which deny the relevance of geography, economics or social factors. In contrast to models of understanding crime that locate criminality, risk-taking and victimhood within economic models of poverty/affluence these articles locate criminal proclivity and threat as the consequence of moral choices rooted in the individual subject.

The erosion of boundaries and diffused criminality

The picture of widespread crime generated by these smaller articles is reinforced by the *Digest*'s special reports that often take their cue from new government or academic surveys. These reports adopt a much broader vision of the relationship between criminality and the social order than the articles already discussed above – but it is a vision still rooted in moral rather than socio-economic explanatory models. In these articles once again statistical information is the launch pad used to relate crime to ordinary readers' lives. For example, a 1994 report entitled 'Fear in the Streets' by David Moller (1994: 41) was the first article in the three-part 'shock report' on crime in Europe. The use of statistics in a pan-European context flattened out the picture of crime into a generalised 'problem' of lawlessness. It also foregrounded the problems inherent in the erosion of national sovereignty and of geo-graphical boundaries in the political landscape of contemporary Europe. The contradictions inherent in the magazine's depiction of the symptoms of crime and its remedies are most evident in this attention to boundaries. While the free market demands the erosion of bound-aries (geographical, fiscal and legal) the worry is that this may lead to an opening of the floodgates to the products of rogue capitalism (i.e. organised crime). Hence Moller's article focuses upon crime in a near-federal Europe rather than in Britain alone. Other *Digest* articles address other kinds of cross-border crime such as animal smuggling, Internet porn and the importation of drugs (e.g. 'Computer Porn, a Degrading Menace' and 'Kids and Drugs', both 1994). The removal of travel restrictions in Europe, the transgression of animal quarantine regulations and the unpoliced traffic of the information superhighway are all offered as evidence of the diffusion of crime.

In the Moller article the breakdown of both physical boundaries (national borders) and symbolic bulwarks (the family) seemed to threaten a new anarchic criminality. The report sought to ask: 'what is behind this anarchy, and what can be done to stop it?' The article is framed with a mock-up photograph of a fearful white woman wearing a wedding ring. It leads with a short, rather stark account of the now-infamous murder of James Bulger by two young boys. This leads into a seven-page diagnosis of the seeds of lawlessness which includes violence in the media, uncontrolled youth, fatherless families, drugs and drink, and a general lack of civic responsibility.

Whereas in the articles cited above criminality is the responsibility of the rogue individual, in this series the family is presented as the basic unit of society and the 'unstable' family is the locus of criminality and other anti-social behaviour. Under the subtitle 'Bad Seed', Moller pursues the theme of the lone-parent family and its production of criminal youths. Here the idea of genetic criminality is explored as an explanation of crime (and as a critique of lone parents' apparently inherent incapacity to discipline their offspring adequately). Moller quotes the clinical and forensic psychologist Masud Hoghughi who avers: 'fatherless families are particularly prone to producing angry and violent children' (Moller 1994: 43). This view is reiterated with contributions from three other experts who are portrayed as substantiating Moller's vision of the dangers of non-traditional family units. Moller adds: 'as the restraining and guiding hand of the family has weakened, neither church nor the state has been able to fill the gap. Church membership and attendance have declined across Europe' (ibid.: 44) The article closes with the warning that it is 'payback time for the permissive society' (ibid.: 47):

> We need to reassert adult authority over children and do so through a compact that entitles them to our generous help *in return* for their orderly and pro-social behaviour. Stressing rights without corresponding responsibilities is a recipe for the disorder we increasingly face. (Hoghughi, ibid.)

This roll call of factors of lawlessness – genetics, lone-parent families, youth culture and permissiveness – is substantiated with a patchwork of quotations from a range of European academics and policing professionals. The organising discourse of the article is one of opposition and conflict, most explicitly expressed in the uneasy tension between youth and responsibility, between the civilising process and those subjects who must be civilised, harnessed and directed. The discursive interrelation of issues of crime, moral rectitude and questions of discipline within the family arena suggest that the 'problem' of crime and criminality is perceived to be part and parcel of a broader problem of societal (in)disciplinarity.

Reader's Digest presents opinion that is keen to locate the responsible and self-sufficient individual and the family that support him/her as the lynchpin of the good society. Its values are economic libertarianism (evident in its commitment to the market place and to enterprise culture which sustains it) and social conservatism (evident in its support of traditional family values). As such they graphically present a contradiction held in tension within the discourses of Thatcherism. As a consequence of this double agenda, its libertarianism is tempered with the fear of indisciplinarity and both are foregrounded in the magazine's treatment of criminality and social disorder. Here crime and the fight against crime become the arena in which dominant discourses about entrepreneurialism, individualism and choice are tested. In one sense the paradoxes and tensions expressed here are unsurprising. Stuart Hall (1995: 63) has argued that 'political identity and subjectivity are inherently fragmented' and so, for example, resentment of the 'nambybamby' state can be married, albeit uneasily, to a lament for the decline of community policing, while the championing of individualism can be married to concerns about the social consequences of the atomisation of the social order. But as Hall also notes there must be a discursive logic to these contradictory political positions. In this context the logic is founded upon everyday experience and 'commonsense' values as the base line and measure of all moral judgements and social action. The practical values for everyday life espoused by *Reader's Digest* in relation to the threat of crime are embedded in commonsense notions such as value for money (in policing, in legal procedure and in penal policy), the importance of personal responsibility (in criminal action and in the prevention of crime) and quid pro quo punishments for those who abnegate that responsibility. It is this agenda of common sense that holds together apparently oppositional tenets.

Concluding comments

All the examples discussed above – law and order programming, true crime programming, privatised crime prevention and popular journalism – point to the ways in which debates about criminality and the social order are also debates about the contemporary social and political moment. They illustrate the ways in which both the criminal subject and the moral subject are discursively produced and held in tension in a range of different but related configurations. All these discursive formations inevitably construct and define the good citizen in relation to its others: miscreants, criminals, immigrants, spongers and fraudsters. Law and order programmes invite the viewer to provide information and to 'make a difference' in the detection of atypical and dangerous individuals. Initiatives such as Neighbourhood Watch invite the citizen, through vigilant community action, to deter small-scale and opportunist criminal behaviour. The discourses of true crime programming offer viewers the crime story as morality tale, rehearsing the successes of state policing over relentless criminality. And popular reportage such as *Reader's Digest* invite readers, through the discourses of common-sense and everyday politics, to assume individual responsibility and consequently to police themselves. All these initiatives and texts therefore help to produce, define and test out the relationship between the moral subject and the criminal subject. As dominant discourses about crime and law and order they offer the reader/viewer/citizen a range of potentially appealing, albeit limited, subject positions that posit a degree of individual agency, initiative and security against what is perceived as a rising tide of criminality and social fragmentation. Taken as a whole they produce a useful, complex and sometimes contradictory picture of the discursive context in which specialist true crime publications are produced and consumed.

Part II
Stories, Bodies, Criminals

4
Crime Magazine Stories: From American Idiom to an English Vernacular

Part I began to unpack the ways in which true crime literatures and other mass media products help to produce certain knowledges and tell particular stories about crime, policing, disciplinarity and social control. The unravelling of historical and political discourses of crime and of true crime highlighted the ways in which concepts of lawlessness, of citizenship and individual responsibility have been articulated and perpetuated, underpinning the rhetorical division between the moral subject and its others. These concepts, always highly charged, became ever more loaded in the articulation of a return to what Philip Rawlings (1999: 173) calls 'eighteenth-century values': a renewed emphasis on community responses to crime, on private policing and on the deterrence of criminals through imprisonment. And we have seen the ways in which these strategies have been advocated not only in new government and quasi-government initiatives, but also in the media in law and order programmes, true crime series and in the magazine *Reader's Digest*. It might be assumed, in the light of this, that specialist true crime magazines and books must constitute an even more robust arena for the production of these kinds of stories about crime and its prevention. True crime magazines are certainly shot through with by now familiar discourses about law and order and disciplinarity and their integral relationship to the common weal; in fact they often adopt a much more overtly retributive position on issues such as capital punishment. However, the following chapters show how a more complex and ambivalent picture of true crime and its regimes of knowledge about crime and the social can emerge through a close reading of both written language and visual signification.

In contrast to the last chapter, in which the emphasis was almost wholly on how subject positions such as the 'citizen' or the moral subject are constituted through a range of discourses about crime, this chapter begins to unpack the likely pleasures of true crime magazine stories and the positions potentially adopted by readers in relation to this kind of material. Consequently, it considers the deployment of a verbal and visual vernacular of true crime from the importation of a US-inspired idiom to the development of a more home-grown style and its relation to other popular generic forms.

'Yank Mags' at Woolworth's

The successful introduction of 'middlebrow' titles such as *Reader's Digest* into Britain was accompanied by the increasing presence of more denigrated popular publications such as the pulp fiction paperback – what George Orwell (1940) referred to as the 'Yank Mag' – and the true crime magazine. Perhaps the first modern true crime, whose presence is still visible and relatively unchanged today, was the true crime monthly magazine launched in the 1950s. Its initial commercial success owed much to the Americanisation of popular and ephemeral literature which began some two decades earlier.[1] While popular American journals such as *Reader's Digest* attracted a large market without attracting significant concern, these other genres called into question the 'influence' of American and American-inspired popular entertainment upon certain readers (see Webster 1988: 186ff; Petley 1997). From the outset, concerned cultural critics conflated crime literature with real crime, reading the degradation of the former as symptomatic of the latter. Orwell's famous essay 'The Decline of the English Murder' (1945) (still frequently invoked by journalists deploring the passing of an earlier era) is exemplary. Here Orwell laments the end of the Golden Age of Murder (roughly 1850–1925), an era that supplied readers of the Sunday papers with the modest thrill of the small-scale domestic murder. These crimes set within a middle-class milieu mixed adultery, respectability and a small dose of poison to provide perfect after-lunch entertainment. But more recent cases, such as the infamous 'Cleft Chin' murders, suggested that a new kind of senseless American-inspired violence had entered the English landscape (and the English popular press). This true case involved a young 'partly americanised' waitress and an American army deserter embarking on a series of random murders during the blitz: it was a 'meaningless story, with its atmosphere of dancehalls, cheap perfume, false names and stolen cars' (Orwell 1945: 100–1). The murders themselves bore all the hallmarks of an un-

British criminality – involving a shift from the domestic to the public sphere, from middle- to working-class protagonists, from motivated to seemingly random criminality.[2]

There was a growing perception that it was not only US-style crime that insinuated itself into British life but also the excesses of US crime literature. In his well-known article on boys' weekly magazines ('penny dreadfuls'), Orwell (1940: 505) addresses the commercial success of a long series of magazines known as 'Yank Mags', imported 'shop-soiled' from America and sold for twopence halfpenny or threepence. In this essay he anticipates Richard Hoggart (1957) in his recognition that cheap reading genuinely reflects popular taste and as such cannot be ignored by cultural critics. Considering the proliferation of the local newsagent he suggests:

> Probably the contents of these shops is the best available indication of what the mass of the English people really feels and thinks. Certainly nothing half so revealing exists in documentary form. Best-seller novels, for instance, tell one a great deal, but the novel is aimed almost exclusively at people above the £4-a-week level. (Orwell 1940: 505)

It is the 'smallish circulation and specialised' weekly paper that reflects 'the minds of their readers as a great national daily paper with a circulation of millions cannot possibly do' (ibid.). While the correlation between the thoughts of readers and the 'special interest' material would need to be demonstrated, Orwell's basic contention is quite proper – the majority of working-class readers (adults and children) were not reading Dorothy L. Sayers or even Edgar Wallace, but the often unknown writers of pulp magazines and the popular press. US-imported and US-inspired crime and adventure magazines were cheap and easily obtainable and Orwell observes that English magazines came a poor second in the skilful expression of violent adventures:

> There is a great difference in tone between even the most blood-thirsty English paper and the threepenny Yank Mags, *Fight Stories, Action Stories, etc.* (not strictly boys' papers, but largely read by boys). In the Yank Mags you get real blood-lust, really gory descriptions of the all-in, jump on his testicles style of fighting, written in a jargon that has been perfected by people who brood endlessly on violence. A paper like *Fight Stories*, for instance, would have very little appeal except to sadists and masochists. You can see the comparative

gentleness of the English civilisation by the amateurish way in which prize-fighting is always described in the boys' weeklies. (ibid.: 522)

In spite of the huge commercial success of these stories, and their apparently formulaic construction, English writers seemed unable to master the formula (ibid.: 523). In a book review of 1936, Orwell exhibits serious reservations about the dominance of American-style representation of violent action in popular magazines and its influence on the popular market. Quoting a paragraph from an American thriller in which a floored man is continually kicked while he is down, Orwell (1936: 249) states:

> Some of the threepenny Yank Mags which you buy at Woolworth's now consist of nothing else. Please notice the sinister change that has come over an important sub-department of English fiction. There was, God knows, enough physical brutality in the novels of Fielding, Meredith, Charles Reade, etc., but, our masters then/Were still, at least, our countrymen.

This rather odd formulation suggests that home-grown literary brutality has at least some indigenous (probably 'literary') quality which renders it more palatable. Certainly, as Jeff Nuttal and Rodick Carmichael (1977: 107–8) have noted, the very timbre of the American true crime and true adventure narratives was dependent upon 'a culture of popular pain' quite alien to the British sensibility:

> The purpose of the supposedly true narratives ... is to legitimise violence. The men are the comic-book, big-chest, square-jaw Rock Hudson character. The girls are the suffering victims ... [in a story] set in Stalag 13, in which heightened situation their bras and suspenders are brutally revealed by guard dogs as the blood trickles down their shackled wrists.

Stories such as the one just referred to, entitled 'TONIGHT WE HIT FEMALE TORTURE STALAG 13' (from *Man's Epic* magazine) do not stand alone, but are part of a broader American aesthetic which also encompasses gun culture, horror comics and films and the bloody grotesqueries of joke shop toys, together with a new and distinctly un-English vocabulary and idiom (Nuttal and Carmichael 1977: 107).

The fear of the importation of a new kind of cultural 'master', one epitomised by lubricious popular music, raw illustration and relentless violence, is one that dovetails with the enduring tradition of critical concern with Americanisation and mass culture evinced since Matthew Arnold (Webster 1988: 174ff). These new-style formulaic stories certainly introduced a different kind of representation of violent action to the British reader; one rooted in the immediately controversial imagery of Hollywood gangster movies. The far from gentlemanly fights which were at the heart of the American crime and adventure magazine were the consequence of the emergence of what John Cawelti (1977: 61) has called 'two major formulaic patterns' in the literature of crime during the 1920s and 1930s. These patterns converged around two new figures who surfaced in pulp magazines such as *Black Mask*: the hard-boiled detective who, operating in the margins of the law, does not hold back from violent action or the breaking of conventions and the Capone hoodlum who rises above urban decay and corruption through relentless gangsterism. Interestingly, both these types are figured as lower class (or outside the social boundaries of respectability within the American context) and consequently able to operate efficiently, if brutally, in violent underworld cultures. It has been argued that the stories in *Black Mask* were reminiscent of the tradition of nineteenth century *feuilletons* – 'cheap, popular, and with some degree of class-based radicalism underpinning them' (Worpole 1984: 50). Clearly, the popularity of cheap literature, which blatantly rejected the upper-class values of the virtuous amateur investigator or the cerebral plotting of the evil arch-criminal in favour of these protagonists, was bound to be regarded with suspicion (see Leavis 1932), its adherence to violence not traceable even to simple 'sadism', but in Orwell's (1936: 150) enigmatic phrase, 'to a subtler and more ignoble cause'.

Thanks to the deregulation of paper in the late 1940s British paperback publishing began to expand rapidly with post-war pulp fiction crime writing investing heavily in the cultural imagery of the United States. These books were written to a popular formula and packaged with the twin invitation and threat of the *femme fatale* on the front cover. The pungent use of demotic language drew on the gangster slang of Hollywood movies, with such un-British titles as *The Corpse Wore Nylons* and *Johnny Gets His* (Holland 1993: 76). British authors adopted the more thrilling personas of their American counterparts. One Mancunian writer is imaginatively described in a back-cover potted biography:

BART BARNATO grew up on the sidewalks of the East Side of New York. He learned the facts of life in a hard and vicious school – and writes as he has lived – brutally, truthfully, and without fear of the public enemies whose evil lives he exposes. (in ibid.: 74)

After the Second World War Britain also imported adult-oriented fiction 'comics' in bulk from the United States in addition to the pulp paperback. However, government restrictions after 1950 meant that small British publishers began to produce the comics themselves with print-runs of up to 50,000 per publication (Barker 1984: 8). As Martin Barker's research demonstrates, crime comics were obviously popular, with over 40 titles on record, including a successful publication entitled *Justice Traps the Guilty* which was published in over 50 editions between 1950 and 1955 (ibid.: 146). Whereas contemporary campaigners and critics launched the now familiar argument that these publications lent crime a certain glamour that could lead to imitative criminal behaviour, Barker's own reading suggests that, on the contrary, these stories actually stood as a warning against the 'slippery slope' towards criminality. His analysis of *Justice Traps the Guilty* suggests quite convincingly that these stories portray a threshold between lawfulness and lawlessness, 'and once past this threshold, there is (virtually) no chance of a return. What follows is a gradual but almost inevitable destruction of the individual' (ibid.: 148). This scenario of temptation and inevitable decline rings true, perpetuating in a different idiom, the conventional cautionary message of far earlier true crime.

Exposed! Sex and violence, disciplinarity and control

The 1950s saw a proliferation of magazines that more closely resemble the true crime monthlies of today. British titles such as *Street and Smith's Detective Monthly* and *True Police Cases*, together with US imports such as *True Crime Detective*, carved out and maintained a steady readership. The British magazine *Exposed: True Crime Cases*, which was launched in January 1959, is fairly typical in its presentation and coverage of true crime. This magazine, slightly larger in format than a pocket paperback and about 30 pages in length, is heavily illustrated. Its covers are restricted to crude blocks of primary colour, with monochrome photographs. Both the images and tone of the articles resemble the popular 'French' sex novelettes of the period and these, together with its adverts, clearly imply a young male readership. The illustrations are a mixture of genuine photographs of criminals and scenes of crime, together with posed photographs, usually depicting glamour models. The headlines in Issue 1 are indicative of the range of articles within: 'Green Light for Red Light District?', 'Murder Stalks the Strip', 'She Fell for a Love Swindler' and 'They Raped and Escaped!'. Only the launch issue of *Exposed* (of those viewed) made any attempt to address crime as a social issue. Here two male writers (one American, one from a more liberal Benelux country) are asked to put the case for and against legalised prostitution, a controversial topic which was obviously intended to attract readers to this new magazine (No. 1: 3–4). The two columns of text are flanked by posed photographs of two rather alluring prostitutes, which suggest glamour photography rather then photo-journalism.

Magazines like *Exposed* need to be examined closely before they can be identified as British publications. All the features in the first nine issues are set in the United States, except for the photo exclusive 'Sex Market of Spain' (Issue 2: 12–5) and 'Green Eyes Can Kill' set in France (Issue 4: 6–9, 22). Features include Hollywood tie-ins such as a re-telling of the Barbara Graham story in Issue 6, which includes three film stills of the actress who plays Graham in various states of undress. Only the adverts' British addresses undermine the magazine's construction of a hard-nosed US sensibility. Notices for body-building products and courses are common, trading on the reader's sense of physical inadequacy; cartoon strips relate the social embarrassment of the puny man who tries to make an impression on the girl of his dreams. Naturally the protagonist gets the girl only after he takes a Charles Atlas Bodybuilding Course. Promotions often include a wide range of 'educational' books including, 'A Massive Chest for You!', 'Intimate Sex Discussions!' (both Issue 1: 2) and British Glandular Products' euphemistic call to 'Wake up your reserve of natural strength' (Issue 2: 33). As Hoggart notes, these adverts surely construct the young working-class male as the typical reader. Of the nine issues I examined, there was only one advert (for a sewing machine) that could have been construed as aimed at female readers. The promotion of bodybuilding and assertiveness courses spoke to the aspirations of the individual male subject towards self-improvement and increased upward social mobility, also signified by the use of a seemingly classless American idiom (Hoggart 1957: 207–8). The look, language and content of the magazines construct an imaginary United States, whose components are small-town suburban life, Hollywood, Chicago and New York City; all already well established in the filmic imagination of movie goers across Europe as places where the small man can make it big.

In *The Uses of Literacy* (1957) Hoggart registers similar concerns to Orwell's about the proliferation of these US-inspired true crime magazines. In all, he offers eleven representative titles whose formats included glossy covers, crude print and recycled stories. He notes that these magazines often sported law and order slogans such as 'published in the cause of the Reduction of Crime' (Hoggart 1957: 206) in order to ward off fierce criticism that they glamorised and trivialised crime.[3] Hoggart (ibid.: 205) deduced that the magazine retailers, who were situated in working-class shopping areas, were in the business of providing 'entertainment literature' for what he called 'The Juke-Box Boys'. He himself clearly regrets the substantial popularity of 'spicy' magazines, arguing that their consumption is evidence of the 'denaturing' of the 'moral fibre' of young unskilled working men (ibid.). The overriding concern here is framed around the influx into Britain of mass-produced popular *American* culture and its rapid erosion of home-grown, localised working-class cultures. He also chronicles the encroaching Americanisation of the cultural life of working-class youth. These avid readers of pulp literature tend to meet in the new-style milk bar:

> Most of the customers are boys aged between fifteen and twenty, with drape-suits, picture ties and an American slouch. … The young men waggle one shoulder or stare, as desperately as Humphrey Bogart, across the tubular chairs. … Many of the customers – their clothes, their hair-styles, their facial expressions all indicate – are living to a large extent in a myth-world compounded of a few simple elements which they take to be those of American life. (ibid.: 203–4)

What Hoggart does not acknowledge is how the juxtaposition of old and new cultures actually creates something new, facilitating a modification of a 'structure of feeling', a fusion of transatlantic mores, attitudes and vernacular rather than merely mindless mimicry. These accounts of crime are framed in a quite different register from the everyday language of law and order encountered in the daily or Sunday press, and there is no reason to think that readers failed to differentiate between the British and American experiences of crime and disorder. That the same readers often consume these two quite different kinds of reading suggests that the US experience of crime depicted in these magazines offers a mode of comparison, a yardstick for the calibration of the British experience. As Nuttal and Carmichael (1977: 110–11) suggest, the juxtaposition of English and American popular cultural forms: the rustle of sweets while watching a Hollywood movie, the knitting resting next to the Hank Janson novelette, arguably undercut any wholesale investment in the American dream.

It seems likely that even in crime and adventure magazines, sex was as seductive to the reader as violence. As early as the 1930s Orwell noted 'the frankest appeal to sadism' directed against women in 'Yank Mags'. These magazines featured:

> Scenes in which Nazis tie bombs to women's backs and fling them off heights to watch them blown to pieces in mid-air, others in which they tie naked girls by their hair and prod them with knives to make them dance, etc. (Orwell 1939: 523)

Magazines such as *Exposed* relentlessly sexualised the female protagonists of its stories whether they featured as the victim or the murderer. But it is the detailed descriptions of female corpses, producing a sort of post-mortem glamour, which underlines the inherent voyeurism of both imagery and text. Alan Masters' feature, (*Exposed* Issue 7: 10) entitled 'The Devil Loved Gloria', is exemplary here:

> A young girl lay dead among the leaves. Her brownish-blond hair streamed maplike from her cracked and partially decomposed scalp. Her face, bloated and gnawed by insects and rodents, was shapeless, like a lump of grimy dough, fixed with blobs for eyes, and pierced with a parted, livid slash for a mouth.
>
> A net brassiere had been pulled up so that it lay like a lace bib above her ripe, protuberant breasts. The elastic waistband of her aquamarine nylon panties was pulled down so that it girdled her fleshly hips some inches below her navel.

The marriage of sex and death is striking if wholly commonplace within true crime of the period. Masters' detailed description of the victim's undergarments – the synthetic materials and gaudy colours – exhibits a fetishistic attention to the accoutrements of glamour photography and a subordination of the wearer's identity that is akin to pornography. As Steve Holland's (1993) history of post-war pulp publishing illustrates, true crime was by no means unique in its voyeurism. Most popular genres, from science fiction to juvenile delinquency novels, were laced with sexual innuendo and were promoted with cover illustrations of glamorous half-naked women. A short selection of titles by the prolific pulp writer Hank Janson is indicative of the rhetorical link between 'dames' and death: *This Woman is Death, Kill*

Her If You Can, The Filly Wore A Rod [gun] and *Hotsy, You'll be Chilled* [killed] (Holland 1993: 199). It is arguable, however, that the structures of the porn magazine resemble the true crime magazine rather more closely than the pulp fiction novel (see Miles 1991). Aside from true crime's prolific utilisation of the image (absent in novels aside from the cover illustration), it also presents a variety of short features that tend to be repetitive and virtually interchangeable. This provides number-less opportunities for variations of the theme of women and death. The body of the woman, whether as *femme fatale* or bludgeoned victim of murder, is constructed as both polluting and alluring. 'The Devil Loved Gloria' amply illustrates this point. While the victim's face is dirty and shapeless, its 'parted, livid slash for a mouth' is highly suggestive of the story's sexual connotations. The rhetorical linkage between femininity and polluting sex sits in opposition to the generally wholesome por-trayal of the male body in adverts that advocate self-discipline, invok-ing the 'natural strength' and cleanliness of the masculine body. Advice is offered on the safeguarding of sexual potency through the control of 'night emissions' and the improvement of 'muscle control'. Clearly the illustrative content and especially the 'soft-porn' covers of these magazines (which continued up until the early 1980s) attests that a predominantly male readership is being confronted with confusing and contradictory messages about sex and sexual control, as well as about the gendering of violent crime.

Among those true crime titles launched in Britain during the 1950s several widely distributed monthly titles are still extant, including *True Detective* (1950–) and *Master Detective* (1952–). *True Crime Detective*, a US publication launched in 1951 and distributed in Britain, is illustrative of the features that were standard to the new real-life crime magazines of the period. This quarterly-issue periodical was the convenient size of a pocket paperback. True crime is strongly visual; replete with glamour models either holding weapons or posing as the victims of crime, Hollywood stills and press photos of women involved in real life crime. The presence in true crime magazines of adverts for periodicals such as *Gent* and *Jem*, written 'for your pleasure', point up the potential crossover in readership from true crime to girlie entertainment. The matte covers were luridly coloured, usually featuring an inset-bordered photograph of a woman posed as either the perpetrator or more often as the victim of violence. The cover for Winter 1952, for example, carried a tinted photograph of an apparently naked woman lying on her back on the floor, her head propped up on some wooden blocks. The image shows her only from the shoulders up – her hair and make-up are glamorous, immaculate and contemporary. There is no caption to anchor the image and no apparent connection between the picture and the stories inside. In contrast, an issue from 1953 (Spring) bears a mono-chrome photograph which signifies that the crime is a 'classic' or period event. Here a plain young woman wearing a severe night-gown and Victorian ringlets brandishes a cut-throat razor. To her left the caption reads 'The Tragedy of Samuel S. Kent'. The caption links the image to the story of Constance Kent who murdered her infant step-brother in the middle of the night. In both issues the covers offer the reader a quite bizarre cover girl, explicitly linking death with the feminine.[4]

The impact of these voyeuristic moments was probably lessened by the sheer variety of features in each edition. For example, in the 1950s *True Crime Detective* carried both classic and contemporary true crime stories, juxtaposed with the occasional book review, editorial and the kind of four-line anecdotes and cartoons which feature most famously in *Reader's Digest*. Their commercial success drew criticism to both their literary value and their perceived influence upon vulnerable readers that seemed to incite a response. Hence sensational stories were often framed by a broader, overtly didactic discourse of moralism and self-instruction. In addition to the law and order slogans trumpeted by the magazines some feature articles took to expounding the rewarding and socially responsible reasons for reading about crime. For instance, a book review in *True Crime Detective* (Spring 1953: 83) ponders on the record number of true crime books sold in the previous year. The author argues that 'fact-crime' books are socially useful for their 'vivid exposition of defects in the very society in which we live'. Here a true crime book by the well-known detective writer Erle Stanley Gardner is commended because it enables readers 'to painlessly absorb a great deal of rewardingly mature thinking on criminalistics, penology, the nature of evidence and the true meaning of justice' (ibid.). This rhetoric of citizenship, individualism, amateur scholarship and murder buffery, as will be seen in some detail, is fully sustained in the magazines of the 1980s and early 1990s.

True crime, therefore, operates as both entertainment and also, quite self-consciously, as a source of knowledge for the informed citizen on all things 'criminous'. From their inception until the 1980s these mag-azines were wedded to a growing permissiveness in the representation of sex and crime. The use of glamour models, voyeuristic reports about prostitution and the centrality of women as the sexualised victims or perpetrators of crime all heralded the entrance of a new 'permissive populism' into British culture (Hunt 1998: 16ff). The established true crime monthlies *Master Detective* and *True Detective*, along with the newer magazine *True Crime* (launched 1982), shifted in tone, subject matter and visual style from an American vernacular that poached the register of 1950s 'hard-boiled' fiction to one that is more indigenous and closer to the forms of address employed by the (post-1960s) British popular press, a tabloid style that emphasises the sexy and the sensational (Cameron and Frazer 1987; Cameron 1990). It was not until the mid- to late 1980s that the entrance of new magazines into the market-place and a growing recognition of the large number of female readers finally engendered a move away from overtly sexualised imagery. While there is still evidence, especially in the traditional monthlies, of a pornographic aesthetic both these, and especially the newer publications, appear to be in the process of engaging with new ways of representing crime, the criminal and the body of the victim. Deborah Cameron (1990: 137) has argued of more contemporary British magazines: 'what true crime magazines like this offer readers is a balance of licit and illicit pleasures, the one defusing the anxiety of the other.' As will be seen in a later chapter these illicit, usually visual pleasures, were redirected from the sexual body to the forensic body. As new technologies altered production, leading to the provision of computerised graphics, enhanced colour and improved production values, they also allowed for the depiction of more complex forensic and investigative procedures, which gradually replaced the spectacle of sexualised crime. A mixture of disciplinary discourses, of criminology, surveillance, forensic medicine, penology and so forth ('fact-crime'), together with the exposing strategies of explicit corporeal and visceral imagery, now constitute the bedrock of these magazines. One recent promotional leaflet for Time-Life true crime publications offers twin invitation and caution: '[S]ome text and photographs are explicit. These disturbing details are not for the faint-hearted.'

'Read all about it!': the construction of a popular vernacular

> Fear in the face of absolute death turns inward in a continuous irony; man disarms it in advance, making it an object of derision by giving it an everyday untamed form, by constantly renewing it in the spectacle of life, by scattering it throughout the vices, the difficulties, and the absurdities of all men.
>
> Michel Foucault (1961: 16)

Despite the emergence of new, more 'professionalised' discourses of crime, detection and punishment in contemporary true crime, the monthlies launched during the 1950s and more especially their Summer Specials, continue today to employ an intimate vernacular in their address to the reader.[5] The grim humour, voyeurism and sensational tone of the story titles signals the generic pleasures and the generic relationship between true crime magazines and the popular press. Some publications, such as *Murder Most Foul*, even feature crime-related cartoons such as the one featuring an apparently contented couple in their middle years at breakfast – except that the wife is reading a book entitled *Poisons* (*MMF* No. 23: 52). Themed editions such as the *Master Detective Summer Special* (1997) entitled 'Murder at the Seaside' underline the role of some true crime publications as arenas for black humour. This edition, emblazoned with a cover-girl[6] sitting in the sun and framed by bright yellow typography, offers a range of wryly presented murder stories including 'A Grim Find in Scarborough', 'No More Trips to Cleethorpes' and 'The Kids' Last Holiday in Bognor'.[7] As noted in the quotation above, here death becomes an object of derision as well as fear, it is mocked and domesticated even though it is the unchallenged protagonist of every story. The monthlies also present incongruous titles that marry death and the 'absurdities of men' such as 'Devon Love Bungalow Killing' or 'Last Tango in Sussex: the Burgess Hill Tea Dance Murder' (*MD* June 1996). These titles problematise any notion of earnest reading, the impropriety of humour in this context signalling the lowliness of true crime as a literary genre (Bakhtin 1965: 67). The use of vernacular in particular recalls the pungent address of popular Sunday papers such as the *News of the World* or the daily tabloids. This is especially apparent in editorials such as this one which echo a sales pitch famously deployed by the *Sun*:

> There's blood and gore and so much more!. ... What can be better than lazing around, reading a Summer Special? Give yourself a pat on the back for thinking of such a thrilling way of cooling off – by reading these blood-chilling stories! (*TDSS* 1995: 4)

The use of anachronistic terminology in the description of period crime also evokes the flavour of tabloid reportage and lends an old story a contemporary inflection. The inappropriate deployment of terms such as 'serial killer', 'gang rape' and 'psychopath' in accounts of early crime is common place. Stories such as 'Southport's Serial Killer Doctor'[8] (set in 1947) and 'The Axeman Got Away with Murder' (both *MD SS* 1996: 3–10, 79–82) are typical in this regard. The latter story, set in 1862, is a dramatised account of the murder of a servant, Jessie McPherson, by her elderly master, James Fleming. Here the writer Robert Carat deliberately draws attention to how the murderer James Fleming, living a 'sleazy' existence, would be described in today's colloquialisms: 'At least one event had occurred ... which today would have earned him the title "dirty old man".'[9]

In these magazines the vulgar, the bizarre and the excessive are brandished shamelessly, jostling with, and sometimes undercutting, the often relentlessly grim tales of domestic violence, acid bath murders and robbery gone wrong. Their excessiveness may be understood as a clear signifier of the complexity of engagement that the text potentially offers readers and of the possibility that these stories are being read 'against the grain'. For while dominant discourses, especially since the early 1980s, have promoted notions of self-development, personal responsibility and progress, these accounts, through a mixture of seriousness and irony, prepare the reader to say 'goodbye to all that'. In the above examples the juxtaposition of English parochialism, working-class holiday resorts and cosy domesticity (Devon bungalow, Scarborough, Cleethorpes, the couple at breakfast) and excessive drama ('love killing', 'last tango', 'a grim find', the book entitled *Poisons*) mocks the banality of the everyday and the exceptional crimes that punctuate it. The promise of gratuitous violence is potentially diluted by the excessiveness of its presentation. The establishment of a credible portrait of everyday life that forms the backdrop to the eruption of violence is crucial.[10] For example, the narrative's emphasis upon the 'ordinariness' of the murderer and of his/her victims foregrounds the unprecedented nature of violence. A story entitled 'Triple Horror in Sunderland' (*MD* December 1996: 2) is characteristic of this strategy. It begins: 'Thomas Kelly seemed a normal teenager ... and like many young people he was unemployed ... he was hoping for something to turn up. What did turn up was death at the hands of a stranger.' Here, and in many other narratives, the horror of the story is founded upon the victim's encounter with a personification of death rather than with a particular killer. The founding scenario is one in which the ordinary and the banal are disrupted by figures of mortality that simply 'turn up' uninvited. In this sense these accounts are not so much crime stories as thanatopses, reflections on the likely incursion of sudden death into the lives of the unsuspecting and the unprepared. Stories often turn, therefore, on the incongruity of the juxtaposition of death with the quotidian. Again, the appeal of the story 'Last Tango in Sussex' (*MD* June 1996: 13–6) stems from the unpromisingly ordinary context from which the murder arises. The story relates the 'love trian-gle' between three older people 'the killer was 67, the victim 80 and the *femme fatale* 52' who met at tea dances and singles' nights, where 'beneath the surface of these genteel gatherings passions seethe' (ibid.: 13). The photographic head-shots of the male protagonists are anchored with text that underlines the apparent incongruity of the case:

> Warwick Batchelor was a vigorous 80-year-old with class, charm and money. He was just the kind of man a woman with troubles could lean on …
> Edward Martin, 67, virile and affectionate, was a handyman, especially with a screwdriver … (ibid.: 13, author's ellipses)

Excessive headlines and stories such as these are examples of 'the inability of the "normal" (and therefore of the ideology that produced it) to explain or cope with specific instances of everyday life' (Fiske 1989: 116), such as ardour in old age and the violence that it engen-dered. These stories reveal the bizarre undertow beneath the everyday, thus interrogating the limits of how the 'normal' is conceptualised. Here, human nature is flawed, and not always in the sense of 'tragedy', but also quite often in a random, almost comic way. The eruption of violent events and passionate emotion in the stories constitute a chal-lenge to the dominant discourses discussed in the last chapter that offer models of behaviour (disciplinarity, individual responsibility, community action, home security) that are supposed to mitigate against becoming the victim, or indeed the perpetrator, of crime. In these narratives the consolatory ordinariness of everyday life is frac-tured by 'bad luck' and by grotesque, unpredictable and terrible events. 'Human nature' and unforeseen circumstance are the rogue elements that cannot be successfully factored into the precautions advocated by the media, the private security industry and the state. Hence these stories are evidence of the false promise seemingly embedded in the discourses of crime prevention, law and order policy, citizenship and individual responsibility.

5
Period True Crime: History from Below?

In the last chapter the emphasis was on the recent history of true crime and the ways that the entrance of pulp fictions into the English market resulted in the mimicry of US idiom, inspiring panic about the destabilisation and erosion of indigenous culture. Orwell and Hoggart, while giving much-needed intellectual weight to the study of denigrated popular forms, drew on codes of taste, quality and value to register concern for the diminishment of home-bred culture and the broader sensibilities of the English. The fear of the importation of violence voiced by these and other cultural critics is both literal and metaphorical. A new language of violence breaks into and contaminates components of the English imaginary – its fictions, its language and its cultural references – and its presence is seen to inaugurate a different, more brutal, physical violence of weapon and fist into the English landscape.

We also saw, however, that with the emergence of a new permissive populism and the resonance of the popular press, this US-inspired sensibility in true crime gradually gave way to a new kind of English vernacular which has lasted the course from the 1950s to the present day. Long-running British publications renewed the emphasis in English crime literature on indigenous murders, on the everyday, on grim humour and on the incongruous and the bizarre, returning constantly to contemporary and period *English* true crime stories. This chapter asks how *True Crime Detective, Master Detective* and *Murder Most Foul*, magazines launched in the 1950s, continue to appeal to readers today.[1] What is their enduring appeal in a market where new-style competitor magazines have made their mark by leaving behind the ordinary and the everyday for the new frontiers of psychological profiling and forensic technologies? The focus is on period stories, analysing how they organise and structure the past through story-telling and photography to render complex historical events with an appealing directness and simplicity that successfully addresses modern readers. It examines the representation of history, of the quotidian, of class and gender relations and thinks through the ways in which the issues that they raise are grafted nostalgically but effectively to the present moment. It explores the extent to which these stories, which persist in speaking about people often excluded from official history (robbers and child-murderers, beaten wives and prostitutes, conscripts and delinquents), provide a space for readers to engage with forgotten and marginalised lives.

True crime: past into present

Geoffrey Pearson (1983) has argued that popular memory plays a significant role in the public perception of the contemporary state of law and order. The experience and the perception of crime is measured against a notional golden age which occurred some two decades earlier and against which crime today is inevitably judged to be more virulent, less controlled and less punished. However, narratives of past crimes occupy a much more paradoxical position within the parameters of true crime magazines. For while the editorial, letters page and articles on recent shocking crimes construct the present as the most dangerous period in criminal history in contrast to some ill-defined earlier moment, 'classic' cases usually present past crime as equally ubiquitous and horrid. Having said this, nineteenth-century and early twentieth-century working-class experiences of crime are not simply cast in a rosy hue, nor are they overtly contrasted with the more 'civilised' conditions of today. Rather, crime is the dramatic motor for a variety of stories whose apparently timeless 'human interest' speaks to the current reader. For example, the full-page preview for *Murder Most Foul* (No. 20 April 1996) presents a special feature on prostitution entitled 'Soho: the murderous years – evil beyond belief ... when the white slavers ruled the streets of fear.'[2] The story, which is undated, appears to be set in the 1940s – as evidenced by the hairstyles of the three women ('street-girls') featured in the in-set photographic portraits: 'Black Rita', 'Russian Dora' and 'Ginger Rae'. A full quotation provides the flavour of these period stories:

> In a slummy flat the wireless is blaring. Usually the job is done with a stiletto. Almost always it is a woman; a prostitute who has stepped out of line. The murder gets just a column on a day when news is thin. At other times it rates only a paragraph. Another murder in Soho, and a shrug. The murderous years saw evil beyond belief. The Micheletti,

Castanar and Messina gangs brought terror to the square mile where fear ensured silence and street girls were expendable; a commodity to trade in. Don't miss this eye-opening double-length story ...

Here the minutiae of everyday life, conveyed in a register that recalls pulp fiction and *film noir*, constitutes part of its appeal. The sound of the wireless, the visual detail of the women's faces and the Soho street lighting ground the story in imagery that is familiar at least from old movies and popular memory.

Similarly, a story called 'Horror in the Blackout' (*MDSS* 1995: 64–7) by Norma Cooper, chronicling the rape and murder of Gladys May Appleton by 18-year-old Private John Davidson in Lancashire in 1944, actively invokes popular memories and imagery of wartime Britain. This is done not simply to establish the scene, but also most importantly to provide the frame of reference through which the murder and its aftermath are read and evaluated. The small details of the story serve to set the violence and death meted out to Gladys Appleton within a knowable context, offering the reader a point of identification with the victim and her world. Hence Cooper (ibid.: 65) offers the reader poignant details of Appleton's life such as that she worked for the Co-op as a cleaner, that 'she could never be accused of being the flighty sort' and that 'she had been putting away odds and ends, week by week, for her bottom drawer'. Yet in spite of this blameless life she is found raped and murdered in a deserted lane. Once again prosaic details jostle with the grotesqueries of death:

> The ground around the body had been badly disturbed by numerous footprints. A false set of teeth belonging to the dead woman lay nearby. ... Her coat was drawn loosely over her body and her shoes lay four feet away. A scarf was wound tightly round her neck, so detectives could only conclude that it had been used to strangle her. (ibid.: 64)

This account locates this single act of violence against the backdrop of a broader, idealised structure of feeling emanating from a much wider experience and 'public memory' of state-sanctioned violence – war:[3]

> A common enemy, the devastation that affected all regardless of class, sex, age or religion brought a sense of unity throughout the nation. Every Briton, including civilians, had a common aim – to win the war, comfort the bereaved and get back to normal. But many who recall those years do so with great affection. That sense of camaraderie between each and every citizen, the togetherness and

feeling of belonging was like a wonderful spell that no enemy bomb could destroy. What kind of man could kill one of his own during all this? (ibid.: 66)

In this case the murder is presented as an aberration that actually affirms the veracity of popular memories of wartime social cohesion: 'With a savagery he should have reserved for the enemy, Davidson turned on the helpless victim' (ibid.: 67). Davidson inspires anxiety, not simply because he took a life but because the 'docile', disciplined and directed body of a soldier spun out of control at a time that has been recalled as one of unified community values (Foucault 1975: 135ff). In the context of this story the message is clear that Davidson deserved to be hanged, not only for viciously raping and murdering Gladys Appleton, but also for puncturing the 'wonderful spell' of both civilian mutual support and military courage that purportedly united a nation. Finally, it is noted that if Davidson had committed the crime only a fortnight earlier when he was still only seventeen years old, his life would have been spared. But in these special circumstances he was rightly executed for 'Britain had no place in it for such cowards during those troubled years' (Cooper 1995: 67). Despite the certainty of the dominant narrative voice in this and other similar stories the narrative is scored with fault-lines around the moral implications of individual violent criminal acts and judicial punishment. Insoluble contradictions and unanswered questions abound, such as why is it that state-directed violence is right and individual violence wrong? Why is the violence of righteous warfare misdirected ('savagery he should have reserved for the enemy') by a soldier towards a civilian 'who provoked him simply be being visible and unprotected' (ibid.)? How might a vicious rape and murder be reconciled with an idealised 'golden age' of social cohesion? And finally how could the killer's judicial fate (death or life imprisonment) be predicated upon the date of his birth? The story works hard to reconcile these tensions, to make sense of contradictions inherent in the discourses that sanction and direct violence within specific arenas such as war and judicial punishment. Here, as elsewhere, the act of murder highlights the knotty intersection between licit and illicit violence, between murder and warfare. As Foucault (1973: 205) has remarked:

From the far side of the law the memorial of battles corresponded to the shameful renown of murderers. ... When all is said and done, battles simply stamp the mark of history on nameless slaughters, while narratives make the stuff of history from mere street brawls.

The contrast between the violence that Davidson should have undertaken and the violence that he chose to undertake displays the unease
inherent in much true crime (and in the broader discourses of law and
order) about the relationship between individual (spontaneous and/or
random) and state-sanctioned (premeditated and directed) violence.

While many of these stories, like the ones discussed above, employ a
strongly retributive discourse of 'just deserts' (albeit shot through with
contradictions), some choose to dwell on miscarriages of justice that
lead to wrongful executions. Other articles even turn on the refusal of
criminals to meet death with contrition. A short piece entitled 'Last
Laughs' exemplifies this last point. This features three, undated, period
monochrome photographs of men laughing or smiling as they face
execution:

> On the left is murderer Jack Sulivan, sentenced to die in Arizona's
> gas chamber. He went to his death grinning and smoking a cigar. As
> unconcerned is [*sic*] Charlie Birger, who smiles and chats with
> officials seconds before he was hanged. And above Kenneth Neu is
> pictured singing the song he composed for the hangman: 'I'm fit as
> a fiddle and ready to hang.' (*MDSS* 1995: 7)

In this article, and others akin to it, fascination stems from the apparent irrationality and defiance of the criminal subject who seems whole-
heartedly to embrace state execution. Their animated conditions
(laughing, smiling, singing), which suggest continuing action and
vivacity, are caught like motion film stills rather than static portrait
photographs. In this sense these images are like 'quotations' from a
longer, now inaccessible performance of absurd bravado (Barthes 1970:
67). Laughter always seems unfitting in the face of death and up
against the limit of the law's power, for as Bakhtin (1965: 67) notes:
'that which is important and essential cannot be comical' for the
'sphere of the comic is narrow and specific (private and social vices)'.
Here the laughter occurs in an official and even political context,
overtly refusing to play the retributive/confessional game of public
punishment. In this sense the laughter captured in these images, like
the use of ironic titles referred to above, seems to cut death and its
agent the law down to size.

An even more dramatic example of the criminal subject who seems
to embrace death at the hands of the law is a story entitled 'He Talked
His Way to the Scaffold' (*MDSS* 1996: 32–8). This is an account of

Charles Henry Cort, a violent robber who was sentenced to 15 years' imprisonment in August 1879:

> Cort didn't like the prison life, which in the last decades of the nineteenth century was harsh and extremely punitive. He was sure he'd never last 15 years, and the prospect of death itself was a happier one than the rest of his days spent in that gloomy, rat-infested institution. (*MDSS* 1996: 36)

Consequently, Cort made a false confession to an unsolved murder that occurred 13 years earlier in order to be sentenced to death. In articles such as these the criminal subject is a figure of defiance, not only of death, but also of the procedures of the law. The fact that Cort actively sought to deceive legal process into ending his life and succeeded reveals the fallibility of the law and its violent aspect. To an extent Foucault's (1982: 205) observations of nineteenth-century murder tales are apposite: 'All these narratives spoke of a history in which there were no rulers, peopled with frantic and autonomous events, a history below the level of power.' But unlike the accounts examined by Foucault, these stories are retold as 'classic', mass-produced tales, without the 'meaningfulness' of contemporaneity and cultural proximity appreciated by early audiences (see Galtung and Ruge 1973; Hartley 1982: 72). Instead, the 'meaningfulness' of such stories for the contemporary reader has to be shaped through other factors such as the formation of popular memories of past times. So the subtext of a clash with the law 'below the level of power' which Foucault goes on to suggest, characterised these discourses in earlier centuries, is arguably present, but may well be neutralised in modern true crime magazines. For although the broad division between what is licit and illicit remains fairly constant, the objectives of punitive justice such as 'the quality, nature, and in a sense the substance of which the punishable element is made' change over time (Foucault 1977: 17).[4] The forms of law, their functions and their effects shift and alter over time, producing different articulations of the triad of criminality, the people and the law. Thus while historical accounts of the criminal who mocks the gas chamber, sings to his hangman or seeks execution represent some sort of defiance of the apparently rational procedures of the law, the 'meaningfulness' of any 'clash' with the law is arguably clouded by its abstraction from the 'structures of feeling' and of jurisprudence within which it was embedded.

True crime as melodrama: the case of Kitty Breaks and Frederick Holt

> Abstracted and redeployed, history seems to be purged of political tension; it becomes a unifying spectacle, the settling of all disputes.
>
> Patrick Wright (1985: 69)

The appeal and fascination of period true crime literature may well reside in the ways in which it both reveals and smooths over the tensions and contradictions evident in professional and popular discourses of crime and punishment, and law and order and the place of the subject in relation to them. Even as true crime begins to unpack and think through social histories of crime, poverty, morality and respectability, class and gender relations, it seems to close down their implications for contemporary readers. A more detailed scrutiny of several stories will demonstrate how this works.[5] Many of the stories, as already mentioned, are set in working-class holiday resorts, drawing on a reservoir of popular memories of simple pleasures: hard-earned leisure, seaside romances and youthful diversions. It is against backdrops such as these that the drama of murder is often played out. An account entitled 'Corpse on the Beach was Worth a Fortune' (*TCSS* 1996: 48–51) provides a flavour of the material on offer to readers, revealing how readers are positioned and the ways in which relations of class and gender are negotiated. The story is one of two featured in a 'Blackpool Double Bill' of seaside murders which begins with a full-page illustration of Central Beach in the 1920s. Superimposed over the picture is the statement: 'They came to the famous seaside town with their lovers ... and left them as corpses' (*TCSS* 1996: 43). The story 'Corpse on the Beach ...', which is set in the 1920s, tells the true story of how 'ex-mill girl' Kitty Breaks fell in love with demobbed Lieutenant Frederick Holt, the man who was eventually to murder her on a Blackpool beach. The account relates their affair from his perspective, underlining her naivety, emphasising his greed and vicious manipulation of Kitty, and his attempts to insure her life for a considerable sum of money. This, like most true crime stories, presents a unified and apparently incontrovertible reading of past events consolidated through the use of stock characterisation, common-sense interpretation and popular generic conventions. The story begins in *media res*, harnessing the discourses of nineteenth-century stage melodrama to set the scene:

> Six foot tall, good-looking Frederick Holt smoothed his moustache and sidled up to the pretty little wide-eyed girl standing alone on the edge of the dance hall floor. 'May I have the pleasure?' he murmured in a clipped, cultured accent. Kitty Breaks fluttered her eyelashes. With a weak, slightly awed smile she gave her consent. (*TCSS* 1996: 48)

Holt is clearly coded as a predatory cad within a narrative that the reader already knows can only end in murder. From the outset Kitty Breaks is marked out as an unlucky victim of circumstance – a 'wide-eyed girl'. The account stresses the vulnerability of a woman of Breaks' social class and limited experience compared to Holt who, in her eyes, was the model of refinement and security with an 'income twice the national wage'. She sends Holt a long 'illiterate' love letter in which she confesses to a divorce (described here as her 'sordid affair'): 'The epistle was both drooling, disjointed, and something of a literary shambles, and when Freddie read it, with one eyebrow slightly lifted, he metaphorically shrugged his shoulders' (ibid.: 48–9). The letter itself is not reproduced. Yet the reader is invited to peep over Holt's shoulder as he reads it, to share vicariously his contempt. In this context Breaks' illiteracy is not so much a mark of her class as the sign of her natural victimhood and her inability to save herself from a threat which seems (in retrospect, of course) so obvious to current readers. That the letter is 'drooling and disjointed' seems explanation enough for Breaks' hapless inability to avoid death. In stories such as these, power, autonomy and vitality reside with the villain, whereas the victim is predetermined as a passive object of power. The appearance of death in the figure of Holt is posited as the most exciting and indeed vital thing in her life. He transforms her life, introducing her to the thrill of motor cars, dining out and holidays. Breaks' joy in travelling from Bradford to Blackpool is noted: 'for holidays at seaside hotels had not figured much in her drab life' (ibid.: 49). It is in this place that she meets her apparently certain end, battered and shot by Holt. He, with equal inevitability in a story whose end is made clear at the outset, is executed for murder.

   In this story and in many others class and gender relations underpin the narrative even as they seem to elude scrutiny. They slip between the competing and sometimes conflicting discourses that true crime habitually deploys: melodrama, police procedural, reportage and who-dunit. The historical advantages and disadvantages of class and gender which might still resonate with contemporary readers are arguably 'purged of political tension' (Wright 1985: 69), recast into those of character, individual agency and drama. In this example true crime is fused with the most denigrated type of melodrama – the 'debased or failed tragedy' that seems to preclude serious critical attention (Gledhill 1987: 5). This story constitutes a 'failed romance' within the terms outlined by the readers of popular romance (Radway 1984: 158).[6] For these readers an unsuccessful romantic novel is one in which the usual attributes of the hero – 'independence, taciturnity, cruelty and violence' – are too exaggerated for comfort (ibid.). Here the 'mildly disturbing' behaviour of the romantic hero becomes genuinely dangerous and the 'transformation from enemy to lover', which is the substance of the ideal romance, is revealed to be a sham (ibid.). In this true crime story, as in the romance, masculine power is equated with social power, and feminine innocence with social disadvantage, producing a *sotto voce* dialogue about the role of capital in social and gender rela-tions.[7] Christine Gledhill (1987: 21) observes of this relation within melodrama:

> Innocence and villainy construct each other: while the villain is necessary to the production and revelation of innocence, innocence defines the boundaries of the forbidden which the villain breaks. In this way melodrama's affective and epistemological structures were deployed ... to embody the forces and desires set loose by, or resist-ing, the drives of capitalism.

In this story, as in the one discussed above in which Private Davidson attacks Gladys Appleton, Kitty Breaks' ingenuousness is fundamental to an effective delineation of the murderer as villain. Essentially it is the problem of capital, of her penury and his greed, that explains, motivates and finally closes down the narrative. Breaks is encouraged by Holt to cross boundaries of class and propriety and is then punished for undertaking this passage. There is self-consciousness or at least 'obviousness' at work in the deployment of such melodramatic tropes that simultaneously holds the reader and holds him/her at a distance (Ang 1982: 96–102). It is difficult to express clearly this reader's sense that it is in fact Breaks who has somehow failed to uphold her end of the dramatic deal here. The thrust of the narrative implies that the real tragedy lies in Breaks' pathetic failure to recognise that she has strayed into a fatal but crudely obvious crime melodrama and that her role is, quite simply, to be killed by a villain.

Representing working-class violence: the case of George Vass and Margaret Docherty

It is clear from the examples discussed that most period true crime stories do little to explore overtly the political and economic context of crime and punishment. At most they present a cursory and haphazard social history of the few issues which directly relate to the events in question: prostitution, penology, temperance, the Elizabethan 'underworld', and so on. Stories of 'classic' crime bear headlines that lend social history the spurious currency of today's news. For example, events which occurred in 1862 are flagged: 'Newcastle woman stripped naked, raped and murdered in street' (*TDSS* 1996: 38–9). This refers to the case of George Vass and Margaret Docherty: 'A sex-crazed brute with rape on his mind, a drunken housewife, and New Year's Eve in Newcastle is a lethal cocktail. It ended with the violent death of housewife Margaret Docherty and the hanging of killer George Vass.' The story, part of a 'Tyneside Double Bill', tells how George Vass followed a trajectory of violent criminal behaviour which ended with the rape and murder of Margaret Docherty. At 21 years old, Vass, who was illiterate, was a well-known figure in Newcastle. He had a history of violent criminality including sexual assault, rape and pub fights. As a reprobate 'he would drive the most patient reformist to drink' (ibid.: 38). Margaret Docherty was a 'housewife' who usually did not drink much, but who was out drunk on New Year's Eve. Docherty had an altercation with her husband, who tried to take her home, which was only stopped when passers-by intervened in the belief that he was molesting her. She was staggering away when Vass spotted her: 'watching her from the shadows, George Vass's cruel lips tightened. "She'll do," he said to himself' (ibid.: 41). Again, as in the murder of Kitty Breaks discussed above, Docherty is styled as the natural victim of a man destined to kill. In other words 'she'll do', but so would the next available woman; 'available' signifying the victim's own 'complicity' in her demise. In both accounts, class and especially gender are not the explicit determinants of events, but the given, naturalised and unspoken backdrop. Docherty, drunk and refusing to return home with her husband, was a working-class woman who had temporarily eluded the regulation of moral behaviour, which was being instituted during the period (Skeggs 1997: 42), she had evaded the domestic 'ideal' which putatively guaranteed her safety (Hall, C. 1980). Away from the alleged safety of the domestic realm, she is dragged to the West Wall which has its own history of violence, rendered more ironic by her earlier fight with her husband:

> With some kind of superhuman effort she still managed to cry 'Murder!' But the West Wall was badly lit. ... It was a place where husbands frequently beat their wives, and the wives frequently cried 'Murder!' and no one took any notice. (ibid.: 41)

Both the Kitty Breaks story and this one beg the question of how such a story speaks to the modern reader, who is likely to be working-class and female. In this account there is no heroine to outwit and outlive the murderer. If there is a 'hero' it is Vass, cheered on in court and afterwards by Newcastle's 'biggest villains', temporarily allocated the role of anti-authoritarian rebel. In both the Breaks and Docherty narratives readers are textually aligned with the male predators right up until their executions: 'Vass listened intensely to the chaplain reading the Bible to him ... he was visited before his execution for the last time by his tearful family; his mother ... had to be torn away from him' (ibid.). Only at the end is the reader torn away also, joining the crowd who watched Vass hang (ibid.): 'as his body shuddered for a few minutes on the end of the rope a woman shouted, "God forgive him all his sins!"' Only now is the female reader textually positioned with the female witness to Vass's punishment. The reader's only apparent consolation is that she is *still* here, even if Mary Docherty is not. In a culture where randomised male-on-female violence is perceived by women to constitute a real threat, and familial male-on-female violence an actuality, true crime narratives (and other crime narratives such as TV reconstructions) can at least affirm readers' present security and contain the sense of threat (while also, of course, reinforcing the perception of ubiquitous danger). In addition, the construction of women, especially of working-class women, as culpable of their own victimisation, is already naturalised within crime reportage (Radford and Russell 1992; Myers 1997). Overall, true crime fits in neatly with the network of dominant discourses, which aligns women with vulnerability and victimhood. The idea that there has always been violent crime among the working class from men onto women, and that this is the inevitable corollary of class formation (rather than of sedimented gender relations) is embedded in everyday historical consciousness. Its entrenchment is effected in part through stories such as these which, unencumbered as they are with overt political interpretation or even sometimes personal memory, normalise socially conservative explanations of criminal behaviour. Most stories portray a crime-ridden working class in which psychological complexity and even the 'elemental simplicity of class-consciousness' is refused (Steedman 1986: 13). In Walter Benjamin's (1955a: 90) terms they have a 'chaste compactness which precludes psychological analysis' or even, we might add, sociological analysis.

The significance of the image: picturing the past in true crime stories

But these readings of the accounts of the murders of Gladys Appleton, Kitty Breaks and Margaret Docherty are not the whole story. These articles offer the reader much more than a study of their written texts might suggest – for every account is accompanied by drawings, photographs and snippets from police gazettes and new reports. This is notable because aside from the surge of interest in graphic novels, illustrations aimed at adult readers are usually limited to the drawings featured alongside short fiction in women's journals and, of course, in non-fiction forms such as the press, encyclopaedias and popular journals such as *Reader's Digest*. Although these illustrations signal the crime magazine's generic relationship to reportage, they also point to the continuities with far earlier forms of adult literature such as execution sheets, chapbooks and serialised stories. For instance, the Kitty Breaks story is replete with contemporary monochrome illustrations of the period: Blackpool beach, fairground attractions such as the big wheel and the helter-skelter, a Bradford mill, as well as with photographic portraits of Breaks, Holt, the trial judge, defence lawyer and headlines from contemporary newspapers. The photograph's status as evidence and truth underwrites the sensational elements of the story, lending it 'representational legitimacy' (Hamilton 1997: 87). Randomly placed and only tangentially anchored to the narrative, these photographs and scraps of documentation taken together loosely suggest the place and time occupied by Breaks and her murderer and, perhaps, elicit a recognition and sympathetic identification with the victim, which the text itself fails (or does not choose) to invoke. It is likely too that these photographs and their arrangement still bear the traces of a working-class structure of feeling that might appeal to the modern reader. Jeremy Seabrook (1991: 171), writing about domestic and amateur photography, postulates:

> It [photography] certainly helped to reinforce certain kinds of conti-
> nuity and awareness in popular experience; it served to anchor and
> generalise a distinctive working-class sensibility, to affirm a shared
> predicament. At the same time it helped to illuminate some of the
> contradictions of that experience.

Altogether the 'syntax' of these photographs (Barthes 1961: 24) of
Breaks, of Holt, of northern mills and working-class entertainments,
tenuously linked through narrative, speak the predicament of female
working-class vulnerability within a rather vaguely established historical moment. Images of Blackpool in particular present a topos that
itself mobilises discourses of class, of Englishness and of pleasure into
an evocative and even nostalgic configuration of 'popular experience'.
Just as the protagonists are rendered 'familiar' via family photos, so too
locations such as Blackpool are also 'known already' even by those who
have never visited the resort. Yet the poignancy and tension at the
heart of the Breaks story is brought to the fore through photographs
that present Blackpool not only as a site of working-class gratification
and diversion but also as a transitory resort where nobody notices the
sudden absence of Kitty Breaks.

A visualised sense of place then, as epitomised by the liberal use of
photographs (but also maps and drawings), is fundamental to true
crime periodicals. Urban, rural and seaside settings are all far from
idyllic. Period crime stories do not represent the picturesque but the
picaresque, parochial and the popular: high streets, markets, music
halls, servants' quarters, and so on. Region, village, suburb, seaside
hotel, respectable household or slum dwelling are presented as the
topos of the English/Scottish/Welsh people, the source of their
national identity and the location of danger, threat and criminality.
Often there are scenes of degraded public life: 'white slavery' and
prostitution (see above), taverns, mobs and execution crowds, but
they are without the currency or acute social observation of Gilray,
Hogarth or Doré. Photographs born of nineteenth-century fascination with, and surveillance of, the unruly poor are redeployed as the
backdrop to individual stories of criminality. The subjects which
nineteenth-century photography helped to construct appear now to
have always been there. If nostalgia is exhibited, it is not for a golden
age of low-level crime, but for a time when experiences of crime and
punishment were, to all appearances, less complex and conflicted,
when the unruly poor were rendered visible, identifiable and
confinable.

The potency of the image

As already noted (Chapter 3) Richard Hoggart provides some insight into the appeal of what he refers to as 'working-class art'. He notes, for example, the popularity of radio soaps, newspapers and magazines all of which pay close attention to the 'human condition':

> Working class art is essentially a 'showing' (rather than an 'explo-ration'), a presentation of what is known already. It starts from the assumption that human life is fascinating in itself. It ... has to begin with the photographic, however fantastic it may become; it has to be underpinned by ... moral rules. (Hoggart 1957: 94)

Hoggart argues that while the 'ooh-aah' sensationalism of sex or crime is appealing, the fundamental success of such stories is based upon the assumption that 'ordinary life is intrinsically interesting'. This is borne out by advertisements for the True Crime Library which link crime (murder, rape and gangsterism) to picaresque biography in the manner of Daniel Defoe: 'the lives, loves and extraordinary adventures of a host of amazing people will fascinate and excite all who read them' (*MMF* No. 22: 32 undated). True crime is, most often, an entertainment based on 'what is known already'; what is already documented. 'Classic' stories are heavily illustrated, as if to substantiate their version of events but the perceived accessibility for readers of news clippings and photographs also affirms continuity between the text and every-day life. Photographs in this sense enable readers to 'know' the protag-onists. Representative figures such as the 'jealous husband', 'greedy wife', 'master criminal' or 'sex beast' are personalised through the liberal use of family photographs, line drawings, and so on, pointing to links with earlier popular adult literatures such as chapbooks, execu-tions sheets and serialised stories.

It has been shown that the oral tradition of narrating crime through street ballads was not roundly defeated by printed accounts of crime but supplemented. The printed sheet took on the role of *aide-mémoire* to the collective remembering and imagining of scandal, crime and executions (Foucault 1973: 204; Gatrell 1994: 113–19). Hence, as Gatrell (1994: 176) maintains, illustrations undertook an important function, the crude and often stylised woodcuts becoming totemic artefacts linking the reader through 'vernacular images' to the horror of murder and especially the scaffold. The psychic investment engendered by the fear and fascination of crime, but especially of execution, would be symbolised most obviously in the totem of the ideographic gallows, a crude monochrome silhouette that was instantly recognised by every reader. This investment would account for the perennial popularity of ballad sheets whose illustrations were wholly familiar, crude and indeed often inappropriate to the case being chronicled. This argument also pertains to contemporary true crime. The images, albeit crudely drawn or in the case of photographs often only tangentially relevant, are a form of 'vernacular' that is instantly accessible – bearing a stamp of authenticity that is only really available to iconic signification. Thus even when photographs are printed without context, their very status as iconic images, linking the present tenuously with the past, provides readers with points of identification for victims such as Kitty Breaks. Even photographs of unknown criminals or unidentified murder victims feature in true crime magazines, suggesting that the potency of the image stems from something more than the factual knowledge that may or may not support it. For example an advert for a book entitled *Death Row* published in the series *True Crime Library* reproduces the cover photograph of a black man being strapped into the electric chair by three white officials (*MDSS* 1995: 6). The accompanying text invites the reader to 'share' in the last moments of men and women who are sentenced to die:

> Share with the condemned the horrors of the execution chamber, the torture of last minute reprieves. Read the eye-witness accounts of how men and women walked the last mile. Some go with courage, others are half carried whimpering, numb with terror. In one such case a young journalist recalls the night he watched four men die, one after the other, in Alabama's electric chair. 'Anderson shook uncontrollably as they strapped him in ... Anderson's eyes, already wide, dilated in protest as an attendant took off his shoes and tossed them into the pine box ...' '"Have mercy, Lord!" Anderson cried ...'

As it turns out, the photograph below the text is not that of Anderson. Instead it shows an 'unidentified man' and yet, like the gallows ideograms in the earlier ballad sheets, the knowledge that the nameless man was about to face death invites a certain 'psychic investment' in the image. As Walter Benjamin (1955a: 93) indicated, the subject who is about to meet death must be a figure of general fascination:

> Just as a sequence of images is set in motion inside a man as his life comes to an end – unfolding the views of himself under which he

has encountered himself without being aware of it – suddenly in his expressions and looks the unforgettable emerges and imparts to everything that concerned him that authority which even the poorest wretch in dying possesses for the living around him. This authority is at the very source of the story.

Images such as that of criminals facing execution invite readers to 'apply to them the perceptual schemes of their own ethos' which produces 'a bracketing of form in favour of "human" content' (Bourdieu 1984: 44). In this sense the photographs are used here to back up the textual exploration of what it is to be 'human' and its transitory nature. The account of Anderson's execution concludes: 'His hair sparked and sizzled with bluish flame for an instant. Then the humming sound stopped ... and he slumped back into the chair, no longer a man but a body' (*MDSS* 1995: 6). The photograph appears to represent the instant, to render visible the fleeting moment when life leaves the body, when the human evaporates. The interpretation of these photographs requires knowledge that is easily accessed by readers, knowledge rooted in the everyday skills of reading the human face, the signification of clothing and of body language. Moreover with photographs the 'narratives nearly always fall within the competence of women [who are] the custodians of human feelings' (Seabrook 1991: 172) and who are also quite often the readers of true crime magazines.

But more than this, the materiality of photographs arguably has the stamp of mortality upon them. Photographs used to illustrate the still notorious murder of Fanny Adams in the 1830s are exemplary (*TCSS* 1996: 2–8). A full-page sepia-tinted photograph of a little girl and her family hop-picking in Hampshire is superscribed with gothic lettering which advertises the horrible story to follow:

> THE HORRIBLE DEATH OF SWEET FANNY ADAMS. She was eight years old and playing with friends in a meadow when a man picked her up and carried her into a wood. What followed was the night-mare every mother dreads ...

Its presentation is reminiscent of a nineteenth-century theatre poster, signifying an aesthetic usually associated with the exaggerated gestures and heightened emotion of Victorian melodrama. The partial oblitera-tion of the image by the text anticipates the destruction of the family through the assault, murder and dismemberment of the little girl. In a double-movement, it both anticipates and fixes the fatal event within the photographic moment. Here 'photography is a kind of primitive theatre, a kind of *Tableau Vivant*, a figuration of the motionless and made-up face beneath which we see the dead' (Barthes 1980: 32).[8] Barthes (ibid.: 95) contends that the photograph precariously links three points in time: the moment when the photograph is taken, the point at which the subjects of the photographs die and the point at which the viewer looks at the image. The poignancy of the photograph is due to its imbrication with mortality, the viewer looks at the subject and knows both that 'he is dead and he is going to die'. Even a photograph of a stranger from another century speaks to the viewer of his or her own inevitable mortality. Examining an 1865 photographic portrait of a young murderer awaiting execution Barthes comments grimly: 'I observe with horror an anterior future of which the stake is death' (ibid.: 96).

Story-telling and recollection

It could be argued that the traces of archaic genres of story-telling, including ballads and execution sheets, are still extant in the ostensibly uncomplicated forms of the modern printed true crime story. The persistence of these traces or residues does not suggest that story-telling continues as Walter Benjamin understood it. It might be the case that contemporary true crime stories draw upon, or else mimic, oral forms, thereby producing *faux* story-telling that fails to communicate real experience, but is still a mode that none the less speaks powerfully to the reader. The examples discussed in this chapter suggest that the appeal of period true crime narratives is part and parcel of a broader experience of story-telling and its reception through the magazine in its entirety. The deployment in these texts of vernacular, punning and grimly humorous asides all point to this generic relationship with an oral tradition of popular entertainment, as well as with the popular press. Vestiges of spoken story-telling are invoked through a number of tropes, several of which are particular to period true crime narratives. A number of stories are introduced in a manner that suggests that the writer is not simply reporting a story but is actually recollecting the events related to the reader. For example, 'John Cupples recalls ... BIRMINGHAM'S MOON MURDERER' (*TCDM* December 1993: 24–5).[9] This strategy presents the tale as occurring within living memory even though this is often clearly impossible and contrives an intimacy between writer and reader. These 'recollections' seek to establish an experiential and cognitive connection between readers' contemporary experience and perception of crime and criminality and the everyday experiences of crime within earlier eras. Crime and the popular memory of crime are manufactured as a constant and perceptible connection between the present and the 'past'. The cursory social commentary provided to contextualise stories poaches 'human interest' social history. One editor makes the ambitious claim that: 'stories ... hail from a diversity of times and places, allowing the serious reader to plot a chart in social history, from the criminologist's point of view' (*MDSS* 1995: 4). Yet oddly, basic information such as the date of the event, which is needed to orientate the reader in time, is often withheld for pages. Like fairy tales these narratives seem to have occurred 'once upon a time'.

Although the writer of the true crime story may be constructed through the trope of 'recollection' as the story-teller and point of authority for the reader, nothing else is known about him/her and often articles are given no by-line whatsoever. Paradoxically this seems to present 'experience without a subject' (Jay 1993). For this reason there is no sense that the true crime story is told, like the novel, through the voice of a single person who confides in his/her audience even though a preferred reading is clearly presented (Barthes 1968: 143). The absence of a distinct authorial voice signals the non-canonical status of periodical true crime stories. The provision of narrative coherence through characterisation and 'enplotment' rather than through 'referential information and logic' links true crime to fictional modes of storytelling even more closely than to journalism (Dalgren, in Storey 1996: 75). The use of stock characters (e.g. 'the beast', 'the upper-class villain', the 'weak husband' and 'innocent victim') in particular recalls the transmission of fairy tales and folklore, for: 'there is nothing that commends a story to memory more effectively than that chaste compactness which precludes psychological analysis' (Benjamin 1955a: 90).

The relatively stable codes and conventions of a formulaic narrative also signal its relationship to older forms. Umberto Eco (1990: 83) maintains that the pleasurable repetition of an already known pattern 'connotes an entertainment originating not from high art or from industry but from the crafts that preceded industrialisation'. Sold as 'stranger than fiction cases' (*MMF* No. 23, cover) these narratives are promoted as 'good value' *entertainment* with tag-lines such as '15 full-length cases, hours of reading' (*TDSS* 1995). True crime is also promoted as a more traditional, less mechanised way to 'pass time', suggesting a return to an older system of values and the pre-broadcast-ing forms of leisure that fostered them. An advert for Forum Press true crime books, including titles such as *Diary of a Hangman* and *From Wall Street to Newgate* (*MMF* No. 23 undated) states: 'Telly's on the blink, the cat's purring on your knee and you have all these books to read. Are you in heaven? No, you're in *True Crime Library* – the most satisfying entertainment around.' 'Satisfaction' is the avowed aim of the true crime magazine, it claims not only to fill spare time, but also to fulfil it. Promotions such as '*Big* Summer specials'; '*full-length* cases'; '*Extra* True Crime Stories in a 30-Page *Supplement*' (*TCDM* October 1994: 50, my emphases) and images of a cosy, book-lined study with true crime magazines lying open on the desk abound. A photograph of one 'satisfied' reader enjoying the magazine, sprawling alone in his hotel room while on holiday, is even published on the correspondence page of *Master Detective* (December 1995: 29). The promotional discourse of these magazines suggests that the experience of reading true crime is one of enrichment and plenitude; it is framed within discourses of consumption and popular pleasure, of effortless reading and easily gained gratification. In this portrait of literary consumption the reader seems to be an isolated figure, one of many readers individually consuming a mass-produced commodity – the very opposite of the story-telling experience. Like the reader of the novel described by Benjamin (1955a: 99) she/he apparently 'swallows up the material as the fire devours logs in the fireplace', to which he adds disparagingly, 'it is a dry material on which the burning interest of the reader feeds'.

It seems that the aspects of early true crime literature that made them meaningful for contemporary readers are still present in the stories discussed above, albeit to a far lesser degree. The use of vernacular, the depiction of people 'below the level of power', the 'clash' between the criminal and the law are all present. To borrow Patrick Wright's distinction, these stories recall the 'past' rather than 'history' and as such they draw upon the techniques of oral and written story-telling, the myths of popular memory and a vernacular idiom which addresses ordinary people (Wright 1985: 142–3). Yet here the 'past' is repackaged for modern-day readers: the manufacture of 'recollections' of crime, the mimicry of oral story forms and the fostering of 'human interest' rather than collective experience builds the bridge that spans the divide between readers and the protagonists of period true crime. Generally speaking then, these stories gloss the past, commodify it, abstracting history and/or reducing it to exemplary figures. Through these operations the treatment of period cases arguably reiterates the view of crime and punishment as rooted in individual and isolated acts of personal responsibility and culpability. But in stark contrast to the heritage culture that has swelled into entertainment and spectacle since the 1980s – where history is extracted from a 'denigrated every-day life' and fashioned into a notable event – here it is the denigrated and the lowly that finds a place within the discrete borders of throw-away magazine culture (Wright 1985: 69).

6
Daring to Know: Looking at the Body in the New True Crime Magazine

True crime as esoteric knowledge

As we have seen, true crime literature has been defended and promoted on the grounds that the genre has something unique to say about the shared condition of being human. The appeal of true crime books has been informed by reflexive questions: 'Do I have the potential for this evil in me too?' Or, are we all murderers 'under the skin?' (Pitman 1961: 50). As seen in the previous chapter, the appeal of even the most ephemeral journalistic accounts of crime is grounded in 'human interest', in stories and images of ordinary people in extraordinary circumstances, either meeting death through murder or capital punishment or meting out death to others. Explicit connections are made between the experiences of readers and the subjects of true crime. Often these stories ask readers directly what they would do in particular circumstances or they connect past crimes with contemporary fears. In this most general sense, then, true crime, like many other narrative forms, aims to speak of the human condition.

Most specifically, however, all true crime murder narratives also hold the promise, to a greater or lesser degree, of the revelation of a more esoteric knowledge. As thanatopses they provide a space to address, without flinching, the idea of mortality and its implications of finitude and decay. True crime asks bizarre and socially unacceptable questions on behalf of the reader. It aims to explain, for example, what the criminal thinks or feels before his/her execution; how long the brain functions after decapitation; how the corpse decays and the kinds of clues revealed in its decomposition. True crime biography in particular, as a 'study of mankind', undertakes an explicitly ontological investigation, exploring the substance of what it is to 'be' through the pursuit of questions of individual psychology, motivation, culpability and victi-mology.[1] Its pursuit of 'human nature stained' is intended by its authors to reveal something about human nature in general and in the particular. In this sense true crime promotes itself as inquiring and *instructive*. As noted in Chapter 2, its pedagogical function was at its most explicit in the religious injunctions that accompanied early true accounts of crime and punishment. While concepts of evil and of a fall from grace still hover at the margins of true crime, modern authors, especially of 'quality' criminal biographies and case studies, frequently invoke educational objectives that stem from secular, usually pseudo-scientific or philosophical discourses.[2] This has already been illustrated in an earlier discussion of true crime authors' recourse to Pope's *Essay on Man* and the assertion that 'the proper study of mankind is man' as justification for writing about the more macabre details of murder and atrocity (see Chapter 2). Moreover, authors make much of the connec-tion between their own work and the more prestigious work of those in the medical profession, implying that the nature of their enterprise requires an amnesty from the strictures of good taste and discretion. Hence the writer often presents his/her role as analogous with that of the qualified clinician. Emlyn Williams (1967: vii), author of the groundbreaking book about the Moors Murderers, writes: 'For me, just as no physical aberration can ever be too extraordinary to interest the medical scientist, so no psychological phenomena can be forbidden to the serious and dispassionate writer.' Similarly, in the introduction to his collection of articles on murder, Brian Masters defends his interest in and illustration of murder by invoking the objectivity and detach-ment of medical inquiry:

> *Medicine, Science and the Law, The Journal of Clinical Psychopathy* … contain essays and studies which set out precisely to examine the gruesome results of compulsive murder … [they] also have pho-tographs of the victims of attack which would never be allowed in a more generally available publication. (Masters 1994: 12)

The medical and corporeal metaphors and analogies used to explain the function and fascination of up-market true crime biography suggest introspection, emphasising that these enquiries into murder and atrocity are not focused on the social or the collective but rather upon the interior realms of mind and body. The true crime writer's aim to 'enter the mind of the murderer'; to be skilful in 'worming his way into the darkest places in the human psyche' (Masters 1993: cover notes) and to unpack the similarity of criminal subject and moral subject 'beneath the skin' is predicated upon the idea that the cause and meaning of criminality, violence and homicide resides within the individual subject. While the new-style magazines maintain a stronger emphasis on the body and its indices than up-market biographies that strive to access the mind of the murderer, both forms look to medical science as the paradigm of good practice.

The latest true crime magazines to enter the market particularly reinforce the presumption that questions of violent criminality and its effects must be inwardly directed, a look into the mind of the criminal and the body of his/her victim. In this sense, they constitute a distinct difference from the publications discussed in the last chapter where criminal psychology and forensic science are both notable by their absence. The new magazines, like the more up-market criminal biographers, appropriate the privileges of the clinician or the scientist that permit the pursuit of knowledge together with a relentlessly enquiring gaze, sanctioning the textual and pictorial display of the opened or decaying body, of blood-stained weapons and forensic X-rays. This penultimate chapter addresses the collect-and-keep partwork magazine, focusing on the ways in which it orders knowledge about violent crime and its aftermath. These publications are different by virtue of their adoption of a more authoritative voice, of the approved discourses of police and forensic science and of the systems of knowledge and representation common to culturally privileged forms such as the encyclopaedia, the dictionary and the textbook. The *apparently* logical and positivist presentation and ordering of knowledge evident in these periodicals permits the reader to scrutinise and think through the mortality of the body and its ontological implications, albeit in a highly limited and controlled way. Their appearance and popularity is the logical result of the shift in the spectacle of real-life crime from a scrutiny of the body of the criminal to the body of the victim.

The body of the criminal and the body of the victim

Towards the end of the eighteenth-century physicians had begun to observe morbid phenomena and to diagnose from concrete observations rather than abstract speculation, signalling the emergence of modern anatomical-clinical medicine (Foucault 1963; Gay 1973). There was a new emphasis upon the dissected body, changes in nosology and a shift in the very style of medical discourses from decipherment to description. The change in medical discourse was itself part of a broader configuration that included the professionalisation of medicine and the elevation of its status and a change in attitude towards health, leading to growing public provision of economic and medical care (Cousins and Hussain 1984: 144). A growing conviction that medical science would produce new knowledge and concomitant technological advances underwrote the desire for longevity and good health. Moreover, the health of the individual was linked to the health of the social body, leading to 'the imperative of health: at once the duty of each and the objective of all' (Foucault 1976a: 170). This new emphasis upon the health of the individual as a vital component to the smooth running of the nation also signalled a shift in power relations and in the procedures of the law:

> Power would no longer be dealing simply with legal subjects over whom the ultimate dominion was death, but with living beings, and the mastery it would be able to exercise over them would have to be applied at the level of life itself; it was the taking charge of life, more than the threat of death, that gave power its access even to the body. (Foucault 1976b: 142–3)

The growing perception that the function of power was to administer and order life rendered capital punishment a 'scandal and a contradiction' unless the monstrosity of the criminal as recidivist and social threat could be invoked. It was only in this last event that 'one had the right to kill those who represented a kind of biological danger to others' (ibid.: 138). The growing tension, still evident in true crime, between the law as the engine of retributive justice and as the guardian of life and liberty displayed itself in a somewhat contorted picture of the criminal body and its uses. If the criminal was going to be punished, to be the subject of legal violence, then perhaps this might be doubly justified if the punishment is also used to benefit medicine and so enhance life. Reason itself dictated that the body of the criminal, either living or dead, should be made available to medical experimentation. Diderot suggested that a judicious assessment of the alternatives would surely convince the convict to submit (in Arasse 1989: 3):

> Who, rather than undergo execution, would not submit themselves to the injection of liquids into their blood. ... Who would not allow their thigh to be amputated at the joint; or their spleen to be removed; or some portion of their brain to be extracted ...?

Here the discourses of medicine and retributive justice intersect, high-lighting the centrality of the body to the transition from an older para-digm of judicial power to a new one of 'bio-power', 'a power whose highest function was perhaps no longer to kill, but to invest life through and through' (Foucault 1976b: 139; see also Rose, N. 1989). Eventually execution, even as last resort, was removed and the body of the criminal had to be maintained within the penal system where it disappears from public view.[3] The last public execution in Britain took place outside Newgate on 26 May 1868 rendering the penal system finally and completely private (Emsley 1987: 279). By 1965, capital punishment was, to all intents and purposes, abolished. By this period the penal system, in theory at least, was grounded in a philosophy of directing and shaping the offender's life: 'the purpose of the training and treatment of convicted prisoners shall be to encourage and assist them to lead a good and useful life' (Rawlings 1999: 144).

The state's power is always underpinned ultimately with reference to the 'sword' because armed response is still the final prerogative of law enforcers and the military. Yet as a consequence of the sequestra-tion of the convicted prisoner from the public arena the modern citizen has little sense of the law's physical power and authority over the individual. Also, while there is a general perception that the role of the police force is the proactive pursuit and prosecution of crimi-nals, its primary function is, in fact, a more general one of the mainte-nance of order (Reiner 1992: 212). The disjunction in particular between the media mystification of policing as aggressive law enforce-ment and the police's actual, far more diffused role, can produce a general dissatisfaction and scepticism that the criminal is allowed 'to get off lightly' rather than be visibly punished. As Leon Radzinowicz (1977: 147) has commented:

> It would be wrong to underestimate the hold capital punishment retains upon the public imagination. It is still seen as an indispens-able adjunct to the maintenance of law and order and it offers to satisfy the deeply felt need for retribution and expiation in relation to certain atrocious crimes.

Today it is only through press and television reportage that the specta-cle of the infamous criminal is still made available to the general public. Even then only court illustrators, not photographers, are per-mitted to portray the trial appearances of criminals in England. The opprobrium heaped on criminals outside the courtroom by onlookers, and in the press after they have been sentenced and reporting restrictions have been waived, is the final trace of a public ritual that played out the clash between the law and the outlaw.[4] Now power has to 'qualify, measure, appraise, and hierarchise, rather than display itself in murderous splendour' upon the body of the criminal (Foucault 1976b: 144) leaving the moral subject with only a fantasy of corporal punishment and Old Testament justice. These fantasies most certainly do exist, although the public outlets for their expression might be few or repressed. For example, the true crime author James Neff (1988) tells how a group of rape survivors gathered for a party after the American rapist Ronnie Shelton was sentenced to life imprisonment. A life-size cardboard cut-out of the man hung in the apartment of one of the women (Marian), which they attacked and taunted before setting it alight in the garden:

> As the flames shot up, Marian and her friends danced around the burning effigy, chanting, 'Burn, Ronnie, burn! Burn, Ronnie, burn!' Marian ran back inside and came out holding a gun high, and the crowd cheered. She moved in close and shot the Shelton figure through the crotch, and everybody howled. (Neff 1988: 338)

This impromptu symbolic revenge is all the more pointed since Shelton was actually sentenced to 3,198 years imprisonment, an impossible sentence that seems to reveal the limits of a law that cannot or will not resort to capital punishment. The conspicuous absence of state-sanctioned violence against the criminal body leaves a gap that for survivors, their families and the general public is liable to be filled with symbolic action or fantasies of revenge. For example, a victim of Peter Sutcliffe (known as the Yorkshire Ripper) recalls:

> Somebody has suggested putting him in a room and throwing away the key. Another person, who I was very surprised at, a doctor, suggested removing both his eyes and giving them to somebody who needs them, taking away his kidneys for somebody who needs them, cutting his vocal cords and putting electrodes to his head. (Burn 1984: 359)

Without the final sanction of death by the state the only remaining option seems to be a Poe-like fantasy of immurement, of 'throwing away the key'. The doctor's fantasy of justice puts a modern spin on the equitable judicial arrangement of an eye for an eye. It is in the discourse of revenge that the potential alliance of violent retribution with medical progress, each one legitimising the other, is still to be found.[5]

In real life, however, the body of the criminal has faded from public view, removed from the public scaffold to the privacy of the prison and prison hospital. Hence the spectacle of public punishment, which situated the criminal body at the centre of true crime, has all but disappeared from the new true crime whose interest lies in forensics and pathology.[6] The preceding chapter showed how traditional magazines continue to draw on period stories and cases from the US, which offer the reader the privatised spectacle of capital punishment, of hangings and the electric chair. The new true crime magazine, however, concentrates on a broader range of recent cases where capital punishment is less likely to have occurred (i.e. post-capital punishment cases and cases outside the US). Whereas the body of the criminal was in various ways constituted as a visible sign of the crime that he/she had committed now interest has turned to the victim's body as evidence of the atrocity of crime. As a consequence, the corpse is more important than ever as the sign and site of violent crime, not only to be looked at in police scene-of-crime photographs but also now increasingly in post-mortem examination. This displacement of attention is also part of a process of 'interiorisation' of the public gaze, a refocusing away from public criminality to the hidden secrets of the body of the victim.

Science and the body in *Real-Life Crimes* magazine

The most obvious difference in terms of content between the long-established true crime monthlies and the newer collect-and-keep partworks such as *Murder in Mind* (launched 1996) and *Real-Life Crimes … and how they were solved*[7] (launched 1993) is the latter's privileging of science and technology as the motor of criminal detection. Each issue of the weekly publication *Real-Life Crimes* is approximately 50 pages long and heavily illustrated with higher production values than the more traditional true crime monthlies. Like *Murder in Mind*, the quality of the paper, reproduction of photographs, abundance of coloured graphics and maps all signal the magazine's affinity with other culturally respectable partwork magazines that are aimed at the autodidact and hobbyist. Colour-coded indexes and the pseudo-scientific categorisation of topics underlines the seriousness of the magazine's presentation as a conduit of knowledge and self-instruction. The contents are divided into the following categories: 'Crime Case Study', 'The Investigators', 'Forensic Mysteries', 'Mind of Evil' and 'Incriminating Evidence'.

The periodical uses a variety of representational models to deliver information and stories. A variety of insets, drawings, photographs and maps punctuate the text and divert the eye from pursuing a more conventional linear pattern of reading. Thus the reader is offered not only a literary account of the crime but also a constellation of duplicate and supplementary information which both surrounds and/or punctuates it. So too the reader is at leisure to move from image to text or to dwell on particular photographic moments. In this way the magazine's display of photographs and graphics helps constitute the reader as 'the master of the look' who chooses how long to spend studying or glancing at an image. The construction of this magazine allows the reader to browse, yet it maintains an air of instruction and useful learning through its organisation and labelling of knowledge. Photographic sequences, probably taken from forensic or police manuals, are used liberally to illustrate different modes of death (e.g. poisonings, strangulation) or indices of time of death (e.g. post-mortem body changes). The attention to detail is far more rigorous here than in the traditional monthlies and more strongly embedded in the discourses of scientific knowledge.

The section entitled 'Crime case studies' is straightforward enough, offering a conventional (in true crime terms) presentation of the crime story. For example 'The Bamber Family Murders' (*R-L C* Issue 2: 31–9) case study contains within it a full-length account of Jeremy Bamber, who shot his parents, his sister and her twin children at home on their farm in Essex in 1988. This story is tightly structured through relations of cause and effect, clue and revelation. It sets out in a logical manner the crime and its aftermath, moving from the 'horrific scene' of the murder, Bamber's exhibition of 'high living' after the death of his family, the 'first doubts' of family and friends about his innocence and finally his arrest. The teleological momentum of the narrative is in part due to the requirement to tell a tale within the codes and conventions of a simple realist narrative formula. These stories sacrifice the random, the contingent and the unexplained to the objective of producing a clear account in which no detail is insignificant to the plot. This emphasis on linear development may also be visually represented in the chronological run of snapshots of murder victims (Issue 10: 213) or the numbered images of witnesses (Issue 27: 591).

Less conventional, perhaps, is the sequencing of significant moments of the story in the manner of a strip cartoon that often accompanies the main story. For example Issue 10 (pp. 207–19) devotes its case study to the American serial killer Ted Bundy who kidnapped, attacked and killed countless women up until the late 1970s. A short account of

Carole DaRonch, the only woman to escape a kidnap attempt by Bundy, is reiterated beneath, with a black-and-white graphic sequence spanning two pages (ibid.: 208–9). The six moments provide snapshots of the significant points of the encounter from Bundy's initial approach to the woman, made by impersonating a police officer, to LaRonch's escape with her attacker in pursuit. These frozen reconstructed moments of graphic illustration are strongly reminiscent of the sketches that accompanied crime journalism in the periodicals of the nineteenth century, providing a visual counterpart to the written text. They also contribute to a general sense of abundance of material for the reader, reiterating and complementing the narrative rather than supplementing it in any way.

Most of the cases in *Real-Life Crimes* are related with a high level of redundancy, with various inset boxes and strip cartoons layering on differently framed versions of the same events. This strategy may be read in several different ways. As already noted, they offer a certain graphic pleasure, allowing digressions from a simple linear account of the case. This excessiveness, however, also pinpoints the problem of affect, the inability of true crime literature to convey the power and feeling of unprecedented criminal behaviour. The Bundy cartoon should grip the viewer since it represents, like the slasher movie, that rare moment when the woman escapes the killer. Yet the sequence seems only to underline the cognitive distance between reader and criminal event, the impossibility of being sutured into the crime scene in the way that a good horror film can involve the spectator in an irresistible identification. Finally, it is also possible that the repetition of information acts as a kind of compensation or cover for what cannot be shown or said directly. It is striking that these illustrations rarely show the moment when atrocity occurs. In one attack Ted Bundy bit his victim on the buttocks and breasts. The crime case study includes a special feature (ibid.: 214–15) explaining how the bite marks were matched with Bundy's own teeth. Included in the illustrations are post-mortem photographs, one of a bite on the victim's rear being measured with a ruler and another close-up of the bite itself. Three other photographs show X-rays and a close-up of Bundy's mouth. Yet none of the drawn illustrations attempts to portray this or any other explicitly sadistic incident – it is clearly unrepresentable. The true crime magazine's claim to educate and inform reaches its limit at the point where it encounters the forbidden scene, the moment of criminal violence that must remain just out of reach of pictorial representation. Instead it offers the reader multiple routes into and out of the

moment when the crime occurred, a variety of 'before and after' scenarios that compensate for never quite arriving at the crime itself.

The emphasis, in the Bundy story, on looking at the victim's wounds
signals the way in which the body can be read as clue in true crime. The
most distinctive feature of *Real-Life Crimes* is its adoption of scientific
discourses and its emphasis upon the body as an object of scientific
inquiry. The allocation of scientific features to certain categories is
somewhat arbitrary; for example in Issue 2, features on time of death
and rigor mortis placed under 'The Investigators', could just as easily
have appeared under 'Forensic Mysteries'. The section on 'The
Investigators' focuses on pathologists and forensic experts rather than
the police, signalling the usurpation of detection by science in the
popular imagination.[8] It also, however, underwrites the authority of the
law, emphasising how its progressive commitment to science and technology bolsters the work of the law's executives. In these magazines
stories of crime are also often stories about the body and its place as an
object of knowledge in the science of detection. Titles featured in *Real-
Life Crimes* such as 'The Exploded Body' (Issue 15: 330–3), 'The
Headless, Handless Corpse' (Issue 21: 460–3), 'What Sex is Your
Skeleton?' (Issue 12: 270–1) and 'Blood, Sweat and Tears' (Issue 17:
370–3) are indicative of the centrality of the (victim's) body and bodily
fluids to the new true crime.[9] These stories demonstrate the mastery of
science over the body and its mechanisms; if murderers have the power
to destroy the body (to explode it, decapitate it, dismember it, and so
on) it is scientists who have the power to decode its remains and reconstruct its story. The story of science, then, is also the story of progress,
for while a putatively unchanging human nature ensures that murders
will always happen, science at least can solve the crime and discover the
perpetrator. It now seems that the tiniest clue can no longer escape the
attention of the scientific detective. One article notes:

> The subtlety of the test available for the determination of blood
> constituents – not only in the blood, but equally in sweat, semen,
> urine and even, some researchers believe, in the tooth pulp – is now
> so great that the medical examiner for New York has claimed that
> he can distinguish between the blood of his twin daughters by the
> different antibodies present following their various childhood ail-
> ments. (*R-L C* Issue 17: 373)

This features microscopic photography which allows the reader to
examine biological phenomena invisible to the naked eye, foreground-

ing the increasing internalisation and medicalisation of criminal detection. The role of photography is of course crucial here, paradoxically demystifying the human body by reducing it to its smallest chemical components and also making it vivid and extraordinary. As Walter Benjamin (1931: 243–4) notes in 'A Short History of Photography':

> Details of structure, cellular tissue, with which technology and medicine are normally concerned – all this is in origins more native to the camera than the atmospheric landscape or the soulful portrait. Yet at the same time photography reveals in this material the physiognomic aspects of visual worlds which dwell in the smallest things, meaningful yet covert enough to find a hiding place in waking dreams, but which, enlarged and capable of formulation, make the difference between technology and magic visible as a thoroughly historical variable.

These images reveal the relationship between the microscopic world and the wider world of bodies, a material world subject to empirical analysis. Yet these images also remain strange and unclear. As Benjamin noted, to the lay reader the objects of microscopic photography can only be read through their resemblance to knowable things, they look like eggs, snakes, branches, and so on. These images would seem magical if an expert did not explain their 'true' meaning and value to the processes of criminal detection. Scene-of-crime pictures, microscopic photography and medical textbook illustrations, together with the scientific discourses that frame them, call to mind the medical encyclopædia which is both instructive and visually fascinating. For example, a four page feature entitled 'Time of Death' (*R-L C* Issue 2: 40–3) deploys a variety of codes and conventions which break down and classify scientific knowledge of post-mortem body changes. Photographs include a rear view of a supine murder victim, a pathologist discovering a skeleton (both Issue 2: 40), a post-mortem photograph showing skin discoloration (ibid.: 43) and a sequence of four smaller photographs illustrating the stages of body decomposition from hours to years (ibid.: 42–3). These divisions operate at a basic level within a positivist paradigm of understanding of the natural world, their specificity foreclosing more broadly abstract or metaphysical enquiries. The natural world, which includes the corpse returning to a state of nature, is required to yield up its answers to reason. The answers (meanings or clues) discovered there are then compartmentalised into the containing boxes and sequences that form satellites around the main story-line. This 'Time of Death' feature, like many others in the series, clearly locates the body as the central object of legal-scientific inquiry. Here the body can be read like a book. The body of the victim (and sometimes of the murderer) is presented and read like the natural phenomenon that it is.[10] Its condition (temperature, weight, position, damage sustained), its fluids (blood, semen, mucus), its surface (skin, hair, fingerprints) and its mutations (rigor, corruption) all contribute, in the discourse of forensic science, to its demonstrable legibility. One monochrome photograph shows a male corpse supported only by two trestles (without a connecting plank) proving the point that profound rigor 'will leave a body as stiff as a board' (Issue 2: 40). Beneath the picture, text of approximately 200 words chronicles the relationship between body chemistry, time and temperature. The picture is morbidly entertaining, a conjuring trick-cum-medical lecture that hints at the more covert pleasures of the new true crime, at its licit display of biological conundrums, corporeal anomalies and physical horrors.

The victim's body as horror-spectacle

Sometimes the study of the body as a natural phenomenon, as in the above example, tips into its opposite – a spectacle of the body that looks anything but natural. The incongruities of the damaged body can appear quite ludicrous despite the straight-faced prose that anchors them. A feature on the 1935 case of Buck Ruxton, a doctor who murdered and dismembered his wife and maid, notes that more significant than the shocking nature of the murders is that the case represents 'one of the earliest major triumphs of medical detection' (*R-L C* Issue 5: 114–18). A sub-feature entitled 'Do the Shoes Fit?' contains photographs of two severed feet, and two photographs of shoes with the feet in them. The bizarre image of these two left feet, upright, be-stockinged but *sans* their bodies, and lodged firmly in their shoes resembles nothing more than a still from a Méliès film, representing the second, perhaps, before their owners hop back to collect them. The prose works hard to recuperate the moment for science, but is closer to grim fairytale than pathology report:

A useful confirmation of the two bodies' identities was to see if the feet of the two bodies fitted shoes that had belonged to the suspected victims. The left foot of each body was dried and powdered, inserted into a stocking, and tried in each shoe. The foot of 'Body No. 1' was

much too small for Mrs. Ruxton's shoe, but fitted the other shoe perfectly; 'Body No. 2's' foot would not fit into Mary Rogerson's shoe
but seemed to fit the other very well. (*R-L C* Issue 5: 118)

I use the word 'moment' advisedly here, for this static image smacks of
the 'exhibitionist' moments of the early 'cinema of attractions' rather
than of an extended, closeted voyeurism (Gunning 1989 and 1990). It
produces an uncanny story of dismemberment, of ghostly bodies and
animated objects. As in the film *Boxing Helena* (Lynch 1993 USA) no
matter how reduced and truncated, the body insists on 'speaking'
mockingly to its audience.

In general, however, the exhibition of body parts is more clinical
than bizarre, although no less disconcerting for all that. The 'Time of
Death' feature mentioned above also contains a four-picture sequence
depicting the long-term decomposition of cadavers. This compartmen-
talises the body in order to close in on important details: a suicide's
hand still grasping a blunt cutlery knife, a torso displaying 'marbled'
skin discoloration, a hand in the process of mummification and, last in
the sequence, the upper body of skeletal remains. Read as a whole
these images seal off and abstract a particular moment in time,
showing body decomposition after hours, days, months and years. The
reading of each photograph is partially determined by a brief commentary on the processes of decomposition and role of the body as object
of evidence. A longer essay that essentially repeats the information
housed in the boxes tops these images. In this description, however,
the mutation of the body through putrefaction is freed from the stasis
of two-dimensional representation by a present tense description. So
when discussing the early signs of decomposition:

> The first signs generally appear in the skin of the lower right
> abdomen, as bacteria from the gut begin to decompose the haemo-
> globin of the blood into greenish compounds. Then the body begins
> to swell as gas forms in the tissues. The veins on the thighs and
> shoulders become outlined in red or green as bacteria grow in them.
> ... Eventually the skin blisters and peels off. The gas in the body
> causes the tongue and eyes to protrude ... (Issue 2: 42)

And so on. The new true crime demonstrates, like the horror film, that
the condition of being dead is not final and unchanging, but a continuing biological process of change, decay and disintegration; a process
usually rendered invisible by the removal of the deceased soon after

death. The bulging tongue and eyes signal the horror-comic potential of the revolting autonomous human body, taping into the lewdness, aggression and mockery historically displayed by gargoyles and fools (see Paul 1994: 353ff; Warner 1998: 240–5).

The true crime magazine describes the on-going destruction of the dead body in the kind of detail that it would never use to describe the violence inflicted by the criminal on the living body. This description of a drowned body is typical:

> When a body is recovered after a period of immersion, there are no external signs to distinguish whether it was alive or dead at the time it entered the water. The skin will be 'goosey', and the feet and hands sodden and wrinkled – the so-called 'washerwoman's hands', After about two weeks the skin loosens from the hands and feet, and in three to four weeks the entire skin may come away from the hands like a glove. (*R-L C* Issue 10: 223)

In both these examples the corpse takes on a new form of animation, the protruding tongue and eyes, the loosening skin connoting the offensiveness of the monstrous undead. This story of the physiological changes after death, accelerated for the reader, also calls up that disconcerting idea of the body displaying itself for the instruction of the viewer in Renaissance medical texts. Thomas Laqueur (1990: 77) describes how anatomical drawings portrayed figures holding open their flesh for 'our viewing convenience'. He notes (ibid.: 75) that these were 'advertisements for their own truth', a visual certification of the scientist's knowledge.

One of the most important elements in the presentation of knowledge is the visual image, the magazine taking a 'strong pictorial approach' to its subject matter (loose section Issue 1). A central pleasure here is that of looking and of looking at a range of images relocated within an entirely new and somewhat disconcerting frame of reference. In her discussion of the 'public taste for reality' in nineteenth-century Paris Vanessa Schwartz (1994: 87) demonstrates the centrality of vision, of 'the mobilised gaze' to leisure, entertainment and the new amusements. The taste for what she calls 'the realism of spectacle' manifested itself in the popularity of visiting the Morgue's exhibition room, where the identification of bodies was turned into a free show for the public. Here people could see, rather than simply read about, the *faits divers*, all kinds of horrible and sensational accidents and crimes (ibid.: 90). Crowds were even keener when the press reported that the case was unsolved and that a real-life murder mystery was at hand. The theatricality of the scene licensed curiosity and a frank unabashed gaze at the corpse. The bodies were not simply laid out, as for an autopsy, but packaged and displayed. For example a four-year-old girl who, it turned out later, had died of natural causes was dressed and seated in a little chair to be looked at by visitors. But as Schwartz (ibid.: 93) also indicates, this entertainment was not simply about looking at the dead. While this certainly was its unique quality as entertainment, the exhibition was also part of a broader 'catalogue of curiosities', 'of things to see' such as the Eiffel Tower, waxwork tableaux, panoramas, and so on. These shows, whether of corpses or waxworks, were not simply looked at as isolated, frozen moments or things, but as still points in a longer narrative of crime and sensation. It is only in this sense, as a collection of 'curiosities' and sensations rather than facts, that the organisation of knowledge in true crime magazines 'makes sense'. Certainly the murder casebook presents its knowledges coherently – as 'things relevant to the crime' – but they are contained within a schema that allows for the sensational, the diverse and the unpredictable and just as importantly its liberal visual representation.

Both the visual and written detail in the new true crime magazine operates as a kind of theatrical anatomical display and nothing might seem less erotic than this morbid exhibition. Yet 'disgust always bears the imprint of desire' (Stallybrass and White 1986: 191), causing the reader to glance away only to return for a second look. This emphasis upon the body in true crime is analogous to the visual aesthetic of pornography, reducing the body to a fleshy object that invites a sadistic gaze. Pornography, like true crime, is devoted to 'propriety violations of every shape, manner, and form' (Kipnis 1998: 157). As the images and verbal descriptions of the bite marks caused by Ted Bundy on his victim's body illustrate, true crime too tests the limits of acceptable and invasive corporeal imagery.[11] Moreover, as Maurice Charney (1981: 54–5) demonstrates in his study of sexual literature, the linguistic animation of an autoerotic scene works through just such strategies as those used in true crime: the use of present tense description and a language 'deliberately simplified and stripped of any emotive words'. To illustrate this point he quotes from the anonymous erotic novel *The Image*. One passage describes a photograph of a sadomasochistic scene, showing the wounds inflicted on a woman:

> One extends from the tip of the breast to the armpit. ... The blood
> pours down one whole side in little rivers of varying force which

run together and separate again in an elaborate network which covers one hip and a good part of the stomach. It even flows into the navel. (ibid.: 54)

In pornography the look may be illicit but in true crime the invitation to look, and look closely, at a display such as this is legitimised by the objective discourse that frames it. The commentary in 'Time of Death' is couched in the medico-scientific discourses of the forensic examination, which situate man/woman as the object of knowledge and which invite readers to confront him/her as a cadaver rather than as a person. In these sections of the partwork adjectives such as 'gruesome' or 'ghastly' are rarely used, strongly contrasting with the more traditional true crime features in other sections of the issue that speak of 'hideous' or 'gruesome' deaths. Instead, they are grounded in observable facts, the relations between them and the more general laws of natural science extrapolated from them.

The emphasis upon body maintenance within consumer culture is posited upon a dichotomy between the inner and outer body. The inner body is the subject of concern about disease and ageing, the outer body about appearance and attraction within the space of the social. In a culture where health, fitness and longevity are promoted through the discourses of consumerism, medicine and government, the visibility of the victim's corpse is also therefore a warning of the precariousness of these ambitions, a new form of *memento mori*. In true crime the divisions between inner and outer body break down, as the body itself breaks down and falls apart after death. Peeling skin, marbled fat, the contents of the stomach, the condition of the heart, outer flesh and inner organs are equally subject to scrutiny. Moreover, in true crime, medicine commonly associated with health concerns itself with death. Any image of a corpse has as its invisible counterpart the image of the perfect body, healthy and undamaged by violence or disease. This double-body epitomises what Adorno and Horkheimer (1944: 234) call the 'love-hate relationship' with the body. They note: 'the body cannot be remade into a noble object: it remains the corpse however vigorously it is trained and kept fit. The metamorphosis into death was simply a part of that perennial process which turned nature into substance and matter.' The point has often been made that the killer, especially the serial killer, treats the bodies of his/her victims as objects. But Adorno and Horkheimer (ibid.: 235) suggest that it is not the murderer but those who extol the perfect body that are actually closest to treating the body as an object:

> They see the body as a moving mechanism, with joints as its com-
> ponents and flesh to cushion the skeleton. They measure others,
> without realising it, with the gaze of a coffin maker ...
>
> They are interested in illness and at mealtimes already watch for
> the death of those who eat with them ... Language keeps pace with
> them. It has transformed a walk into motion and a meal into calo-
> ries just as the English and French languages make no distinction
> between living and dead wood. ... Society with its death statistics
> reduces life to a chemical process.

Here the division between the living and the dead, the subject and the
object is revealed to be a sham through language that fails to distinguish between them. The new true crime also erodes the distinctions
between the living and the dead, animating the corpse while reducing
the *person* of the victim to a cartoon character. It reveals too that medicine's avowed interest in 'life' is really an interest in 'death' to the
extent that the living body and the cadaver are equally objectified. The
new true crime unveils and even celebrates the obscene underside or
counterpart of the managed, aestheticised body. Bizarre images of dried
and powdered feet, of the skin turning inside out, of human bite marks
in human flesh, of fat laid bare by the scalpel all suggest that the
boundaries of the well-maintained clean and proper body are permeable
and vulnerable to damage from violent crime and from scientific practice even post-mortem. The rationalism of instrumental science, which
legitimates the spectacle of the abject body in true crime, is always
accompanied and undercut by the strange and wonderful natural phenomena of somatic entropy and decay. The point of true crime, and
therein lies its appeal, is that its stories relate the moment in which the
subject becomes the object, in which the living being: 'the father of
two', 'the bubbly blonde' or 'the serious student' becomes the victim of
attack, the object of atrocity, the cadaver. Whereas popular therapeutic
discourses enjoin people to 'find their inner self', to 'become whole' or
to 'be their own person' this literature depicts the many ways and
means by which people fall apart and become non-people. This is displayed literally and graphically in magazines such as this, not only in
stories that tell how murderers attack and mutilate living and dead
bodies, but also in their detailed attention to the natural processes of
decomposition and the unnatural procedures of post-mortem medical
intervention. The final chapter of this book explores how the tenuous
hold on notions of the integrated subject, on 'personhood' signalled
here are greatly elaborated in a more displaced and complex manner

through the depiction of the notorious killer and his motivations in crime biography. Here true crime's portrayal of the murderer as split personality, as living a double life, as someone who both lives life to the maximum but is also an agent of death and destruction offers a different route into some of these same issues by illustrating how 'falling apart' is a psychic as well as corporeal dissolution.

7
Figure in a Landscape: The Dangerous Individual in Criminal Biography

New times, new crimes

> While at the heart of the matter stands the 'un-British' crime of violence.
>
> Geoffrey Pearson (1983: 209)

Eric Hobsbawm (1994: 13) begins his book *Age of Extremes* by describing the twentieth century as the 'most murderous of which we have record' and one that has witnessed an 'accelerating return to the standards of barbarism'. He identifies a strong feeling of insecurity and disorientation which, in the two 'crisis decades' from 1973 onwards, has manifested itself in acts of multiple murder. Drawing on a *New York Times* report he comments:

> These were times when people, their old ways of life already undermined and crumbling in any case ... were likely to lose their bearings. Was it an accident that 'of the ten largest mass murders in American history ... eight have occurred since 1980', typically the acts of middle-aged white men in their thirties and forties, 'after a prolonged period of being lonely, frustrated and full of rage', and often precipitated by a catastrophe in their lives such as losing their job or divorce? (ibid.: 416)

Is it possible, enquires Hobsbawm rhetorically, that these men were the products of a 'growing culture of hate in the United States?' To which he adds: 'This hate certainly became audible in the lyrics of popular music in the 1980s, and evident in the growingly overt cruelty of film and TV programmes.' Hobsbawm's profile of the multiple murderer, both driven to violence through changing socio-economic conditions and also nurtured in a culture replete with representations of violence, is in keeping with the now dominant perception of the serial killer in the US and British press. Philip Jacobson writing in 1985 draws the 'common knowledge' picture: 'So far, known serial killers have all been male, almost all white, often unusually intelligent or extremely cunning' (in Cameron and Frazer 1987: 27).[1] Within popular representations this figure's acts of mutilation and murder are facilitated by his status as an intelligent and mobile white male. They imply a crisis of white masculinity in which the inability to cope with new ways of living, with declining security in employment and declining status in the home, has resulted in the perpetration of a new kind of violent crime, a 'new compulsion' – serial killing. To some therefore the serial killer is a 'commonplace lethal creature whose presence has increased to alarming proportions as social units and concepts – the family, organised religion, the perception of law and order – have woefully decreased in importance' (Nash 1992: i–ii).

Serial killing may be differentiated from other types of multiple murder such as spree killing in that a minimum of three, some say four or five, *separate* premeditated murders are committed with a significant lapse of time between them. The serial killer selects carefully and pursues one particular type of victim. The murder is planned: 'representing an endeavour to extract the maximum pleasure by proceeding deliberately from one stage to the next, for example from abduction through mutilation to termination and then ritual rearrangement of the corpse' (Cyriax 1993: 547; see also Ressler with Schachtman 1992; Norris 1988). Hobsbawm's chronicle is not unusual in making connections between these individual acts and the broader cultural and political climate.[2] Certainly the serial killer has been taken as a sign of change, a token of social flux and instability. He has also inspired a sub-genre of true crime, a sub-genre of the crime novel and a specialist field of reportage in which the weekend press in particular will serialise books devoted to particularly notorious criminals.[3] Diana Fuss (1993) suggests that press coverage of serial killers is the true heir of the nineteenth-century serialised crime story. Fuss maintains: 'Indeed, tales of serial killers in our newspapers have become our new serial literature, with regular instalments, stock characters, behavioural profiles, and a fascinated loyal readership' (1993: 199). The very pattern of serial murder, the inevitable progression from one crime to the next, each one seemingly more grotesque than the last, lends itself well to true crime by instalment. Sequences of portrait photographs of the killer's victims that accompany non-fiction accounts are landmarks in the serial killer's journey from first crime to dénouement. In serial killer fictions in particular, the accumulation of murders as 'variations on a theme' produces especially effective narrative cliff-hangers.[4] Even the coining of the term 'serial killer' by Robert Ressler of the Behavioral Science Unit of the FBI in Quantico, Virginia during the 1970s stemmed not only from the pattern of the crime but also from childhood memories of adventure serials in the cinema (Seltzer 1998: 16).[5] According to Richard Dyer (1997: 14), it is 'the amplified desire for seriality' fuelled by the commercial imperatives of press and television, which is best satisfied by the serial killer story. The sequence of killings that characterises the serial killer story also fits into a much greater serialised media spectacle: 'In turn, each killer is fitted into the wider phenomenon of "serial killing" itself, with its stars, fact, fiction or both ... and its featured players, the police, victims, witnesses and acquaintances' (Dyer 1997: 14; see also Leyton 1986; Jenkins 1994: 114; Seltzer 1998: 63–4).[6]

The serial killer is often regarded as emblematic of a changing order of crime, in which skilful domestic killers such as Crippen have made way for killers for whom 'quantity' is more important than 'quality' (Campbell, D. 1993: 13). Serial killing has been styled a twentieth-century phenomenon, as a new kind of 'motiveless' or 'pure' murder not driven by jealousy or greed but by existential or metaphysical impulses (Masters 1985; Cameron and Frazer 1987: 58–65; Black 1991). Crime fiction and true crime depict the serial killer and other multiple murderers not only as a symptom of late twentieth-century malaise, but also as powerful criminal agents in their own rights. Crime literature and film, in particular, have done much to imbue the serial killer with mythical qualities; for example the ability to lure victims into a trap, to remain undetected, to live a double life and to have a specialist knowledge of the 'dark side' of the psyche (Jenkins 1994: 111–20). The serial killer is also often figured as somewhat supernatural: a vampire or a virus that slips unnoticed through society, a kind of freak of nature who can cross any boundary (social and physical) without being detected (Winder 1991; Fuss 1993).

The dominance of these mythical and literary features, together with high level of violence and atrocity committed by them, underpins the perception that the killer is in possession of the kinds of esoteric knowledge already outlined in the previous chapter: a knowledge about death (or the limits of life) and the body. The extreme nature of these crimes seems to constitute a puzzle that cannot be explained through biology, psychology or sociological thought. Professor Canter, a psychologist engaged in aiding criminal detection, comments:

> The inner, secret nature of violent crime, the very 'alternativeness' of the criminal stories they live, is possibly one of the strongest challenges to the social learning perspective. If the violence is a secret part of the hidden thoughts of the criminal, how can it be shaped by contact with other people? ... Social processes are open to view. Yet the brutal actions of Duffy,[7] Dahmer,[8] and thousands of other violent men, are secret creations of their own. (Canter 1994: 284)

This emphasis upon secret and occluded knowledge stems from an extreme transgression of acceptable limits, a crossing of boundaries that seems to command a search 'into the mind of the murderer'. Epigrams such as *truth dwells in the inner man* (ibid.: 300) abound in both crime fiction and true crime although the nature of this truth is rarely specified. Whereas Canter seeks to understand the stories those killers tell themselves in order to make sense of what they are doing; others explore the roots of mental disorders in behaviourism and biology, tracing them in children as young as three years old (e.g. Moir and Jessel 1995). Of these two routes into the matter of criminal atrocity – the psychological/discursive and the biological – it is Canter's approach that is most prominent in media representations of notorious murderers. Canter usefully advocates an analysis of crime as narrative, its outward signs telling a story about the significant moments in the criminal's 'personal narrative'. He comments (1994: 302): 'the narratives with which we are concerned are expressed in violent actions and the traces left in the aftermath of those crimes. They are like shadow puppets telling us a story in a stilted, alien language.'

The almost legibility of the serial killer and his narrative is an important component of his high media currency. In fiction especially, the serial killer often operates through encryption, offering highly coded erudite clues about his identity and that of his next victim. As such he demands a high level of scholarship, leading detectives through libraries and museums, art galleries and bookshops in pursuit of the obscure reference that will close up the gaps in the narrative of serial homicide. The serial killer then has become a conundrum and a cipher. He is both an intellectual puzzle and a clear symbol of changing times; a contradictory figure who signals 'the decline of the English murder' and the diminution of civilised values; a figure who crudely privileges 'quantity over quality' but also commits the 'pure', intellectually driven murder. He is regarded as a badge of the erosion of older, more civilised ways of living or as an Americanised interloper onto the British scene. John Mortimer's tongue-in-cheek introduction to a new selection of the Penguin *Famous Trials* series sketches the British pleasures still extant but soon to be pushed aside by these new crimes, painting a portrait of English life that has changed little since the days of T. S. Eliot (1948):

> Colour supplements devoted to *nouvelle cuisine* have failed to make any great change in the English Sunday, which goes with a joint in the oven, the all-pervading smell of boiled cabbage, and an account of the charred remains found in a burnt-out Ford Poplar as described on page one of the *News of the World*. (Mortimer 1984: 7)

This description of a common culture, further augmented by 'the plays of Shakespeare, the full breakfast, the herbaceous border and the presumption of innocence' is solidly domestic and parochial.[9] It harks back, somewhat wistfully, to the pre-permissive moment when murder was an 'act of intimacy' between family members, friends and lovers, landlords and tenants; people who could not break the bonds of their association in any other way.[10] Its scenarios of domestic strife, jealousy and greed were crystallised in the golden age of detective fiction and given a new lease of life during the 1980s, when television adaptations of Agatha Christie's[11] work and the appearance of *Inspector Morse*[12] vied for attention with increasingly gruesome police procedurals. Consequently, the police procedural and the more traditional lone-protagonist detective series constituted a discursive contest between two opposing models of criminality and more importantly perhaps between two opposing visions of modern British life.

Robert Winder's (1991: 27) full-page article entitled 'When Murder is not Enough' harks back to that scene eulogised by John Mortimer, citing Orwell's 1945 essay which mused on the passing pleasures of reading about domestic murders in the Sunday papers (see Chapter 2). Winder's Orwellian reference is made precisely in order to provide a nostalgic contrast between older small-scale domestic murders and the proliferation of serial murders that hit the headlines between 1980 and 1984. He observes with concern the notable increase in the numbers of serial killers and significant developments in their *modus operandi* throughout the 1980s, quoting criminal psychologist Elliott Leyton's somewhat estranging phraseology: 'the mid-Eighties were years of unprecedented growth, experimentation and innovation among multiple-murderers'.[13] In Britain this 'innovation' was marked by the emergence of murderers such as Peter Sutcliffe and Dennis Nilsen, whose appearance fuelled the public appetite for true crime and fictional crime stories. Winder's concern is that Britain, stimulated by these crimes and influenced by the United States, is now immersing itself in books and images of the 'new demon' serial killer (see also Jenkins, S. 1994).

Winder's article is typical of commentators who tend to muddle issues of crime, the representations of crime and the Americanisation of British culture. The coinage of the term 'serial killer', as already noted, is part of an imported North American idiom used to describe a criminal activity that undoubtedly preceded this nomenclature. However, the deployment of such a label carries with it a 'whole referential context', providing not only a lexicon through which random murder may be understood but also a framework in which these crimes may be positioned as un-British (Hall *et al.* 1978: 19). Recent press debates about true crime, random homicide and unprovoked violence clearly reflect longer-term anxieties over the Americanisation of mass culture. Here, and elsewhere, the British public's penchant for non-fiction and fictional crime narratives, together with the perceived rise in all kinds of 'stranger killings', is regarded as an index of a national malaise. Winder's article followed the success of the British television crime drama *Prime Suspect*[14] and anticipated, with some trepidation, the release in Britain of the serial killer film *The Silence of the Lambs* (Demme 1991 USA). It conflates real crime with a boom in the consumption of a 'viceberg' of explicit TV crime drama, true crime and reportage. The argument is also typical in judging both crime and the narration of crime as symptomatic of some kind of undiagnosed condition of England. The elision between crime and its narration leads the journalist to ask rhetorically whether serial killers should be viewed as evidence of a culture in decline or as its clearest metaphor. The slippage between true crime entertainment and the perceived boom in random crime is typical of the debates surveyed for this book. Indeed, true crime writers themselves seem no more able to differentiate between the two. Brian Marriner, a prolific true crime author, offers a particularly unhelpful explanation for the commercial success of true crime that equally fails to clarify or differentiate its terms. Marriner notes: 'we are going through a decadent period similar to the one at the end of the last century and it's going to get worse. There is a vast increase in true crime' (Campbell, D. 1993: 13).

The random murderer as symptomatic of the condition of England also appears in Hugh Barnes' more thoughtful article, 'The death of the English Murder' (1993: 16–22). Here too, murder is clearly an 'index of social decline' (ibid.: 20), a ruler against which to measure cultural change and social breakdown. Barnes again contrasts Orwell's essay on the pleasures of an old-fashioned domestic murder story with the high media currency of random, seemingly unmotivated killings in order to ask what this says about 'our way of life' (ibid.: 16). For him the humanism inherent in domestic crime and the detailed reportage that made it so fascinating and comprehensible is inevitably absent in stranger-killings. This unexamined and unexplained notion of 'humanism' is the criterion against which contemporary murder and its narration are evaluated and found wanting. The 'randomness of street violence' exhibits a lack of depth of feeling that, according to Barnes, the public does not want to know about. He comments (ibid.: 23):

> The murder-loving public does not want to hear that murder is a flawed genre drawing us into a kind of complicity with itself, and giving off the suggestion of real, human mystery below the surface – a constant sense of something about to be revealed. But, of course, it never is.

The meaninglessness of most contemporary violence – speedy, random and unmotivated – holds no mystery for Barnes, and it is the mystery, inherent in the 'humanist' old-style crime narratives, that arguably attracted readers. Barnes spies an 'affectlessness' in the new age of murder (which was inaugurated in the 1960s) and an increase in random crime that makes its reportage a meaningless and boring exercise.[15] As an example, he relates the story of the unprovoked murder of Reg Woof in east Lancashire in October 1993, an event which is now considered to be too common or garden to merit a place in the national news. In the classic true crime style of which Orwell would have been proud, Barnes begins with a detailed description of Woof's home town of Waterfoot, pushed through industrial decline 'beyond history' (ibid.: 16). 'Murder,' he writes, 'like other things is subject to fashion, and in its randomness, its unyielding brutality, the Reg Woof story seemed to be a product of our era' (ibid.: 18). Here the frequency and anonymity of contemporary murder are the markers against which cultural decline may be calibrated. The lament for a time when murder was more personal and less frequent is harnessed to a mythology of Englishness, of middle-class domesticity, subdued passions and an old world courtesy that leads the poisoner to mutter 'excuse my fingers' as he hands the fatal scone to his guest. For Barnes, as for Orwell, it was the tiny details of everyday life that rendered crime so fascinating. Even in the case of Reg Woof, it is the ordinary details of his life and death that should make the story meaningful to the reader:

> Banality acquires a kind of objecthood, a sort of immanence. Often it connects the murderer and the victim with the rest of society. It also connects the extreme and the whimsical with ordinary life, with England, with the decade, with the type. It serves, it you like, as a kind of history. (ibid.: 18)

Homicide constitutes an alternative history, a history of ordinary people in extraordinary circumstances. Even the English landscape, that touchstone of English heritage, has become sullied by murder, turned by crime into 'killing grounds', a 'theme park' of atrocity whose first point of contemporary reference must be Saddleworth Moor. Rather like a number of contemporary British novelists, Barnes tries to read the near-invisible scars of atrocity upon the land, reading the temperature of England by the barometer of contemporary murder.[16] 'The whole country', as described by Barnes, 'was connected by a network of more or less secret or known or almost known wickedness' (ibid.: 18).

The idea of a cartography of murder is most common and most acceptable when it is articulated through the fictional murder story or historical murder rather than those still painfully fresh in popular memory. The Wests' house in Cromwell Street was razed to the ground to deter murder-tourism, but tours of Morse's Oxford or the Ripper's Whitechapel fall within the rubric of 'heritage' geography, along with Bram Stoker's Whitby or Thomas Hardy's Wessex. City tours invite walkers to 'take a journey into terror' around London's East End or to engage in a 'darker, danker brand of underground experience' at the Clerkenwell House of Detention (see Samuel 1994: 284–5).[17] Guidebooks trace topographies of historical murder and public execution as local or regional history (e.g. Butler 1992; Tibballs 1993).

Sometimes, however, the imaginary landscape of fiction fuses with the landscape of true crime to produce a new kind of topos of murder, one that permits the construction of a literary cartography of modern atrocity. Nicole Ward Jouve's bold analysis of the Peter Sutcliffe case entitled '*The Streetcleaner*' (1986) (so called because Sutcliffe claimed that he killed prostitutes to 'clean up the streets') locates Sutcliffe's crimes within a Romantic gothic scene – Yorkshire as 'Ripper Country'.

Peter Sutcliffe murdered 13 women and injured a further seven between 1975 and 1980. Jouve's feminist account of the murders, of the machismo culture that underpinned them, together with that of the mismanagement of the investigation, is an insightful critique that occasionally slips into its opposite – a romanticisation of the serial killer who is, more particularly, a killer of women. Jouve, drawing on Lacan and Barthes, self-consciously attends to the connections between madness, crime and literature, producing a complex portrait of the notorious killer which includes a portrait of the killer as romantic anti-hero. Her attempt to 'demystify the construct of murder' (ibid.: 37) founders most overtly in the places in her account where murder intersects with the literary landscape. Sutcliffe operated mainly in the red light districts of cities such as Bradford and Leeds: 'sleazy run-down slums where junk shops and sex shops, betting offices and minicab rooms were interspersed between patches of broken ground left by random demolition' (Cyriax 1993: 535). Yet Jouve depicts a violent and dark literary geography:

> I, a French woman, had settled in Yorkshire, because myths like the Brontës, spaces like the moors, had appealed to me as deeply nurturing, promising freedom and scope. Now, other places and a new myth that were uncomfortably close to those I loved, were threatening murder. The place was spelling death to me as a woman. (ibid.: 18)

Jouve presents the mythic figure of the 'Ripper' as the dark side of the Yorkshire landscape of the imagination. Awkwardly, she attempts to reconcile her vision of what is essentially a literary gothic sublime topos with images of the violent deaths under consideration: 'Rocks, stonewalls. On the moors you can see the bones of the earth. You are close to what is most real – most essential: the oldest, that which lasts the longest.' Jouve depicts Nature that is harsher and more enduring than the killers who scar her:

> I could not think of Brady and Hindley and their secret moorland cemetery. I felt sullied. What had always meant cleanliness and expanse had been violated. Then time and the wind and the heather won. The silence washed over the sickness. (ibid.: 19)

The fact that Sutcliffe was an urban killer jars with Jouve's portrait. In her own Brontë-inspired depiction it was an accident of fate that led

Sutcliffe to kill in cities rather than on the moor, belying the obvious logic of murdering in the busy metropolis where everyone minds their own business. Jouve deals with this inconvenience by commenting: 'Sutcliffe steered clear of the moors. Just' (ibid.: 20). In an extraordinary juxtaposition she wonders whether Heathcliff may have pursued a route similar to Sutcliffe's along the Aire Valley, creating a literary link between the moody, swarthy Sutcliffe and Heathcliff, the brooding gypsy foundling. The linguistic theory judiciously employed by Jouve offers a fresh and challenging perspective on the Ripper case; however, her invocation of Mrs Gaskell, *Wuthering Heights* and George Eliot presents a curiously romantic configuration of literature, landscape and appalling homicide. In her commitment to illustrating how myths are made to supplement our scant knowledge of the unidentified and therefore mythical serial killer, Jouve creates her own.

Villainy as privilege

The highly dangerous individual, the 'new' kind of murderer, the 'serial killer' is formed, as we have seen, from opposing models of criminality. He is styled as banal and unsophisticated, preferring 'quantity over quality' and also as the romantic anti-hero and outsider. He is presented as being both a nobody and someone very remarkable indeed. Jouve's epigraph for '*The Streetcleaner*' is a poem by Antonin Artaud entitled 'Van Gogh, le Suicidé de la Société', a choice that signals the way in which Sutcliffe's 'sickness' is also the malady of society at large. But of course it also, by implication, arrogates to the criminal the privileged insight of the artist as someone on the margins of the social.[18] This portrait of the criminal as artist *manqué* is inherent in criminal literature from Thomas De Quincey onwards. The depiction of, and fascination with, the murderer as a privileged subject and powerful agent is a phenomenon noted by a variety of academics (Mandel 1984; Senelick 1987; Black 1991; During 1992). Laurence Senelick's *The Prestige of Evil* (1987) examines the nineteenth-century roots of the murderer-hero who, leaving gallows sheets and 'true accounts' behind, moves into a new fictional criminal literature to become a romantic hero: an 'emblem of irrevocable rebellion' (Senelick 1967: 366). Foucault (1975: 68–9) notes of this new literature:

> Crime is glorified, because it is one of the fine arts, because it can be the work only of exceptional natures, because it reveals the monstrousness of the strong and powerful, because villainy is yet

another mode of privilege ... there is a whole aesthetic rewriting of crime, which is also the appropriation of criminality in acceptable forms. In appearance, it is the discovery of the beauty and greatness of crime; in fact it is the affirmation that greatness too has a right to crime and that it even becomes the exclusive privilege of those who are really great.

In Foucault's account of developments in criminal literature the aesthetic rewriting of crime (e.g. De Quincey, Walpole, Baudelaire) represents the usurpation of the popular status of 'rustic malefactor' by the wicked and intelligent criminal of a different social class.[19] The development of the detective story completes this process of transformation. In this new genre 'the great murders had become the quiet game of the well behaved' (Foucault 1975: 69). Foucault posits a divergence between what was to become the intellectual combat between the criminal and the detective and the 'unheroic details of everyday crime and punishment' still presented in the press. The notorious criminal is no longer the anti-hero of the working people but a figure of the literary imagination and a cut above the rest.

In 'Prison Talk' Foucault (1980: 46) offers us Pierre-François Lacenaire as an example of a real-life criminal anti-hero, a new class of criminal subject who emerged in the 1840s. Lacenaire was a petty criminal whose inflated view of himself helped to create a mythic persona of the murderer as dandy, artist and public celebrity (see Black 1991).[20] The consequence of such notoriety, notes Foucault (1980: 46), is that: 'The bourgeoisie constitutes for itself an aesthetic in which crime no longer belongs to the people, but is one of those fine arts of which the bourgeoisie alone is capable.' He addresses in particular the aestheticised criminal act that, in effect, conflates life with art. It could be argued that this elision is privileged as the founding moment of the 'attitude' of modernity (Foucault 1984a). 'From the idea that the self is not given to us, I think that there is only one practical consequence: we have to create ourselves as a work of art' (Foucault 1984b: 351, see also Dreyfus and Rabinow 1986).

Joel Black (1991), like Foucault, dismisses detective fiction as a kind of ruse and digression from what he calls a 'criminal literature' in which the criminal takes centre stage. However, for Black, criminal literature is synonymous with literary fiction rather than true crime. He argues (1991: 45) that even within literary fiction, texts that treat the artist-as-detective are 'the most inauthentic and artificial of all the varieties of crime literature', proposing that the criminal-as-artist or the artist-as-criminal should be the proper focus of a criminal literature. His contention that these narratives are in some way 'inauthentic' is questionable, but he is right to note that the hermeneutic and episte-mological foundation of the detective story is one that must relegate the criminal to the margins.[21] In this genre and in commentaries on the genre the criminal is either marginalised or else melded with the figure of the investigator; an elision indicated by motifs of dualism and doubling in the texts. This gaping absence of the criminal as protago-nist allowed a new emphasis on the law as the prime mover in detec-tion and as the final arbiter of guilt or innocence.

Alongside the growth of the detective genre there developed what Black chooses to call a more 'authentic' criminal literature (see also Foucault 1975; Senelick 1987). The argument is that the experience of murder, unless we are directly involved, is primarily aesthetic; however, an 'ideology of moral reason' denies and closes down these aesthetic experiences (Black 1991: 4). His book is an attempt to theo-rise this murder aesthetic through an examination of nineteenth- and twentieth-century texts. De Quincey's *On Murder Considered as a Fine Art* is, naturally enough, marked out as the founding literary moment of the murder aesthetic. De Quincey marries his own vision of Kantian aesthetics to an assessment of the possibility of certain acts of murder to be designated fine art; thereby introducing the term aes-thetics into the English language. In this significant moment Black (1991: 3) identifies: 'the duplicitous, macabre associations that attended aesthetics at the moment it was incorporated into the English language, that contributed to its delayed assimilation by Anglo-American philosophy, and that continue to haunt Western culture today as never before.' Aesthetics in general, as well as the aes-thetics of murder, is a tainted and thereby transgressive philosophy; infusing a network of murder writing originating with De Quincey. Black identifies two significant movements. The first is the nine-teenth-century representation of the criminal-as-artist which includes the romantic tradition of Hoffmann and Poe and the art for art's sake theme in works by Baudelaire and Gautier. The second movement is launched by Wilde's *The Picture of Dorian Gray* (1890) – its publication the herald of the modernist movement wherein the artist is himself (rarely herself) portrayed as a criminal opposed to the norms of society (Black 1991: 39). This second movement turns on work by Nietzsche: 'the figure in whose name the crime of murder has been rationalised and raised from merely passive aesthetic experience to outright epistemological pursuits, and ultimately, to pure, often outrageous, spontaneous action' (ibid.: 82). These points mark the shift from the notion of the disinterested spectator to that of the disinterested artist. It is in Nietzsche's work, for example, that Black perceives the modernist forms that typify a disinterestedness that was to manifest itself in fascism. Black has, therefore, made two periodic correspondences with Foucault's own observations: the high romanticism of the nineteenth century correlates with the 'aesthetic rewriting of crime' and certain twentieth-century modernist forms correlate with the notion of greatness having a right to crime.

Fascism is one of the modernist forms informed by the idea of the artist or intellectual as outside the norms of ordinary human interaction and responsibility. Depictions of the serial killer arguably touch upon this *übermensch* formulation; the serial killer has already been identified as the horrible but logical extension of Aryan privilege and even of an Aryan aesthetic (e.g. Taubin 1991; Fuss 1993). Both fictional and non-fiction depictions of the serial killer foreground this notion of 'privilege'. Bret Easton Ellis's yuppie serial killer novel *American Psycho* (1991) portrays Patrick Bateman as a man obsessed with the cultivation of a pure and perfect body. Bateman's status as a young, handsome and privileged WASP is reiterated by the book jacket's illustration of a besuited male model from the German edition of the life-style magazine *Vogue* for men – *Männer Vogue*. Bateman is repulsed by the poor, the dirty and, more specifically, by the ugly, although he also kills a vast number of people from his own milieu.

The serial killer as a scourge of social outcasts (and as a symbol of fascist power) is rendered most explicitly in Christian da Chalongé's film *Docteur Petiot* (France 1990) which fictionalises the true story of the doctor who murdered many Jews in occupied France (see also Maeder 1980). Petiot's mobility and apparent status allowed him access to, and authority over, his many victims trapped in their hideaways. The film's imagery, including lingering shots of heaps of clothing and possessions removed from Petiot's victims, deliberately recalls the broader decimation of the Jews in the Holocaust. Likewise, references to killers such as Jeffrey Dahmer as a murderer of 'German descent' most of whose victims were black and Peter Sutcliffe's own notion of himself as the 'scourge of God' simply cleaning up social outcasts, abound in the press and true crime. The killer, as a stock character, has all the accoutrements of privilege and autonomy within Western society – white, mobile, male, intelligent, perhaps professional – and is in some respects therefore a powerful figure within these narratives. Moreover, the killer is often depicted as relentlessly and supernaturally invincible, casting a shadow over the city like Fantômas. Doctor Petiot's gothic image in Chalongé's film is overtly reminiscent of Nosferatu, a figure with whom serial killers, such as Jeffrey Dahmer, are sometimes conflated in the press (see Fuss 1993).

It is in true crime biography, above all, where the criminal has remained central to the narration of crime and the detective is largely absent, that the legacy of these criminal literatures and imagery may still be found. Although for Black (1991: 26) 'true confessions' have the greatest impact when transformed 'into the more powerful stuff of fiction' it is, in fact, the denigrated genre of true crime that has had consistently to accommodate this influential tradition of aestheticised murder with its own agenda of 'moral reason'. The tracery of criminal literature mapped out by Black, in terms of aesthetics and other philosophical discourses, arguably persists not only in the contemporary narration of murder, but as an optic through which the media attempts to understand the motivation of the notorious murderer. The true crime author proclaims his or her 'disinterestedness' in the ghastly details of homicide and yet often also makes the murderer the heroic centre of the story (rather than the victims of the crime, for example, or even the detective). The remainder of this chapter looks at one exemplary text, Brian Masters' 1985 account of serial murderer Dennis Nilsen, in order to unpack the variety of discourses that attempt to put together a credible and coherent picture of the notorious murderer. It engages with the question of how the notorious killer is constructed through various discursive practices, including those of his own memoirs and confessions. It unpacks the range of literary, popular and professional discourses – journalistic, legal and medical – that attempt to understand and categorise the notorious criminal subject and which also, inevitably, position his story as the most important in the narrative of a crime and its aftermath. Masters' book is one example of the discursive clash between a literary heritage that depends upon the aesthetic of murder and a moral-ethical imperative in which the true crime author must be seen to condemn the criminal subject. It demonstrates how the utilisation of a sublime and/or gothic aesthetic immediately frustrates any idea of the non-fiction crime story as a genre apart. In fact, it is its adherence to the conventions of high literature that prevent it from finding a new way to talk about modern murder and its consequences for victims and for society at large.[23]

Brian Masters' *Killing for Company*

> Through his actions the criminal tells us about how he has chosen to live his life. The challenge is to reveal his destructive life story, to uncover the plot in which crime appears to play such a significant part.
>
> David Canter (1994: 299)

> Nature had mismatched me from the flock.
>
> Dennis Nilsen (in Masters 1985a: 53)

The British serial killer Dennis Nilsen has been regarded as a landmark in the appearance of the 'increasingly bizarre crimes' that have occurred in Britain since the 1970s (Begg and Skinner 1992: 263–78). Between 1979 and 1983 Nilsen killed up to 16 men in his small London flat. He was charged with 15 counts of murder and nine charges of attempted murder. After undertaking certain rituals with the bodies of his victims he either burned them or dismembered them and pushed them down the lavatory. In 1985 Brian Masters wrote the definitive biography of Nilsen entitled *Killing for Company* (1985a). The book was well received, winning the Crime Writers' non-fiction award and high praise in the press. Beryl Bainbridge (1985), writing in the *Observer*, praised the author's objectivity and restraint, calling the book 'a bloody masterpiece' rather than a 'shilling shocker'. Masters (1985b: xiii) himself makes no bones about the moral position that must be adopted by the writer in relation to the unpleasant and disturbing revelations made in the book. A moral acuity is especially needful bearing in mind the kudos gained by the author through his position as a 'murderer's confessor', brought about in this instance by the book's inclusion of material gained in interviews with Nilsen, the inclusion of facsimiles of his drawings and poems (Masters 1985b). *Killing for Company* was presented by its author as an object lesson, as something that would 'leave its mark' in the history of criminal homicide. The inclusion of Nilsen's own writings are defended as one way in which to determine the criminal's emotional development and, notes Masters (1985a: xv), 'if we cannot so determine, then we are left with the miserable conclusion that a man becomes a murderer by chance'.

In *Killing for Company* fictional discourses play a significant role in signposting for the reader Nilsen's physical and emotional journey from childhood to sociopathic adulthood. Masters dramatically structures his narrative by beginning with Nilsen's arrest in February 1983 and the suspense that he endured while waiting for the police to apprehend him. The scene is set with a description of the quiet suburban area of Muswell Hill where Nilsen was then living. This is effectively contrasted with the hideous picture of Nilsen desperately attempting to hide the body of his latest victim by dismembering him in the tiny flat and boiling the flesh from his head for hours on end. At this time tenants who occupied the house with Nilsen were insisting on an investigation of the drains after prolonged problems with the plumbing. When flesh was discovered in the drains the police were called in to investigate. Meanwhile, Nilsen sneaking down in the middle of the night to remove the offending material, is captured by the author in a scene reminiscent of De Quincey's famous description of the maid servant listening behind the door in the Ratcliffe Highway murders:

> [Tenants] Fiona Bridges and Jim Allcock were by now more than apprehensive; they were seriously alarmed. They had heard the footsteps on the stairs, the front door opening, the manhole being removed, more clanking and scraping, the sound of someone walking down the side of the house towards the garden. Fiona has said to Jim, 'There is somebody having a go at the manhole. I bet it's him upstairs.'

This depiction of the suburban nightmare touches upon a variety of disturbing narratives such as the popular Stephen King horror novels, David Lynch's *Blue Velvet* (USA 1986) and the enduring tradition of British domestic murder reportage. Masters' first chapter and those that follow draw on this and a number of other, sometimes conflicting registers to explain what happened to Nilsen. The opening chapter and the concluding chapters on the trial form a frame, portraying Nilsen to some degree from other people's points of view. Within this frame, however, the story is definitely Nilsen's alone. Chapters 2–5 deal in biographical fashion with Nilsen's life-story; chapters 6 and 7 with his victims and the difficulties of body disposal; chapters 8 and 9 concern his remand and trial, before the final chapter offers a range of 'answers' which might account for such a 'calamity'. A postscript by the well-known psychiatrist Anthony Storr is indicative of the serious intentions of the author.

Chapter 2, in which Masters concentrates on Nilsen's ancestors and his childhood, is structured by the popular conventions of Romantic Gothic.[24] Nilsen himself is noted as saying that he was a 'child of deep romanticism' (ibid.: 196). Masters maintains that knowledge of Nilsen's birthplace in Aberdeenshire and of his Buchan roots is fundamental to any analysis of his subject's personality. He paints a picture of an inbred and fatalistic population harnessed to a harsh and unforgiving environment: 'Good and evil are realities for them, not thin religious concepts, and it is sometimes said, not fancifully, that the fisherfolk have markedly different personalities at night' (ibid.: 28). He paints a portrait of blunt, independent and radical iconoclasts who have 'above all a deeply-ingrained respect for the irresistible forces of nature' (ibid.: 27). His account of the Buchan legacy of mental instability hails back to complex intermarriages dating from 1699. Special mention is made of the Stephens family, some members of which moved to London and produced the manic-depressive J. K. Stephen, who was a suspect in the Whitechapel murders, and the writer Virginia Woolf (ibid.: 35–6). Tales of other notable Buchan 'eccentric' fisherfolk pepper Nilsen's childhood, signalling a criminal predestination that is reminiscent of early English true crime. Here 'images of death, and images of love' (children go missing, the Laird's daughter dies in a suicide pact with her lover, and a man drowns after his 'sanity had cracked') were to collide and produce a homicidal subject who is also a natural disaster (ibid.: 59). Nilsen's Norwegian father, posted to Aberdeenshire during the war, also contributes to Nilsen's sinister inheritance. Olav Nilsen had a 'hint of cruelty about the eyes' (ibid.: 39) and he produced a misfit son by deserting his wife and family. The landscape is peppered with burnt-out castles: 'left open to the sky, like ghastly skulls in the landscape. Children, Dennis included, have for generations played amongst the ruins of their people's past. They are never far from reminders of their history' (ibid.: 31–2).

In this narrative the seagulls 'scream' in the high lonely places of Nilsen's childhood. The cruel sea and harsh coastal environment are the chief protagonists in the tale of Nilsen's early years; they provide the gothic and sublime experiences of Nilsen's youth. The death of Nilsen's vigorous and patriarchal grandfather provides the corpse which will become the object of his obsession and which will, suggests Masters (who takes his cue from Nilsen), sow the seeds of the killer's necrophiliac fantasies. His grandfather was 'protector' and 'hero', and even when he saw him laid out in the house he could not believe that he was gone. The killer is delineated as the progeny of a harsh geography. The cycles of nature, of death and rebirth are shown to be integral to the Buchan character. Masters quotes Nilsen's recollection of his dead grandfather: 'He took the real me under the ground and now I rest with him under the salt spray and the wind in Inveralochy Cemetery. Nature makes no provision for emotional death' (ibid.: 47). In this way Nilsen is transformed into the freak of nature so beloved of the tabloid press, one of the living dead whose origins Masters shrouds in tales of local suicide and drowning.

The narrative here signals a subsequent theme: Nilsen's necromantic impulse to achieve a consummation with death that in the early chapters is symbolised by a destructive nature. The primeval sea, as Nilsen points out (ibid.: 49) is the site of our origins; 'Origins' is the title chosen by Masters for this childhood chapter. Nilsen, like Jouve, stresses the harsh but purifying redemption of nature. In Nilsen's fantasy of a boy's (perhaps his own) death by drowning, the site of violent death is wiped clean like the moors after the visitation by Brady and Hindley: 'when the last man has taken his last breath the sea will still be remaining. It washes everything clean. It holds within it forever the boy suspended in its body and the streaming hair and the open eyes (Nilsen, in ibid.: 49). The imagery here suggests a Darwinian nightmare in which the protagonist features as a 'throwback' or 'mismatch', a product of genetics and environment that seems to have very little to do with the familial and social realm.

The dualism of the landscape, of water and wind – both intimidating and cleansing – anticipates and is analogous with the dualistic depiction of the serial killer as both outside the law and also as the counterpart of the law. For it is arguable that the multiple murderer remains undetected because his victims are often considered to be of little account within society. The notion of the killer, just 'cleaning up the streets' in the case of Peter Sutcliffe or 'releasing' victims from a 'miserable life' in the case of Nilsen, owes much to a vulgar Social Darwinism in which the killer is portrayed/portrays himself as society's 'social hygienist'. The killer, like the virus, is figured here as a force of nature, unalloyed with the civilising influence of social relations, but enabling them to function more efficiently through the eradication of outcasts and ne'er-do-wells.

Nilsen as artist *manqué*

> I did it all for me. Purely selfishly ... I worshipped the art and the act of death, over and over. It's as simple as that.
>
> Dennis Nilsen (in Masters 1985b: 277)

Masters, even as he acknowledges Nilsen's dark, romantic writings as retrospective fantasies, chooses to reinforce them. As the narrative progresses through Nilsen's army days, the author once again couples sublime scenery, this time of the Shetlands where Nilsen was posted after Aden, with the portrait of the future killer as freak of nature. He says of Nilsen's secret homosexuality:

> As far as he was concerned, his very nature was marked with a scar
> of abnormality which he could do nothing about. Like a club foot,
> it would be with him forever, but at least it was not so visible. (ibid.:
> p. 70)

The image of the club foot connotes a deviant sexuality; as a demonic
symbol of moral and spiritual deformity it recalls tales of the devil, of
Byron and of a misshapen Mr Hyde. Masters suggests that it is this dark
side of Nilsen, the devious and demonic figure, which will be repressed
only to emerge with catastrophic effect at a later date. In *Killing for
Company* the dark figure becomes Nilsen's *alter-ego* or double, loosely
substantiated by Nilsen's obsession with mirrors and play acting.
Masters' narrative (and quite possibly Nilsen's narrative also) owes
much to such authors as Stevenson, James Hogg, Nathaniel Hawthorne
and above all to Edgar Allen Poe. The uncanny atmosphere of Nilsen's
childhood produces a fissure in his character that cannot be masked
over indefinitely, an alterity that has to be accommodated. Masters, like
Jouve (above), employs the pathetic fallacy in representing Buchan's
harsh geography and weather as the externalised indicator of the
turmoil within the boy and his fractured personality.

Dr MacKeith, in his capacity as the expert medical witness in the
trial of Nilsen, corroborated this view of a fissured personality albeit in
a different lexicon: 'He had the ability to separate his mental functions
and his behaviour to an extraordinary degree ... [for example] when
two parts of him appeared to operate a few minutes apart in total dis-
crepancy' (ibid.: 221). Nilsen also describes himself as a divided 'monochrome man' (although it must be noted that, like his biographer, he
tries on a range of explanatory categories in order to account for his
bizarre and destructive behaviour). Aside from the more commonplace
illustrations used in true crime biographies, *Killing for Company* also
includes a facsimile of Book 9 of Nilsen's prison notebooks entitled
'Monochrome Man Sad Sketches' which consists of poetry, notes and
line drawings of his victims. Here Nilsen (ibid.: 306) writes:

> The monochrome man in a dream
> It is the black and it is the white of life.
> He is the cameo that activates now and then
> Can't cope with metropolitania. (ibid.: 306)

At another point, however, this view of a personality which is severely
inhibited and unnatural gains a heroic twist more in keeping with the

existentialist anti-heroes of true crime – the serial killer becomes a worthy opponent of 'metropolitania' (ibid.: 196). Other killer confessions, such as those collected in Foucault's (1973) dossier on Pierre Rivière and in the memoirs of Rivière's contemporary the poet-assassin Lacenaire, also locate criminals in conflict with the vapidity of modern life. The notorious murderer is often depicted as undertaking violent action as a form of self-assertion and to reject the stultifying and life-draining forces of convention. In spite of this self-indulgent hubris (and because of it) the serial killer continues to be depicted as intelligent, imaginative and even as the psychological twin of the artist. Within Masters' own text Nilsen accrues powerful vampiric qualities (signified by the whitening of his face to simulate death, for example) that seem to account for his unconventional and voracious appetite for murder and its aftermath. Nilsen himself describes his relationship with his victims as one of an 'assimilation' of their spirits. Like a *revenant* exposed to the light of day, Masters says of Nilsen: 'it was difficult to believe he was human at all. He himself wondered, he wrote, if the jury could see him decomposing slowly in the dock' (ibid.: 218).

In this narrative there are a number of motifs that are born of the legacy of philosophy and aesthetics outlined by Foucault and Black above. The romantic and gothic imagery points indirectly to the initial formulation identified by Black of the murderer-as-artist. Kant's promotion of aesthetic disinterestedness, which according to Black takes on a radical and subversive form in De Quincey, casts a faint shadow on non-fiction accounts such as this. This can be read in the references not only to Nilsen's apparent detachment from his acts, but also to his distorted artistic or creative (in the sense of both art and the generation of life) impulses. Like a modern-day Frankenstein, Nilsen is depicted attempting to bring injured animals back to health and life. Nilsen calls his corpses 'my tragic products' (ibid.: 149) and Masters asks the reader to decide whether he 'is he killer, victim, or producer' (ibid.: 144). This last question is asked in response to Nilsen's description of himself as a central camera, framing and recording acts of murder, and unflinchingly arranging his corpses. Masters lends significance to Nilsen's film-making while posted in the Shetlands. Here Nilsen directs a comrade, 'Terry Finch', in numerous short films. Nilsen undergoes a crisis of frustration when he realises that 'Finch' is unattainable:

He went alone to the high overhang at Fitful Head and thought of throwing himself over, to the sound of the ever-present screeching birds. Then he walked back to base, finally dejected and hopeless. ... All the films which he had made with such care and pride over the last year he threw into the incinerator and destroyed. (ibid.: 78)

Diana Fuss (1983: 189) argues in her article on Hannibal Lecter and Jeffrey Dahmer that film as a technology of 'dismemberment and fragmentation' formally corresponds with medical pathology:

> This formal correspondence ... may explain why, in narratives of serial killing, the film director has virtually become a cliché ... the killers [in films] are often amateur filmmakers, filming their kills so they can watch them over and over again, trying to recapture, through cinematic replay, the experience of the actual killing.

Amy Taubin (1991: 16) makes a similar point when she shows how cinematic voyeurism (and film theory's own concept of 'distanciation') employed in serial killer films from *Psycho* (Powell UK 1960) to *Henry: Portrait of a Serial Killer* (McNaughton USA 1990) 'is creepily revealed as the emotional framework of murder'. Nilsen's films of 'Finch' playing dead occur long before he commits murder. However, the notion of the killer as a film director objectifying the bodies of his actors is implicit. He is portrayed as the tortured artist who wreaks havoc on the bodies of his victims in order to create his own distorted scenarios of love and desire. Here the imagination, unfettered by reason or morality, becomes a malevolent amoral (rather than immoral) force. In the course of Nilsen's trial, an expert witness, Dr Gallwey, describes Nilsen's objectification of his victims in terms of a misdirected imagination:

> A normal person enriches experience and life with imagination. A schizoid personality indulges imagination for its own sake. This can produce artists, but in schizoids it can be dangerous. ... Nilsen's imagination eventually took him over, causing recurrent breakdowns. (Masters 1985a: 226)

In *The Shrine of Jeffrey Dahmer* (1993) Masters devotes a much longer passage to the dangers of the imaginative capacity which can alienate the dangerous individual from the social strictures of 'real life'. He notes (ibid.: 41): 'It is virtually impossible to exaggerate the dangers of this kind of withdrawal (unless, of course, it promotes the creative isolation of artist, who is, in this respect, the antithetical twin of the murderer).' In the film-making episode and at various other points in the narrative Nilsen is represented as a murderer-artist succumbing to his fantasy of choreographing both life and death. Nilsen's filming, photography, his obsession with posing himself and his corpses in tableaux and the reproduction of his sketchbooks in the book foreground his role as demonic artist. In addition, Masters makes much of his subject's interest in the works of Oscar Wilde while on remand, spying a narcissistic love that smacks of artistic decadence. His evidence includes Nilsen's reworking of Wilde's poems that indicate, 'the almost inconceivable and unpalatable possibility that the act of murder was, in this case, a diabolical act of love' (ibid.: 144).

The connotations of decadence, narcissism and self-fashioning recall Joel Black's promotion of *The Picture of Dorian Gray* as pivotal in the transition from the artistic criminal to the artist as criminal. As already indicated the use of a romantic aesthetic in the representation of Nilsen's early years dovetailed at one point with the issue of sexuality: 'his very nature was marked with a scar of abnormality ... like a club foot' (ibid.: 70). Now Masters' account reinforces this imagery of the tortured artist who is also deviant and criminal by attempting a brief analysis of Nilsen's homage to 'The Ballad of Reading Gaol' (which, incidentally, was sent to him by the author) from which he quotes (ibid.: 145):

> It's now the turning tide of time
> When all will ask me, why?
> I sleep, the only company
> Forever with me lie;
> And is there love in such a thing
> When everything must die?

Unspoken in Black's account of early criminal literature, but implicit in his references to Lacenaire, Wilde and Genet and so on, is the cultural yoking together of decadence, narcissism and the cultivation of the self as an artwork within literary explorations of homosexuality. The textual imbrication of sexual deviance with death is developed throughout *Killing for Company* in the stories of Nilsen's love for his dead grandfather and for some of those whom he despatched. But this is also more specifically apparent in his narcissistic obsession with mirrors and the makeup that he would use to simulate his own demise. In Masters' text Nilsen becomes the unique but flawed protagonist of a *Bildungsroman* that descends into tragedy, a darkly romantic figure that belies the author's own construction as dispassionate commentator.

Subjects and objects

The *frisson* of horror that accrues to the figure of Nilsen may also be attributable, in part, to his role as an ostensible representative of law, order and authority. He was variously a soldier, NCO, policeman and civil servant – all counterparts of the law. According to Masters, Nilsen's status as an employee with some degree of power and rank remains unrecognised so that he must resort to strange acts of murder in order to shore up his uncertain authority. Masters comments (ibid.: 25): 'The sad paradox of his unremarkable life was to discover that he was, after all remarkable.' How is Nilsen 'remarkable' within the terms of Masters' book? Nilsen explains popular interest in his story by claiming that he is a 'rare type' enacting what everyone secretly wishes but fears to do (ibid.: 25–6). His discourse of the uniquely daring individual foregrounds the aura of power and esoteric knowledge accrued by the serial killer within the terms of the narrative. Certainly, the depiction of Nilsen and others mentioned above, as a revenant, vampire or thwarted artist who transgresses the laws of nature, adds something to this notion. Also, the notorious criminal may also be a 'remarkable' or 'rare' type within the story of 'criminal history' wherein certain notable individuals propel the narrative onwards and 'make things happen'. Masters comments (ibid.: 293) on these lofty individuals: 'They are themselves aware of their uniqueness, and look upon the attempts by the rest of us to distil their characters into a shape that we can apprehend with something like amused disdain.'

The national press carries a number of examples of this perception of the serial killer as an 'expert' or 'specialist' in the field of murder. During the Colin Ireland investigation of 1993 the press carried a number of articles speculating upon the usefulness of the serial killer as an informed expert.[25] The *London Evening Standard* (2 July 1993: 22) carried a full-page article on the news that Nilsen had *not* been approached to speculate on the identity of the perpetrator of a number of murders of homosexuals within the London area. None the less most of the piece is devoted to a letter from Nilsen in which he offers his unique services to the law. Nilsen warns: 'Before I could make any full assessment of his [the killer's] psychological profile I would require an appreciation of the details at the scene of the crime and key facts flowing from forensic pathology.' Ironically, Nilsen employs the discourses of criminal psychiatry and 'police procedurals' rather than responding in a manner or in a lexicon which would suggest a 'unique' knowledge base. Later Nilsen begins to draw a portrait of the elusive serial killer:

He is reliving the indelible imprints of the traumas of his childhood with a ritual which requires him to render his victim into a state of extreme passivity [i.e. dead] so that he views the nude, unresponsive body in the frisson of an image which oscillates between two vivid self-images – his fantasy vision can embrace himself as both victim and doer.

Here Nilsen replicates, in the assessments of the unknown killer's motivation, those that were formed by Masters and others to account for his own murderous activities. Within the article Nilsen maintains the position of oracular authority; a seer whose portrait photograph is larger than the video still of the unknown murderer who was later to be identified as Colin Ireland. This redeployment of professional lexicons by the criminal is difficult to interpret; it suggests a mimicry (or perhaps a mockery) of legalistic discourses. It might also be interpreted as a counter-discourse, a strategy that robs the law of its authority to speak and identify the criminal subject. Lastly, it may be understood as evidence that the criminal can decode violent crime only through the discourses of the human sciences that have already constituted him as a modern criminal subject. Clearly, the criminal is himself inscribed within these discourses as an object of knowledge and cannot leave them behind. Masters' comments, as well those of medico-legal professionals, illustrate the confusing collision of discourses seeking to penetrate the enigma of the multiple murderer as the object of knowledge. Despite this confusion, the validity of the infamous killer as an historical object of analysis remains central to the legitimisation of detailed non-fiction accounts. Masters insists (1985b: 294): 'If the death penalty were still in force, it would now be idiotic to kill Nilsen, for that would destroy the only evidence worth exploring.'

The existence of Nilsen as living 'evidence' and as an exhibit is central to Masters' account. This suggests a double function of true crime narratives: to set up the killer as a witness of evil, a witness of what, for those operating within the discourses of reason, is simply unknowable but also to present the killer as an enigma to be decoded, an object to be studied. Here, the journalist simulates the role of the anatomist in his/her avowed intent to produce 'a study of a murderer's mind that is 'unique of its kind' and 'to treat his material with ... objectivity and restraint' (jacket notes). The gridding of Nilsen's face by the metal bars of the prison van window and the reflection of camera lighting on his spectacles in the image featured on the book's cover reinforces this notion of the killer as a pinned-down object of evidential scrutiny.

Similarly, the cover graphics of a weekly magazine depicted Jeffrey Dahmer's head as an anatomical object of clinical enquiry – divided into labelled coloured grids (Fuss 1993: 198). The scrutiny of the brain, face and eyes of the murderer not only objectifies him but also recalls his objectification of his victims through dismemberment or consumption of body parts. This tilts towards our collective fears of becoming the objects of consumption. Reversals and elisions of the distinctions between subjecthood and objecthood, between the individual as powerful agent and the individual as the object of violence or even consumption are arguably central to popular interest in this material. True crime describes bizarre forms of seizure, both corporeal, spiritual and in terms of property (through the collection of totems or trophies). Propp's (1968: 32) description of the villain who demands or lures his/her victims into an attack involving mutilation explicitly links body parts with other property:

> It is interesting to note that these forms [of story] ... are also forms of seizure. The eyes, for example, are placed by the servant girl in a pocket and are carried away; thus they are consequently acquired in the same manner as other seized objects.

Seizures of all kinds are given considerable significance in serial killer stories. Masters, for example, notes Nilsen's 'oft-repeated contention that he had absorbed the essence of the dead into himself', thus committing the ultimate spiritual plunder (1985b: 192). But the body itself is the more obvious and tangible object of theft. The psychologist Jane Firbank (1994: 22) wrote in *Hello!* magazine during the events surrounding the Fred and Rose West case:

> Some [serial killers] collect the belongings of their victims – underclothes, jewellery. Some gather their statistics; one German serial killer wrote the name, date of death and dead-weight of each victim into a ledger. And some collect the bodies themselves.

David Canter (1994) discusses this corporeal objectification in a chapter entitled 'Objects of Murder'. Here the attempt by the killer to sever the head and hands of his victim is commented upon by a clinical psychologist new to crime: 'Wow! What a wonderfully symbolic act. A real attempt to turn the victim into a non-person, to remove her personality' (1994: 237).[26] As already noted, the complex relationship between subjecthood and objecthood in *Killing for Company* revolves around the story of Nilsen's own perception of himself as dead or decomposing;

contrasting with other images of Nilsen as assertive, powerful and capable of turning his victims into object-corpses. Foucault argues in *The Order of Things* (1970: x) that with the emergence of the human sciences 'man' emerged as a discursive construct – he is both the subject and the object/sacrifice of knowledge – one of these knowledges being 'the knowledge of living beings'. True crime represents a popular and repetitive re-enactment and exploration of the implications of this double role within modernity. Studies such as Jouve's *'The Streetcleaner'* and Masters' books on Nilsen and Dahmer chronicle the killer's drive to understand the mechanisms of victims' bodies. The killer's interest in anatomy (e.g. Sutcliffe's viewing of anatomical wax models, Nilsen's sketches of corpses, Dahmer's interest in reconstructing bodies and listening to the sounds of the living body, Fred West's fascination with the sexual body) justifies the centrality of the body as the object of investigation, knowledge and control within true crime. Indeed, as noted in the previous chapter, other kinds of true crime literature focus solely on the corpse, both as an object of evidence and as a sign of mortality. So too, the body of the serial killer itself can become an object of spectacle, not only in terms of the face of the killer mentioned earlier, but also more literally. For instance, the US tabloid *Weekly World News* (27 December 1994) (a paper not renowned for its seriousness) carried the headline: 'The picture EVERY American wants to see! INSIDE: FIRST PHOTO OF JEFFREY DAHMER'S DEAD BODY'. Among the articles surrounding the authentic-looking photograph of Dahmer on the mortuary slab is one proclaiming 'Human flesh found in Dahmer's stomach during autopsy'. Here even the specularised body of Dahmer can continue to be an object of fear because he has ingested the body of another. In this way the objectified body of true crime cannot be identified in any simple way as always the body of the victim. The bodies of both victims and criminals may be represented as objects of investigation and fascination.

Who are you? Categorising the killer

> The accused evades a question which is essential in the eyes of the modern tribunal, but which would have had a strange ring to it 150 years ago: 'Who are you?'
>
> Michel Foucault (1988: 126)

> It's now the turning tide of time
> When all will ask me, why?
> Nilsen (in Masters 1985a: 145)

The notorious killer is not in any simple way merely the object of inquiry and of the discursive practices that underpin investigative procedure. He or she may also be seen to be a participant who resists easy definitions and therefore disrupts attempts to categorise and contain. As an object of knowledge the presence of the criminal subject serves as much to highlight the limitations of scientific and popular enquiry in making sense of violent crime as to substantiate them. As the above quotations indicate the notorious criminal is an enigmatic figure, an object of inquiry of whom several key questions are asked including, 'what was your motivation or why?' and underlying this another more fundamental question 'Who are you?' The central role of the modern judicial system (as well as that of the crime journalist) is to ascertain from the criminal the true answer to this metaphysically important and all-consuming question. The injunction to the criminal is to speak, to confess, to enumerate and explicate his/her crimes. This injunction may be founded upon the unacknowledged conviction that the 'cold blooded' murderer has an esoteric relationship with and knowledge of the forces of life and death which is somehow more 'authentic' than anything that may be inferred from everyday life. To borrow a phrase from Foucault (1961: 7) the multiple murderer in particular is perceived to be a 'hieratic witness of evil'. Categorising the criminal is a function of the discourses that attempt both to contain the unease emanating from the subject of such terrible knowledge and to maintain the authority of the law.

Both the inquisitors (judges, psychiatrists, journalists, and so on) and the killer himself are aware of the range of previously established categories into which he must be made to fit. *Killing for Company* is exemplary in its delineation of the various professional and popular lexicons which frequently clash during any attempt to solve the enigma of who Nilsen is and what motivated him. Nilsen himself remarks: 'I can't think of any slot to place myself in. … I wish there was a clear view on motive, conventionally speaking, then I could come to grips with the problem' (Masters 1985a: 141–2). He then proceeds to try on various labels only to reject them as inappropriate or inaccurate, including sex maniac, robber, sadist, necrophiliac, avenger and madman. Later still (ibid.: 184) he sums up a host of other labels which he has borne at one time or another including: 'job finder, peace campaigner, amateur film maker, mine of useless information, administrator, penpusher, detained prisoner, solitary reaper, killer of the innocent, unremorseful, reformed character, enigma … warped monster, mad man, ungodly, cold and alone.' At yet another point he comments astutely:

'Society has a right to call me a cold mad killer. No other category fits my results' (ibid.: 188).

As *Killing for Company* demonstrates, professionals such as Masters together with legal and medical experts experience much difficulty in finding a category to fit the criminal subject rather than simply the results of his actions. It is partly for this reason that the notorious killer remains a source of anxiety and fascination. Not only is he encouraged to speak, but also this discourse has a disproportionate impact amongst the many other voices of the legal-media spectacle (including especially those of the victims and their families). As a result, the rhetoric of normality versus deviance has to be sustained in spite of rather than because of the presence of the notorious homicide. In Nilsen's case, although he did not speak in court, he was quoted at length; for example, the court heard Nilsen's confessional piece entitled 'Unscrambling Behaviour' (ibid.: 214–15). Both Masters and Janet Malcolm note not only the killer's tendency to talk compulsively and at length about themselves, but also, more significantly, how media celebrities such as these are never short of listeners. Arguably, murderers are invited to make their own interventions into the procedures of power and thereby become, discursively at least, a source of fascination, turbulence and disruption.

Foucault (1975) observed that as the spectacle of punishment gave way to the processes of interrogation and confession, so too both professional and public attention shifted towards a renewed scrutiny of the soul and of the mind of the murderer. This will-to-know has multiple origins: it is apparent not only in the discourses of the medico-legal professions but also in the narratives which appeal to the popular imagination. Foucault (ibid.: 21) argues that each judgement of the accused is founded upon the degree of abnormality of the accused; it is quite evident, however, that the perceived abnormality of these killers gives grounds for both reassurance and anxiety. They become the focus of public fascination and repugnance that is compounded by the contradictory ordinariness of their everyday lives. They are 'other' but not sufficiently so.

Masters' account of Nilsen's trial in 1983 shows how, as in the case notes of Pierre Rivière (Foucault 1973), a proliferation of discursive practices, each conforming to its own knowledge base and lexicon, clash in the attempt to situate the criminal within its own particular hierarchy of categories. Of the various discourses which cross-hatched the events of the Rivière case, Foucault (1973: x) explains: 'But in their totality and their variety they form neither a composite work nor an exemplary text, but rather a strange contest, a confrontation, a power relation, a battle among discourses and through discourses.' This 'strange contest' is clearly enacted at Nilsen's trial. The trial begins inauspiciously enough with a complicated episode of 'logical nonsense' that is imposed upon the jury through the inconsistencies in the language of the judicial process. Ivan Lawrence for the defence was to argue for a charge of manslaughter on the grounds of diminished responsibility. He did not, however, try to prove Nilsen insane in 'either the medical or legal sense' (1985a: 219). It is possible to argue that Lawrence's refusal to offer a defence which was solidly based within the established medico-legal frames of reference led to the jury's decision to find Nilsen guilty of murder rather than manslaughter on the grounds of diminished responsibility. Lawrence called in Dr MacKeith as an expert witness for the defence. MacKeith argued that: 'Nilsen's trouble was an unspecified type of personality disorder, which did not fit any particular category. He showed signs of disorder in all categories, but insufficient to diagnose when taken alone' (ibid.: 220). Following this comment a contestation of definitions arises. The legal form of words used by the prosecution is too narrow to be acceptable for Dr MacKeith, leading to a contretemps over the words 'mind', 'personality' and 'character'. A series of discursive oppositions arose which could not be resolved. Dr MacKeith favoured the terms 'personality', 'repression', and 'dissociation'. The prosecuting counsel Alan Green offered the following alternatives: 'character', 'suppression', 'very good actor'. Finally, unable to respond within the parameters of the appropriate discourse, Dr MacKeith was 'unable' to formulate a judgement as to Nilsen's mental condition at the time of the killings. As Masters (ibid.: 224) shrewdly concludes: 'The lawyers and the psychiatrists did not speak the same language.' This conflict arises once again in the form of an exchange between an expert witness, Dr Gallwey, and Mr Justice Croom-Johnson. The Justice inquires of the doctor: '"By reason of his [Nilsen's] emotions not being involved, he is acting in cold blood. Is a cold-blooded killer not responsible for his acts?" Dr Gallwey replied that such words were not within his discipline' (ibid.: 228). Later still Ivan Lawrence draws yet another discourse into the courtroom – that of common sense. He asks (ibid.: 236), '"Does not common speech oblige one to say of the perpetrator of those killings, he must be out of his mind?"' Again this seems to offer no common lexical ground for the experts.[27]

What is ably illustrated in *Killing for Company* is the insubstantial persona of the killer when read through the inadequate and conflicting discourses which seek to understand him. The argument here is not that other, more 'adequate' discourses are required; rather that the notion of a coherent subject is, in this example, revealed to be a chimera. It is arguable that these professional discourses founded upon the hegemony of modern reason, which persists against all obstacles to render the human subject knowable, foundered upon the subject who eludes the delimiting definitions of (legal) language. The 'monstrous' criminal can 'pass' as an ordinary member of the public because the only outward sign of his/her derangement is the enactment of the crime itself. Here the prominent but elusive murderer appears to be 'a fragment of ambiguous space' (Foucault 1966: 314), cross-hatched but never fully-formed by either analytic, medico-legal or literary language.

It could be argued that Dennis Nilsen's deployment of professional lexicons to profile other murderers foregrounds the fragmentation of the self into both the subject and the object of knowledge. Nilsen, as Masters shows in some detail, presents a problem for professionals and for the public alike because as an object of knowledge he seems to refuse to surrender the psychological secrets of motivation and impulse that led him to the murders and their aftermath. Nilsen himself recognises the considerable limitations of medico-legal enquiry into these matters. Yet when he is asked to account for the actions of another, apparently similar murderer, he seems to become the subject of that knowledge, picking up and wielding the discourses that pathologise the killer with skill and verve. This doubled and precarious balancing act is a good example of the ambivalence of true crime as a genre. As seen most particularly in the last two chapters, true crime adopts just such reflexivity. It invites readers-as-subjects to deploy knowledge to expose the mind of the killer and the body of the victim to scrutiny. But at the same time readers are told that they are actually exploring themselves (readers-as-objects) since true crime implicates everyone ('there but for the grace of God go I') as either victim or perpetrator.

The nightmare scenario of Nilsen decomposing in the dock or the sequential photographs of the body that literally falls apart in true crime codifies and contains fears of psychical and corporeal dissolution. While true crime narratives mark out an individual who is 'remarkable' or 'rare' within history, reinforcing perhaps, the promises of infinity and renown inscribed within the positive knowledges of modernity; his *mode* of self-substantiation reveals the 'watermark' of the knowledge of our own finitude – the mortality of the body. Foucault (1966: 315) calls this 'a finitude which rests on nothing but its own existence as fact'. The literary depiction of the serial killer (e.g. Easton Ellis) may be said to represent the killer as symptomatic of a postmodern *Zeitgeist* and this may well be in line with the appearance of the 'serial killer' as a late twentieth-century phenomenon. None the less, a closer look at the common-or-garden variety of true crime texts reveal that they are still firmly embedded within the discourses of the human sciences which engendered both 'man' and the modern criminal subject and made them both the objects of study.

8
Concluding Comments

This book has investigated the relationship between the prominence of contemporary true crime and the social and political moment of its commercial success. It has analysed how various non-fiction accounts of crime and punishment, law and order programming, quasi-government initiatives, popular journalism, true crime books and magazines – speak about and interrogate issues of criminality and victimhood in the contemporary moment. It has argued that the ability of true crime to harness and explore current concerns about law and order, mortality and individual vulnerability, all within a highly accessible format, constitutes part of its popular appeal. The analyses undertaken here unravel the subtle and complex differences in the ways in which fear and fascination are articulated in the discourses of true crime. The readings made in this work take into account the specificity of particular genres, discourses and imagery in the production of knowledges about crime, policing and punishment, trying to understand them in the context of the social and political moment of their production and reception. This has involved identifying how politically inflected subject positions, most notably that of the 'dangerous individual', the 'moral subject' and the 'good citizen' are constituted through a range of discourses about real-life crime.

In thinking through these themes, it is perhaps the issue of personal vulnerability in the face of crime, especially but not only violent crime, which has come to the fore most often. In a work written specifically to disabuse the public of the notion that violent crime is rife in Britain Elliott Leyton notes that his objectives come up against the fact that, 'public fear is universal, palpable, apparently justified' (1997: 1–2). The presenters of *Crimewatch UK* comment that: 'Fear is the greatest penalty we pay for crime. ... Society has been frightened by crime throughout history, and nothing we do is likely to change the pattern much' (Ross and Cook 1987: 157–8). In addition, as John Keane suggests, social and economic factors such as ethnic discrimination or poverty create so-called 'no-go' zones, 'archipelagos of incivility within an otherwise civil society' that attract and focus differently inflected fears of social discord (1996: 115). The importance of fear as a factor in policing the country has also been widely acknowledged, with at least one Police Force explicitly promoting its role to reduce 'crime, *fear* and disorder'.[1] Richard Sparks (1992: 11) points out that this apparently diffused 'fear' is in fact made up of a range of different and differently weighted anxieties dependent upon circumstance and type of person, so that the fears of the elderly, of male youth or of women differ not only in '"quantity" but in kind.'[2] None the less a generalised fear remains the mobilising reference point, the touchstone of 'common-sense' political rhetoric, of government crime surveys, of private and individual policing initiatives and media critiques of violent representation. In the run-up to the 1997 general election press coverage of the 'rising tide of lawlessness' was as prominent as ever (see Ackroyd and Miller 1997).[3] Chester Stern (1997: 32) of the *Mail on Sunday* still felt the need to ask: 'If crime is falling, why don't we feel safe in our beds at night?' He comments: 'public perceptions of crime have never been worse ... our personal experiences seem hopelessly at odds with official figures.'

Many of these issues – the appeal of true crime, its mobilisation of fear and fascination with crime and violence, its exploration of mortality and vulnerability – hinge to a lesser or greater degree on the status of the genre as representation of real events. True crime functions as sensational testimony 'which confronts us with the body of the historical person, heir to all the vicissitudes of life, and subject to the finality of death' (Nichols 1994: 48). The image of the corpse of Tommy Thompson, murdered by his abused and desperate daughters, the TV reconstruction of the 'last known movements' of a robbery victim, a post-mortem display of a drowned cadaver or the nightmarish description of the serial killer disposing of his victims are all more than simply moments of voyeuristic fascination (although they are these too). Their presence attests to the fact that brute offence and personal violation, although uncommon, are present in the most civil of civil societies and cannot ever be wholly eradicated, policed or hidden from view. It is in this sense that true crime fits with and provides a forum for the real concerns of readers about personal vulnerability and physical danger in everyday life.

Notes

Introduction

1. For further publishing details, see Benn's *Media UK* and *Brad* for these years.
2. At the time of writing magazines cost about £1.80 each or £15 for an annual subscription.
3. Magazine and Design Publishing, which produces the main bulk of regular titles, has not to date applied for certification by the Audit Bureau of Circulation.
4. See Benn's *Media UK 1996*. Campbell (1993: 13) says that there is a circulation of 30,000 for *True Detective*.
5. *BRAD*, October 1995.
6. The reader profile for these long-running monthlies is of a readership over 45 years of age, occupying the C2, D, and E socio-economic bracket and largely female (Cameron 1990: 131).
7. Occasionally magazines refer explicitly to this recycling process in order to sell back-copies, e.g. 'Disaster at public execution', in *Master Detective* November 1994: 36, refers readers to the full-length version in a back copy from 1993.
8. This is from the promotional leaflet in the first edition.
9. Author of an investigation into the notorious A6 motorway murder entitled *Who Killed Hanratty?* (1971).
10. In fact, the well-known Penguin *Famous Trials* anthology of vintage cases was reissued as 'social history' (Mortimer 1984).
11. Bedford's book was an account of the longest murder trial to date (1957) of Dr John Bodkin Adams.
12. Hawley Harvey Crippen was hanged on 23 November 1910 for the murder and dismemberment of his wife Cora. He was arrested with his lover Ethel Le Neve (who was disguised as a boy) after pursuit on an ocean liner bound for Quebec. The event inspired a number of true accounts, novels plays, several films and a musical (see Goodman 1985).
13. Florence Maybrick was found guilty of the murder of her husband in 1889 (Wilson and Pitman 1961: 445–6).
14. Blue Books record the visual evidence of every murder inquiry in Britain.
15. These were not the first audio books to enter the true crime market. During the 1970s Ivan Berg Associates (Audio Publishing) re-issued Edgar Lustgarten's true crime radio broadcasts on audio-cassette (see, for example, Lustgarten 1976).
16. Known as the 'Yorkshire Ripper', Sutcliffe murdered 13 women between 1975 and 1980.
17. Christie is now thought to be responsible for the murders of seven women and a baby. He was sentenced to death on 15 July 1953.
18. Information from *The Bookseller* 1992–96.

19. Beverley Allitt was convicted in May 1993 of the murder of four children and of harming nine others (see Davies, N. 1993a).
20. During more than two decades the English couple Fred and Rose West abducted, raped and murdered at least 12 women and girls. Fred West committed suicide in prison while awaiting trial. In the 'trial of the century' Rosemary was convicted of the murders in November 1993 and awarded ten life sentences (Cobain 1995).
21. In August 1994 Roderick Newell was found guilty of the murder of his parents. His brother was convicted for helping to dispose of their bodies.
22. See Brown and Cheston (1994), Josephs (1994) and Wood (1994).
23. While 'instant' books, which are often crudely expanded journalistic dossiers of a crime, attract only occasional criticism for exploiting recent grief and fascination, television and film productions of notorious crimes often have to wait many years before they can be made with impunity. For example, the first British television drama documentary of the Peter Sutcliffe investigation was made in 2000. See *This is Personal: The Hunt for the Yorkshire Ripper* (Granada, UK, broadcast 26 January and 2 February 2000).
24. My understanding of the phrase 'law and order' accords with the definition formulated by Martin Kettle (1983: 218) that it is both 'a policy area covering crime and justice' and 'a belief in and practice of *discipline* in attitudes, behaviour and choices in the home, the streets and the workplace' (author's emphasis).
25. The journalist Nick Cohen (1996) has argued that the British press seeks to make ideological capital out of even the most appalling killings by blaming the permissiveness of 30 years ago. See also my discussion of the ways in which the Moors Murder case of 1957 provided a focus for some of these debates (Chapter 2).
26. It is clear, for example, that there has been a substantial rise in crime (or the recording of national crime figures) in Western Europe since the early 1950s (Central Office of Information 1995: 3). While readers may not be cognisant of these facts of rising crime they will share the perception that crime is rising and that personal risk is increasing.

1 'True stories only!'

1. See, for instance, the highly critical coverage of Gitta Sereny's second book on the child murderer Mary Bell, *Cries Unheard* (1998). See also the concerns expressed by the victims of the serial killer David Berkowitz about the making of the film *Summer of Sam* (Lee 1999 USA). Protestors against the film carried banners reading 'Murder is not Entertainment' (Wilson 1999: 25).
2. See chapter 1 note 14 above.
3. Finally, of course, both the genres of domestic photography and of police photography are situated, in the context of the gallery space, within the cultural category of 'art'.
4. The third book is Tom Byrnes' *Writing Bestselling True Crime* (1997).
5 This problem can be solved through literary ventriloquy but only, of course, when the criminal protagonist is long since dead. See, for example,

Andrew Motion's (2000) recent biography of the aesthete and poisoner Thomas Wainwright (1794–1847), which takes the form of 21 fictionalised confessional chapters.

6. For another, quite different, self-reflexive commentary on the interdependence of actuality and representation, see Simon Schama's account of an historical murder. Here Schama transgresses codes of factual narration to highlight 'the teasing gap separating a lived event and its subsequent narration' (Schama 1991: 320).

7. Cameron and Frazer add the codes of 'existentialism' to those of romanticism.

8. Lennard Davis, for example, in his genealogy of the English novel, describes the 'act of disownment' in which the author denies a creative connection with their work, shifting the 'focus of the narrative ... to the authenticity of the document', as 'uniquely novelistic' (1983: 16).

9. See, for example, the controversy over the 'truthfulness' of the representation of the events surrounding the Stephen Lawrence case following the broadcast of the drama documentary *The Murder of Stephen Lawrence* (Carlton/Granada, UK, 18 February 1999). See 'Television Version of Murder "Distorts the Facts"' (Davenport 1999) and 'The Justice Game' (Redhead 1999).

10. The long history of crime literature, the boom in true crime since the 1980s and the tradition of lurid reportage ('if it bleeds it leads') might belie this assumption of a gentler literature in Britain.

11. Suzanne Moore (1991: 13) has noted that in general the avowed moral concern about violent or offensive literature is often a smokescreen for other concerns. 'We know *American Psycho* is Literature with a big L because Norman Mailer has publicly defended it. ... In other words it is only when these things enter middle-brow culture that we begin to make a fuss about them. ... But the fuss we make often boils down to little more than an argument over good and bad art.'

12. Thomas De Quincey (1890) is famous among true crime writers for his essay on the Ratcliffe Highway murders of 1811. The murders of three adults and a baby at home on the Highway and later of another three adults nearby were described by De Quincey as the 'sublimist' in the art of murder. On murder as art, see also Oscar Wilde (1922).

13. While Jenkins is correct in identifying the strategic use to which serial murder may be put by lobbyists across the political spectrum, this view should be tempered with the recognition that special interest groups may have valid concerns over the way in which the police prioritise certain cases.

14. See also work on gender, misogyny and modern crime by Caputi (1987); Soothill and Walby (1991); Radford and Russell (1992), Birch (1993) and McLaren (1993).

15. See also Smith (1989) and Bland (1992) for commentaries on the Ripper cases.

16. Knox is referring in particular to James Baldwin's *Evidence of Things Unseen* (1985, New York: Henry Holt) and Kate Millett's. *The Basement: Meditations on a Human Sacrifice* (1979/1991, New York: Simon and Schuster).

17. See Burns (1977) for an historical overview of the formation of 'pubic opinion' and Hartley (1992: 183ff) for an analysis of how the modern press forms 'public opinion'.

18. On the problem of violent film images, see 'Violent Anxiety' by Linda Grant (1996) and Brian Masters' 'Are We All His Victims?' (1999). The latter argues that public fascination with the character Hannibal Lecter 'depraves us all'. On the scandal surrounding the Myra Hindley portrait, see Daniels (1997) and Mouland (1997). See also the controversy over the artist Jamie Wagg's use of media images arising from the murder of James Bulger and its aftermath (Walker 1996). For criticisms of true crime programming, see, for example, Cult (1993a, b and c) and Hellen (1993).

19. The best publicised critique of Hollywood film to reach a mass audience is Michael Medved's *Hollywood versus America* (1992) which was serialised in the *Sunday Times* in February and March 1993 (see Medved 1993a and 1993b). Medved catalogued acts of violence perpetrated in mainstream movies as part of a broader argument about the socially and morally destructive effects of some popular films. In contrast, audience research conducted by Annette Hill (1997) found that audiences who watched violent films regularly actually become more sensitised to film violence.

20. See Gauntlett and Hill (1999: 248ff) for a summary of the debate and a concise account of academic work in the area of media violence and its effects.

21. See, for example, Hunter and Kaye's assertion that: 'everyone is a potential niche market. One of the many pleasures of consumer capitalism is that it so perfectly services this fragmented, postmodern individual. Out there in the global pick'n'mix is a text made just for you' (in Cartmell *et al.*, 1997: 3). See also the debate about the role of the cultural critic, populism and the free market between Graeme Turner (1992) and John Docker (1991 and 1994).

22. There has been a growing debate within cultural and media studies about a perceived abnegation of critical responsibility within the field. Connor (1992: 234) has characterised the problem of relations between theory and questions of cultural value as one of a continuing pull between the use of evaluative criteria (selection, preference and judgements of quality) and anthropological imperatives of observation and interpretation (see also Herrnstein Smith 1986). For more on this debate and its implications for the field, see McGuigan (1992), A. Ross (1989), Squires (1993), Tester (1994), Frow (1995) and Miller and Philo (1997).

23. See, for example, Ang (1982) Radway (1984) and Morley (1986) for examples of how popular texts are open to contestation by readers and viewers.

24. For an incisive critique of the ways in which recognition (and consent) is invited in the tabloid press, a form that shares many characteristics with the traditional true crime magazine, see P. Holland (1983).

2   Histories of True Crime

1. Davis notes: 'The evolutionary model [of the development of the novel] is perhaps the most pervasive one. In literary critical works which search for forerunners, precursors, embryos, and missing links the underlying metaphor is a phylogenetic one. ... The obvious flaw in using the evolutionary model for literary analysis is that its metaphor implies a slow,

progressive change based on the key biological notion of adaptation' (Davis 1983: 2–4).

2. For example, there were developments in the new technologies of printing, of travel, of the distribution of goods, the availability of rags for paper-making and the cultivation of mass literacy.

3. See Emsley (1987: 11–13, 248ff) for a concise summary of the progressive (Whig) interpretation of criminal history and of its opponents such as Rusche and Kirchheimer (1968) and Foucault (1978).

4. See also Radzinowicz with Hood (1986) for a progressive stance on the history of punishment and reform.

5. The trial and execution broadsheets sold on the streets were always popular, their sales swelling noticeably in the mid- to late eighteenth century and again in the second quarter of the nineteenth century (Gatrell 1995: 156).

6. This is not to say that the people were always in complete accordance with the rule of law. Distinctions between 'the legal code and the unwritten popular code' were commonplace and were usually rooted in the specific requirements of the community rather than of the country at large (Thompson 1963: 59–60).

7. This could simply be a sound commercial justification for re-issuing stories without any direct resonance for English readers.

8. Their construction is similar to some of the illustrations used in modern collect-and-keep true crime magazines, see Chapter 5.

9. Executions themselves were, of course, a great popular attraction, since 'public punishment was theatre' (Emsley 1996: 256). See also Laqueur (1989), Garland (1991) and Gatrell (1994).

10. For a psychoanalytic reading of the relationship between popular fascination with and repulsion towards the criminal, see Duncan (1996).

11. It also renders explicit the law's relation to sovereignty (Foucault 1979: 47; Hunt and Wickham 1994: 40ff).

12. The image of early policing as haphazard and inefficient has however been challenged recently (Emsley 1996: 216ff).

13. It should be added here that although Colquhoun's plans were not immediately implemented, his conceptualisation of the role of the police chimed with those of later reformers.

14. See, for example, the discussion of crime as organised entrepreneurialism in Chapter 3.

15. As already indicated in Chapter 1, the growing imperatives within literature to distinguish between fact and fiction, biography and the novel, history and news, will impact particularly on true crime writers who attempt to remain objective while also necessarily employing 'imaginative leaps' to realise their stories.

16. Shocking, atypical crimes did sometimes galvanise public opinion into calling for more organised policing; most notably the stealthy murders of two separate families within a week of each other in December 1811. This case instilled rising panic leading to abortive calls for police reform. See De Quincey (1890), Critchley (1970: 40–1) and Critchley and James (1971).

17. There was a resurgence of political radicalism following Waterloo and the introduction of the Corn Laws (both 1815) epitomised in the drama of the 'Peterloo' massacre of parliamentary reformers in 1819. In addition, the

appearance of the Chartist Movement (from 1836) and the growing fear inspired by insurrections across Europe from the 1830s, all helped to construct and bolster another kind of collective criminality – the mob (Briggs 1996: 111–18; Pearson 1983: 156ff).

18. 'Flare-up' may be found at the St Brides Printing Library, Special Collection. For an account of the development of street literature, see Shepherd (1973).

19. Visual signification is still central to the appeal of modern true crime magazines. See Chapters 4 and 5.

20. All the following examples of street literature may be found at the St. Bride's Printing Library, Special Collection.

21. Dates followed by – signify that the date of publication is approximate.

22. For a clear discussion of news values see Hartley (1982).

23. Gatrell's (1996) own research suggests that this popular scepticism of the operations of the Council was well founded.

24. See my discussion of Birkett's selection from the *Newgate Calendar*, above, for a reference to this leniency towards fraudsters.

25. The idea of a 'criminal class' was always present but was most commonly used during the 1860s. The formal category of 'habitual criminal' was created by legislation in 1869 and 1871 (Emsley 1996: 168ff; Wiener 1990: 294–307).

26. For a detailed discussion of the conflicting discourses of medicine and the law, see the discussion of the trial of Dennis Nilsen in Chapter 6.

27. For a comprehensive description of Victorian 'penny dreadfuls' held in the Barry Ono Collection at the British Library see James and Smith (1997), for a list of the various working definitions of the 'penny dreadful' see Springhall (1998: 42).

28. The novel, based on the Whitechapel murders which occurred when Lowndes was 20 years old, remains in print. It has been translated into 18 languages, adapted for five films, a stage play and an opera (Cyriax 1996: 282, Marcus 1996: xxii).

29. For a comprehensive assessment of the 'the permissive moment' and the place of trial cases such as that of D. H. Lawrence's novel, see Weeks (1981: 249–72).

30. Freud distinguishes quite clearly between remorse and guilt (1930: 324–6). The perpetual guilt of civilisation, the 'fatal inevitability of the sense of guilt', is reinforced by the suppression of aggressive inclinations which are carried over to the super-ego (ibid.: 325). Later he notes that the sense of guilt produced by civilisation appears as a kind of malaise or general 'dissatisfaction' (ibid.: 329).

31. See especially my last chapter on the criminal as the subject and object of knowledge in Brian Masters' true crime biography of Dennis Nilsen (1985a).

32. The spate of books about Hindley and Brady, together with full media coverage of the trial, led to press debate about the limits of representation of sensational murder cases. Some journalists were quick to criticise the popularity of books about real crimes (Whelwell 1966: 14). Others such as Ludovic Kennedy entertained the possibility of a 'benevolent censorship' in the light of the Moors case, although he ultimately sanctioned the public's need to know (Kennedy 1966: 489). Kennedy had good grounds for this

defence since his own book about the Christie/Evans case, marrying a challenge to British justice with an enthralling real-life murder story, contributed towards a posthumous pardon for Timothy Evans (see Kennedy 1961).

33. An advert for *Beyond Belief* on the same page as the Fowler review reinforced its literary profile; carrying puffs by Rebecca West, as well as by The *Observer* and *The Times* newspapers.

34. Smith was an unwilling spectator to the murder of the couple's final victim.

35. For Brian Masters, writing nearly three decades after Williams, the same allusion to Pope is still apposite. 'All murder is awful. ... But we may still look at them, and at ourselves, and ponder. "The proper study of mankind is man." Murderers are men too' (1994: 15). It is also the epigram to Elliot Leyton's book *Men of Blood* (1995: 1), although it is wrongly attributed to a prison doctor.

36. This notion of true crime as a mirror or reflection on the self is not new, see my discussion of early modern illustrated editions of true crime stories described above. In addition, several recent books on high-profile crimes have initiated a confessional form of crime writing which is still consistent with the ontological aims of more 'objective' accounts. Both O'Hagan (1996) and Morrison (1997) are introspective, drawing upon their own autobiographies to make sense of violent crime.

3   Discourses of Law and Order in Britain from 1979 to 1995

1. See, for example, Abercrombie *et al.* (1986: 11), who agree, with certain provisos, that British society is broadly individualistic in character.

2. Magazines such as *Killers* (renamed *Ultimate Crimes*) and the newest entry into the market *Murder in Mind* (February 1997–) exclude by definition crimes other than homicide.

3. Jack the Ripper is, perhaps, the most notorious example. See, for example, the special edition of true crime magazine *Murder Most Foul* (No. 22) which presents the mystery of the murderer's identity as its main attraction.

4. I refer to these as 'law and order' programmes in order to differentiate them from other real-life reconstruction programmes such as *Michael Winner's True Crimes* (ITV UK), which should more properly be designated 'true crime' programming. 'Law and order' programmes are those that operate in conjunction with the police and which invite the viewing public to help in investigating crime.

5. The exception to this is *Inside Crime* (Carlton UK 1997), presented by former police commissioner John Stalker. This programme showcases crimes that have remained unsolved for some time (usually years) through a mixture of interviews, visits to scenes of crime, and so on.

6. As Schlesinger and Tumber (1993: 30) indicate, *Crimewatch UK* also helps to disseminate the notion that something is being done about crime since the programme makes evident that these less stigmatised crimes are also being scrutinised by the police.

7. This emphasis upon the viewer as detective also masks the other purpose of the programme – to address the viewer as a consumer of television, to entertain the viewer and to maintain audience figures.

8. Of course it also in the interests of the police to be able to use the media as an instrument in the investigation of crime, see Innes (1999).

9. Private law enforcement agencies have always been reluctant to work with the programme for commercial reasons (stated on *Crimewatch UK* January 1999).

10. For example, police officers perform a whole range of functions aside from law enforcement and crime prevention, but these are obviously unrepresented in the programme (see Reiner 1992: 212; Southgate with Ekblom 1996).

11. These include a donation by Royal Assurance to be spent by Neighbourhood Watch schemes in 1989 and Crime Concern (1988), a crime prevention initiative funded by the Home Office and Woolworth (see Johnston 1992: 138).

12. This was undertaken as part of a government initiative launched in September 1994 called 'Partners against Crime'. The intention was to promote co-operation between the public and the police (Central Office of Information 1992: 5).

13. It should be noted that the Conservative government's fostering of private action against crime did not lead to a concomitant reduction in police power or to a reduction of state control over policing. See Sullivan (1998).

14. Johnston notes, however, that the boundaries of the private security industry are difficult to establish. He divides the industry into three parts: provision of mechanical devices (e.g. locks), provision of electronic devices (e.g. CCTV) and the provision of staffed services (Johnston 1992: 71). While reliable information on the growth in private security is elusive there is substantial evidence that the market has expanded rapidly (ibid.: 73ff).

15. So, too, the number of properties protected by apotropaic signboards stating: 'Beware of the dog'; 'Enter at your own risk'; or more assertively 'Go ahead – make my day' (accompanied by an image of a snarling dog) is also evidence of the less quantifiable, sometimes less legitimate, actions undertaken by individuals to deter intruders and safeguard property. During the early 1990s canine defence turned into criminal threat through the perception that the growing popularity of the pit bull dog constituted a danger to the public. It was certainly the case that the dog was deployed by some owners as part of a defensive public machismo. The dog became part of street armoury, in Iain Sinclair's phrase, an 'heraldic cartoon' embodying courage and aggression (Sinclair 1997a: 55).

16. O'Hagan (1995: p. 163) has indicated, for example, that some police officers privately believe that the computerised records of missing persons will provide a testing ground for a nation-wide system for locating and identifying all citizens.

17. This is a reference to 25 Cromwell Street – the address where Fred and Rose West murdered and disposed of a number of women and children.

18. In fact, the Thatcher government's housing policy was more hesitant and opportunist than Hutton's work suggests, even if its ideological motives were clear-cut. See Stewart and Burridge (1989).

19. For an entertaining and insightful documentary on Neighbourhood Watch, see *Cutting Edge: Street Patrol* (Channel 4, UK, 24 November 1998).

20. In fact, Abercrombie *et al.* (1986: 81ff) offer four constituents of individualism, briefly: 'liberty and freedom from interference, capacity for transformative action, rationality, responsibility and self-motivation'.

21. Foucault suggests also that 'the birth of detective literature and the importance of the *faits divers*, the horrific newspaper stories' contributed to this constitution of the populace as 'moral subject' (1980a: 41).

22. In 'Prison Talk' Foucault suggests that intolerance of the delinquent in now being eroded. Even if this is the case, the discourses of true crime and of law and order programming still deploy divisive strategies in their depiction of the moral subject and the criminal subject (1980: 42–3).

23. The carceral organisations include the school, the military barrack and the mental asylum, see Foucault (1975).

24. Parker's nomination of the habitual criminal who constantly returns to prison as the 'Unknown Citizen' is a reference to the 'Unknown Soldier.' Parker's analysis of the case of Charlie Smith, who once committed an act of theft only a few hours after being released from prison, suggests that the criminal, like the soldier, is a victim of an inflexible and crude system of regulation and abuse. Both soldier and criminal are sacrificed and then forgotten; shoring up the security of the nation.

25. At the 1993 Conservative Party Conference the Home Secretary Michael Howard said: 'We shall no longer judge the success of our system of justice by a fall in our prison population. ... Let us be clear. Prison works' (in Rawlings 1999: 152).

26. Indeed, Mary Desjardins (1993: 143) argues in her analysis of *The Krays* (Medak 1990 UK) that the story 'exposes the connection between free enterprise and criminality'. This is foregrounded in the title of Charlie Kray's book *Doing the Business* (Fry and Kray 1995).

27. True crime books such as Duncan Campbell's *That Was Business, This Is Personal* (1990), depictions of organised crime in London in the 1960s and 1970s, e.g. *The Long Good Friday* (Mackenzie 1981 UK) and *The Krays* (Medak 1990 UK), and the television series *Our Friends From the North* (January 1996–BBC2, UK) are indicative of this kind of portrayal. These texts, both fact and fiction, offer alternative communities in which conspiracy, gangsterism and organised crime thrive.

28. A recent variation on this type of real-life television includes the one-off programme *Rat Trap* (Carlton, UK, broadcast 08 March 2000). This 45-minute programme presented by the newsreader Kirsty Young, lays traps for criminal 'rats' by filming bait such as unattended motorcars to see who 'bites'. The footage is then broadcast to see if any viewer can identify the thieves. The executive producer Sarah Caplin defended the programme, claiming: 'We are not creating the crime, nor are we inviting people to steal. ... We are replicating normal activities ... and using cameras to see what happens next' (*Radio Times* 4–10 March 2000: 103).

29. True crime is, of course, only one of the many factual or fact-based genres that have repackaged 'real life' into mass entertainment (see Caughie 1980; Goodwin 1993; Paget 1998).

30. *In Suspicious Circumstances* is unusually long at 60 minutes per episode; however, there are usually three 20-minute stories told within each episode.

31. *In Suspicious Circumstances* actually credits Edward Woodward as 'story-teller' rather than as 'presenter'.

32. For example, the Channel Four documentary programme *Despatches: The Shame of Cromwell Street* (UK, 22 November 1995) concentrated upon a broader culpability in the failure of society (state services, neighbours, acquaintances) to detect and prevent the murders and abuse committed by Fred and Rose West over several decades.

33. An example of this may be seen in an episode of *In Suspicious Circumstances* called 'Crimes of Passion'. In this episode the presenter concludes the story by judging that the protagonist, for a variety of reasons (the murderer's putative innocence, her alleged pregnancy and the cruelty of capital punishment itself), should not have hanged. In this instance, the call for natural justice to be served supersedes that of official criminal justice.

34. Similarly, Edward Woodward is an actor known for his 'enforcer' roles in series and film adaptations such as *Callan* (Sharp 1974 UK) and the 1980s' vigilante series *The Equalizer*. Both these roles were of law enforcers who were at the margins of the law.

35. Here also, of course, the symbolism of the eyes of the law stands in stark opposition and dialogue with the eyes of the killer so beloved of horror iconography.

36. I am greatly indebted to Research Editor Lucy Wildman and Librarian Victoria Kearns for allowing me access to the *Digest* library and for their help in locating materials.

37. There are exceptions to this – see my discussion of an article by David Moller below.

38. See, for example, Hollway (1981), Bland (1992) and J. Smith (1989).

39. As indicated in my earlier discussion of the Charters developed under John Major, Thatcherite discourses, albeit somewhat reconfigured, continued to inform both political and popular discourses after the Thatcher years. However, it should also be noted here that Majorite campaigns, especially the 'Back to Basics' initiative, were also formulated in order to deal with the 'catastrophes ... which were the direct outcome of the Thatcher years themselves' (Rose, J. 1996: 56). In this sense Majorite political discourse constituted both an extension of, and a rejoinder to, Thatcherism.

40. The most dramatic example of the criminal as venture capitalist is the case of Nick Leeson, whose massive fraud brought down Barings Bank. A 'biopic' entitled *Rogue Trader* (Dearden UK) was released in 1999.

4   Crime Magazine Stories

1. In this instance 'Americanisation' means the importation of new cultural forms and styles, for example, changes in idiom, dress, music and popular literature.

2. For a literary exploration of this shift, see Graham Greene's 1938 novel *Brighton Rock*.

3. This strategy was far from new. The makers of 1930s gangster movies were impelled to add cautionary slogans to their films to defuse criticism of bad effects on impressionable audiences. John Springhall (1998: 100–1) relates how the Howard Hawks' film *Scarface* (1932) became subtitled 'Shame of the Nation' and included a straight to camera speech advocating citizens to fight against crime.

4. Deborah Cameron (1990: 134) notes that the pornographic gaze continued in true crime magazines until the late 1970s and very early 1980s. She notes, for example, the particular influence of pornography on the magazines of the 1960s and argues that the structure of true crime genre was always pornographic.

5. As John Fiske (1989: 106) observes, vernacular speech is not replicated directly by the popular press, instead a form of written language is developed that produce 'resonances' between it and the speech patterns of spoken cultures used by readers.

6. It is increasingly rare to see cover-girls on the front of even the more traditional true crime magazines, but the register and visual signification of Summer Specials in particular tends to hark back to what Leon Hunt (1998: 2, 25–6) has called the 'permissive populism' of the 1970s.

7. Roland Barthes (1977: 27) has noted that the contradiction between image (the smiling cover-girl) and text (the murder story) also appears in true romance magazines, producing a 'compensatory connotation'.

8. The nomenclature 'serial killer' in particular is frequently used outside of its correct temporal and cultural context in true crime and elsewhere. For example, the popular history magazine *History Today* (1986 Vol. 46: 3: 1) trumpeted 'Stuart tabloid horror' in a feature entitled: 'Serial Killers in Seventeenth-century England ... the grisly Stuart Counterparts to Fred and Rosemary West.'

9. Full-length true crime books also use anachronisms to appeal to the reader, see, for example, the recent publication of the autobiography of a Victorian detective called *The Crime Buster* (Caminada 1996).

10. 'Everyday life may be conceptualised in various ways. For example, John Fiske (1989: 47) argues that, 'everyday life is constituted by the practices of popular culture.' I favour Henri Lefebvre's (1958b) formulation that 'everyday life' may be located in work, leisure, the family and in 'moments "lived" outside of culture' (although he then proceeds to problematise this definition [1958b: 31ff]). My reading of Lefebvre suggests that by 'culture' he is actually referring to official or high culture and that consequently 'everyday life' is that lived outside of high culture.

5   Period True Crime

1. True crime magazines will be referenced by their initials: *TC: True Crime; TCSS: True Crime Summer Special; TD: True Detective; TDSS: True Detective Summer Special; MMF: Murder Most Foul* and *MD: Master Detective*.

2. This preview was featured in *Master Detective* June 1996: 17.

3. David Chaney (1993: 88) defines 'public memory' as 'dramatic traces, symbolic artefacts, of the institutionalised forms of social order, in these traces

representations of significant moments, people or ideas will be made available to interpretation and re-interpretation.'

4. Thus, the meaningfulness of a seventeenth-century account of the trial and
punishment of a female killer is eroded not only by temporal distance, but
also by the inability of a leisure interest magazine to address the specificities
of husband-murder at a particular historical juncture.

5. Some of these stories have been discussed in 'Death in the Good Old Days:
True Crime Tales and Social History' (Biressi 2000).

6. For a full-length study of the generic relationship between romance and
true crime, see Knox (1998). Knox (1998: 87) observes usefully that
romance and crime have been, and continue to be, immensely popular
genres that are by no means mutually exclusive. She points out, for
example, that in the 1940s adverts for lonely-hearts clubs appeared in *True
Detective Magazine*. In addition, Chapter 1 of this book noted that a substantial proportion of true crime magazine readers are female and women constitute the bulk of the readership for romance novels.

7. For a detailed exposition on the historical development and relationship
between love, individualism and capitalism see Macfarlane (1987: 127–43).

8. Vanessa Schwartz (1994) has linked the spectacle of tableaux death scenes
to the moving image, albeit not theatre but film.

9. This strategy is analogous to the crediting of true crime television presenters
as 'story-tellers' (see previous chapter).

6 Daring to Know: Looking at the Body in the New True Crime Magazine

1. Victimology is the study of the victims' circumstances, habits and lifestyle.
Here the criminal investigator hopes that the victims' life will yield some
clue about their death.

2. It is not always the case that 'quality' true crime writing seeks to occupy a
moral high ground. See for example Gordon Burn's book about the West
family *Happy Like Murderers* (1998). Here Burn's writing is novelistic, bereft
of the dates, notes, sources or photographs that usually orient readers, lend
authority to the writer and add a didactic quality to the text. Burn's book is
much closer to his own novel-writing such as *Fullalove* (1995) and to
Truman Capote's *In Cold Blood* (1966).

3. It is rare for true crime books and news articles to say much about the killer
after he/she has been removed from the public sphere into prison. The continuing prominence given to Myra Hindley is an exception fuelled by the
Sun newspaper, by subsequent confessions of further crimes, by the
activism of bereaved families and by Hindley's attempts to gain release (see
Soothill and Walby 1991). See also Brian Masters' (1995) exceptional article
which examines the lives of US serial killers following imprisonment and
the serialised 'exclusive on Dennis Nilsen's life behind bars' in the *Daily
Mirror* 4 April (Edwards 1995).

4. Popular opprobrium can turn to carnivalesque celebration when a murderer
does receive the death sentence. In the case of Ted Bundy, 'The execution
was greeted with ghoulish enthusiasm, with "Bundy burgers" and T-shirts

on sale outside' (*Real-Life Crimes* Issue 10: 218). A photograph of Bundy's face, frozen in a howl of despair as he hears his sentence, is one of the most commonly used images of Bundy in true crime.

5. This sort of scenario also emphasises the discursive links between medical science as both life-enhancing and as violent intervention. More broadly still, Evelyn Fox Keller (1990: 177–91) has illustrated how science itself contains within it the double imperative to 'unveil' the secrets of nature ('life') and to develop instruments of death.

6. Forensic detection has constituted a new sub-genre of the true crime book, see Joyce and Stover (1993); Wecht (1993); Miller (1995).

7. References for this magazine will be abbreviated to *R-LC*.

8. For example, it has been suggested that the phenomenal success of Patricia Cornwall's forensic detective novels demonstrate that the scientist is the 'new avenging angel' of crime (Frances Fyfield talking on arts programme *Front Row*, BBC Radio 4, UK, 31 August 1999).

9. Television programmes such as the series *Autopsy* (Channel 5, 50 mins, USA, 29.02.2000 –) examining the work of forensic scientists in the US, and *Forensic Detectives* (Discovery, 60 mins, USA, 09 March 2000 –) also attest to TV audience's interest in this area of criminal detection.

10. The idea of the body as a 'natural' and readable phenomenon is underscored in an episode of *The Natural World* (nature documentary series) entitled *The Witness Was a Fly* (BBC2, UK, broadcast 17 April 1994; see also Davies 1994). Here the relationship between the cadaver and the rest of nature is revealed. The programme demonstrated, among other things, how the presence of a blowfly in a corpse can pinpoint the time of death.

11. There are also clear parallels between pornography and fictional 'slasher film' imagery. See especially, Linda Williams' (1989: 184ff) discussion of the generic confusion between horror films and hard-core pornography. She shows how the supposedly *vérité* film *Snuff*, which seems to depict both real sex and real atrocity, appeared to present a logical extension of pornography's aim to see pleasure displaced onto pain. She notes: 'read in the context of pornography ... a flinch, a convulsion, a welt, even the flow of blood itself' proves that a woman's body can be *seen* to be physically '"moved" by some force' (ibid.: 194).

7   Figures in a Landscape: The Dangerous Individual in Criminal Biography

1. This chapter will refer to the serial killer as 'he' throughout because female serial killers are considered to be extremely rare and in any case popular representation, with which this analysis is concerned, nearly always assumes that the killer is male. Note, however, that the criminal psychologist Candace Scrapec (1993: 241–68) has challenged the assumption that serial murder is a male province and the gendered assumptions that support this view.

2. See, for example, Renata Salecl's (1994: 107–11) analysis of the events around the arrest of serial killer Andrei Chikatilo in the former Soviet Union. He was responsible for the murders of 53 men, women and children

over a period of 12 years. Salecl argues that the pattern of his crimes echoed the logic of the Soviet system, both ignoring the law and also trying to become a law unto himself. See also Jenkins (1994: 121–38) for a survey of the ways in which the serial killing 'problem' has been deployed by various special interest groups as a weapon of social critique.

3. See, for example, the *Guardian*'s serialisation of Nick Davies' book on the nurse Beverley Allitt (Davies 1993b) beginning 22 May, and of Andrew O'Hagan's book on the Wests (O'Hagan 1995) beginning 2 September.

4. See, for instance, the film *Seven* (Fincher 1995 USA) in which the serial killer despatches his victims on the theme of the seven deadly sins, and the novel *Every Dead Thing* (Connolly 1999) in which the killer, known as 'Travelling Man', flays his victims alive and displays them in tableaux resembling illustrations from Renaissance medical texts.

5. According to *Brewer's Twentieth Century Phrase and Fable* (1991) it was the 'Zodiac Murders', a series of unsolved killings beginning in California in the late 1960s, that was subsequently to be acknowledged as the first murders by a serial killer. The case signals the centrality of the media to the amplification of subsequent serial killer crimes since 'Zodiac' maintained contact with the press, police and even a television chat show up until about 1974.

6. For an analysis of the complex relationship between murder, media spectacle and soap opera serials, see Hargreaves (1996: 44–56).

7. John Duffy, known as the 'Railway Rapist', was arrested in 1986 for the murder of three women and the rape of many others.

8. Jeffrey Dahmer was sentenced to 900 years in prison in 1992 for the torture and murder of 16 men.

9. See Anthony Shaffer's 1979 play *Murder* for a nostalgic re-enactment of these classic domestic murders. The play features a protagonist who is also a fan of period true crime; a man who fantasises about committing an old-fashioned domestic homicide.

10. It should also be noted, however, that cases such as that of the West family illustrate precisely how the 'new' kinds of apparently unmotivated murder and atrocity can and do occur within the domestic realm (Wykes 1998: 233–47).

11. For a comprehensive list of films and television production of Christie's work since the 1970s see Light (1991: 234–5, n. 9). Heavily cited texts on the 'golden' period of crime fiction include Watson (1971); Symons (1972); Cawelti (1976); Porter (1981) and Mandel (1984).

12. *Inspector Morse* made by Central Television for ITV (UK) was broadcast between 1987 and 1993, and has been repeated since. Set in scenic Oxford, many of the cases centre on murders within a family, business or other confined area. It is regarded as 'quality entertainment', winning a BAFTA for best drama in 1993 and for best actor (John Thaw) in 1989 (Holland, p. 1997: 290). See also '*Inspector Morse*: The last enemy', an essay that addresses its 'beguilingly timeless' quality (Sparks 1993: 86–102).

13. Leyton's book is *Hunting Humans* (1986). In fact, Britain has a relatively low rate of homicide and few murders are the result of random 'stranger' killings. A later book by Elliott Leyton (1995) was written precisely to

counter the 'moral panic' that Britain has a high rate of homicide and of psychopathic killers.

14. *Prime Suspect* (1991–6) was a television series made by Granada for ITV (UK). Scripted by Lynda La Plante it followed the work of a top woman detective heading a series of murder enquiries.

15. Barnes' comments on post-permissive 'affectlessness' echo those of Pamela Hansford Johnson (1967) voiced in her contemporary account of the Moors Murderers (see Chapter 2).

16. For example, see Iain Sinclair's *White Chappell, Scarlet Tracings* (1987) and also his non-fiction essays 'Bulls and Bears and Mithraic Misalignments' (1997b) and the 'Cadaver Club' (1997c) in *Lights Out for the Territory* (1997) and also Peter Ackroyd's *Hawksmoor* (1985) and *Dan Leno and the Limehouse Golem* (1994). For fictional explorations of more recent murders, see Pat Barker's *Blow Your House Down* (1984) which explores the lives of prostitutes set against the backdrop of Yorkshire Ripper-type killings, and *Another World* (1998), which depicts the haunting of a family by stories of child-murderers such as Mary Bell, and John Thompson and Robert Venables who killed James Bulger.

17. See promotional leaflets for The Jack the Ripper Walk, 41 Spelman Street, London E1 and the House of Detention, Clerkenwell Close, London EC1.

18. For a detailed account of the incompatibility of the individual and the social and its production of artists and criminals, see Martin (1986) where he examines notorious criminality as a partial response to artistic rejection. See also Katz (1988: 8) who makes an argument for the 'genuine experiential creativity' of crime.

19. For an account of the gendering of the aesthete murderer and its implications, see McDonagh (1992).

20. Simon During (1992) suggests that the artist, critic and poisoner Thomas Wainwright would be the British equivalent of Lacenaire. Wainwright, active in the 1880s, was eulogised by Oscar Wilde (1922) because he lived his life as art, killing people upon a whim (e.g. because a woman had thick ankles). During comments (1992: 164), 'he seems a very Foucauldian counter-hero.' See also Motion (2000).

21. For an account of the hermeneutics of the detective story, see Umberto Eco's *Reflections on the Name of the Rose* (1993).

22. Taubin (1991: 16) identifies this image of the serial killer as *revenant* also at work within the structures of the slasher film: 'It is the killer's ability to rise from the dead in film after film – rather than his appearance, his physical strength or even the extreme sadism of his actions – that demonises him.'

23. Since writing this chapter Gordon Burn has published his true crime book on Fred and Rose West called *Happy Like Murderers* (1998). For me, Burn's book is one of the few substantial criminal biographies to avoid the legacy of the romanticism of crime and the criminal discussed here.

24. I refer in particular to gothic as a literary form that privileges the psychological over the social, focusing on the fragmentation of the individual subject and how this interior struggle is often externalised through concepts of nature and the weather (see Jackson 1981: 97).

25. The film *The Silence of the Lambs*, in which the police try to draw on serial killer Hannibal Lecter's expertise in their pursuit of a serial killer, probably inspired this move.
26. Later Canter acknowledges the more prosaic possibility that the killer was trying to obliterate clues to identification.
27. The absence of a common ground here is symptomatic of the way in which jurisprudence works. Douzinas and Warrington (1991: 8) demonstrate the importance of the maintenance of legal discursive boundaries, observing: 'For jurisprudence the corpus of the law is literally a body: it must either digest and transform the non-legal into legality, or it must keep it out as excess and contamination.'

8   Concluding Comments

1. This objective is most visibly promoted by Thames Valley Police Force whose vehicles bear this slogan.
2. Differentiating between the degree of fearfulness within different demographic groups is notoriously difficult especially since findings are often tainted by the stereotyping of different social groups, see for example, Goodey (1997) and Gilchrist *et al.* (1998).
3. Philip Rawlings (1999: 169) observes that during the run-up to the general election New Labour could not afford to be seen as 'soft' on law and order issues and so simply tried to outbid the Tories on retributive policies on crime and punishment.

Bibliography

Abercrombie, N., Hill, S. and Turner, B. (1986) *Sovereign Individuals of Capitalism*, London: Allen and Unwin.

Ackroyd, P. (1985) *Hawksmoor*, London: Hamish Hamilton.

Ackroyd, P. (1994) *Dan Leno and the Limehouse Golem*, London: Sinclair Stevenson.

Ackroyd, R. and Miller, L. (1997) 'Crime, the £16 billion fear that haunts us all', in the *Express*, 24 February: 20–1.

Adonis, A. and Pollard, S. (1998) *A Class Act: The Myth of Britain's Classless Society*, London: Penguin Books.

Adorno, T. and Horkheimer, M. (1944/1979) *Dialectic of Enlightenment*, Trans. J. Cumming, London: Verso.

Adorno, T. and Horkheimer, M. (1944a/1979) 'The culture industry: Enlightenment as mass deception', in T. Adorno and M. Horkheimer (1944).

Adorno, T. and Horkheimer, M. (1944b) 'The importance of the body', in T. Adorno and M. Horkheimer (1944).

Altick, R. (1957) *The English Common Reader: A Social History of the Mass Reading Public 1800–1900*, Chicago: University of Chicago Press.

Altick, R. (1972/1974) *Victorian Studies in Scarlet: Murders and Manners in the Age of Victoria*, London: J. M. Dent and Sons.

Anderson, B. (1983) *Imagined Communities: Reflections on the Origin and Spread of Nationalism*, London: Verso and New Left Books.

Anderson, P. (1994) *The Printed Image and the Transformation of Popular Culture 1790–1860*, Oxford: Clarendon Press.

Ang, I. (1982/1989) *Watching Dallas: Soap Opera and the Melodramatic Imagination*, London: Routledge.

Anglo, M. (1977) *Penny Dreadfuls and Other Victorian Horrors*, London: Jupiter Books.

Anon. (*c.* 1773) *The Newgate Calendar or, Malefactor's Bloody Register*, Paternoster Row, London: J. Cooke.

Anon. (1994) 'Fear at the flick of a TV switch', in *Guardian, Outlook Section*, 26 March: 24.

Arasse, D. (1989) *The Guillotine and the Terror*, London: Allen Lane.

Arendt, H. (1963) *Eichmann in Jerusalem: A Report on the Banality of Evil*, New York: Viking Press.

Armstrong, N. and Tennenhouse L. (eds.) (1989) *The Violence of Representation: Literature and the History of Violence*, London: Routledge.

Artley, A. (1994) *Murder in the Heart: A True-Life Psychological Thriller*, Harmondsworth: Penguin Books.

Bainbridge, B. (1985) 'Supping full of horrors', in *Observer*, Arts and Books Section, 24 February: 27.

Bakhtin, M. (1965/1984) *Rabelais and his World*, Trans. H. Iswolsky, Bloomington: Indiana University Press.

Barker, M. (1984/1992) *A Haunt of Fears: the Strange Case of the British Horror Comics Campaign*, London: University Press of Mississippi.

M. Barker and Petley, J. (eds.) (1997) *Ill Effects: The Media/Violence Debate*, London: Routledge.

Barker, P. (1984) *Blow Your House Down*, London: Virago.

Barker, P. (1998) *Another World*, London: Viking.

Barker, P. (1996) 'Time and punishment', in *Observer on Sunday, The Observer Review*, 4 February: 14.

Barnes, H. (1993) 'The death of the English murder', in *Observer Magazine*, 7 November: 16–24.

Barthes, R. (1961) 'The photographic message', in R. Barthes (1977).

Barthes, R. (1968) 'The death of the author', in R. Barthes (1977).

Barthes, R. (1970) 'The third meaning; research notes on some Eisenstein stills', in R. Barthes (1977).

Barthes, R. (1977) *Image–Music–Text*, selected and translated by S. Heath, London: Fontana Paperbacks.

Barthes, R. (1980/1984) *Camera Lucida: Reflections on Photography*, London: Flamingo.

Bauman, Z. (1993) *Modernity and the Holocaust*, Cambridge: Polity.

Bedford, S. (1958/1989) *The Best We Can Do*, Harmondsworth: Penguin.

Begg, P. and Skinner, K. (1992) *The Scotland Yard Files: 150 Years of the C.I.D. 1842–1992*, London: Headline.

Belsey, C. (1980) *Critical Practice*, London: Methuen.

Benjamin, W. (1931/1978) 'A small history of photography', in *One Way Street and Other Writings*, Trans. E. Jephcott and K. Shorter, London: Verso.

Benjamin, W. (1955/1992) *Illuminations*, Trans. H. Zohn, London: Fontana.

Benjamin, W. (1955a) 'The storyteller: reflections on the works of Nikolai Leskov', in W. Benjamin (1955).

Benjamin, W. (1955b) 'Theses on the philosophy of history', in W. Benjamin (1955).

Bennett, C. (1993) 'Say cheese! The serial killer as celebrity', in *Guardian*, 26 January.

Bennett, T. (1986a) 'Introduction: popular culture and the turn to Gramsci', in T. Bennett *et al.* (eds.) (1986).

Bennett, T. (1986b) 'The politics of the "popular" and popular culture', in T. Bennett *et al.* (eds.) (1986).

Bennett, T. (1986c) 'Hegemony, ideology, pleasure: Blackpool', in Bennett *et al.* (1986).

Bennett, T. (ed.) (1990) *Popular Fiction: Technology, Ideology, Production, Reading*, London: Routledge.

Bennett, T., Mercer, C. and Woollacott, J. (eds.) (1986) *Popular Culture and Social Relations*, Milton Keynes: Open University Press.

Berman, M. (1982) *All That is Solid: The Experience of Modernity*, London: Verso.

Best, S. and Kellner, D. (1991) *Postmodern Theory: Critical Interrogations*, London: Macmillan – now Palgrave.

Birch, H. (ed.) (1993) *Moving Targets: Women, Murder and Representation*, London: Virago Press.

Biressi, A. (2000) 'Death in the good old days: True crime tales and social history', in S. Munt (ed.), *Cultural Studies and the Working Class: Subject to Change*, London: Cassell.

Birkett, N. (ed.) (1951) *The Newgate Calendar*, London: The Folio Society.

Black, J. (1991) *The Aesthetics of Murder: A Study in Romantic Literature and Contemporary Culture*, Baltimore: Johns Hopkins University Press.

Bland, L. (1992) 'The case of the Yorkshire Ripper', in J. Radford and D. Russell (eds.) (1992).

Bloom, C. (1990) 'MacDonald's man meets *Reader's Digest*', in G. Day (ed.) (1990).

Bloom, C. (1996) 'The Ripper writing: A cream of a nightmare dream', in C. Bloom (ed.), *Cult Fiction: Popular Reading and Pulp Theory*, London: Macmillan – now Palgrave.

Boothroyd, J. (1989a) 'Angels with dirty faces', in *Police Review*, 6 January: 16–17.

Boothroyd, J. (1989b) 'Nibbling away at the bobby's patch', in *Police Review*, 13 January: 64–5.

Borowitz, A. (1981) *The Woman Who Murdered Black Satin: The Bermondsey Horror*, Columbus, Ohio: Ohio State University Press.

Bouquet, T. (1995) 'The soft arm of the law', in *Reader's Digest*, December: 61–4.

Bouquet, T. (1997) 'Private clampers, public menace?', in *Reader's Digest*, April: 76–81.

Bourdieu, P. (1984) *Distinction: A Social Critique of the Judgement of Taste*, London: Routledge.

Bourke, J. (1994) *Working Class Cultures in Britain 1890–1960: Gender, Class and Ethnicity*, London: Routledge.

Boyle, T. (1968) *Black Swine in the Sewers of Hampstead: Beneath the Surface of Victorian Sensationalism*, New York: Viking.

Brandt, G. (ed.) (1993) *British Television Drama in the 1980s*, Cambridge: Cambridge University Press.

Briggs, J., Harrison, C., McInnes, A. and Vincent, D. (1996) *Crime and Punishment in England: An Introductory History*, London: University College London Press.

Bromley, R. (1988) *Lost Narratives: Popular Fictions, Politics and Recent History*, London: Routledge.

Brooks, P. and Gewirtz, P. (eds.) (1996) *Law's Stories: Narrative and Rhetoric in Law*, New Haven: Yale University Press.

Brown, L. (1985) *Victorian News and Newspapers*, Oxford: Clarendon Press.

Brown, T. and Cheston, P. (1994) *Brothers in Blood*, London: Blake.

Brundson, C. (1998) 'Structure of anxiety: recent British television crime fiction', in *Screen*, 39:3: 223–43.

Burchell, G. (1991) 'Peculiar interests civil society and governing "The system of natural liberty"', in G. Burchell *et al.* (eds.) (1991).

Burchell, G., Gordon, C. and Miller, P. (eds.) (1991) *The Foucault Effect: Studies in Governmentality*, Hemel Hempstead: Harvester Press.

Burn, G. (1984/1993) *Somebody's Husband, Somebody's Son: The Story of Peter Sutcliffe*, London: Mandarin.

Burn, G. (1995) *Fullalove*, London: Secker and Warburg.

Burn, G. (1998) *Happy Like Murderers*, London: Faber and Faber.

Burns, T. (1977) 'The organisation of public opinion', in J. Curran *et al.* (eds.) (1977).

Butler, I. (1992) *Murderers' London*, London: Robert Hale.

Byrne, R. (1992) *Prisons and Punishments of London*, London: Grafton.

Byrnes, Tom (1997) *Writing Bestselling True Crime and Suspense: Break into the Exciting and Profitable Field of Books, Screenplay, and Television Crime Writing*, US: Prima Publishing.

Cameron, D. and Frazer, E. (1987) *The Lust to Kill: A Feminist Investigation of Sexual Murder*, New York: New York University Press.

Cameron, D. (1990) 'Pleasure and danger, sex and death', in Day, G. (ed.) (1990).

Caminada, J. (1996) *Caminada: The Crime Buster*, London: True Crime Library.

Campbell, B. (1993) *Goliath: Britain's Dangerous Places*, London: Methuen.

Campbell, D. (1990) *That was Business, This is Personal*, London: Secker and Warburg.

Campbell, D. (1992) 'Crime becomes boom industry', in *Guardian*, 17 September.

Campbell, D. (1993) 'How murder is putting new life into publishing', in *The Guardian*, Section 2, 22 March: 13.

Campbell, D. (1994) 'Crime-watching', in *Guardian – Guide*, July 2–8: 11.

Campbell, D. (1995) 'Somebody's neighbour', in *Guardian*, Supplement, 15 December: 14.

Canter, D. (1994/1995) *Criminal Shadows: Inside the Mind of the Serial Killer*, London: HarperCollins.

Capote, T. (1966/1981) *In Cold Blood: A True Account of Multiple Murder and its Consequences*, London: Abacus.

Capp, B. (1996) 'Serial killers in seventeenth century England', in *History Today*, 46:3: 21–6.

Caputi, J. (1987) *The Age of Sex Crime*, Bowling Green, Ohio: Bowling Green University Press.

Carter, C., Branston, G. and Allan, S. (eds.) (1998) *News, Gender, Power*, London: Routledge.

Cartmell, D., Hunter, I. Q., Kaye, H. and Whelehan, I. (eds.) (1997) *Trash Aesthetics: Popular Culture and Its Audience*, London: Pluto Press.

Caughie, J. (1980) 'Progressive television and documentary drama', in *Screen* 21:3: 9–35.

Cawelti, J. (1976/1977) *Adventure, Mystery, and Romance: Formula Stories as Art and Popular Culture*, London: University of Chicago Press.

Central Office of Information (1992/1995) *Criminal Justice*, second edition, London: HMSO.

Chamblis, W. and Seidman, R. (1982) *Law, Order and Power*, second edition, London: Addison.

Chaney, D. (1993) *Fictions of Public Life: Public Drama in Late Modern Culture*, London: Routlege.

Charney, M. (1981) *Sexual Fiction*, London: Methuen.

Chesney, K. (1970/1972) *The Victorian Underworld*, Harmondsworth: Pelican Books.

Chibnall, S. (1977) *Law-and-Order News*, London: Tavistock.

Clarke, A. (1986) 'This is not the boy scouts: television police series and definitions of law and order', in T. Bennett *et al.* (1986).

Clover, C. (1992) *Men, Women and Chainsaws: Gender in the Modern Horror Film*, London: BFI.

Cobain, I. (1995) 'Rose West: guilty of murder', in *Daily Express*, 22 November: 4–5.

Cohen, N. (1996) 'Whodunit? The sixties of course', in *Independent on Sunday*, 14 April: 21.

Cohen, S. (1973) *Folk Devils and Moral Panics*, London: Paladin.

Cohen, S. (1988) *Against Criminology*, New Brunswick, New Jersey: Transaction Inc.

Collison, R. (1973) *The Story of Street Literature: Forerunner of the Popular Press*, London: Dent.

Colquhoun, P. (1797) *A Treatise on the Police of the Metropolis, etc.*, London: Mawman.

Connolly, J. (1999) *Every Dead Thing*, London: Hodder and Stoughton.

Connor, S. (1992) *Theory and Cultural Value*, Oxford: Blackwell.

Cornwell, J. (1984) *Earth to Earth: A True Story of the Lives and Violent Deaths of a Devon Farming Family*, Harmondsworth: Penguin Books.

Cousins, M. and Hussain, A. (1984) *Michel Foucault*, London: Macmillan – now Palgrave.

Critchley, T. A. (1967/1978) *A History of Police in England and Wales*, revised edition, London: Constable.

Critchley, T. A. (1970) *The Conquest of Violence: Order and Liberty in Britain*, London: Constable.

Critchley, T. A. and James, P. D. (1971) *The Maul and the Pear Tree*, London: Constable.

Culf, A. (1993a) 'Home Office seeks to ban murder show', in *Guardian*, 19 January.

Culf, A. (1993b) 'Mass killer "must not be allowed to air views on TV"', in *Guardian*, 26 January.

Culf, A. (1993c) 'TV watchdog upset by Nilsen interview', in *The Guardian*, 12 March: 4.

Cunningham, I. (1990) 'How to beat the car theft pros', in *Reader's Digest*, July: 39–42.

Curran, J., Gurevitch, M. and Woollacott, J. (eds.) (1977) *Mass Communication and Society*, London: Edward Arnold/Open University Press.

Cyriax, 0. (1993/1996) *The Penguin Encyclopedia of Crime*, revised edition, Harmondsworth: Penguin.

Dahrendorf, R. (1985) *Law and Order: The Hamlyn Lectures*, London: Stevens and Sons.

Daniels, A. (1997) 'The Royal Academy is degrading us all. It should not forget many talented artists served Adolf Hitler', in the *Daily Mail* 17 September: 8–9.

Davenport, J. (1999) 'Television version of murder "distorts the facts"', in the *London Evening Standard*, 18 February: 9.

Davies, A. and Saunders, P. (1983) 'Literature, politics and society', in A. Sinfield (ed.), *Society and Literature 1945–1970*, London: Methuen.

Davies, G. H. (1994) 'Dead giveaways', in the *Radio Times*, 22 April: 36–7.

Davies, N. (1993a) *Murder On Ward Four: The Story Of Bev Allitt, The Most Terrifying Crime Since the Moors Murders*, London: Chatto and Windus.

Davies, N. (1993b) 'Childhood of a serial killer', in the *Guardian Weekend* Supplement, 22 May: 7–16.

Davies, R. (1981) 'Viewpoint', in *The Times Literary Supplement*, 5 June: 631.

Davis, L. (1983/1996) *Factual Fictions: The Origins of the English Novel*, Philadelphia: University of Pennsylvania Press.

Day, G. ed. (1990) *Readings in Popular Culture: Trivial Pursuits?*, London: Macmillan – now Palgrave.

De Quincey, T. (1890) 'On murder considered as one of the fine arts', in *The Collected Writings of Thomas De Quincey*, Vol. X: 389–94, D. Masson (ed.), Edinburgh: Adam and Charles Black.

Defoe, D. (1725/1986) *True and Genuine Account of the Life and Actions of the Late Jonathan Wild* reprinted in D. Nokes (ed.), *Jonathan Wild* by Henry Fielding, London: Penguin Classics.

Desjardins, M. (1993) 'Free from the apron strings: representations of mothers in the maternal British state', in L. Friedman (ed.), *British Cinema and Thatcherism*, London: UCL Press.

Didinotto, R. (1992) 'Freed to rape again', in *Reader's Digest*, May: 67–72.

Docker, J. (1991) 'Popular culture versus the state: an argument against Australian content regulation for television', in *Media Information Australia*, No. 59.

Docker, J. (1994) *Postmodernism and Popular Culture: A Cultural History*, Cambridge: University of Cambridge.

Douzinas, C. and Warrington, R., with McVeigh, S. (1991/1993) *Postmodern Jurisprudence: The Law of Text in the Texts of Law*, London: Routledge.

Dove, G. (1982) *The Police Procedural*, Bowling Green, Ohio: Bowling Green Popular Press.

Dovkants, K. and Davenport, J. (1997) 'London crime: the new godfathers', in *London Evening Standard*, 14 March: 12–3.

Dreyfus, H. and Rabinow, P. (1982/1983) *Michel Foucault: Beyond Structuralism and Hermeneutics*, second edition, Chicago: University of Chicago Press.

Dreyfus, H. and Rabinow, P. (1986) 'What is maturity? Habermas and Foucault on "What is englightenment?"', in D. Couzens Hoy (ed.) *Foucault: A Critical Reader*, Oxford: Blackwell.

Duncan, M. (1996) *Romantic Outlaws, Beloved Prisons: the Unconscious Meanings of Crime and Punishment*, New York: New York University Press.

During, S. (1992) *Foucault and Literature: Towards a Genealogy of Writing*, London: Routledge.

Dyer, G. (1994) 'Journey to the heart of darkness', in *Guardian*, 12 March, Section 2: 29.

Dyer, R. (1997) 'Kill and kill again', in *Sight and Sound*, September: 14–17.

Easton Ellis, B. (1991) *American Psycho*, New York: Vintage Books.

Edwards, J. (1995) 'Inside chilling mind of psycho killer Dennis Nilsen', in the *Daily Mirror*, 4 April: 8–9 and 5 April: 22.

Eco, U. (1990) 'Interpreting serials', in *The Limits of Interpretation*, Bloomington and Indianapolis: Indiana University Press.

Eco, U. (1993/1985) *Reflections on the Name of the Rose*, Trans. W. Weaver, London: Secker and Warburg.

Eliot, T. S. (1948) *Notes towards the Definition of Culture*, London: Faber and Faber.

Emsley, C. (1987/1996) *Crime and Society in England 1750–1900*, second edition, London: Longman.

Engel, M. (1996) *Tickle the Public: One Hundred Years of the Popular Press*, London: Victor Gollancz.

Erickson, L. (1996) *The Economy of Literary Form: English Literature and the Industrialization of Publishing 1800–1850*, London: Johns Hopkins University Press.

Ferris, P. (1966a) 'The mind of the murderer – Part I', in *Observer*, Supplement, 24 April: 13–21.

Ferris, P. (1966b) 'The mind of the murderer – Part II: the breaking point', in *Observer*, Supplement, 1 May: 9–14.

Fielding, H. (1743/1986) *The Life of Jonathan Wild*, Harmondsworth: Penguin Classics.

Firbank, J. (1994) 'Comment', in *Hello!* February Issue: 22.

Fiske, J. (1987) *Television Culture*, London: Methuen.

Fiske, J. (1989) *Understanding Popular Culture*, London: Unwin Hyman.

Fiske, J. and Hartley, J. (1978) *Reading Television*, London: Methuen.

Fitzgerald, M., McLennan, G. and Pawson, J. (eds.) (1981) *Crime and Society: Reading in History and Theory*, London: Routledge and Kegan Paul.

Foot, P. (1971/1988) *Who Killed Hanratty?*, Harmondsworth: Penguin Books.

Foucault, M. (1961/1989) *Madness and Civilisation: A History of Insanity in the Age of Reason*, Trans. R. Howard, London: Routledge.

Foucault, M. (1963/1973) *The Birth of the Clinic: An Archaeology of Medical Perception*, Trans. A. M. Sheridan, London: Tavistock.

Foucault, M. (1966/1989) *The Order of Things: An Archaeology of the Human Sciences*, London: Routledge.

Foucault, M. (1969/1989) *The Archaeology of Knowledge*, Trans. A. M. Sheridan Smith, London: Routledge.

Foucault, M. (1972) 'Prison talk', in M. Foucault (1980).

Foucault, M. (1973/1982) 'Tales of murder', in M. Foucault (ed.), *I, Pierre Rivière … A Case of Parricide in the 19th Century*, Trans. F. Jellinek, London: University of Nebraska.

Foucault, M. (1975/1979) *Discipline and Punish: The Birth of the Prison*, Trans. A. Sheridan, London: Peregrine Books.

Foucault, M. (1976a) 'The politics of health in the eighteenth century', in M. Foucault (1980).

Foucault, M. (1976b/1984) *The History of Sexuality: An Introduction*, Trans. R. Hurley, London: Peregrine.

Foucault, M. (1977) 'The eye of power', Trans. C. Gordon, in M. Foucault (1980).

Foucault, M. (1978) 'Body/power', Trans. C. Gordon, in M. Foucault (1980).

Foucault, M. (1980) *Power/Knowledge: Selected Interviews and Writings 1972–1977*, Trans. C. Gordon, L. Marshall, J. Mepham and K. Soper, ed. C. Gordon, New York: Pantheon Books.

Foucault, M. (1982) 'The subject and power', in H. Dreyfus and P. Rabinow (1982).

Foucault, M. (1984/1986) *The Foucault Reader*, P. Rabinow (ed.) London: Penguin Books.

Foucault, M. (1984a) 'What is Enlightenment?', Trans. C. Porter, in P. Rabinow (1984).

Foucault, M. (1984b) 'On the genealogy of ethics: an overview of work in progress', in M. Foucault (1984).

Foucault, M. (1988) 'The dangerous individual', in *Politics, Philosophy, Culture: Interviews and Other Writings 1977–1984*, L. Kritzman (ed.), London: Routledge.

Fowler, N. (1967) 'Sadist studied in depth by Emlyn Williams', in *The Times*, 8 June: 16.

Frayling, C. (1986) 'The house that Jack built: some stereotypes of the rapist in the history of popular culture', in S. Tomaselli and R. Porter (eds.), *Rape*, Oxford: Blackwell.

Freud, S. (1930/1991) 'Civilization and its discontents', in Volume 12 *Civilization, Society and Religion*, Penguin Freud Library, A. Dickson (ed.), Harmondsworth: Penguin.

Frow, J. (1995) *Cultural Studies and Cultural Value*, Oxford: Oxford University Press.

Fry, C. with Kray, C. (1995) *Doing the Business: Inside the Violent Empire of the Krays*, London: Smith Griffin.

Fuss, D. (1993) 'Monsters of perversion: Jeffrey Dahmer and *The Silence of the Lambs*', in M. Garber, J. Matlock and R. Walkowitz (eds.), *Media Spectacles*, London: Routledge.

Fussell, P. (1977) *The Great War and Modern Memory*, Oxford: Oxford University Press.

Galtung, J. and Ruge, M. (1973) 'Structuring and selecting news', in S. Cohen and J. Young (eds.), *The Manufacture of News: Deviance, Social Problems and the Mass Media*, London: Constable.

Garland, D. (1991) *Punishment and Modern Society: A Study in Social Theory*, Oxford: Clarendon Press.

Gatrell, J. A. C. (1994/1995) *The Hanging Tree: Execution and the English People 1770–1868*, Oxford: Oxford University Press.

Gauntlett, D. and Hill, A. (1999) *TV Living: Television, Culture and Everyday Life*, London: Routledge.

Gay, P. (1973/1979) *The Enlightenment: An Interpretation 2, The Science of Freedom*, London: Wildwood House.

Gekoski, A. (1998) *Murder by Numbers: British Serial Sex Killers Since 1950 – Their Childhoods, Their Lives, Their Crimes*, London: Deutsch.

Gerrard, N. (1998) 'Do we really need to know?', in *Observer* Review Section, 13 September: 18.

Giddens, A. (1987) *The Nation-State and Violence: Volume Two of A Contemporary Critique of Historical Materialism*, London: Polity Press.

Giddens, A. (1991) *The Consequences of Modernity*, London: Polity Press.

Gilchrist, E., Bannister, J., Ditton, J. and Farrall, S. (1998) 'Women and the "fear of crime": challenging the accepted stereotype', in *British Journal of Criminology*, 38:2: 283–98.

Gill, M. and Hart, J. (1997) 'Exploring investigative policing: a study of private detectives in Britain', in *British Journal of Criminology*, 37:4: 549–67.

Gledhill, C. (1987) 'The melodramatic field: an investigation', in C. Gledhill (ed.), *Home is Where the Heart is: Studies in Melodrama and the Woman's Film*, London: BFI Publishing.

Godwin, W. (1794/1988) *Caleb Williams or Things as They Are*, Harmondsworth: Penguin.

Goldrei, D. (1967) 'Facing up to violence', in *Illustrated London News*, 11 March: 26.

Goodey, J. (1997) 'Boys don't cry: masculinities, fear of crime and fearlessness', in *British Journal of Criminology*, 37:3: 401–18.

Goodman, J. (1983) *The Pleasure of Murder*, London: Alison and Busby.

Goodman, J. (1984) 'The fictions of murderous fact', in *Encounter* 62:1: 21–6.

Goodman, J. (1985) *The Crippen File*, London: Alison and Busby.

Goodman, J. (1990a) *Bloody Versicles of Crime: The Rymes of Crime*, second edition, Penarth: Hallmark Books.

Goodman, J. (ed.) (1990b) *The Art of Murder*, London: Piatkus.

Goodwin, A. (1993) 'Riding with ambulances: television and its uses', in *Sight and Sound*, January: 26–8.

Gordon, G. (1994) 'Published but not damned', in *The Times*, 29 April: 15.

Gramsci, A. (1985) *Selections from Cultural Writings*, ed. D. Forgacs and G. Nowell-Smith, Trans. W. Boelhower, London: Lawrence and Wishart.

Grant, L. (1996) 'Violent anxiety', in *Guardian Weekend*, 28 September: 22–9.

Graves, R. (1957/1962) *They Hanged My Saintly Billy: The Macabre Life and Execution of Dr Wm. Palmer*, London: Arrow Books.

Greene, G. (1938) *Brighton Rock*, London: William Heinemann.

Grossberg, L., Nelson, C. and Treicher, P. (eds.) (1992) *Cultural Studies*, London: Routledge.

Gunning, T. (1989) 'An aesthetic of astonishment: early film and the (in)credulous spectator', in L. Williams (ed.) (1995).

Gunning, T. (1990) 'The cinema of attractions: early film, its spectator and the avant-garde', in T. Elsaessar (ed.), *Early Cinema: Space, Frame, Narrative*, London: British Film Institute.

Gunning, T. (1995) 'Tracing the individual body: photography, detectives and early cinema', in L. Charney and V. Schwartz (eds.), *Cinema and the Invention of Modern Life*, London: University of California Press.

Haining, P. (1975) *The Penny Dreadful, or, Strange, Horrid and Sensational Tales*, London: Gollancz.

Haining, P. (1977) *Mystery: An Illustrated History of Crime and Detective Fiction*, London: Souvenir Press.

Hall, C. (1980) 'The history of the housewife', in E. Malos (ed.), *The Politics of Housework*, London: Alison and Busby.

Hall, S. (1976) 'Violence and the media', in N. Tutt, (ed.), *Violence*, London: HMSO.

Hall, S. (1980a) *Drifting into a Law and Order Society*, London: Cobden Trust.

Hall, S. (1980b) 'Reformism and the legislation of consent', in National Deviancy Conference (ed.), *Permissiveness and Control: The Fate of the Sixties Legislation*, London: Macmillan – now Palgrave.

Hall, S. (1981) 'Notes on deconstructing "the popular"', in R. Samuel (ed.), *People's History and Socialist History*, London: Routledge and Kegan Paul.

Hall, S. (1983) 'The great moving right show', in S. Hall and M. Jacques (eds.), *The Politics of Thatcherism*, London: Lawrence and Wishart/*Marxism Today*.

Hall, S. (1995) 'Fantasy, identity, politics', in E. Carter, J. Donald, and J. Squires, (eds.), *Cultural Remix: Theories of Politics and* the *Popular*, London: Lawrence and Wishart/New Formations.

Hall, S., Critcher C., Jefferson, T., Clarke, J. and Roberts, B. (1978) *Policing the Crisis: Mugging, the State, and Law and Order*, London: Macmillan – now Palgrave.

Hall, S. and Gieben, B. (eds.) (1992) *Formations of Modernity*, London: Polity Press/Open University.

Hall, S. and Held, D. (1989) 'Citizens and citizenship', in S. Hall and M. Jacques (eds.) (1989).

Hall, S. and Jacques, M. (eds.) (1989) *New Times: The Changing Face of Politics in the 1990s*, London: Lawrence and Wishart/*Marxism Today*.

Hall, S. and Scraton, P. (1981) 'Law, class and control', in M. Fitzgerald *et al.* (eds.) (1981).

Hamilton, P. (1992) 'The Enlightenment and the birth of social science', in S. Hall and B. Gieben (eds.) (1992).

Hamilton, P. (1997) 'Representing the social: France and Frenchness in post-war humanist photography', in S. Hall (ed.), *Representation: Cultural Representations and Signifying Practices*, Milton Keynes: The Open University.

Hargreaves, T. (1996) 'Domestic violence, soap opera and real life', in A. Myers and S. Wight (eds.) (1996) *No Angels: Women who Commit Murder*, London: Pandora.

Harman, J. (1985) 'How you can beat the car thieves', in *Reader's Digest*, November: 119–22.

Harman, J., Slater, S. and Fletcher, L. (eds.) (1992) *Writing for Reader's Digest*, London: The Reader's Digest Assoc. Ltd.

Harris, T. (1988) *The Silence of the Lambs*, London: Heinemann.

Harrison, B. (1997) *True Crime Narratives: An Annotated Bibliography*, London: Scarecrow Press.

Harriss, J. (1994) 'Plague of revolving-door justice', in *Reader's Digest*, May: 77–81.

Hartley, J. (1982/1988) *Understanding News*, London: Routledge.

Hartley, J. (1992) *The Politics of Pictures: The Creation of the Public in the Age of Popular Media*, London: Routledge.

Haste, S. (1997) *Criminal Sentences: True Crime in Fiction and Drama*, London: Cygnus Books.

Hay. D. (1975/1977) 'Property, authority and the criminal law', in D. Hay, P. Linebaugh, J. Rule, E. P. Thompson and C. Winslow (eds.) *Albion's Fatal Tree: Crime and Society in Eighteenth-Century England*, London: Peregrine.

Hebdige, D. (1982) 'Towards a cartography of taste 1935–62', in B. Waites, T. Bennett, and G. Martin (eds.), *Popular Culture: Past and Present*, London: Croom Helm.

Heelas, P. and Morris, P. (eds.) (1992) *The Values of the Enterprise Culture: The Moral Debate*, London: Routledge.

Hellen, N. (1993) 'Warning for BBC on killer nurse story', in *The London Evening Standard*, 22 July: 3.

Hennessey, S. (1995) 'Don't be a victim', in *Sainsbury's: the Magazine*, April: 52–6.

Hill, A. (1997) *Shocking Entertainment: Viewer Response to Violent Movies*, Luton: John Libbey Media.

HMSO (1990) *Victims' Charter*, London: HMSO.

HMSO (1991) *The Citizen's Charter: Raising the Standard*, London: HMSO.

HMSO (1994) *The Citizen's Charter: Second Report*, London: HMSO.

Hobsbawm, E. (1994/1995) *Age of Extremes: The Short History of the Twentieth Century 1914–1991*, London: Abacus.

Hodgkinson, L. (1995) 'Neighbourhood watch foils the burglar', in *Reader's Digest* April: 152–6.

Hogg, J. (1824/1986) *The Private Memoirs and Confessions of a Justified Sinner*, Harmondsworth: Penguin Classics.

Hoggart, R. (1957/1985) *The Uses of Literacy*, Harmondsworth: Penguin.

Holland, P. (1983) 'The page three girl speaks to women, too', in *Screen* 24:3: 84–102.

Holland, P. (1997) 'Documentary and factual television', in *The Television Handbook*, London: Routledge.

Holland, S. (1993) *The Mushroom Jungle: A History of Post-war Paperback Publishing*, London: Zeon Books.

Hollingsworth, K. (1963) *The Newgate Novel 1830–1847, Bulwer, Ainsworth, Dickens and Thakeray*, Detroit: Wayne State University Press.

Hollway, W. (1981) '"I just wanted to kill a woman." Why? The Ripper and male Sexuality', in *Feminist Review*, 9: Autumn: 33–40.

Hopkins, E. (1991) *The Rise and Decline of the English Working Classes 1918–1990*, London: Weidenfeld and Nicolson.

Hough, M. (1988) 'Public attitudes to sentencing', in *Crime UK 1988: An Economic, Social and Policy Audit*, London: Policy Journals.

Hough, M. and Roberts, J. (1998) *Attitudes to Punishment: Findings from the British Crime Survey*, Home Office Research Study 179, London: Home Office.

Hurd, D. (1989) 'Freedom will flourish when citizens accept responsibility', in *Independent*, 13 September.

Hunt, A. and Wickham, G. (1994) *Foucault and the Law: Towards a Sociology of Law as Governance*, London: Pluto.

Hunt, L. (1998) *British Low Culture: From Safari Suits to Sexploitation*, London: Routledge.

Hunter, I. Q. and Kaye, H. (1997) 'Introduction', in Cartmell *et al.* (eds.) (1997).

Hutton, W. (1995/1996) *The State We're In*, revised edition, London: Vintage.

Ignatieff, M. (1978) *A Just Measure of Pain: The Penitentiary in the Industrial Revolution 1750–1850*, London: Macmillan – now Palgrave.

Ignatieff, M. (1991) 'Citizenship and moral narcissism', in G. Andrews (ed.) *Citizenship*, London: Lawrence and Wishart.

Innes, I. (1999) 'The media as an investigative resource in murder enquiries', in *British Journal of Criminology*, 39:2: 269–86.

Jackson, R. (1981/1986) *Fantasy: The Literature of Subversion*, London: Methuen.

Jacobson, P. (1985) 'Rise of the random killers', in *The Sunday Times*, 2 September.

Jacoby, M. (1982) 'If your child is molested', in *Reader's Digest*, March: 139–42.

James, E. and Smith, H. (1997) *Penny Dreadfuls and Boy's Adventures: Barry Ono Collection of Victorian Popular Literature in the British Library*, London: The British Library.

James, L. (1963) *Fiction for the Working Man, 1830–1850*, Oxford: Oxford University Press.

Jay, M. (1993) 'Experience without a subject: Walter Benjamin and the novel', in *New Formations*, 20: 145–55.

Jenkins, P. (1994) *Using Murder: The Social Construction of Serial Homicide*, New York: Aldine de Gruyter.

Jenkins, S. (1994) 'The pornography of fear', in *The Times*, 22 March: 20.

Johnson, J. (1992) 'Let me bury my son', in *Chat*, 26 September: 4–5.

Johnson, P. Hansford (1967) *On Iniquity: Some Personal Reflections Arising Out of the Moors Murder Trial*, London: Macmillan – now Palgrave.

Johnson, P. (1997) 'An obscene picture and the question: will decency or decadence triumph in British life?', in *Daily Mail*, 20 September: 10–11.

Johnson, P. and Reed, H. (1996) *Two Nations? The Inheritance of Poverty and Affluence*, London: Institute for Fiscal Studies.

Johnston, L. (1991) 'Privatisation and the police function: from "New Police" to "New Policing"', in R. Reiner and M. Cross (eds.), *Beyond Law and Order: Criminal Justice Policy and Politics into the 1990s*, Basingstoke: Macmillan – now Palgrave.

Johnston, L. (1992) *The Rebirth of Private Policing*, London: Routledge.

Josephs, J. (1993) *Hungerford: One Man's Massacre*, London: Smith Gryphon.

Josephs, J. (1994) *Murder in the Family*, London: Headline.

Jouve, N. Ward (1986) *'The Streetcleaner': The Yorkshire Ripper Case on Trial*, London: Marion Boyars.

Joyce, C. and Stover, E. (1993) *Witnesses From the Grave*, London: Grafton.

Katz, J. (1988) *Seductions of Crime: Moral and Sensual Attractions of Doing Evil*, New York: Basic Books.

Keane, J. (1996) *Reflections on Violence*, London: Verso.

Keith, M. (1991) 'Policing a perplexed society? No-go areas and the mystification of police-Black conflict', in *Out of Order? Policing Black People*, E. Cashmore and E. McClaughlin (eds.), London: Routledge.

Keith, M. (1993) *Race, Riots and Policing: Lore and Order in a Multi-racist Society*, London: UCL Press.

Keller, E. F. (1990) 'From secrets of life to secrets of death', in M. Jacobus, E. F. Keller and S. Shuttleworth (eds.), *Body/Politics: Women and the Discourses of Science*, London: Routledge.

Kellner, D. (1995) *Media Culture: Cultural Studies, Identity and Politics Between the Modern and the Postmodern*, London: Routledge.

Kennedy, L. (1961/1971) *10 Rillington Place: Christie and Evans*, London: Grafton Books.

Kennedy, L. (1966) 'Liberty's muddy fountain', in *Spectator*, 22 April: 489.

Kent, J. (1986) *The English Village Constable 1580–1642, A Social and Administrative Study*, Oxford: Clarendon Press.

Kermode, F. (1967) *The Sense of an Ending: Studies in the Theory of Fiction*, Oxford: Oxford University Press.

Kettle, M. (1983) 'The drift to law and order', in S. Hall and M. Jacques (eds.), *The Politics of Thatcherism*, London: Lawrence and Wishart/*Marxism Today*.

Kidd-Hewitt, D. and Osborne, R. (eds.) (1995) *Crime and the Media: The Postmodern Spectacle*, London: Pluto.

Kipnis, L. (1998) 'Pornography', in J. Hill and P. Church Gibson (eds.), *The Oxford Guide to Film Studies*, Oxford: Oxford University Press.

Knelman, J. (1998) *Twisting in the Wind: The Murderess and the English Press*, London and Toronto: University of Toronto Press.

Knight, S. (1980) *Form and Ideology in Crime Fiction*, London: Macmillan – now Palgrave.

Knox, S. (1998) *Murder: A Tale of Modern American Life*, London: Duke University Press.

Kolarik, L. and Kennedy, D. (1993) *How To Write True Crime That Sells*, Chicago: Buckingham Classics Audio.

Lake, P. (1993) 'Deeds against nature: cheap print, Protestantism and murder in early seventeenth century England', in K. Sharpe and P. Lake (eds.), *Culture and Politics in Early Stuart England*, Basingstoke: Macmillan – now Palgrave.

Laqueur, T. (1989) 'Crowds, carnival and the state in English executions, 1604–1868', in *The First Modern Society: Essays in Honour of Lawrence Stone*, A. L. Beier, D. Annadine and J. Rosenheim (eds.), Cambridge: Cambridge University Press.

Laqueur, T. (1990/1992) *Making Sex – The Body and Gender from the Greeks to Freud*, London: Harvard University Press.

Leadbeater, C. (1989) 'Power to the person', in S. Hall and M. Jacques (eds.) (1989).

Leavis, Q. D. (1932/1965) *Fiction and the Reading Public*, London: Bellew.

Lee, A. J. (1976) *The Origins of the Popular Press in England*, London: Croom Helm.

Lefebvre, H. (1958) *Critique of Everyday Life*, Volume 1, second edition, Trans. J. Moore, London: Verso.

Lefebvre, H. (1958a) 'Philosophy and the critique of everyday life', in H. Lefebvre (1958).

Lefebvre, H. (1958b/1992) 'Work and leisure in everyday life', in H. Lefebvre (1958).

Lesser, W. (1993) *Pictures at an Execution: An Inquiry into the Subject of Murder*, London and Massachusetts: Harvard University Press.

Leyton, E. (1986) *Hunting Humans: The Rise of the Modern Multiple Murderer*, London: Penguin.

Leyton, E. (1995/1997) *Men of Blood: Murder in Modern England*, Harmondsworth: Penguin.

Light, A. (1991) *Forever England: Femininity, Literature and Conservatism between the Wars*, London: Routledge.

Linebaugh, P. (1977) 'The ordinary of Newgate and his account', in J. S. Cockburn (ed.), *Crime in England, 1550–1800*, London: Methuen.

Lodge, D. (1981) 'Getting the truth', in *The Times Literary Supplement*, 20 February: 185–6.

Lovitt, C. (1992) 'The rhetoric of murderers, confessional narratives: the model of Pierre Rivière's memoir', in *Journal of Narrative Technique*, 22:1: 23–34.

Lowndes, M. Belloc (1913/1996) *The Lodger*, Oxford: Oxford University Press.

Lustgarten, E. (1974) *The Chalk Pit Murder*, London: Hart-Davis, MacGibbon.

Lustgarten, E. (1976) *Murder at the Follies 1907*, Ivan Berg Associates (Audio Publishing) Ltd.

MacDonnell, D. (1986) *Theories of Discourse*, Oxford: Blackwell.

Macfarlane, A. (1978) *The Origins of English Individualism: The Family, Property and Social Transition*, Cambridge: Cambridge University Press.

Macfarlane, A. (1987) *The Culture of Capitalism*, Oxford: Blackwell.

Maeder, T. (1980/1981) *The Unspeakable Crimes of Dr Petiot*, London: Hutchinson.

Malcolm, J. (1990) *The Journalist and the Murderer*, London: Bloomsbury.

Mandel, E. (1984) *Delightful Murder*, London: Pluto.

Marcus, L. (1986) 'Introduction' to *The Lodger*, in B. Lowndes (reprint: first published 1913).

Mark, R. (1977) *Policing a Perplexed Society*, London: Allen and Unwin.

Martin, A. (1995) 'Better read than dead', in *London Evening Standard, ES Magazine*, March: 20.

Martin, S. (1986) *Art, Messianism and Crime – Sade, Wilde, Hitler, Manson and Others: A Study in Antinomianism in Modern Literature and Lives*, London: Macmillan – now Palgrave.

Masters, B. (1985a) *Killing for Company: The Case of Dennis Nilsen*, London: Hodder and Stoughton.

Masters, B. (1985b) 'Is evil contagious?', in *Observer*, Weekend Section, 24 February: 47.

Masters, B. (1993) *The Shrine of Jeffrey Dahmer*, London: Hodder and Stoughton.

Masters, B. (1994) *On Murder*, London: Coronet Books.

Masters, B. (1995) 'Serial killers: can they be cured?', in *Mail on Sunday, Night and Day* magazine, 25 June: 7–11.

Masters, B. (1999) 'Are we all his victims?', in the *Daily Mail*, 12 June: 12–13.

Mathews, R. (ed.) (1989) *Privatising Criminal Justice*, London: Sage.

Mayhew, H. (1851–61/1968) *London Labour and the London Poor*, 4 volumes, New York: Dover.

Mayhew, P., Elliott, D. and Dowds, L. (1989) *The 1988 British Crime Survey*, Home Office Research Study No. 111, London: HMSO Books.

McCann, P. (1997) 'Anger over ad for murder magazine', in *Independent*, 7 April: 2.

McDonagh, J. (1992) 'Do or die: problems of agency and gender in the aesthetics of murder', in I. Armstrong (ed.), *New Feminist Discourses: Critical Essays on Theories and Texts*, London: Routledge.

McGinniss, J. (1983) *Fatal Vision*, London: André Deutsch.

McGowan, R. (1989) 'Punishing violence, sentencing crime', in N. Armstrong and L. Tennenhouse (eds.) (1989).

McGuigan, J. (1992) *Cultural Populism*, London: Routledge.

McKeon, M. (1988) *The Origins of the English Novel 1600–1740*, London: Hutchinson Radius.

McLaren, A. (1993/1995) *A Prescription for Murder: The Victorian Serial Killings of Dr. Thomas Neill Cream*, London and Chicago: University of Chicago Press.

McMullan, J. (1984) *The Canting Crew: London's Criminal Underworld 1550–1700*, New Brunswick, N.Y.: Rutgers University Press.

McMullan, J. (1998) 'Social surveillance and the rise of the "Police Machine"', in *Theoretical Criminology*, 2:1: 93–117.

Miller, D. A. (1988) *The Novel and the Police*, London: University of California Press.

Medved, M. (1992) *Hollywood vs America: Popular Culture and the War on Traditional Values*, London: HarperCollins.

Medved, M. (1993a) 'Hollywood's addiction to violence', in *Sunday Times*, 14 February: 23–5.

Medved, M. (1993b) 'Hollywood: the cure', in *Sunday Times*, 7 March: 23–5.

Metz, C. (1990) 'Photography and fetish', in C. Squiers (ed.), *The Critical Image: Essays on Contemporary Photography*, Seattle: Bay Press.

Miles, J. (1991) 'Imagining mayhem: fictional violence vs. "true crime"', in *North American Review*, 276: 4: 57–64.

Miller, D. and Philo, G. (1996) 'Against orthodoxy: the media do influence us', in *Sight and Sound*, December: 18–20.

Miller, D. and Philo, G. (1997) *Cultural Compliance: Dead Ends of Media/Cultural Studies and Social Science*, Glasgow: Glasgow Media Group.

Miller, H. (1995) *Traces of Guilt: Forensic Science and the Fight against Crime*, London: BBC Books.

Mills, S. (1997) *Discourse*, London: Routledge.

Moir, A. and Jessel, D. (1995) *A Mind to Crime*, London: Michael Joseph.

Moller, D. (1994) 'Crime's spectre haunts Europe: fear in the streets', in *Reader's Digest*, April: 41–7.

Moller, D. (1995) 'The case of the paint-spot murders', in *Reader's Digest*, May: 108–116.

Moore, S. (1991) 'Killjoy culture: the new breed of psycho-killer', in *Marxism Today*, May: 13.

Morley, D. (1986) *Family Television: Cultural Power and Domestic Leisure*, London: Routledge.

Morris, R. (1998) 'Who's Who of candidates for execution becomes a hot seller', in the *Independent on Sunday* 1 November: 3.

Morris, T. (1989) *Crime and Criminal Justice Since 1945*, Oxford: Blackwell.

Morrison, B. (1997) *As If*, London: Granta.

Mortensson, C. (1992a) 'The black widow', in *Chat* 18 July: 12–13.

Mortensson, C. (1992b) 'The romantic poisoner', in *Chat* 19 September: 40–1.

Mortimer, J. (1984) *Famous Trials*, originally edited by H. Hodge and J. Hodge (1941), Harmondsworth: Penguin.

Motion, A. (2000) *Wainwright the Poisoner*, London: Faber and Faber.

Mouland, B. (1997) 'Invitation to an outrage: Hindley's victims' families scorn Academy offer', in the *Daily Mail*, 17 September: 1–2.

Mullen, B. and Taylor, L. (1986) *Uninvited Guests: The Intimate Secrets of Television and Radio*, London: Chatto and Windus.

Murdoch, G. (1997) 'Reservoirs of dogma; an archaeology of popular anxieties', in M. Barker and J. Petley (eds.) (1997).

Murray, C. (1990) *The Emerging British Underclass*, London: TEA Health Welfare Unit.

Myers, A. and Wight, S. (eds.) (1996) *No Angels: Women Who Commit Violence*, London: Pandora.

Myers, M. (1997) *News Coverage of Violence against Women: Engendering Blame*, London: Sage.

Nadelson, R. (1994) 'Why everyone loves a good family killing', in *Independent*, 7 January: 18.

Nash, J. R. (1992) *World Encyclopaedia of Serial Killers*, London: Headline.

Neale, S. (1980) *Genre*, London: BFI Publishing.

Neff, J. (1988/1995) *Serial Rapist*, London: True Crime.

Newman, K. (1985) *A Police for the Police: Report of the Commissioner of Police of the Metropolis for the Year 1985*, London: HMSO.

Nichols, B. (1994) *Blurred Boundaries: Questions of Meaning in Contemporary Culture*, Bloomington and Indianapolis: Indiana University Press.

Nokes, D. (1982) 'Introduction', in H. Fielding (1986).

Norrie, A. and Adelman, S. (1989) '"Consensual authoritarianism" and criminal justice in Thatcher's Britain', in A. Gamble and C. Wells (eds.), *Thatcher's Law*, Cardiff: GPC Books: University of Wales.

Norris, J. (1988) *Serial Killers*, New York: Doubleday.

Nowell-Smith, G. (1987) 'Popular culture', in *New Formations 2*, London: Methuen.

Nuttal, J. and Carmichael, R. (1977) *Common Factors/Vulgar Factions*, London: Routledge and Kegan Paul.

Odell, R. (1965) *Jack the Ripper: In Fact and Fiction*, London: Harrap.

O'Hagan, A. (1995) 'Fred West's spell in Glasgow', in the *Guardian Weekend*, 2 September: 11–22.

O'Hagan, A. (1996) *The Missing*, London: Picador.

O'Neill, E. (1994) 'The seen of the crime: violence, anxiety and the domestic in police reality programming', in *CineAction* 38: Fall: 56–63.

Open University (1981) *Law and Disorder: Histories of Crime and Justice*, D335 2 (1–3), Milton Keynes: The Open University Press.

Oppenheimer, P. (1996) *Evil and the Demonic: A New Theory of Monstrous Behaviour*, London: Duckworth.

Orwell, G. (1936) 'Review of *Bastard Death*', in G. Orwell (1968): 248–50.

Orwell, G. (1940) 'Boys' weeklies', in G. Orwell (1968): 506–31.

Orwell, G. (1945) 'The decline of the English murder', in *The Collected Essays, Journalism and Letters of George Orwell: In Front of Your Nose 1945–50*, Vol. 4, S. Orwell and I. Angus (eds.) (1968/1970), Harmondsworth: Penguin Books.

Orwell, G. (1968/1970) *The Collected Essays, Journalism and Letters of George Orwell: An Age Like This 1920–1940*, Vol. 1, S. Orwell and I. Angus (eds.), Harmondsworth: Penguin Books.

Osborne, R. (1995) 'Crime and the media: from media studies to post-modernism', in D. Kidd-Hewitt and R. Osborne (eds.) (1995).

Ousby, I. (1976) *Bloodhounds of Heaven: The Detective in English Fiction from Godwin to Doyle*, London: Harvard University Press.

Oxford, E. (1995) 'Taking Cromwell Street to Charing Cross Road', in *Independent* Supplement, 3 October: 4–5.

Paget, D. (1988) *No Other Way To Tell It: Dramadoc/Dowdrama on Television*, Manchester: Manchester University Press.

Palmer, G. (1998) 'New police blues: police shows on British television', in *Jump Cut*. 42: 12–18.

Palmer, J. (1991) *Potboilers: Methods, Concepts and Case Studies in Popular Fiction*, London: Routledge.

Parker, T. (1963/1966) *The Unknown Citizen*, Harmondsworth: Penguin Books.

Paul, W. (1994) *Laughing, Screaming: Modern Hollywood Horror and Comedy*, New York: Columbia University Press.

Pearson, G. (1983) *Hooligan: A History of Respectable Fears*, London: Macmillan Education.

Pecheux, M. (1982) *Language, Semantics and Ideology*, New York and London: St Martin's Press/Macmillan – now Palgrave.

Petley, J. (1996) 'Fact plus fiction equals friction', in *Media, Culture and Society*, 18:1: 11–25.

Petley, J. (1997) 'Us and them', in M. Barker and J. Petley (eds.) (1997).

Pitman, P. (1961) 'Why an encyclopaedia of murder?', in C. Wilson and P. Pitman (1961).

Playfair, G. (1967) 'Beyond Emlyn', in *Spectator* 1 August: 160.

Poe, E. A. (1839/1984) 'William Wilson', in *Tales of Mystery and Imagination*, London: Dent.

Pope, J. and Shaps, S. (1992) *Michael Winner's True Crimes*, London: Boxtree/LWT.

Pope, S. (1989) 'Cold revenge', in *New Statesman and Society*, 27 January: 44.

Porter, D. (1981) *The Pursuit of Crime: Art and Ideology in Detective Fiction*, New Haven: Yale University Press.

Propp, V. (1968) *Morphology of the Folktale*, Austin: University of Texas.

Provost, G. (1991) *How to Write and Sell True Crime*, Ohio: Writer's Digest Books.

Raban, J. (1988) *Soft City*, London: Collins Harvill.

Radford, J. and Russell, D. (eds.) (1992) *Femicide: The Politics of Woman Killing*, Buckingham: Open University Press.

Radway, J. (1984/1987) *Reading the Romance: Women, Patriarchy, and Popular Literature*, London: Verso.

Radway, J. (1992) 'Mail-order culture and its critics: the book-of-the-month club, commodification and consumption, and the problem of cultural authority', in L. Grossberg *et al.* (eds.) (1992).

Radzinowicz, L. with King, J. (1977) *The Growth of Crime: The International Experience*, London: Hamish Hamilton.

Radzinowicz, L. with Hood, R. (1986/1990) *The Emergence of Penal Policy in Victorian and Edwardian England*, Oxford: Clarendon Press.

Rawlings, P. (1991) 'Creeping privatisation? The police, the Conservative government and policing in the late 1980s', in R. Reiner and M. Cross (eds.), *Beyond Law and Order: Criminal Justice Policy and Politics into the 1990s*, London: Macmillan – now Palgrave.

Rawlings, P. (1999) *Crime and Power: A History of Criminal Justice 1688–1998*, London: Longman.

Rayment, T. (1996) 'Bolt-down Britain', in *Sunday Times* 7 January: 12.

Reader's Digest (1972) '50th Anniversary Album', in *Reader's Digest*, March: 108–15.

Redhead, M. (1999) 'The justice game', in the *Guardian*, Media Section, 15 February: 9.

Reeves, G. (1993) '*Tumbledown* and *The Falklands Play*: The Falklands faction', in G. Brandt (ed.) (1993).

Reiner, R. (1992) *The Politics of the Police*, second edition, Hemel Hempstead: Harvester Wheatsheaf.

Reiner, R. (1995) 'Selling the family copper: the British Police plc', in 'Crime and punishment: a special report on policing', in *Independent* Section Two, 12 October: 2–3.

Ressler, R. with Shachtman, T. (1992) *Whoever Fights Monsters*, New York: St. Martin's Press – now Palgrave.

Reynolds, J. (1621–2) *The Triumph of Gods Revenge Agaynst the Crying, and Execrable Sins of Murder in Thirty Tragical Histories*, n.p.

Roe, M. (1994) 'Magazine panders to cult in Britain', in *Observer*, 24 April: 18.

Rose, D. (1992) *A Climate of Fear: The Murder of PC Blakelock*, London: Bloomsbury.

Rose, D. (1996) *In the Name of the Law: The Collapse of Criminal Justice*, London: Jonathan Cape.

Rose, J. (1996) 'The English at their best', in *States of Fantasy*, Oxford: Clarendon Press.

Rose, N. (1989) *Governing the Soul: The Shaping of the Private Self*, London: Routledge.

Ross, A. (1989) *No Respect: Intellectuals and Popular Culture*, London: Routledge.

Ross, N. and Cook, S. (1987) *Crimewatch UK*, London: Hodder and Stoughton.

Ross, P. (1993) '*Crimewatch, Crimestoppers, Crime Monthly* ... Crime Overdose?', in *Bella*, 7 July: 11.

Roughead, W. (1943) *Art of Murder*, London: Sheridan House.

Rule, Ann (1980/1989) *The Stranger Beside Me*, revised edition, USA: Warner Books.

Rumbelow, D. (1971) *I Spy Blue: The Police and Crime in the City of London from Elizabeth I to Victoria*, London: Macmillan – now Palgrave.

Rumbelow, D. (1981) *Jack the Ripper: The Complete Casebook*, Harmondsworth: Penguin Books.

Rusche, G. and Kirchheimer, O. (1968) *Punishment and Social Structure*, New York: Russell and Russell.

Salecl, R. (1994) *The Spoils of Freedom: Psychoanalysis and Feminism After the Fall of Socialism*, London: Routledge.

Salgado, G. (1977) *The Elizabethan Underworld*, London: Methuen.

Samuel, R. (1994) 'Pedagogies', in *Theatres of Memory*, Volume 1, London: Verso.

Savage, M. and Miles, A. (1994) *The Remaking of the British Working Class 1840–1940*, London: Routledge.

Schama, S. (1991) *Dead Certainties (Unwarranted Speculations)*, London: Granta Books with Penguin Books.

Schlesinger, P., Dobash, R. E., Dobash, R. P. and Weaver, C. K. (1992) *Women Viewing Violence*, London: BFI.

Schlesinger, P. and Tumber, H. (1993) 'Fighting the war against crime: television, police and audience', in *British Journal of Criminology*, 33:1: 19–32.

Schlesinger, P. and Tumber, H. (1994) *Reporting Crime*, Oxford: Oxford University Press.

Schwartz, V. (1994) 'Cinematic spectatorship before the apparatus: the public taste for reality in fin-de-siècle Paris', in L. Williams (ed.) (1995).

Schwarz, B. (1996) 'Night battles: hooligan and citizen', in M. Nava and A. O'Shea eds. (1996) *Modern Times: Reflections on a Century of Modernity*, London: Routledge.

Scrapec, C. (1993) 'The female serial killer: an evolving criminality', in H. Birch (ed.) (1993).

Seabrook, J. (1991) 'My life in that box', in J. Spence and P. Holland (eds.) (1991) *Family Snaps: The Meaning of Domestic Photography*, London: Virago.

Seltzer, M. (1998) *Serial Killers: Death and Life in America's Wound Culture*, London: Routledge.

Senelick, L. (1987) *The Prestige of Evil: The Murderer as Romantic Hero from Sade to Lacenaire*, New York: Garland.

Sereny, G. (1995) *The Case of Mary Bell: A Portrait of a Child Who Murdered*, London: Pimlico.

Sereny, G. (1998) *Cries Unheard: The Story of Mary Bell*, London: Macmillan – now Palgrave.

Shaffer, A. (1979) *Murder – A Play in Two Acts*, London: Marion Boyars.

Sharpe, J. A. (1990) *Judicial Punishment in England*, London: Faber and Faber.

Shepherd, L. (1973) *The History of Street Literature*, Devon: David and Charles.

Sinclair, I. (1987/1988) *White Chappell, Scarlet Tracings*, London: Paladin.

Sinclair, I. (1997) *Lights Out for the Territory: 9 Excursions in the Secret History of London*, London: Granta Books.

Sinclair, I. (1997a) 'The dog and the dish', in Sinclair (1997).

Sinclair (1997b) 'Bulls and bears and mithraic misalignments: weather in the city', in Sinclair (1997).

Sinclair (1997c) 'The cadaver club', in Sinclair (1997).

Skeggs, B. (1997) *Formations of Class and Gender: Becoming Respectable*, London: Sage.

Slater, S. (1995) 'My terror in the darkness', in *Reader's Digest*, September: 155–79.

Smith, A. Duval (1994) 'Making a killing at the bookshops', in *Guardian*, 20 August: 25.

Smith, B. Herrnstein (1988) *Contingencies of Value: Alternative Perspectives for Critical Theory*, London: Harvard University Press.

Smith, D. J. (1994) *The Sleep of Reason: The James Bulger Case*, London: Century.

Smith, J. (1989/1990) 'There's only one Yorkshire Ripper', in *Misogynies*, London: Faber and Faber.

Smith, J. (1997) 'Unnatural born killers', in the *Independent on Sunday*, 31 August: 4–7.

Sobchack, V. (ed.) (1996) *The Persistence of History: Cinema, Television, and the Modern Event*, London: Routledge.

Soothill, K. and Walby, S. (1991) *Sex Crime in the News*, London: Routledge.

Southgate, P. with Ekblom, P. (1986) *Police-Public Encounters*, Home Office Research Study No. 90, London: HMSO.

Sparks, R. (1992) *Television and the Drama of Crime: Moral Tales and the Place of Crime in Public Life*, Buckingham: Open University Press.

Sparks, R. (1993) '*Inspector Morse*: 'The last enemy', in G. Brandt (ed.) (1993).

Spierenburg, P. (ed.) (1984) *The Emergence of Carceral Institutions: Prisons, Galleys and Lunatic Asylums*, Rotterdam: Erasmus University Press.

Spierenburg, P. (1984) *The Spectacle of Suffering: Execution and the Evolution of Repression from a Preindustrial Metropolis to the European Experience*, Cambridge: Cambridge University Press.

Springhall, J. (1998) *Youth, Popular Culture and Moral Panics: Penny Gaffs to Gangsta-Rap, 1830–1996*, London: Macmillan – now Palgrave.

Spurling, H. (1998) 'Urban nightmare', in *Telegraph*, 26 September: 3.

Spurrier, R. (1990) 'Making crime pay', in *The Bookseller*, 30 November: 1635–6.

Squires, J. (ed.) (1993) *Principled Positions: Postmodernism and the Rediscovery of Value*, London: Lawrence and Wishart.

Stallybrass, P. and White, A. (1986) *The Politics and Poetics of Transgression*, London: Methuen.

Stasio, M. (1991) 'The killers next door, we can't get enough of them', in *New York Times Book Review*, 20 October: 46–7.

Steedman, C. (1984) *Policing the Victorian Community: The Formation of English Provincial Police Forces 1856–1880*, London: Routledge and Kegan Paul.

Steedman, C. (1986) *Landscape for a Good Woman: A Story of Two Lives*, London: Virago.

Stern, C. (1997) 'If crime is falling, why don't we feel safe in our beds at night?', in the *Mail on Sunday*, 16 March: 32.

Stevenson, R. L. (1886/1964) *The Strange Case of Dr. Jekyll and Mr Hyde*, New York: Airmont.

Stewart, A. and Burridge, R. (1989) 'Housing tales of law and space', in A. Gamble and C. Wells (eds.) (1989) *Thatcher's Law*, Cardiff: GPC Books/ University of Wales.

Storch, R. (1981) 'The plague of blue locusts: police reform and popular resistance in Northern England, 1840–57', in M. Fitzgerald *et al.* (eds.) (1981).

Storey, J. (1996) *Cultural Studies and the Study of Popular Culture*, Edinburgh: Edinburgh University Press.

Strinati, D. and Wagg, S. eds. (1992) *Come On Down? An Introduction to Theories of Popular Culture*, London: Routledge.

Sullivan, R. (1998) 'The politics of British policing in the Thatcher/Major state', in *The Howard Journal of Criminal Justice*, Vol. 37, No. 3: 306–18.

Sutherland, J. (1982) *Offensive Literature: Decensorship in Britain 1960–1982*, London: Junction Books.

Swingewood, A. (1977) *The Myth of Mass Culture*, London: Macmillan – now Palgrave.

Symons, J. (1972) *Bloody Murder: From Detective Story to the Crime Novel – A History*, London: Faber and Faber.

Tagg, J. (1988) *The Burden of Representation: Essays on Photographies and Histories*, London: Macmillan – now Palgrave.

Taubin, A. (1991) 'Killing men', in *Sight and Sound*, May: 14–19.

Taylor, E. (1994) 'Secret of the sands', in *Bella*, 16 March: 39.

Taylor, I. (1997) 'Crime, anxiety and locality: responding to the 'condition of England' at the end of the century', in *Theoretical Criminology* 1:1: 53–75.

Taylor, L. (1984) *In the Underworld*, Oxford: Blackwell.

Taylor, S. J. (1992) *Shock! Horror! The Tabloids in Action*, London: Black Swan.

Tester, K. (1994) *Media, Culture and Morality*, London: Routledge.

Thompson, E. P. (1963) *The Making of the English Working Class*, London: Victor Gollancz.

Thompson, T. and Cumberbatch, F. (1993) 'Citizen's army', in *Bella*, Issue 42, 20 October: 11.

Thorpe, V. (1997) 'Readers give true crime books the axe', in *Independent on Sunday*, 9 November: 6.

Tibballs, G. (1993) *The Murder Guide to Great Britain*, London: Boxtree.

Tithecott, R. (1997) *Of Men and Monsters: Jeffrey Dahmer and the Construction of the Serial Killer*, Wisconsin: University of Wisconsin.

Tomasulo, F. (1996) '"I'll believe it when I see it": Rodney King and the prison-house of video', in V. Sobchack (ed.) (1996).

Traini, R. (1984) *Home Security and Protection*, London: Willow Books.

Tumin, S. (1997) *The Future of Crime and Punishment*, London: Phoenix.

Turner, E. S.(1975) *Boys Will Be Boys*, second edition, London: Michael Joseph.

Turner, G. (1992) 'British and Australian cultural studies', in N. Grossberg *et al.* (eds.) (1992).

Wagner, P. (1994) *A Sociology of Modernity: Liberty and Discipline*, London: Routledge.

Walker, J. A. (1996) 'Press humbug: the Jamie Wagg affair', in *20/20*, Issue 4, Spring, Comment Section.

Waites, B., Bennett, T. and Martin, G. (eds.) (1982) *Popular Culture – Past and Present*, London: Croom Helm.

Walker, G. (1996) 'Demons in female form: representations of women and gender in murder pamphlets of the late sixteenth and early seventeenth centuries', in W. Zunder and S. Trill (eds.), *Writing in the English Renaissance*, London: Longman.

Walkowitz, J. (1992) *City of Dreadful Delight: Narratives of Danger in Late Victorian London*, London: Virago.

Wallace, J. (1998) 'Editorial', in *Keywords: A Journal of Cultural Materialism*, 1: 5-11.

Warner, M. (1998/2000) *No Go the Bogeyman: Scaring, Lulling and Making Mock*, London: Vintage.

Watkins, L. (1981) 'You can foil the pickpockets', in *Reader's Digest*, December: 99–102.

Watkins, L. (1982) 'Watch out! There's a burglar about', in *Reader's Digest*, June: 48–52.

Watkins, L. and Fletcher, L. (1985) 'Anatomy of a burglary', in *Reader's Digest*, December: 57–61.

Watson, C. (1971/1979) *Snobbery with Violence: English Crime Stories and their Audience*, Revised Edition, London: Eyre Methuen.

Watson, J. (1982) 'Let's stop punishing the victims of rape', in *Reader's Digest*, December: 146–51.

Watt, I. (1957/1987) *The Rise of the Novel*, London: The Hogarth Press.

Weaver, C. K. (1998) '*Crimewatch UK*: Keeping Women off the Streets', in C. Carter, G. Branston and S. Allan (eds.) (1998).

Webster, D. (1988) *Looka Yonder! The Imaginary America of Populist Culture*, London: Comedia.

Webster, D. (1989) '"Whodunit? America did!": *Rambo* and post-Hungerford rhetoric', in *Cultural Studies*, 3:2: 173–93.

Wecht, C. (1993) *Cause of Death: The Final Diagnosis*, London: True Crime.

Weegee [Arthur Fellig] (1945) *Naked City*, New York: Essential Books.

Weeks, J. (1981/1989) *Sex, Politics and Society: The Regulation of Sexuality since 1800*, Second Edition, London: Longman.

Wexler, P. (1990) 'Citizenship in the semiotic society', in *Theories of Modernity and Postmodernity*, ed. B. Turner, London: Sage.

Whelwell, H. (1966) 'Murder in the press', in *Guardian*, 23 April: 14.

Wiener, M. (1990/1994) *Reconstructing the Criminal: Culture, Law and Policy in England 1830–1914*, Cambridge: Cambridge University Press.

Wilde, O. (1922) 'Pen, pencil and poison', in R. Ross (ed.) *The Complete Works of Oscar Wilde*, Vol. 4: 61–99 (4 volumes), New York: Bigelow, Brown and Co.

Williams, E. (1967/1968) *Beyond Belief: A Chronicle of Murder and its Detection*, London: World Books.

Williams, L. (1989) *Hard Core: Power, Pleasure and the 'Frenzy of the Visible'*, California: University of California Press.

Williams, L. (ed.) (1995) *Viewing Positions: Ways of Seeing Film*, New Jersey, Rutgers University Press.

Williams, J. (1991) 'The trouble with serial killers', in *The Face*, March: 58–60.

Williams, R. (1958a/1993) *Culture and Society*, London: The Hogarth Press.

Williams, R. (1958b/1989) 'Culture is ordinary', in *Resources of Hope*, London: Verso.

Williams, R. (1961/1992) *The Long Revolution*, London: The Hogarth Press.

Williams, R. (1974/1991) 'Drama in a dramatized society', in R. Williams, *Writing in Society*, London: Verso.

Williams, R. (1977) 'A lecture on realism', in *Screen* 18:1: 61–74.

Williams, R. (1981) *Culture*, London: Fontana Press.

Williams, V. (1994) *Who's Looking at the Family?* London: Barbican Art Gallery.

Wilson, A. (1999) 'A film too far: a new movie about the serial killer who terrorised New York has outraged both the victim's families and the murderer', in the *Mail on Sunday, Night and Day* magazine, 13 June: 25–31.

Wilson, C. (1961) 'The study of murder', in C. Wilson and P. Pitman (1961).

Wilson, C. (1971/1975) *The Order of Assassins: The Psychology of Murder*, London: Panther Books.

Wilson, C. and Pitman, P. (1961/1984) *The Encyclopaedia of Murder*, London: Pan Books.

Winder, R. (1991) 'When murder is not enough', in *Independent*, 27 April: 27.

Winship, J. (1987) *Inside Women's Magazines*, London: Pandora Press.

Wood, B. (1994) *A Blood Betrayal*, London: HarperCollins.

Worpole, K. (1984) *Reading by Numbers: Contemporary Publishing and Popular Fiction*, London: Comedra.

Wright, P. (1985) *On Living in an Old Country: The National Past in Contemporary Britain*, London: Verso.

Wykes, M. (1998) 'A family affair: the British press, sex and the Wests', in C. Carter, G. Branston and S. Allen (eds.) (1998).

Young, H. (1989/1990) *One of Us: A Biography of Margaret Thatcher*, London: Pan Books.

Zehr, H. (1976) *Crime: The Development of Modern Society*, London: Croom Helm.

Zipes, J. (1979) *Breaking the Magic Spell: Radical Theories of Folk and Fairy Tales*, London: Heinemann.

Index